LEGEND OF THE RAVAJA

JULIEN LEVANGIE

ILLUSTRATORS

Yanli ◆ Brandon LeVangie ◆ Dima ◆ Danny Ramirez

SEAL OF RAVAJIAN AUTHENTICITY

Text Copyright © 2020 by Julien LeVangie

Published by Julien LeVangie

For Christ Jesus, and Brandon LeVangie

ACKNOWLEDGMENTS

To Megan Ontiveros and her family, Erik Schiemann, Brian and Julie Santerre, Joseph St. Amand II-III, Joseph and Silvia "Tia" Batres, Danny Ramirez, Jeremy Carbajal, Donovan Corprue, Daniel Maldonado, my Hume Ninjas, and several more without mention though just as special as the aforementioned contributors, thank you for believing in this story, and I as a writer.

"By the sweat of your brow you will eat your food until you return to the ground, since from it you were taken; for dust you are and to dust you will return."

—Genesis 3:19, NIV

CONTENTS

PART I

FORGOTTEN FATHER

I

HUNTED

IN THE town of Sol Puesta, not one dared to venture outside their home, in cowardice watching from the sills of their fogged windows, very few peeking through the leaking cracks of their walls. Sunset had long passed; thunder preceded heavy rainfall, and the crescent moon commanded view, a portion of the storm diminishing as the great luminescence presently endowed a shimmering to the settlement's bogged grounds.

"You're not welcome here."

The thief grinned. "No. I'm not, but I go where I damn well please…"

Within the widened road, the two stood, across from them establishments such as the bunking house and saloon gathering a host of viewers from inside. "Tell me, bandit," said the young man, a constant stream of fire releasing from his eye sockets, "what are you after? If it's gredo we got in the bank, you might want to look elsewhere…The last two punks that tested their luck tryin' to take our local funds found their mouths at the end of this here barrel."

Illuminating the thief by the flames emanating from his eyes and by a secondary outlet of light from the young man's mouth, a wispy strand of cloud lingered beside his left eye. From his attire he was recognized as a vaquero of sorts, the local tongue for *cowboy*, *gunslinger*, with a belt and nothing more than an iron that hung from his hip. His poncho was diamond in shape; a jagged blue pattern reminiscent of lightning formed a V reaching the bottom of the gold cloth, connecting to the pattern cast from his opposite shoulder, slightly darker than his cerulean skin. The felt hat on his spherical head matched appropriately to the russet brown boots he wore, additionally, loose-fitting gloves that were grimier than the former articles.

Grinding his heels in the dirt anticipating his antagonist's draw, the vaquero's hand hovered just above his unlatched holster, a grin playing about his lips.

The thief was undaunted by the vaquero's words. His desire, to hunt the last of the Judean tribe, brought an opportunity of seizing the throne, or so he lied to himself enough times believing this would be so; never was he promised such a thing. "A keeper of her word, she is, she is," the thief muttered deeply. "No doubt, I look forward to what ravishes will come from this kill of mine.—All mine, none left for the Zealot!"

His face, one half of his features absent of any muscle, resulted in his one eye sagging onto his cheek, and his cheek draping onto the portion of his lips where he drooled without control, repeated wiping from his hand to momentarily subdue the leakage. The rusted staple situated within the crease of his mouth and onto his cheek hadn't helped with the outpouring of spit, but was sufficient in granting him recognizable speech. The end of his tarnished coat was dripping with a black substance, as were certain cuts in his red skin, damages that never closed but remained as festering wounds. About his neck, a bandana hummed, marked with peculiar sigils emanating a violet hue.

The vaquero looked at the thief curiously, the falling rain becoming streams of vapor as they touched his eyes.

"Hey," he chuckled, "havin' fun over there talkin' to yourself?"

The thief shouted: "Quiet! I advanced before your fallen brother…the kill is mine to claim."

The vaquero tried to stay silent, swallowing his laughter. "Look, buddy," he exclaimed, "whatever grudge you have, I don't have the slightest recollection of who you are—!"

"Boy…what's your name?" requested the thief.

Raising his chest, his eyes crackled suddenly, his breath of white wavering. "Tycho…horrified to make your acquaintance."

Lowering his hand slightly more to his gun's handle, he waited.

"I believe you're the first bandit to ask that of me," said Tycho. "…Huh, weird. Suppose I should ask the same of you then…not that I care—"

"Call me Dargan—" The staple upholding the side of his mouth released, a stream of blood from the puncture holes mixing with saliva.

"Wonderful," said Tycho, shuddering at the grotesque scene though quickly regaining his former demeanor. "Well since we're all getting to know each other, I'd like you to meet Havoc. Don't think she takes too kindly to cravens, stranger."

Pulling back on the hammer of the revolver, his arm rose with the iron in-hand. Striding across the barrel of the gun, three spikes of lightning were crowned, flaring with a thunderous snap.

Dargan snatched his gun from the waist of his trousers and lifted it high, aiming at Tycho's head.

"I'll make her proud," he slurred, lifting his bandana over his mouth.

From the chamber of Dargan's gun a bullet scraped against Tycho's cheek, scarce entering through his mouth and neck, foolishly underprepared to strike before his assailant; then again, the vaquero hadn't much to lose. Before he could bleed, a white light seared the graze closed, his face appearing untouched. Tycho smirked, the boy without surrender, without any evince of humility or self-preservation.

He leveled his aim once more at his foul adversary, just short of chortling. There was a source of strength to be found in battle, veritable drunkenness from triumph and dominance that Tycho could not get enough of.

The thief and vaquero fired simultaneously, their bullets chancing collision. The azure cast from the Havoc chewed and spat out the lesser projectile, the lead missile torn to shreds, shards of the bullet shattering nearby windows, befallen to shards and dust given the exceptional force from Tycho's lightning-based round.

Tycho emptied the remainder of electrically condensed rounds within his chamber, roaring, puncturing holes into the thief's torso, pockets of oil popping out with gust. Dargan howled.

The spikes along Tycho's gun depleted, signaling him to reload. Taking the chamber out from its slot, he spun it back inside of the revolver, recharging it for another six shots. The spikes shone anew, erected in ascending height. Its lightning-crowned frame granted transparency when its barrel had been aligned with the caster's eye that the spikes would not be a hindrance as an outlet for drawn earth currents—alternating rather than direct.

Electricity scrambled over Dargan's chest and shoulders, holding his hand over the holes that poured black, his reflection in the pool he cupped in his hand. Raising his gun once more, it escaped from his grasp, a bolt from the vaquero's Havoc smacking it to the ground far from him. Issuing a damning bellow, Dargan charged forward with what strength of his remained. Yawning, Tycho patted his mouth and closed his eyes, turning his head aside. Dargan advanced vigorously, Tycho awaiting his approach; blood spewed from the thief's cuts and holes, smelling as volatile as tar, trailing down to his hand, whetting his fingers to a refined black. Before he could take the young man, a chilling pain enveloped his stomach—his core had been shot by the cocksure vaquero, oil splashing out from the freshly-torn rupture in his gut. His body was becoming cold, numb. Tycho spun his revolver back into his holster.

Before he could fall, Tycho caught him by his bandana, still turned away from him—the rune cloth slipping past Dargan's mouth. He moaned, wailing thick.

"Hold on," said Tycho. "Where do you think you're going?"

Tycho grinned, his eyes slowly opening as the raw intensity of light crept past his lids, subjugating Dargan to sightlessness.

"You left yourself wide open. Still…you lasted longer than most."

Looking back, he squinted at the thief's flashing bandana—cautious. He saw the bright markings, sigils of some kind, their purple glare veiling his thumb. As he pulled it closer, the cloth began to crumble, becoming flakes of white, Dargan slumping until collapsing onto the dirt.

Kneeling, the fire receded within his eyes, the cloudy wisp of white withdrawing back into his mouth; his eyes returned to their sapphire shade, the freckles circling about his eyes presently discernible. He gazed at Dargan, enthralled, drawn as to where this thief hailed from, who he was. A first for Tycho—he never much cared for the dull, savage slavers. But with all circumstances at hand, it was doubtful Tycho would be alone in his inquisitiveness for answers.

"Dargan, right? Where did you get that bandana from…? Never seen anything like it."

He coughed. "It comes."

"Who...? Now you've got me all impatient."

His eyes filling black, he chuckled, "Is it now you worry? If I were you...the child that you are—"

Tycho rolled his eyes.

"—...I'd run."

With his ceasing breath, the light that gleamed outward from the puncture in his stomach faded.

A hand rested on Tycho's shoulder.

"Got his core good. Even those thugs who left you for dead weren't that cruel...then again, maybe they just forgot." He scratched his beard.

Tycho kept his eyes on Dargan. "He had it coming, acting rash like that..."

"Like you?"

The folks of Sol Puesta exited their homes, scouring the scene.

"I heard that bandit say something to you, what was it?"

Tycho was quiet—unresponsive.

"Tycho," he said, "don't get spooked on me now. Wha'd he say?"

"Someone else is on their way, Bill...guessin' he was trying to beat the other guy to the punch."

Smiling, Tycho looked up at him.

"Not that it'll be a problem."

"The Shine," said Bill. "How is it?"

"Same as always."

The glowing flare had a name, given by Bill when Tycho had first met him, but that was long ago.

"Good...that's good," said Bill, scarcely muted from the rolls of thunder, nodding. "His hand, you saw what happened...?" He glanced at the damned cutthroat.

"No, I…"

"Right, right," Bill smirked with impudence. "The boy was too concerned with indulging matters pertaining to his ego than anything else. Ever get tired of it?" He intended the vitriolic jab to have Tycho provoked.

"Nothin' I do is ever good enough, isn't that *right*—?"

"Tomorrow—"

"Ah…don't say it," said Tycho under his breath.

"You'll be putting in new windows around town, bright and early."

"Yeah…I knew you'd ask somethin' like that of me."

"You know me all too well then."

Bill smiled.

Tycho's head dropped—an overdramatized attempt of exuding despair.

Bill chuckled. "Get some sleep. You still need to help with the saloon before heading out for the day…I'll make sure Kat prepares breakfast."

"Great, thanks," groaned Tycho—though in his mind, he was in a sensation of delight. *What would it be*, he thought, *Brench toast—maybe bacon and eggs on the side? Always.* Rambling to his inner self the most obvious of meals that constitute a morning feast, the nonsense stopped when he took a glance at the fallen thief yet again. He was puzzled, remembering quickly of Dargan's unspecific and vague caution—at the least, how soon was the other to arrive? Tycho thought this, but more so captivated by the bandana Dargan had strapped to his neck, with what remains of it in ash.

Greeting everyone that left from their homes to return inside, Sheriff McBrady, a white-suited bot with a scruffy stache, was busy comforting the concerns of the many. Disgruntled hags and codgers, just miserable people, busied him with shouts—complaints of Tycho's recklessness; although valid, he reminded them that it was Tycho that maintained the peace, whether they liked it or not. Without him, Sol Puesta would be nothing more than a ghost town.

Dusting his boots, Tycho ignored Sheriff McBrady as he neared him, shuffling home with his eyes to the ground. The sheriff was eager to give thanks but could see Tycho wasn't in the most approachable of moods, looked like something was bothering him. Besides, he was there to clean up the mess and get that body out of town, having his boys heave the carcass for him. Time and time again, he was always grateful for the kid, as was Bill.

With the night relinquishing its reign by the first light of dawn, rays of the sun warmed the alpines set far from where the small town made living, its face brightening Zodain's surface to exude white, the Wasteland sparkling. And as the land was brought again to life, there was an exception for a mountain whose height ascended beyond its contemporaries, the serrated agape jaws of *Titan Summit*'s slope continually black, disparaging onlookers by its mighty void.

Easily against the relativity of Sol Puesta's name, its inhabitants prospered during the morning rather than evening's pervasion, leaving vagabonds and merchants to scurry elsewhere from the howls of vectras, to the deafening, horrid spills of laughter echoing from bandit encampments seemingly closer than they were. Sol Puesta was a small town, but very much abundant with life and an economy that was getting better with each day.

Bill rose from his bed that morning with the appetizing thought of fashioning his day to his liking, flailing his blanket aside—Kat bare, she sluggishly grabbed it by a corner and pulled it back onto the bed. From the balustrade of the second floor, as always, Bill was pleased to see people walking around town, keeping their minds young with memories of the past, some waiting for Bill's saloon to open its doors for that very reason, elegantly named *Papa's Retreat*. None seemed too fussed about the disturbance earlier that morning, but for the residents of Sol Puesta, a bandit looking to make some quick gredo,—that, or looking to chain someone,—was nothing of spectacular excitement or a notable event to those desensitized of such things, the town very much plagued with a history that renders them so. Regardless, their fear never subsided.

Hurrying back into his room, Bill hastened to his closet and began picking which clothes that would suffice his taste to make this day somehow contrastingly different from the last.

Around him, walls of coats, shirts, union suits, Kat's dresses, and the occasional sack suit—above, a displaced scuttle door to the attic, whilst fitted to return to the ceiling's indentation by his hand.

"What's got you all antsy?" Kat grumbled, her face turning from her pillow.

"What do you think?" asked Bill, stepping out from the closet, alternating between two thermals against his chest. "Brown, or the needlemouse blue?"

"I like the brown," she began to smile. "But that's only because you never wear it."

"I wear it…you just never see me with it on."

"Uh-huh…right," she chuckled softly. "You gonna answer my question?"

Tossing the other thermal back in the closet, he pulled the chestnut article of clothing over his head, grabbing a pair of trousers from the dresser across from the bed. The window behind the dresser warmed Bill's skin of grey, matching well with the brown buttoned thermal Kat saw fit to her liking, not so much his own. The sheen of his jagged, wiry black hair had almost been diluted of color from the sun's radiance, his scraggly beard without exception. From the surface of the dresser, Bill grabbed his harmonica where he'd placed it the two previous nights—misplaced, habitually it would never leave him. A keepsake, something invaluable of his son's to be always with him.

"To answer your question," said Bill, glancing back at her, "I plan to seize the day. First thing, I'm going to rearrange all the tables downstairs and make rows of two instead of smaller rows of four."

"How daring." Kat prodded.

In the dresser's lowest drawer, he shuffled through piles of socks and undergarments. "I'm sure it'll bring some life to the place, haven't moved things around since...I believe when Tycho and I got new furniture."

"And I'm sure everyone will notice your change in display," she said grinningly. "...Tycho, how's he doing after last night?"

"He's holding up," said Bill. "Nothing seems to faze that kid. I know he's brave and with all that gusto but...it's becoming clearer to me that he doesn't understand how precious his own life is. It's just too easy for him..."

Bill became quiet, waiting for Kat to respond. She did not. Bill continued.

"I know he doesn't remember how he wound up here a corpse, but after telling him about it...you'd think he'd be a little more cautious for it to not happen again. He stills runs out there, thinking he can save the world. Sooner or later, it's gonna catch up to him..."

Bill lifted a pair of black socks.

"The black socks," smiled Kat. "Those will look nice on you."

Bill paused.

"Sure thing, honey."

Plopping on his boots, he hopped over to her briefly.

"I told him to be here around the same time as usual for scrubbin', and that you'd be making breakfast."

"How kind of you to ask."

Bill kissed her.

"You know his favorite right?!" He hollered as he made his way down the stairs.

"Yep…" She slowly rose, sitting on the edge of the bed. "After so many years, how could I forget."

With a clamor of the town at the steps of *Papa's Retreat*, men hung their heads inside as they watched Bill from the square slots along the walls of the saloon, empty of glass. Politely, Bill greeted them with a smile, and swung his curtains to blind them until he was open for business—there was much cleaning to do. But first, there was something else needing taking care of.

Exiting through the side door near the end of the saloon, he walked around to the back and grabbed a wheelbarrow of hay.

"Hey, Meseron," he said, clicking his tongue. "How we doin', girl?"

Attached to the back of the saloon, there was a stall for holding Bill's mustang—white, a blotch of grey tainting her thigh. They used to ride together, but Bill was beginning to tire, his youth slipping away from him. Most of the time, Bill would check up on her and reminisce of their springtide days, regrettably most if not all within wartime.

"Hope the loud noises didn't upset you last night. Nah, you're used to it, huh?" He chuckled. Using the rope from the pulley within her stable, he lowered her feeding bag and filled it with hay, emptying the wheelbarrow of the suntanned grass.

"Looks like I'll have Tycho pick up another bale." He wiped the sweat from his forehead.

Meseron lowered her head from the stall door. Patting her head, he pulled a sugar cube lodged within the crease of his pocket, dusting it of lint as he fed it to her. Meseron nuzzled her nose beside his head.

Walking back inside, noticing how messy the place was, it came to him that preparing the saloon the night before might be a better, more effective method—allowing more time in the day, be it an hour, to strike gold with perhaps customers …and that's where his thought ended. Stepping on a chunk of glass from behind the counter, striking through the sole of his shoe, he pulled out his broom and began to sweep. He did well to brush off the pain, the sporadic curse to soothe the cut; later when he would return to bed had he considered mending the intrusion.

After clearing the floor of glass, he readjusted the furniture within the space given, Bill having to lift chairs to make them fit elsewhere, and secured them in the space that gave him delight in his subtle accomplishment. He began straightening the chairs around the tables of the saloon incessantly, waiting for Tycho.

Returning to the counter, as he wiped it down of grease and spills of rum, and the occasional shard, he glanced at his reflection. Leaning, he peered into the streak.

Bill turned his face in the reflection, grinning. "Not half bad…"

About noontide Bill grew curious as to where Tycho was, and it was half an hour later when he started to become frustrated at his forgetfulness and sloth behavior, refusing to wake the boy due to his own incompetence.

Tapping his fingers on the counter, slouched, contemplating whether to undertake Tycho's chores, Bill peeked at the rustling of the curtains. Brushing past them, Bill saw him; overjoyed, he remained expressively stern. Seeing him washed away any irritation he had for the boy, pleased he showed nonetheless, although this was the fourth time he'd decide to sleep-in than arrive when instructed.

"Sorry I'm late," said Tycho. "What's up with the curtains?"

Bill said, staying behind the counter, "Don't worry 'bout it, and I don't want an apology. Just be here on time…That's all I ask."

Kicking a chair around to sit in, Tycho bounced to the seat, his arms at rest on the cresting rail.

"So whaddya have planned for me today?" he asked.

"I've already swept the floor and watered-down the counter, but you, I need you to sweep out the stall, clean the dishes and wipe down the tables and chairs—"

"You didn't already do that?" said Tycho. "Not that…I—"

Bill hardened in his gaze.

"No, I did not…I left that to you. This time, I ain't doing your share of work; so get goin', I've already kept our guests waiting out there for long enough."

"Right…," sighed Tycho.

Bill leaned over the counter. "Stop being lazy, and get scrubbin'— I don't care what order you do it in, just get it done."

"What about breakfast?" said Tycho, his head gently lifting.

"It's not exactly morning anymore, is it?" said Bill, grinning.

Tycho put down his head, feigning discontent: "Wow…this could be the worst day of my life."

"I can see you're deeply upset." Bill aware of the boy's irreverence, smiled.

"Regardless, you get cleaning now," said Bill, "I'll ask if Kat will ready you up some grub afterward. But the sooner you start, the better the chance—"

"Yep, got it!" said Tycho, springing out from his chair.

Bill chuckled beside himself.

In a flurry, Tycho snapped the cap off from the dish soap and got to scrubbing, bubbles and an avalanche of twinkling foam pouring out from over the sink. The back kitchen became flooded.

Swinging open the back door, Tycho rushed to the stable and began cleaning Meseron's less-than-desirable mess. Shoveling the waste from out of the stable, Tycho held his breath until he could no longer. "Geez, Meseron," said Tycho, "what else has Bill been feeding you?"

Tycho's back to her, Meseron grabbed his hat with her teeth, flaunting it away from him. "Hey," he chuckled, "give that back!" He reached with hops, Meseron seemingly grinning, teasing the bot.

Eventually, Tycho was able to get his hat back, swiping it from her. Locking the stable door behind him, smiling, he said some words to her, readjusting his hat as he made his way back inside.

Next, the chairs and tables.

Grabbing a mop, Tycho hopped onto a table, almost tipping it over with his swift land. As he began to swab the tabletop, Tycho dancing around the watered streaks beside his feet, Bill stared, not in the least amused. As fast as he leaped onto that table, Tycho settled himself on the floor and put the mop back, grabbing a rag and a sponge Bill held out for him to take instead.

Those waiting very patiently outside struck a chain of yawns, scratching their rumps in harmony. The road beside them was beaten from the pounds of hoofs and stomps of feet as town markets and general good stores flooded with travelers. Particularly, hunters and miners would trade their skins and crystalline chunks for pounds of gredo; the small rhombus-like cubes supplemented the need for attaching weighty gold nuggets and ores to one's person, and in some occasions, other establishments and merchants only accepted payment in gredo, refusing gold, as they would rather not chance it being a forgery of the scarce rock.

Preparing the saloon, Bill overheard the chatter of his customers, surprised at their vigilance to stick around for so long, but more than anything he was thankful for them. He had good people around him to keep him going, either Lojus, the drunkard who told tall tales of his youth, or his quick-witted wife, Kat, he knew he'd be in the best of company.

From behind the counter, Bill watched Tycho, continuing to wipe down the tables.

"You did good out there last night," said Bill. "I'm proud of you, kid."

"When aren't I?" Tycho smirked.

"I wouldn't get too ahead of yourself," said Bill. "Don't forget who taught you everything you have to know. You were dumber than most when we first met. You remember, don't you?"

"Hey," said Tycho. "That's not exactly fair, I—"

"I don't know," said Bill, scratching his beard. "Depends."

Bill smiling, Tycho grew a frown.

"Regardless of your fugue," he jeered, "you were still stupid enough to almost get yourself killed. There you were…in pieces—"

"If I hear this story one more time…" muttered Tycho under his breath.

"I found you," said Bill, "your limbs torn, strewn from your body, your core hidden beneath the sand. Most hadn't a clue you were out there, keeping themselves indoors; they feared those bandits, those Congregation thugs who came around these parts, having them too afraid to leave their own homes…well, that was until you booted them out."

"Was that me?" Tycho raised the question, conceitedly.

"Shut it," said Bill. "So, one night, I snuck out, keeping out of sight from those desperados, gathering up taxes from the folk around here…taking our women, sons, and daughters to be chained if they didn't pay up."

Tycho slowed his wipes.

"The Congregation," said Bill, "after all this time since you've been here, they still don't seem to get the message that we don't want them in these parts no more. I guess its ignorance, thinking the guy who came before deserved his fate; they all tend to think like that. They're all a bunch of animals."

"As if they weren't before," said Kat, her burgundy dress fluttering softly as she made her way down the steps of the stairs to the kitchen.

"Sure," chuckled Bill, "only now they're counting the gains of their wealth rather than acting upon that ideology they once worshiped so passionately…putting this town and other settlements into a depression."

Intrigued, the young bot quelled himself to blare out a question. Looking from Kat, he put his eyes back on Bill.

"If they caught me out there," said Bill, his eyes placed on the woman briefly, "they would've taken the both of us, but seeing you out there, I couldn't…I had to get you. I left Kat in the dark about the whole thing, until she wised up." He caught her glare, smirking.

Resting with his elbow, Tycho leaned on the side of the table, and listened.

"I brought you here, into town, and rebuilt you. All I did, with every morning till night, I would work on you until…that day you awoke."

Bill's eyes glistened.

"The first time you opened your eyes…the Shine proudly made its presence known, watching over you…almost as if it were your guardian angel. You then sat up and looked to me, smiling."

He poised his hands on the counter, his arms stiffened.

"In a way, you became my passion project…and I can see that my hard work has paid off splendorously."

"Splendorously isn't a word, Bill."

"Whatever, you know what I mean…!"

Bill and Tycho began cracking up, laughing restlessly.

They returned to their chores, Tycho scrubbing away as Bill dusted the shelves below the counter, lining each mug perfectly. Deciding to pull back the curtains, Bill saw noon dwindling as evening approached with its setting light; nevertheless, eager Sol Puestans brought his establishment to life, flooding the counter; he considered extending opening hours to make up for the day's loss. Tycho was about finished with wiping down the furniture, at times distracted which slowed his pace. But a scent had him reinvigorated, rising out from the kitchen, an aroma, a ferociously, delectable scent snagged all of Tycho's motor skills and had him drifting towards the precious smell. Placed on the table nearest to him, a dish of Brench toast, doused in thick, amber syrup, the viscous rivers of sugar shimmering, jiggling soft as the plate gently tapped against the table's surface.

Bill started letting people in, *Papa's Retreat*, open for service. To be honest it was about time.

Sitting beside him, Kat smiled as she watched Tycho devour his afternoon breakfast feast, her head resting in the palm of her hand.

"How is it?" said Kat, her chocolate crescent-cut eyes shrouded underneath her golden bangs. Her freckles peeked through the cracks of her fingers, the brown specks upon her deep blue cheeks a seashore to the ocean in her eyes.

"Awesume…!" He relentlessly chewed.

She chuckled. "I always make good Brench Toast, huh?"

Tycho nodded.

"So," said Kat, "I have this yogurt and waffle parfait waiting in the kitchen, and…no one has tried it—yet! I was hoping someone, maybe the young man sitting beside me, would try it and tell me if it tastes good or not. Interested?"

In heaven, Tycho gently turned his head to her, his eyes glazed, and said, "Yesh, that sounds…amazing."

"I'll go get it right now." Kat grinned, walking to the back kitchen.

"Also," she hollered over the men beginning to fill the bar, "when doing the dishes, don't use so much soap! I almost slipped when I walked in here!"

Tycho looked up from his plate, swallowing his last bit of food. "My bad! I'll make sure not to do that next time, promise!"

"You better…or else!" She pointed her finger at him, leaving Tycho with a smile proceeding into the kitchen.

"Hey," said Bill, surprising Tycho from behind. "Here's some gredo, go get some glass from the shop and tell me when you've finished fitting all the windows in town. If you need help, I'll see if Chester can lend a hand."

"But—"

"It can wait, I'll let Kat know."

"Always know when to ruin a good moment, huh, Bill?"

"No one better."

"*Buzzkill…*"

"What was that?"

"Nothing," Tycho cleared his throat. "Weird how words can just come out sometimes…"

"Mhmm, sure thing, kid. Now get to it."

With evening onset, Tycho began to work in the cooling hours of daylight. Much of the folks sauntering through the town of the falling sun retired from their business, some aiding Tycho in his tedious task, those whose homes had been marred in the scuffle. But, a greater part of townsfolk slurred words of hatred as he kept his tongue tied to a blistering knot, half-shells of peanuts and thick wads of chewing tobacco thrown and spat in his face. He was tempted to raise his fists, fantasizing their teeth crushing in-between the gaps of his knuckles, but held back. Bill taught him better, that others without guidance know not what they do, whether actions callous or malicious are done it is better to spare them than to grow fond of beating the blind— bandits, on the other hand, are aware of their intentional cruelties and the agendas they follow, and so should be protected against and dealt with without forgiveness. Besides, he could never have the stomach to touch a hair on any of them. For he was the guardian of Sol Puesta, it's champion, he would fight for them with his last ever-enduring breath.

Tycho pushed throughout the night, with rancid dribble covering his eyes, using the poncho's tail to repeatedly wipe them clean.

II

UNWANTED VISITATION

FOUR days had passed. Behind the bunking house, a freshly made carcass of some slain vectra was emptied of its bowels as its limbs intermittently jerked, discarded parts of its entrails draped on the roof's eave.

Hunched, the predator's head gave rise. From the bunking house's raised center of roofage, still, it gazed forward. In its paw, it devoured the flesh of the wolf; the stripping of its skin and the crunch, the chilling echo of snapped bones gave further crave to its feast. Its snout dripping redder and redder, the smacking of its mouth against the tender muscles culminated its throat lodged with gluttonous amounts of meat that it could barely swallow.

With its gorging at an end, its wetted lips and snout steaming, it became upright, and gradually its spine cracked foully as it became erect. It was idle for a time before lunging for the establishment across from where it stood. Dust fell from the ceiling of *Papa's Retreat*, Bill looking up—curious; he subdued his subtle intrigue and returned to sweeping.

All at rest none proceeded to walk the grounds of Sol Puesta; the shops closed, their candles quenched, those afoot or on carriage hauled by mares of behemoth stature had their business ceased. The chairs on the porches of neighbors screeched, swaying methodically to the arid wind, curling waves of dirt impacting against their porch steps from the road. For the roars of the pounding wind had deafened the crawls of this creature.

Fitting its claws into the fissure of the plywood layers of the roof, it tore, cracking back the sheets; nails ripped away from the beams, clattering as they flung outward, rolling down from the roof. It slunk into the gutted hole it mangled wide, landing faint within the attic of the saloon. Hearing echoes, it pressed its head slowly against the floor of the attic, listening to Bill's muffled talk.

"He's been gone for some time…Mhmm," he grumbled. "What's taking him so long?"

"Should I be concerned, honey? I'm finding you more and more mumbling obscenities."

From out of the back kitchen drying a plate Kat blew a few strands of hair away from her eye, looking to her beloved with heart.

"Am I always one to champion a sailor's mouth?" He smiled. "But I'm alright, love—sorting through thoughts is all I'm doing."

"And by *sorting through thoughts* does that involve whispering on like some madman?" Kat taunted him.

The old man chuckled.

"What's on your mind, Bill?"

The creature overhead, it pried to hear more.

"It's nothing," he said.

"Really now"—Kat curled the back of her hand against her waist—"think you can get away that easy? You should know better. What's up?"

Pulling his eyes away from the sweeping bristles of his broom, becoming still, he turned his head to his shoulder and looked to her.

"He's still not back after two days. He's never been out this long on a patrol." He rested on his broom.

"You're worried, aren't you?" She smirked.

Bill's eyes darted to the floor.

"You have to let him do his thing. If he thinks it'll keep us safe—"

"Safe…" he snickered. "Yea, and in the meantime, he's jumping in head-first. All the kid cares about is getting to blow open some guy's head and call it a day. Sometimes I think that Shine of his does more harm for him than good."

"Don't talk like that," said Kat. "He cares for us, you know that. That's why he even goes out there in the first place. Sure he's…a little spirited at times—"

"A little—?"

"Let me finish," Kat interjected gently. "Tycho isn't one for foresight, I'll give you that, but he sure as hell gets the job done. He protects this town regardless, no matter who or what comes trespassing through these parts, just like you had too…*when my man was a lil' slimmer at the waist.*"

Bill gestured with his hand. "You hear that…it's the echo of the same ol' crap I've heard a thousand times."

"Don't be a jerk." Her features wrinkled at her scowl.

Bill nodded. "Maybe I should have gone with him…"

"Next time you should," said Kat, rather irritable. "You'd probably whine less."

Bill chuckled. Looking up at her, he smiled at a short length.

"I feel like he's all we ever talk about."

Kat huffed faintly, regaining her formal demeanor. "Yeah…sure seems like it."

"Honey," said Bill. "I appreciate you staying up with me, to clean up the place a bit."

Rosy became Kat's face.

"You don't have to thank me; I'm going to bed."

Leaning, Bill awaited his kiss.

Looking back, Kat chuckled with a playful expression. "Think again."

She walked from him, leaving Bill stranded until he took a hold of her hand, easing the woman near with a gentle tug, and, placing his hand at her chin lifted her precious lips against his own, rough and cracked kiss. Enamored, she placed the dish within the drying rack of the kitchen resisting her giggling fit, thereafter making her way to the stairs. Reaching the second floor, Kat paused.

"Bill, honey…"

He looked gradually to the balustrade where Kat leaned.

"Stop thinking about him, he's fine. There's no reason you should be worrying."

Bill shifted his eyes away from her and smirked, moving his broom in the pattern he'd fallen entranced to previously. "Even if it were in my power, I wouldn't…" He mumbled.

Crawling, it dragged its body from its waist down as if it were limp, its ossified hips knocking gently against the ridge of the support beams—for the attic was without complete flooring. From its hide, a black excretion spilled over the wooden beams, thick and stomach-knotting as tar's stench, furthering its ghastly drag towards the door that hung above the closet room.

Undressing, Kat put her clothes away and closed the closet door. The sound of Bill's sweeping was soothing, lying in bed, listening to the bristles scratch against the cracks of the floor. It wasn't long until she fell asleep to the unremitting scrapes of the night.

The scuttle door to the closet lifted. There was a subtle thump. It stood in the closet room, staring at the wooden door, ere scrabbling at its surface until reaching for the knob. Its paw-like hand slipped, the doorknob jerked. It grabbed it again, and slowly turned it. The door unfastened from its jamb quietly. It spied her, Kat's form given to the creature by the blanket.

Through the agape shadow of the mouth of the door, it dropped to its hands and began to crawl. It pulled itself onto the bed, the sheets pulling gently underneath her. It placed its hands beside her head and purred. Holding itself over her astraddle, it started to smell—along her neck to her bosom, it breathed. Its throat clacking faint, the reverberations of its purr intensified, not to be heard by her as she was a sound sleeper.

From the end of its spine, a nub sprouted. Thickening, it grew, protruding into a tail-like appendage. It curved upwards, a hook of a shadow cast against the floor of the room. Kat's blanket became arisen, the tail ridding of its shadow to caress forward along her haunch. Her eyes shot open to the touch. Before she could scream, the tail constricted around her throat in a sudden thrust, leaving her eyes to water. It growled, head shaking in place. In this arrest, Kat was galvanized to seize her knife from the periphery of her mattress—a precaution, if ever a fellow was to bring himself within the confines of their abode unexpected. She clawed for the hilt of the knife, scratching her grabbling, mad fingertips against its wooden surface. But with each touch to drag her leverage in hand, her attempts brought only further distance to the point, becoming sunken into the bed's center. The impacts from her drubbing absorbing into its skin, Kat strenuously removing her hands and feet from the sludge-like hide, she decidedly flailed her tarred arms and legs against the mattress, hoping Bill would hear, pulling against the side of the bed in the yearning of becoming free from the intruder's strangle.

Her voice squeaking until silenced, Kat looked into the eyes of the creature, attempting to remove the constriction about her throat as she gasped for air. She could see the image of a woman in stifle—dying, not wanting to believe that this hapless reflection belonged to her.

The creature lifted its hand out to her, cutting into her delicately. Kat raising her quaking eyes, she watched as the creature carved into the canvas that was her forehead, oil from her torn flesh running alongside her eyes, dripping from off her lips.

Whimpering, Kat felt its finger press upon her wetted lips.

"*Shh...*"

It uttered this to her gently. Smiling, its gums receding as its jutting dentition glinted, the waft of the digesting craw of slain kill permeated.

Gliding its tail past her clenched lips, prying open her jaws, it struck violently down her throat. It was then its appendage begun to throb, the end of its tail spitting its substance inside of her. Turning into a husk—void of fear—her mouth drooped wide. Channeling up through her eyes, the secretion flooded them of light, pulling to the wound that began to illuminate on the crust of her forehead. The mark, as it had been but a laceration before, dazzled the room with its horrid light, the creature's searing anew to the flesh upon its forehead.

Bill had heard nothing. Extinguishing the blaze from the candle near the end of the counter, he was done for the night. He made his way up the stairs.

In their bedroom, the creature turned its head hurriedly to the door of his approach, the burning sigil mark ceasing with its glow.

Bill opened the door.

The stench of rotting flesh and the bitterness of tar struck him odd.

At the edge of the bed, Kat sat looking to the window, its white curtains washed in the moon's light.

"You're still up?" Bill yawned, rubbing his eye. Slowly, he shuffled towards her.

Her hands were not propped on the bed, or her lap, or knees; they hung, arms suspended. Her back rolled inward, her head jerking in convulsion. Bill confused, became unsettled the closer he approached.

"Honey," said Bill, slowing his steps, "is everything alright?" He presented the question sternly, reserving his instantaneity of dread.

It watched him from the ceiling's corner.

Bill put his hand on her shoulder, glancing out the window to where she gazed. "The night terrors getting at you again——?" He looked down to see her face. A black, tarry substance came bubbling to her lips.

A crack echoed throughout the room—twisting her head brutally, she bellowed tremendously, opening her mouth to Bill's hand. Her fangs split through the palm with her bite, ripping the hand from his arm. Oil spouted, holding his arm down. Light-headed, he pocketed the severed wound into his armpit to block the jolting outflow. He stumbled and fell back against the wall, watching as Kat slowly lifted from the bed, seemingly unaffected by the former's bloodcurdling cries of pain. She turned and walked towards the agonized Bill. The black tar now drenched beyond her mouth, soaking into the crease of her bosom.

"Reven…en…ce?" Her breath rattled. Hiding within the corner of the ceiling beside Bill, the creature became her puppeteer, manipulating her speech, its lips and tongue mimicked by Kat, the cursed blood its strings. The creature itself could speak, but it could not reveal furthermore of its presence, Kat used as its oracle.

"Dece rö…" She walked nearer.

Bill struggled to keep his eyes open, watching Kat fade into darkness.

"Reven en ce?!" she roared. "Reven en tcöng Verumshaï?!"

The window shattered. Kat looked back, beginning to howl as she became enveloped in light. The muck on her lips and breast burned, blasting away in flakes, free of its control. Her legs quivering, she suddenly blacked out, Tycho catching her fall. The creature scurried to the closet room, away from the smoldering flash of the Shine; the wailing winds tittering with the closet door, surging from the vaquero's blindsiding entry.

"Bill," said Tycho fearfully calm. "What's going on…?"

Bill weakly pointed to the closet.

The Shine lessening, the creature pounded past the closet door, lunging onto Tycho; its quarry present there was no longer a need to hide, furthermore the light retarding. Kat dropped to the floor, Tycho pushing back strenuously against the thrusts of its claws.

Dragging himself over to Kat, Bill pulled with his forearm, pushing forward with his feet. His thermal soaked, smeared with oil from the breast down, his arm bled a path against the floor from where the appendage had been severed.

Bill crawled next to her, combing his shaky fingers through her hair. "Kat...you with me, baby?"

"Wha...what's happening?" Tar oozed from the corner of her mouth.

"It's okay, babe. Tycho's here...Tycho's here." He looked up to him, uncertain whether the vaquero would be the decisive victor. "No...Kat—Kat open your eyes. Keep talkin' to me."

The creature forced its weight on Tycho, the tips of its claws masking his face in cuts as he resisted. Tycho dipped his head to the side, its claw crashing through the wooden floor, splinters, and chunks of wood bursting with its slash. Swiftly, Tycho pulled the Havoc from his holster and cracked a round into its gut. Snapping through its spine, its stomach bursting, eroded bones and shriveled organs clotted in undigested fur spurted out from its blown open backside, splashing viciously against the ceiling to the floor.

It howled horridly—miserably.

Looking through the excavation his bolt had made through the lower end of its torso, he saw the bottom half of a sphere lodged above the opening—engraved, absent of light. His bolt had scarcely threshed past it. It appeared to him that it was indeed a core, although its lack of colored palpitations struck him in the certainty that it was no longer active. The opening beginning to tether shut, black whips of tar sowing its void closed, Tycho was curious, but more so in a panic that his attempts of slaying the creature hadn't worked.

The jaws of the creature began to lengthen, a deafening pop as its lower mandible released. Slamming its hands down on Tycho's arms, the Havoc tumbled across the floor away from him. Holding his head back from its fangs that festooned and webbed saliva, a trickling ray of light shot into Tycho's eyes—he squinted at its forehead. Cracking through its skull, a glow bled through its skin. The sigil that bore its markings on the bandit's bandana branded itself upon its flesh anew.

Tycho finding himself deepened in the abyss of its maw, its tongue lashed forward, wrapping around his knees. Painfully, freeing one of his arms from its hold, he squeezed his hand around the constricting tongue, pulling effortful to sever it from its mouth. It only lengthened the further he pulled, tightening its grasp around him. From the scattered shards of the window lain beside them, Tycho grabbed a chunk of glass, slashing open its tongue—a spray of black from the dividing underbelly of the muscle washing beside his legs.

Erecting sinuously from its rear, the tail lashed forward, whipping the chunk of glass from the vaquero's hand, the tongue becoming un-torn. Placing out its arms in a brace, it pulled him inward—its upper mouth peeling back with the gradual tearing of its palate.

"Shine, now would be the time…!" Tycho grunted, holding back from his drag into the hauntingly gaping chasm of the creature.

It became clearer to see the back of its throat, its tongue slathered in sludge as it jerked. Its gullet excitedly began to convulse, spitting black tar from its bowels to lubricate its swallow.

"C'mon, don't let me down now, buddy!"

His feet pushed—slipped against the back of its gullet.

"Shine!"

In a blazing rupture of white, the creature expelled Tycho from its capture, its tongue in rapid disintegration as it cried.

"There we go, much better!" Hastening, he pushed back with the light.

Falling from the verge of its mouth, the creature trembled and cried terribly as it skipped away from Tycho on all-fours, cowering.

Pushing up from his knee, Tycho,—cuts on his cheeks and mouth sealing,—looked to the creature, slinking awry from where he wanted it to be. Bill became insensible upon Kat, both tired and without strength to keep themselves attentive. The creature stepped beside them, Tycho following its movements very carefully. The Shine beginning to wither, his eyes darted to Bill. The creature noticed this.

Taking Bill by the collar, it leaped out of the room dragging him behind.

"No," Tycho uttered, grabbing the Havoc as he raced after it. "Let go of him!"

Through the entrance of the saloon, it pulled him as it fled. Tycho close behind, the creature began to gallop—running vectra-like, clenching its fangs into Bill's arm as it carried him afar.

Tycho chased after it, following into the desert.

People had gathered outside of *Papa's retreat*, wondering what the commotion was all about—the screams and sudden silences, they just stood and listened, waiting for someone to do something. They watched as Tycho left the saloon, curious as to what he was chasing after—*a bandit perhaps*, they thought. For the grotesque image of the creature was incomprehensible, as for it being a bandit was the only concluding thought that made sense. *What else takes people from their homes?*

Tycho shot at the creature, pushing himself forward, his core pounding as he launched his feet from the ground. Panting, his breaths becoming sharp, he watched as the creature disappeared into the silhouette of the mountains, jutting against the darkened blue sky of night.

"Bill!" He shouted out of breath. "Bill!"

Tycho didn't stop running; he continued to chase after the creature. But eventually, he gave in to his body's demand, stumbling to his knees, his chest tightening.

Tycho began squeezing the dirt, sand gritting through his fingers. His lips quivered. Looking out, a dreadful glare arose upon him—his teeth gnashing. Making his way back to town, to the stable behind the saloon, he released the lock from the stable door and took Meseron.

"Hey, where you off to?!" said the sheriff commanding, in spite of being concerned. Tycho riding his way through town said, "Kat's badly injured, get her to the infirmary now!"

"But…"

"Get her out of there!"

The sheriff snapped out from his hesitation and ran in with his men, ordering but a few to secure the area as the rest of them made haste for the lifeless woman.

Leaving Sol Puesta, he regretted in being so far in his hunt during his patrol for the man whom he was warned of, waiting for his arrival, by the end of his search taken aback by Kat's damning cry. He promised her, to himself, that he'd return with Bill—that those bandits would have hell coming their way.

That mark, where did it come from…? No, who is it coming from— who's branding these people? If it's the Congregation—but how?

For Dargan and the creature bore the same mark, it was his only assumption that the Congregation was tethered to such a being, using it in their hunt to enslave peasant men—taming it, like their vectras. It did cross his mind that it came to abduct for a ransom, whether this was an often tactic by the Congregation, there were still stories fluttering about through the Wasteland by the mouths of defected thieves that would tell you so.

The flesh of that creature coming out from Kat, he thought, *it burnt to ash like Dargan's bandana. And that mark, how was it capable of burning through its skin?*

"Alright, girl." Tycho recaptured his focus. "Let's bring Bill back home."

Lashing on the reins, Tycho shouted, Meseron bolting as she pounded against the earth. Heading for the mountains, they would pass through the crevices many merchants and bandits took to reach the isolated settlement. If they were to find themselves on the other side, Tycho would need forbearance—he would not last without.

TYCHO PYRON, CHAMPION OF SOL PUESTA

III

THE RAVAJA WASTELAND

ORNING'S light flooded in-between the base of the mountains' walls, each crevice granting passage yellowing until shimmers began to reflect on the vaquero and mount's skin, the wonderful sear of the sun baking their backsides. From the late evening of his departure, the venture through the range was accompanied with perseverance, passionately fueled by a fit of unrighteous anger to see to the end that he'd find Bill, and very careful observation of what was to come to surround him as he furthered his way into the cragged paths that followed.

"It's already dawn?" murmured Tycho agitatedly. "How could I've let this happen?! Bill is probably gone by now—no, you can't think like that! You can't think like that…" He sighed, bowing his head.

Tycho tried sticking to one trail, where most prints of that he could see remained from traders and their horses, the defined softened streaks of wheels from carriages pressed into the sand from recent excursions. He wondered if he would find a merchant or a band of them on his way that could guide him to reach the other side, but to his disappointment, none had passed through—or simply they were on separate paths, for there were several passageways one could become lost to. Traders fascinated themselves with the horror of casting the title *Minotaur's Run* to these range of mountains, sickly making light of a fear that enraptured all their hearts. For many found themselves cornered by dead ends, hunted by stampedes, hordes-worth of bandit raiding parties, thusly left to rot in the labyrinth of earthly horns. For Tycho's sake, it would be in chance and careful observation that such inconveniences would not come his way.

Tycho stayed on the path he trusted, the most traffic of feet and other distinctions that would direct him to have egress from the range. Soon, less and less of the bent brown walls of stone that became accustomed to Tycho's sense of sight—a dull sight—was becoming much more linear, strengthened light seeping against the edges of the pathway as it straightened. Ahead, a blinding wall of radiancy awaited Tycho. Past it, he would find the Wasteland.

His stomach began to jitter, his core pattering mildly. Tycho had never been this far from home, repressing the fear that may have arisen inside. Leaving the pathway, he remembered the stories the merchants told him of the Ravaja, Tycho's curiosity striking many conversations and questions as to what lied on the opposite side of town. In those times Tycho would toss in bed, sleepless, gazing at the ceiling in fantastical thought of yearning to know more, what else was out there. All of it, every question he'd envisioned, was about to be answered.

Passing through the veil of light that screened the Wasteland, looking out from Meseron, the imposing venue was more than satiable, at the least overwhelming for him to fathom. From the sprawling dunes speared by glimmering crystals of variegated light, cactuses, shrubbery, and emaciated beasts roaming the flatlands, goliath obstructions of stone pervaded. Buttes and tremendously vast mesas conquered over the plains of the Ravaja, defaced luminary guardsmen carved into the side walls of these uplifted stone masses, towering above everything else—their presence disheartening, foreign to him. And in isolation, piercing the rim of the horizon, *Titan Summit* sat—the sun graciously rising from its bow.

Tycho began to chuckle. "Would you look at that…it's more remarkable than I ever pictured it being."

Meseron pawing the ground, her hoof digging into the sand, Tycho looked to her and said, "Well aren't you the impatient one? Alright, hold on—just…give me a moment."

He sat there looking out for a few more seconds and was then satisfied. "Okay," he exhaled. "Let's be off then, eh Meseron?"

He chuckled.

"Alright…here we go," said Tycho, anxious to look back from the crevice he had exited. "There ain't returning home until I find him."

Taking a deep breath, he took off, leaving Sol Puesta indefinitely. He thought of Kat as he plunged into the heart of the Ravaja, if she was doing any better than the condition he left her in. Tycho felt sick about not staying to help her, telling himself that Kat would have it this way—Bill was abducted, the longer he would have waited, the more strenuous his venture would be to get him back. His chances of finding him were minimal, but he didn't waste time to have the obvious mend his actions; there was no room for doubt.

The mountains, once a formidable blockade from the threats of the outside world, though, not a very good one at that, became great in distance once more as Tycho delved into the arid plains of the Ravaja Wasteland. Racing past the dunes that pocketed themselves among the barren grounds, an odorous breeze rushed past him—foul, yet exciting in the whiff he'd caught. Placing his hand out, he swept his fingers along the edge of the protruding crystals as he hastened beside them, shimmering to his touch. Stupidly, he left his hand out to be pricked by the cactus that followed.

Gazing at the monolithic sculpture that neared, seemingly looming ever closer to him, Tycho was enraptured by the scale of its image; he was but a grain of sand held to such a colossal figure of sovereign proportions. It began to tremble, shaking violently as the ground began to quake. Ascending from the crust of the earth, the butte obtruded, the guardsman swaying to its pull. Its ankles tore from the land, its feet left remnant—swallowed by the opening depression consequently, the ground surrounding sinking to its consumption. Streams of sand and rock slid from the uprooted butte, the hollowed depression spreading as some giant's haunches exerted force against the rough surface. Its continental paw colliding down onto the surface, dunes erupting with its pound, Meseron became unsteady, Tycho tightening his hands on the reins as he witnessed the baffling scene.

Pushing itself out from the deep confines of Zodain, a resounding snap uttered from the butte that reached as far as the Wasteland's fringes. A crack struck swiftly along the center of the butte— spontaneously, it snapped in two. The giant's beaked mandible yawning wide, it howled with might, the guardsman shook to rubble from the reverberation of its roar. Leveling the plains, placing its foot clumsily on the cusp of the hollowed crater, trembling to its knee as the earth below sunk to its step, the severed remains of the butte began to fall away. Two rows of sails increasingly stretched alongside its back, the cast of the molded stone showering to dust. From hibernation, it awoke, from slumbering dormant in maturation it stood on its newly developed feet. It began to stravage the plains heedlessly. After such a long hibernation, its hunger ripened, there was but a single determining force that drove the behemoth. It sought to find a mate.

Tycho continued on his way through the Wasteland, dunes softening as they flattened to sheets over the arid expanse. A smile crept to Tycho's face, but for a short time; he reminded himself why he was out there to begin with. His eyes and fine hairs shimmered, the sun toasting Meseron's hide.

Gnawing at the carcass of one of their fallen, stripping away what withered skin remained, their ears erected to the thunderous pounds. Flying past, the breaths of the desert following in her run, their heads steered to her gradual passing. Howling, their chase had begun.

Tycho alerted, he spun his head around and watched as shadows in the dust-clouds approached upon Meseron. Coming up on her sides, snarling as they gnashed their teeth, the brutish wolves slathered their jaws in anticipation. One directed itself closer to Meseron's hind leg. Tycho pulled out the Havoc and shot underneath the vectra—flailing forward, it collapsed onto its side. Running ahead of the pack, to the right of Tycho, a vectra, its assurance much more evident, locked eyes with him briefly. On its forehead, there looked to be a crown, a white patch of fur embedded on its tawny hide. Tycho began shooting at the wolf. Evading two of his shots, the last almost hitting it, the crowned vectra lessened in its sprint, staying seconds behind Meseron with the rest of its pack—they too began to wane in their hunt, cowering in the chase.

Meseron overpowered them, her speed becoming unmatched. But soon, all desires of fleeing from the starved curs would end. Tycho looked out, the land slowly beginning to pull apart. A canyon awaited them, wide and abysmal. Nearing the cliff, the vectras persevering onward, there wasn't much he could do. Tycho shouted, yanking on the reins—Meseron rearing. She brayed, stepping back as the crowned vectra and its pack slowly approached, beginning to surround the vaquero and his mount. Glancing over the step that would lead them to the canyon below, tent rocks amass, Tycho returned to keeping his eyes on the gathering of wolves.

They crept closer. Tycho reloaded his gun, eyes burnished by the light of the torrid spikes. Lunging, they tore into Meseron's heels, violently pulling down on her. Tycho swung his arm down and pulled the trigger on the vectra nearest to him, popping its head open, shooting the others hemmed beside it. Beginning to claw up her frontal leg, chomping gnarly as they snapped for Tycho's foot, Meseron staggered. Tycho continued to hold them off, but in his narrowed focus, the crowned vectra lunged at him in his blindside. Tycho fell into the canyon, along with Meseron and the wolves attached to her save the crowned, scrabbling to the surface ere his flight. Reluctant to shout, Tycho tumbled in his descent, formulating a means of an escape—charming. Above him, racing downwards to the plunge, a frightened vectra smashed into Tycho's head, knocking him out cold. There was nothing but black.

The croaks from settled ravens drowned the canyon with their bellows, perched they were on their bodies. Pecking at their skin with intrigue, they became that much more aroused. They began plucking away at their fur coats, punching their beaks into their carcasses— steam flowed from the outpour of the warm blood. Dragged out from the pile as it began to sodden, its hand took him by the leg, tossing him over its shoulder.

The stale musk from its fur swaddled him in its odor. Becoming conscious of the sunlight on his lids, his eyes opened—he looked to the beast that held him. Hulking, its shoulders the width of the arms of an anchor, shaded by the shadows of the canyon walls and other formations surrounding, Tycho was certainly limp in his motivation to break free from its hold, he was much too drowsy for activity. But then, he began to hear it speak, listening to it wander in its words.

"Bednyy bot," he said looking over to him, "ya budu imet' vas zdorovyy—Oh, you're awake!"

Tycho gave it the most unsatisfied look of confusion. Slowly, he began to tire, enshrouded in the coming darkness of slumber.

"Rest, blue bot—all will be well." It chuckled.

The beast had returned to its home. Hanging in-between two columns of stone, acuate as they were thick, a nest wreathed by bone and branch drooped. Two ropes held its suspension, decorated with hollowed crystal chunks that burnished white as the sun's gaze reflected off the shimmering things, uttering sounds of chiming bliss with the wind's pass as they knocked against one another. The remains of an airship hedged on the outskirts of its home, its corpse sunken to the sands. Placing Tycho on its bed, wrapped in pelts of various game, it lathered a clear cream on his forehead to bring him relief of the bruise. Sauntering over to the stove as he swung down his gunny sack from his backside, humming jubilantly, it began preparing a meal for the weakened bot.

Putting its hand behind Tycho's head, he lifted his mouth to the soup. Slowly beginning to sip from the cusp of the bowl, Tycho began to awaken, the warming broth wetting his tongue and throat as he swallowed.

"Feeling better?" said the beast.

Tycho turned his eyes to it, but remained silent.

"Quiet, are we?" It grinned slightly.

Able to see the beast with much better focus, assisted by the light penetrating through the nesting's cracks to determine its form, strewn rays from the sun left golden streaks on its hide for Tycho to grasp its Herculean features. Its ears resting back alongside its head, it smiled as it scratched the bridge of its muzzle. Its eyes encased within a tinted pair of goggles Tycho hadn't determined their color, noticing the blackened spectacles matched its fur well enough that it appeared he hadn't eyes at all, the hair from his large head sheathing the band wrapped around it. Several strands of sunshine splotching its hide grey, the same brilliance revealed the network of veins running through his inky wing, similarly when raising a leaf to the sun to uncover its venation. And about his immeasurable shaggy throat hung a bandana rippled with white circles, weathered at its ends.

"Who are you?" said Tycho weakly.

"I am Sarkas…Sarkas Severov," the giant replied.

Tycho rubbed his forehead, the cream slightly sticking to the tips of his fingers.

"I saw you fall with your horse from the surface," said Sarkas. "Thankfully, I was able to catch you two in time. Here, finish your soup, there is not much left."

Tycho quickly downing what was left, he wiped his mouth and said, "Meseron, is she alright?!"

"She is being cared for," he said. "Those bites from those vectras were deep, but she will heal."

"You're a bat…aren't you?" Tycho asked.

"What gave it away…? Was it the fangs," he said as he closely lifted his flew to him, "or the wings?" He proudly displayed, exemplifying his grand stature.

Chuckling, Sarkas placed the bowl beside him on the table.

"If you don't care of me to ask," he said, "how did you end up on the other side of this canyon, or haven't you come far at all…Are you a mountain man?"

Tycho was hesitant, but thought he should say something regardless.

"No. I'm looking for a friend," he said, circumventing the question.

"'A *friend* is vague," said Sarkas. "What's this fellow's name, blue bot?"

Tycho refused to say anymore.

Sarkas chuckled. "Perhaps I should ask of yours first, no?"

Sarkas saw Tycho's irritation, the worrisome language his face expressed to him. Gently, Sarkas lifted the goggles from his hazel eyes and rested them on his brow, his smile drooping.

"Forgive me if I seemed…eager in knowing. This friend of yours, I'm sorry to hear that he has gone away from you. I can understand to an extent as to what you're feeling."

"Why do you care?" Tycho spoke softly, irritable.

Sarkas shook his head, but swiftly halted its sway.

"It does not matter…If you wish to no longer be bothered, be on your way."

Tycho looked out from the orifice of his home, taken aback by the elevation he found himself at. Looking down from over the bed, through the slits of the branches and knotted femurs, Meseron was partially visible; herself small as a rock, she was darkened by the shadow cast down upon her. Turning his head to see the rest of the room, Tycho saw an Aberican flag hanging from the wall, the national flag of Brussia hung alongside it. There was a rack that held more than a few medals, a shelf above that held photographs and a Faberge egg of crimson embroidered with jewels, crowned with two small portraits. The steam from the bowl remained steady, a savory scent that lingered with it. From the table to the plump quilted sack Sarkas sat on, a rug was laid out underneath—edged with a foreign text that Tycho could not read. Sitting behind Sarkas, an iron stove hissed, heaps of junk and glittering shards of crystals lining the walls around it—price tags slathered to their surfaces. Some of the trinkets appeared to be falling through the woven flooring.

"So," said Tycho, adjusting his attitude to be more amiable, "did you make this place all yourself...?"

Sarkas raising his head, repressing his growing smile, said, "No, I found it. It was left abandoned.

"I just moved everything that I had with me at the time within...this roost. I am thankful that whoever once dwelled here has not returned. After so many years...I don't think it ever will." He gazed at the space around Tycho.

Tycho looked to the egg on the shelf.

"Those portraits...are they of your family?"

Sarkas glanced at the portraits of his son and wife. He nodded, turning his head back to him bowed.

"Sarkas...why do you live all the way out here?" asked Tycho.

"I find it easier to be alone. The wastes give me that satisfaction."

Sarkas had a grim expression with the rise of his face.

"Then, why are you bothering yourself with me?"

Sarkas slowly grinned. "Chto zh...I don't know. Perhaps fate brought us here."

"Uh-huh," said Tycho. "But by your choosing, right?"

"More or less," he said. "But perhaps you are right; after all, I did drop you after you had been caught."

"Why—?"

"Do not worry, it's very simple to explain," Sarkas quickly interjected to say.

Sarkas inched closer in his pulpy seat.

"You see," said Sarkas, "I was in search of small treasures that had been brushed into this here canyon from the surface—then, out of the sky, I saw you!" He laughed.

"Of course, I'm being a bit dramatic, but I did indeed become alerted to your timely predicament! I had caught your horse…and then you, and then not you—"

"Any day now." Tycho crossed his arms.

"Breaking your fall, you somehow managed to evade my grasp. It was after I brought your horse here that I noticed you were not of presence. So I went back, and I found you—where I had dropped you! All is good now, no?"

Tycho moved his hand along his belt to his holster, pulling out his gun, checking to see if there were any cracks struck along the barrel. Spinning the chamber, the spikes of lightning flared.

"What iron is that?" Sarkas awed. He dipped his head closer to the spikes, smelling the dew-like evaporation that fumed from their eruption.

"It's called the Havoc," said Tycho. "Without much of a depleted source of ammunition, I can—"

Sarkas leaping out from his seat, the roost jolting, he clasped his nose as it bled, seeping out from the palm of his hands. Sarkas had stuck his nose too close to the spikes, his flesh becoming seared.

His back to Tycho, his face twitching, he began to hear the crackling of flames. Slowly, turning around with his hands remained held to his nose, his eyes widened to the sight. Flames of white, scorched eyes, the Shine revealed itself. Tycho looked along his arms and hands for any harsh scrapes or gashes, but he was fine.

"Hold on…," said Tycho in-question. "Why is it—?"

Tycho slowly looked to Sarkas.

"Come here…," he said. "It's okay; you'll be fine—promise."

Sarkas apprehensive, especially after being burnt, he sidled cautiously over to him.

"Now…let's see if this works."

Holding out his hand, Tycho pressed his palm against Sarkas' nose as it flashed white with varying rays of light. Stanched, all blood and scaring had vanished.

Tycho chuckled. "Awesome…didn't know it could do that," he said.

"I did not know eye-lights could do such miracles." Sarkas tapped his nose, his eyes crossed momentarily. "I have fought with many comrades that were bots in my past, and I have never seen such things but from the prophet…"

"Yea, well it's not exactly—never-mind."

Tycho and Sarkas talked for much longer, unaware at the time that had passed. He spoke of Sol Puesta, that he came from beyond *Minotaur's Run* in hope of finding his friend—albeit Tycho was absent on the details of what took him and what had happened prior, which eventually became easier for him to discuss in his journey onward. Tycho detailing the event to a summary, he failed in keeping Bill's identity discrete any further.

"So that's the name of the one you seek, is it not?!"

Tycho huffed, disappointed in his slip.

Sarkas excitedly rising from his quilted seat, looking out from the orifice said, "Then what are we waiting for?! Let us find him so you two can be reunited!"

Tycho waiting for the shaking to ease, he scooted from off the bed and landed lightly on his feet. "It's not that easy, Sarkas. I don't even know where I should be looking."

"You don't know where he is, hm?" Sarkas turned his head around to him.

Tycho opening his mouth to speak became quiet. He wiped his hand against the side of his face, lowering his eyes to the floor.

"I shall assist you in the best way I can then, blue bot."

Looking up, he saw Sarkas with a brimming smile of fangs—his wings crossed.

"We should leave now for the surface," said Sarkas, turning back to the orifice. "Once I land you up there, head west facing the canyon—there you will find the small town of Crest View. Maybe there you will find answers in regards to where your friend has gone. Most if not all who come through these parts of the Ravaja make stops there, even bandits, unfortunately."

Tycho's eyes lit up.

"Do you remember everything I have told you?"

"Ugh, yea—yea," said Tycho alerted.

"But…with Meseron," he said, "how are you gonna carry us all up there? I imagine going up ain't as easy."

"Mal'chik, you underestimate me."

Sarkas smiled back to him.

Tycho followed on Meseron as Sarkas guided them to the opposite side of the canyon that was a far reach from where they'd originally fallen—fourteen miles from Sarkas' home. The hike was bearable, but long, the sun at its setting. Meseron's wounds were still healing, but the bandages Sarkas applied to her ankles and legs helped her performance. Eventually, they reached the other side, Sarkas gazing up along the canyon wall, Tycho glancing at him before doing the same. A faint line, asperous, he could hardly make out the surface. Stretching vast like a glimmering vein upon the sky, the evanishing cliff of the canyon flickered pale, smoldered by the moon's light.

"Alright, big guy, show us what you got."

Sarkas hunched and spread his wing on the ground for Tycho to walk onto.

"Hop on," he smirked.

Leaping off from Meseron, Tycho ran up his wing and climbed onto his back, holding onto the brim of the gunny sack. "Good to go," he said, patting him on the shoulder.

Sarkas fitted his goggles over his eyes. "Then let's be off."

Sarkas began to beat his wings against the ground, clouds of dust rising at the pounds. Taking to the air, he grabbed Meseron by the saddle, the talons of his feet wresting ahold the leather seat. Lifting higher, Tycho looked down from Sarkas' back and saw Meseron jointly paddle her legs for escape.

"Oh no," said Tycho, chuckling. "Meseron—hey Meseron, it's fine! Calm yourself, girl!"

She neighed incessantly in rebellion.

"Will she be fine? She'll be fine, yea she's good," Tycho convinced himself, looking back to Sarkas.

"Ready?" Sarkas said impishly as if he were hiding something.

"Ready for what…?" Tycho hesitantly spoke.

Sarkas turned his head up. "Hold on," he said.

Elongating out his wings further, blanketing the wall of the canyon, Sarkas' rapidity began to build—it was until Tycho had almost lost consciousness he realized the velocity they were traveling at. A resounding boom thundered throughout the skies, a ripple of air popping beneath Sarkas as he soared along the canyon wall. Tycho couldn't get enough of it, a brazen grin stretched along his face as he held onto his hat.

"How are you doing this?!" shouted Tycho smilingly.

Sarkas' flew flapping wildly, he shouted, "Survival! If bat wishes to fly, he must teach himself to fly fast—to be burdened not by breath, but limitations! Without such drive, one such as myself may very well be without life!"

As the cliff faded in its reflecting glare, Sarkas bolted past the edging of the canyon, beginning to hover above the surface with his descent.

"And here we are!"

Placing Meseron on the ground of the surface, Tycho quickly jumped from Sarkas' back and ran over to her, trying to place his hands gently on her neck as she frantically gaited in circles. Soothed enough, Tycho leaped onto the saddle and looked up to him.

"You still haven't told me your name, blue bot!" He smiled.

"It's Tycho," he shouted to him over gusts that came from his wings. "Thanks for helping me out, for whatever the reason, I appreciate it!"

"Not needed, for it was a pleasure…Tycho."

Gradually flying away, Sarkas shouted back to him, "Good luck finding your friend—I mean Bill! Remember what I told you, go west—Crest View shall be in wait!"

"Where you off to?!" Tycho shouted.

"To sell, my friend. I am a merchant, am I not?"

"I don't know, are you?"

Sarkas bellowed with laughter. "I don't carry this bag with me for fun! For what purpose would it serve?!"

"I dunno, carrying stuff!"

"And what do you suppose I'm using this bag for?!"

"Oh…right, gotcha! But, I thought you didn't like…you know, being around others!"

"I have to feed myself somehow," hollered Sarkas, "and certainly will not be feasting on those vectras down there!"

Tycho's eye-lights materializing as the moon gave further rise, Sarkas became calm and stern.

"That reminds me, as for that *fire* in your eyes…?"

Tycho smiled, bobbing his head down. He looked back up to him.

"I'll tell you all about it when we meet up again one day...hopefully, I'll have a better understanding of it," said Tycho scratching the back of his head.

"So be it...Until we meet again!" The bat's hollering trailed afar.

Tycho nodded, waving so long.

By the streak of the moon inundating the desert land, Tycho rode onward through the silver glare of the glimmering grains of sand as if a road of heavenly light marked his already predetermined path. How fantastical. Regardless, Tycho and Meseron shortly became fatigued; Tycho throwing his head up from his tiresome slumps, fighting the voracious urge of slumber to keep his eyes alit. He couldn't be out if they were to be preyed upon once more.

Tycho asleep on Meseron, he awoke to the sun far from its rise, realizing he had failed in his troublesome duty to be alert throughout the rest of the morning hours. Fortunate, Meseron kept at her pace without faltering in their westward journey. And it wasn't very long until they reached the settlement, its foundation grounded at the edge of the canyon.

Tycho gazed at the structures, his eyes slowly widening. "Sarkas didn't say anything about a hanging city..."

Pillars of wood erected from the face of the canyon's wall, at an upwards slant they bore the weight of several shacks and structures. Upheld around the hollow center of an excavated tunnel, these shanty abodes boomed with echoing shouts as the tunnel shrieked of grinding steel. Bridges crafted of rope and thinned crystal shards for stepping swung attached to each of these miner's homes, each working denizen equipped with cable guns, *grappler dashers*, to access their suspended city and excavation routinely.

From the mouth of the tunnel minecarts rode on the outskirts of a maintenance staircase, hopping and jouncing down and about the rails as they sped from the port that would garner their troves and back again into the mine; some, more daring than others, would ride within their minecarts as they would plummet down the fine crystalline dusted railways, neck-deep in the stash of their harvested shards. As they collectively piled their share of quarry onto the lift attached to the port's end, stately-thick ropes were used to raise the lift as their heaps upon heaps of twinkling shards would spill into the canyon on occasion, leaving a host of them grumbling. Those who collected the crystals on the surface were set up within a warehouse that hung partially over the side of the canyon's precipice,—terribly dilapidated,—gathering the treasures of their brothers from below and began refining the commodity ere packaging and weighing, as crystals were sold in bags for cheap ammunition.

There was still a surface town to be seen, regrettably not much of one. Nothing more than a few establishments, such as a bank and a bustling saloon, but most of their structured buildings were either sagged over the cliff face or constructed about the excavation itself.

A steam whistle cried; the piercing blare swelled eardrums as Tycho furthered into town. Riding on through, he spied concubines on the porch of the saloon propping their breasts, their resplendent hair lavishly draped over their shoulders, mischievously grinning as they advertised themselves to the men coming through the doors of the warehouse, which they'd had a lift from the port. The bats and boars heeded no interest in them, their market attuned to the indolent bots. This was unusual for Tycho to witness; accustomed to Bill's saloon solely it felt strange and erroneous to him seeing one as racy as this. Walking past him, he saw bats in grimace—weary, making their way to the saloon.

They don't nearly look as pleasant as Sarkas, thought Tycho.

Boars towering in height with their fellow bats and bots came too; they yearned to have the taste of liquor on their lips. It appeared for those dozens it was their mealtime.

Tycho tied Meseron to the post and entered the saloon, welcomed to the sour perfumes of lust and stench of sweat steaming out from fatty creases of those miner's backs, the fingers of the concubines flowing down from his arm, whispering, *Mammon*. Not nearly as spacious as *Papa's Retreat*, crests of chairs continually knocking against each other, the tables were crammed tightly together as they fitted themselves manageably for less than reasonable space. The hairy guts of boars would hang over the table, arms from bots pinched to stay at the surface. Dim, the only light came from behind the counter—the lopped head of a bot fixed with red eye-lights flickering, shading the walls crimson.

"What'll it be? Dabiels, Mup...you're not from around here, are you—?" The bartender peered.

Tycho approached the counter, and said, "I'm not here for a drink...but I appreciate the hospitality."

He lifted himself on the stool, raising its height to the counter until sitting.

"You see a bot come through here," he said, "old, black hair, greyish skin, wearing a blue thermal—being dragged and whatnot? I suspect that the Congregation kidnapped him, but—"

An obnoxious roar of laughter erupted from beside Tycho at the counter.

"What's his name?" said the bartender, drying a mug with a fold from his wing, turning Tycho's attention back to him.

"Bill—"

"You say the Congregation took your friend?!" One of the bats at the counter slurred out from his mouth, his scrunched muzzle twitching. "He's no better than a slave by now...hogtied in chains!"

"I ain't got business with you," said Tycho. "Unless you've seen my friend, I'd prefer it if you'd keep your mouth shut."

The bat scowled. "Your friend...*Bill*, they probably sold him. More than likely," he glanced over at his peer, chuckling, "he's being picked and striped to pieces by those birds in the north, selling him for parts, perchance smelting him to the ground!"

"Lucky if he winds up even being used, maybe he'll end up being my next roscoe!" cracked the bot sitting beside him.

Tycho flung out the Havoc from his holster, quickly standing on top of the stool, pointing his piece at their roused glower. "You two feel like saying anything else? Please, you now have my utmost attention."

Behind, Tycho heard the reverberations of hammers cocked. The entire saloon had their aim on him. Gradually looking back to the bartender, he looked down the barrels of his coach gun, his claw locked on the trigger. The bartender cocked the hammer.

"Can I at least get a bucket of water?" Tycho asked him.

Thrown out from the saloon, they tossed him a pail of water as Tycho quickly turned to catch it with both hands, the bucket smacking against his chest. The curvaceous four lowered their pieces, giving him a spiteful glare with their leave from the porch into the saloon.

"And here I was thinking they liked me." He slowly grinned, carrying the bucket to Meseron.

Untying her from the post, he held the bucket steady on the ground for her to drink from. Putting his hand on his knee, he wiped his brow with the other, fiddling with the moisture between the tips of his finger and thumb.

Reflecting, he was disappointed in the actions he took. He went against what Bill had taught him, knowing that any threats he should make shouldn't be directed to anyone who wasn't a bandit or a scare. Tycho felt terrible—he told himself he wouldn't slip up the next time if a similar situation were to occur. Although, another part of him argued he was in the right, the cackling of mockery justifying his antagonistic impulsivity to defend his friend's honor.

"Don't worry, girl. We'll find Bill, it's just gonna take us some time," said Tycho solemnly. Looking from the bucket, he glanced at the road through town, a man shrouded in a black robe standing distant in-watch. Setting his eyes on the bucket again, he quickly spun his head around to him in realization, watching the stranger depart into the alley of the bank and warehouse.

"Maybe that guy knows something." He muttered under his breath.

Brushing his hand across her muzzle, Tycho walked down the center road—slowly, he approached the alley. Languor, the air's stillness ensnared Tycho perplexed. The robed man had his back facing him, gazing into the canyon. Then, he turned his head to his shoulder.

Overwhelmed with silence, Tycho was struck with an intimate familiarity, the shadow of the hood veiling the stranger's defined features. Only through the shade was his emerald skin discernible. Stoking his eyes to a small blaze, the Shine permeated in subtle activity without Tycho's notice. The Stranger was alerted by this. In haste, he dashed from idleness, bolting onto the partial beam that edged the wall of the warehouse until reaching the partial end that hung deep past the cliff.

"Wait!" Tycho proceeded to give chase.

Carefully but quickly, Tycho leaped onto the brink of the beam that stretched along the outside wall of the warehouse, sidling impatiently to meet the back-end; he hoped the lift would be there in wait for him. Glancing along the wall, he said, "Now, if only I could run like that…it'd definitely be making things easier right about now."

His boots scratching against the beam, sand stuck to his soles scrapped into the sun rinsed chasm, he tried to keep his eyes solely on the movement of his feet. "Should have just gone through the entrance," he grumbled.

Turning the corner, his back pressed uncomfortably tight against the wall, the lift to his misfortune was far in its course to the port. The Stranger gazing at him, he waited as he stood in his descent.

Tycho breathed deep, smirking wide. "Tryin' to lose me, huh? Ain't gonna happen."

Flicking his foot forcefully from the beam of the back wall, Tycho dived to reach the falling platform. His feet smashing against the surface of the lift, rising from his hunched brace, a tremendous howl echoed with his impact.

"Look, fella'," said the temerarious vaquero, taking a step in his approach, "whatever you're hidin', it would be in your best interest to—"

Hissing snaps blared as the ropes to the lift began to untangle savagely. The Stranger casting his gaze up once more, Tycho too turned his head in ascension to the warehouse. The foundation to which upheld the warehouse, the wooden pillars bolted to the undersurface snapping inward asudden, the base of the warehouse became severed by the canyon's cliff from the force of the lift's jerking pull. Half of the warehouse began its collapse into the canyon, Tycho and the Stranger racing downward with the loss of suspension from the lift.

Tycho keeping his gaze in terror, maintaining his balance in freefall aboard the lift, a flood of deposited crystals from the tear of the warehouse flowed out in a landslide. He could see and hear the hollers of men carried by the monumental discharge, threshing their shacks to splinters in its downward course.

Casting his hand out, eyes glinting with light, the Stranger beseeched whispering, enveloping the trapped souls in spheres of fire—booming with an inward collapse, dematerializing, the miners were safely taken back to the surface. With a sudden outward disperse the shards of crystals cracked and popped from their hastened vanish, only to return in their fall within the flood.

In moments of colliding with the port, Tycho and the Stranger propelled themselves from the inclining lift, their skin grinding against its crystal-coated layering. Striking at the edge of the port with a bellowing crunch, its frayed ropes lashed in between Tycho and the Stranger with its plummet. "This place is really built like crap," said Tycho groaningly.

Struggling to push up on his forearms, he saw to the Stranger with an opening eye, uttering, "How did you—?"

Rushing to grab him by the collar of his poncho, the Stranger pulled Tycho to the maintenance stairs as the debris from the warehouse threshed the port to ruin. The staircase beginning to collapse from under their feet, the scaffolding base crumbling from underneath in the vicious dismemberment of the port, a part of its foundation aside from the precipitous face of the canyon, they hurried in their steps. With the dilapidation of the riving scaffolds, the railways came undone, near to shearing their scalps as the two quickly ducked. The rails swayed and snapped, shrieking—moaning unkind to their departure from the mine.

Reaching the mouth of the mine's excavation, the Stranger and Tycho ran through into the voluminous tunnel, the miners watching in woeful awe as the flood of crystals poured over the canyon's wall, rushing over the tunnel's opening in a blinding cascade. Their mouths agape, few smashed their hats against the ground blaring the surliest of oaths.

Tycho following him, it raced through his mind where those people went, there vanish from the flood unparalleled to anything he could have expected, taken aback from the light he cast. He reached for his arm—his cloak was elusive.

"Hey! Hey—where are you going?! Who are you?!"

The Stranger bled into the shadows of the mine, dispersing phantom-like. Tycho shouted Bill's name as he fled, asking him if he knew of him and his whereabouts. His only response was the echo carried by his voice.

Tycho huffed. "Great."

Before turning to exit the mine, a puddle of muck glared beside the railways from the eye-lights of bots as they hurried to the outside roar. He brushed past them, Tycho walking against the furor that came with their stampede to reach the exit of the mine. Kneeling gently, their furious rush now past him, he saw its tar mulched throughout the shale. At its surface, Bill's oil bowled—its brown contrast spilling against the creature's own thick shedding.

All of the miners crowded themselves at the ending of the spectacle, grouped in belligerent chatter, pointing fingers at each other in the result of the destruction. Tycho kept himself crouched near the railway, eye-lights flashing in operation.

That man, he thought, *who was he…? Is this why he led me here?*

He looked into the broad gullet of the mine, where the Stranger presumably dashed into oblivion. Below, a conflicting shimmer piercing from the puddle retracted his attention to observe it anew. Placing his hand into the coarse wetted heap, he reached for the dissimilar obstruction—the clacks of shale chips smacking against the rail and ground as they fell from his pull. He held up Bill's harmonica, succumbed to the creature's ichor. His harmonica became asphyxiated in his hand.

His anger quick to consume him, Tycho slowly began to scowl and made his descent into the mine.

Diluted, a smearing handprint slathered across the surface of the shale chips before him. Its trail ended at the turn to the rail line, its crown imprinted freshly with Bill's handprint, his fingers appearing once clenched along the sides of the rail. Tycho quickened his pace, following the dense puddles ahead galled.

Fireworks, the thoughts of finishing off the creature and finding Bill ideated with excitement in Tycho's mind. Vivid, ghastly depictions of the creature's slaughter enriched his mind in an enraged madness, thinning the surface of his teeth—grinding them effortful—hungering for vengeance. More so, the idea of hunting the creature was more prevalent to him than returning Bill safely back home. Tycho did not want to acknowledge such apathetic callousness, for his own sake he knew no better.

Withal, the Stranger returned to his thoughts to be questioned with his mind beginning to furiously exhaust itself, failing to seize a constant meditation of ire.

Whoever that guy was, he poorly referenced to the Stranger, *Is he the one in control of that beast...no— I'm more than certain he brought me here to find Bill. If those are the chances, then why didn't he just tell me? Why keep himself elusive? Could be a defector...though there aren't many of them these days.*

Maybe he hopes for something in return once I find Bill. Doesn't make much sense to put one's own neck on the line like that... as for everyone else out there, assuming whatever he did was to help them. I had that situation under control though...I just didn't get a chance to prove myself.

Tycho recalled the light of the Stranger, but dismissed such notion of the indistinguishable familiarity it brought to the mind. Perhaps the luster from the crystals encouraged by the sun's brilliance enshrouded his vision, or so he began to tell himself.

A glare came from the end of the tunnel from his eye-lights. His choleric temperament gradually subsiding, reaching the end of the tunnel, he gazed out at the vast extent of a basin plumed with a plethora more of crystals extending out from the deepened waters. Streaks of coloration painted the surface of the basin, slivers of light glistening through the cracks of the surface. Scaffolds were built among the mountainous crystals, chipped away at their peaks from miners until they would be left to become stumps. Rafts, conglomerated at the edge of the basin touching Tycho's feet, were used to drift between scaffolding sights. Seeking to find further traces of the creature, he chanced upon a small passage in skimming view, lying behind an elongated hedge of un-harvested crystals.

"How did a person get dragged through here…and no one notice?"

As he moved onto the rafts, he was struck delirious, his sight fogging as the Shine remained hidden, becoming disorientated. Legs kicked inward, Tycho fell to his knees.

A cloth was pulled around his mouth, fitted tightly around the back of his head. They chained his wrists and ankles, took his hat, and placed a sack over his head to shroud his sight. Dragging him to the rafts, Tycho squirmed to loosen the man's grip around the collar of his poncho, mumbling incoherent shouts. The man clouted the boy's stomach, knocking the wind out from him, keeping his fist long enough in his gut to expel any air that was left—Tycho's agape mouth lined the sack. Aboard the rafts, they rowed onto the other side of the basin. Tycho had made it a burdensome day for them, more than quite the annoyance.

IV

ENCAGED

HOUSED in huts of steel, chained to the ground, soaking in their excretions, men underwent cruel subjugation insofar that nails bolted down through the apex of their cages were used to keeping them kneeled. A woman cried.

Through the door, a brute pulled her by the hair, the woman pleading for release as his grip tightened. Tycho awakened to her nightmarish shouts, and he too found himself imprisoned in the huts that circled about the chamber. He looked to the bandit that arrested his grip around the woman's locs, jesting despicably of her outcome about her not fitting within the car of a train. He then saw that he'd fastened the Havoc to his person. Tycho was not happy with this, not at all. Not only was his piece removed from him, but fancied was the bandit by perching his hat upon himself. Tycho's eyes swelled passionately.

Thick and stagnant was the air around him, bringing him much discomfort. He suspected with this humidity that he was taken further into the mine, far below from where he came. Above, there was a sliver of light; flickering, it cast its distancing streak from its ostensibly aerial position through the encirclement of huts, wavering faintly before the threshold of the door. It reminded him of a star he'd see hanging over Sol Puesta on some nights, moreover, its radiance unmatched by its siblings.

Tycho turned his head to the man a hut away from him.

"Where are we?" Tycho said grimly.

The man did not respond, looking away from him, his tongue trembling.

"I shouldn't be here...I shouldn't be here." The man chanted.

Denying his present circumstances initially, Tycho came to accept his predicament. Fearful, the hope of finding Bill in this hold kept him focused. Turning his gaze to the bandit, his eyes began to drift in the morbid curiosity that clenched his stomach sufficiently to have him feeling unsettled. Bound by barbed wires, amass of folk were fitted tightly within the confines of the same hut, their faces sliced from the barbed netting. Their cheeks and lips scabbed around the surfeit weaving of their capture—the oil once shed from them had become encrusted on the surface of the hut, trailing to the darkened shadow of a dried puddle that lied before them congruent to the shape of a sycamore's crown.

Tycho could not stand to look much longer, hoping they hadn't seen his stare.

Beginning to turn his wrists in the manacles that chained him to the ground, he eased in his pull as the bandit strode past him with the opening of the door. Eavesdropping on their conversation Tycho found their discussion worrisome.

"Execute the excess merchandise. The cars have been shipped," said the messenger heavily.

"What—?! Dispose of them, just like that?!" hollered the other brute. "You realize the loss we'll be taking—"

"The Outset brings jurisdiction from Halcón."

The bandit silenced himself.

"Do what you will."

As the door came to a slamming close, the bandit lifted the Havoc from his side—ill-content with a huffing pout, aiming to the hut closest, he turned the bots head to mulch with a cracking lash from the bolt sent out from its chamber. They began to scream, the people chained within the encirclement of huts crying deafening, the bodies in conglomerate writhing concordantly in panic.

Seeing his gun used to down an innocent man, Tycho's lips quivered with exceptional wroth, his eyes following the next victim beside him. The man's oil splashed against his cheek and eyes. Tycho slowly reopened them.

"How about that," said the bandit over their bellows, gawking at Tycho, "the man who thought he could sleuth his way in here and come out alive—shut it!" He horridly discharged. Their shouts quelled, momentarily.

Tycho placing his hands behind his back, he tugged subtle against the chains. The bandit crouched to further speak with him.

"We were supposed to question you, but we got bored waitin' for you to wake up, so we locked you in here with the rest of the chattel."

Tycho kept his expression of fury, wrestling with the manacles as calmly as possible. The chains gradually eased in their uprooting.

"You cost us a lot of money with that stunt you pulled back there," said the bandit, earnestly tapping the nose of the Havoc against the ground. "…With the warehouse and whatnot. This place is supposed to be a secret, you know? But now, you've gone and attracted all this attention here we never asked for to begin with."

The bandit leaned closer.

"Now, if government officials do come by, and most likely they will, there gonna come here wonderin' what happened to cause this mess, stickin' their noses in places they shouldn't be! How'd you suppose we deal wit' that, huh?!"

Tycho kept to his silence.

"Well, thinking about it now, it don't matter. We'll be gone before anyone stumbles upon this abode of ours. Of course, all thanks to you, considering.

"I'm taking a liking to your gun here…real special, ain't she?" He strode his eyes along the barrel, pointed upwards. "Don't suppose I've ever seen an iron quite like this, no sir. But don't you worry; I'll take proper care of her—"

Tycho churned the phlegm from his throat, spitting it in his face.

The bandit chuckled, wiping the muck from his lower lip, his expression becoming somber.

Gradually, he stood up as the whimpers of the encaged folk began to heighten. The bandit aimed at the vaquero, grinning slowly.

Lashing through the venation of the hut, Tycho ensnared the bandit's wrist by the chain attached to his manacle, thrusting him forward unexpectedly. The bandit's torso and face became impaled on the barbed wiring; his arm torn through the brush of weaved steel.

Tycho grabbed a hold of the Havoc, releasing her from his grip.

"Suppose this is mine."

Shouting before his life's end the bandit's head softened into a sudden dashing wave of oil, the electric discharge from the blast drawing out the currents from his corpse—they danced like careless bolts of lightning, striding from his chest to his shoulders.

As planned, the doltish thief became lured to Tycho's plan of becoming released. Stepping out from the widened hole left from his blast, Tycho scuffled to find a key in the body's pockets that would unlatch the manacles from his wrists. With plenty of searching, he found the small key in the arm-sleeve pocket, of all places. The chafing fetters falling onto the ground as he messaged his wrists, thugs of the Congregation pummeled their way past the door into the chamber, accompanied with vectras, barking hellishly. Tycho, quick to draw, blew their heads open in quick succession excluding the wolves outrunning his aim. Closing its teeth around his ankle the vectra yanked Tycho onto the ground, throwing its head from side to side until exposing his bone, the other lunging onto the vaquero's chest, snarling as it went for his throat. As blood no longer flowed from the boy's jugular and fire warded the wolf from continuing its predation, Tycho slew the last of his irritants and stood anew, shoving the warm body from off of him. He noticed the slowness of the Shine's reaction to healing both his wounds, and wondered why. Something as of late, he thought, was amiss with his deific friend.

Fanning out his hat of the residue with its pickup from the body of the bandit he'd first slain, Tycho would stifle his bed-head of blue once more.

"Well, all that was disgusting."

Wiping his face clean with the tail of his poncho Tycho looked at the small domes, hearing their sorrowful moans.

He went over to the hut that disturbed him greatly, and began to pull the wiring apart. His hands giving way to the tear it brought, his eyes glimmered with the Shine as he continued to widen enough space for them all to withdrawal. Flowing out, malnourished and diseased with rust, Tycho's hands had begun to heal, helping the feeble individuals onto their feet. To them all, he healed their wounds and infections, releasing the others from their huts as well. They were amazed at the power he exerted, questioning if he was from the Tribe of Judah, or a descendant of the prophet, all while Tycho was still in amazement at the Shine's miraculous splendor of preservation onto others. Looking amongst them, not a glimpse or remnant of a previous stay of Bill was to be seen. This depressed him considerably.

Questioning each person, he detailed Bill insofar that his milky iris received mention. None had replied with an instance of familiarity. Tycho consoled them to stay within the chamber, his departure from them only momentarily, but was responded with an upsetting uproar. One of the children that had been caged with her father grabbed Tycho's wrist with her hand, her eyes gibbous. Tycho looked back to her, lifting his eyes to her hand. Seared by the claw of Al Halcón, the outer skin from the branding bubbled in a crisp lining to the encirclement of her mark.

He said to her, "Everything is gonna be alright."

She stared at his gentle smile, and slowly began to let go.

Leaving the door to a crack, he smiled at her again and exited from the remote chamber of the hold, proceeding to its grander space at the end of the eroded hallway of stone. At the brink of his step from out the hallway, Tycho beheld. An immeasurable wall fastened with rows of walkways upon its surface puzzled him, but having found hundreds of dens bared with copper rods, sullied by flakes of verdigris, within the facing wall he quickly realized they had been used to contain the slaves prior to their shipping. Crossing into the center of the hold Tycho looked back and found he'd come from underneath a wall similar; shortly after he questioned where the path had been that led him down into this prison. He looked again to the wall he saw first and scanning the base of it found another hallway across from him. Suddenly his attention was diverted to the incoherent and garbled echoes of few in discussion; the vaquero pursued after the noise's source.

To his right, there had been a third path, hollowed out underneath the wall that connected the other two he discovered upon entry.

The ceiling of the path was low, a caramel-esque glaze of spilled blood on the floor glistening from the vaquero's eye-lights as he observed the place. Before he made a single step into this hallway, an unpleasant feeling dissuaded him to venture from those he had freed. The vaquero would keep his word on returning, and ignored his fear of abandoning them.

As Tycho avoided the glaze from sticking onto the soles of his shoes he thought of where the corridor would lead him, how much more of this hold was there? The vaquero had become suspicious of this facility's placement, foreign yet observable to ascertain the purpose of chambered walls, within the depths of the Crest View excavation. He reasoned this hold could not have been built by the hands of bots or beastmen alike, it was much too grand for such theories. If taken into reasonable consideration, then construction wouldn't have gone without its notice, tremors aplenty.

Struck afresh with former anxieties as he furthered his way down the hallway Tycho discarded the hindrances, but not so easily, challenging himself to keep onward to have Bill's kidnapper slain as he overcame the ambiance and uncertainties that lied ahead.

Reaching the end of the corridor his eye-lights scathed the darkness of the upcoming cavern, fanged with an abundance of stalactites that gleamed from the boy's projected luminescence.

Far-left of the cavern, a yawning cavity emitted profuse groans from the bowels of Zodain. Coursing out from its mouth, a railroad trailed to the other end of the opened expanse.

Tycho turned to his left and spotted a staircase, above him a lookout.

Climbing the stairs, he began to gingerly take his steps as the intelligible voices became clearer to interpret than just echoing grunts and hisses. Finding two figures in conversation within the room of the lookout, he flitted to the wall beside the entrance, peeking past the threshold, watching.

"They're bein' dealt with as we speak," said the fatter one, stout and short compared to the person ahead of him. "A sad assortment of events...I really enjoyed the company of havin' chattel around."

Diamond-shaped buckles secured around the face of his hat, the globule bot would fitfully place his hands within his coat pockets until provided with excitement in his speech.

"I expect by tomorrow we'll be seein' those inspectors, but when they start askin' questions—"

"Be calm, brother," spoke the other, looking out to the railroad. "Bother yourself with holding your position here at the excavation as he's instructed. This mine is under your name, no less."

Fitted with a forested smeared trench-coat, it blended with his weathered green flesh, as with his helm. Slick and bowed—convex—it shone at its honed tip. A teardrop; that's how Tycho pictured it, finding himself intrigued at his guise. Surfaced on the facial carapace was a slim crimson visor, notched inverted at its ends. Inches from scraping into his chest, a pair of sizable incisors was decorated underneath the visor. For his entire head was enshrouded within this helmet.

"As I've told you...a simple explanation of your stumbling of this *catacomb* came from the excavation. Be as ignorant as your miners when it comes to this place, the knowledge you possess surface level."

Eloquently spoken, his tone was harsh—a voltaic rasp from his helmet.

The rotund fellow chuckled hesitant. "Well, in all honesty..."

The armored bandit appeared displeased, gradually turning his head back to him.

"You see," he said as he began to scratch behind his head, "I had some of my men work an evening shift because there wasn't enough stockpile collected earlier in the day and—"

Losing focus, he turned his head to his other shoulder, analyzing the entrance curious. Tycho slowly pulled his head back, his core throbbing in his throat, suspended in unease if he'd been seen.

"So when they saw bodies being dragged through this mine," continued the rotund man, "I gave them a sufficient bonus to keep their mouths shut! It was my fault, I swear on it."

The armored bandit returned his attention to him. "Fields...you enlighten me. That bot that came down here..."

"What abou' him?" he said.

"Did you place him with the remnant stock?"

Field's revoltingly smiled. "Without fault," he said.

"Good..." said the armored bandit, closing near to Fields. His hand collapsing within, from his forearm a blade concreted to a stunning point. Tenderly, he placed his other hand behind Field's head, grazing the tip of his blade within the circumference of his face.

"Those who trample upon the institutions of our commerce, purposeful or not, should be dealt with in sever measure. Because of our guest, we're in the position we're in now. Unfortunately"—he stared at the blade in adoration as it traced the creasing wrinkles that mapped Field's face—"you're partly to blame for his uninvited quartering."

He glided the blade of his arm against his cheek. "If it was to happen again because of your incompetence, I will surely kill you...without the bother of a doubt.

"Let this mark be that of a reminder to you." Stanching Field's cut with the cuff of his sleeve.

Tycho peeking past the threshold of the entrance anew, he obtained a glimpse of the armored bandit as he approached steadfast, departing from his subordinate. He turned his sights away and thought of a means of concealing his whereabouts. To his right, there was the opened door—a skip away from him.

"Fields," he said, halting at the doorway, "do not forget we commence our incursion at the second rise of the sun—this plight has changed nothing. Seal this cavern shut after your leave. We wouldn't want them following it to our succedent hold, now would we?"

Fields slowly began to nod, oil beginning to pour from his cheek.

Exiting the lookout, Tycho regarded the seal his back bore as he hid behind the flayed door. Embossed centered on the back of the armored bandit's coat, an emblem positioned with a cap—a skullcap—with daggers beside it. Written underneath:

Eid Mar

Around the erected collar of his coat, in small black letters, read:
Sic Semper Tyrannis.

Tycho would not forget the seal and credo. In question, he watched the blade of his arm return to form as he swung his arm down beside him. Pondering short, the subject of the bandit's proposed raid fascinated him intrigued. He relinquished this matter from his concentration until another time.

When the cavern was clear and absent of the armored bandit's sound, Tycho crept past the threshold into the lookout, causing Fields' opening mouth to success in the motion of a cry before quieted by the spark of the Havoc's mane.

Tycho placed his finger to his lip, wagging it pendulum. The Havoc was lined in aim at him. Slowly, he closed the door behind him, approaching Fields fervently as his temperament returned to him.

"How did you—"

Tycho roughly grabbed him by the collar of his shirt, nudging the barrel of his gun against Field's bottom jaw.

"The creature," he grunted low, "the one with your branding, where is it?"

Forced into a position of compliance, Fields' still expressed concern for the matter of the subject of his interrogation, becoming bewildered in how to respond.

"That man who just left, does he know of it?" His eyes darted aside.

"What in the hell are you talkin' about, kid."

Cocking back the hammer, Tycho chuckled. "Now is not the time to be coy.

"Whatever that thing is you sent out there, it took my friend and brought him back here. You really should clean up after it, wasn't hard to see where it fled off to."

"Is that why you came down here?" said Fields. "Here I was thinkin' you were some klutz of a vagrant. You know, you cost us a lot of—"

"So I've been told. I'm sure you'll make it up in thrall trades."

Removing the Havoc from underneath his head, he signaled him with the wave of the gun to sit at the chair behind him. Tycho kept his aim on him, leaning against the wall.

"Look, whatever—this creature that kidnapped your friend, I don't have the slightest damn clue!"

"That's a shame," said Tycho. "Those miners…you think they'd know?"

"What are you tryin' to say—?!"

"I heard the whole talk with you and that gaudy bandit, picked up on a few things here and there. Assuming I'd get an answer from one of them, how many do you think I'll have to go through until I find one of the shills that's been paid to keep their mouths shut—supposing they'd seen it dragging him through here."

"You wouldn't—!"

"Then you best answer everythin' I've got to ask.

"Someone of your cult, Dargan I believe was his name, came into our town lookin' to cause trouble—nothing unusual, all except for the rune bandana he wore about him. I know you fellas like to brand your merchandise, if you can even call it that—a label like that really takes the soul out of someone doesn't it ?—I couldn't quite figure out the marking on the bandana or why he'd even carry the marking with him."

Tycho continued to speak as he made his way from the wall to the view of the lookout over the cavern, peering into the cave tunnel.

"I kinda just guessed that the Congregation was distributing a new design for their sears on their merchandise…then things got weird." The vaquero chuckled.

Walking over to Fields, he said, "The creature, bearing the same mark as him, invaded the home of my friend and took him from his wife…"

Tycho stopped himself from telling further of the event. He became sick.

"That bandit warned me of another that would come. To be honest, I didn't take him seriously. Bandits come and go, but who would've guessed the Congregation to send a behemoth like that for one guy. So you're gonna tell me," said Tycho, crouching before Fields, the Havoc lazily pointed at his head, "where are you guys hiding this thing, and where are you keeping my dear ol' compadre?"

Fields mumbled.

"What?" said Tycho sternly.

"Dargan," he said. "You actually…came across him?"

"Yeah, somethin' I should know?"

Fields lowered his head. "He went away from us forty years back…"

Tycho bemused, he listened further.

"After one of our raids, we took to a valley so that we could save some sunlight on our expedition in return to this here hold. Regrettably, that's where we lost him, with a cavalcade of chattel. Sorrowful, dusk came, troubled himself lost among the fog. A surprise to hear you're the one to put him down, then again after so much time that has passed, I'm befuddled that he'd still be alive. Why didn't he ever come back to us…? Ah hell, who's to say I wouldn't do the same if the gredo weren't as good as it is."

Tycho's eyes had drifted to the floor, unsure of what to make of Fields' tale. He considered it valid, but became more skeptical the further he pondered it.

"I don't know about this creature you've spoken of, or of the brand Dargan donned upon himself, but…I can tell you where your friend might be indeed heading."

"Spill it."

"Hasty, are we?" He smiled. "But only with the circumstance that you speak to none of my workers about this place when you leave. With that agreement, I can begin."

Sighing, Tycho popped onto his feet, returning to his rest against the wall, arms crossed.

"You may begin," said Tycho considerably sarcastic.

"As director of this hold," he said, "I have men assigned here to look after the income of chattel as my part in all of this is to keep things running smoothly. I don't get to see all of the merchandise; if the men stationed here hadn't hightailed it, I'd say you'd have better luck with askin' them if they saw him. If you didn't find him in the back room, then there is a chance we shipped him aboard the train but an hour ago."

"The train, where's it slated for?"

Fields straightened his back in the chair, Tycho easing the Havoc with a raise.

"I was just getting there," he said, glancing at his piece. "It'll be stopping in Duranché for a recount before reaching our other storehouse; we have men stationed there for those sorts of purposes. Its east of here, though it might take you some time before you find yourself in town. If you leave now, you might be able to reach him before it's *adios* for good." He figured this naïve vaquero would die at the hands of the Duranché cutthroats, telling him what he wanted to hear to leave him be.

"I'm curious," said Tycho, "how long has this mine in Crest View been a front for the Congregation?"

"Boy, you got an ear on ya', dontcha?" He bared his yellowish teeth. "Before the Kingdom of Rahnth opened trade with us…yeah, that was a time when we were flaying and peeling the flesh from bots, melting skin down to puddles to make brick. Our buyers never caught on, though it was easy gredo at the time, a bot in itself brings in an income that's tenfold—that is, if there's a market for it."

Tycho scowled at his irksome grin.

"Tell me," said Fields, chuckling, "before you go, how was it you escaped? I heard gunshots."

"I took back my gun."

Fields waited for Tycho to further expound of the situation, but was left with a solemn stare.

"Ah...I can see that," he eventually replied. "That's too bad, perhaps they'd know for certain if your friend came through here."

Fields smiled ghoulishly.

"How do we get out of here?" asked Tycho.

"On the right wall of the hold, there is a second hallway lateral from the one which you came that will take you to a lift. From there, you'll find yourself at the crag that touches the basin—cross it, and at the mouth of the tunnel there should be a flight of stairs on the right-hand side that leads to the surface, given an emergency were to occur. Had the boys use it when night came around ..."

"That would have been helpful to know earlier..."

"What's that—?"

"Nothing, don't worry about it."

Tycho leaned his shoulders back, stretching his backside.

"Remember our deal, you can't say nothin'! Is that clear?!"

"Oh, I won't. But you can."

Tycho grinning, Fields' eyes began to widen.

"But that wasn't—"

"Part of the deal? Yea, I know. But I'm sure once you get everything off your chest, you'll feel much better about all of this...if they don't leave you to be hung that is."

Fields trembled to his knees, knocking back the chair. Grabbing Tycho's gun, he held its barrel against his forehead, shouting, "No! End me! They're savages, savages! They'll tear me to pieces—!"

"Calm down," said Tycho.

Ripping the Havoc away from his grasp, Tycho paused, suddenly clocking him at the back of his head with the butt-end of his gun.

Tycho asked himself, looking down at Fields, "Why did I do that? Now I'm gonna have to carry him. Well... it's better than having to hear him whine the whole way there."

Tycho heaving Fields onto his shoulders, struggling with every step to stay balanced, he reunited with the peasant men and women, guiding them to the hallway Fields directed him in. The staircase had been hidden underneath a wooden trapdoor, a sparing distance from where the bank was stationed. Locked, a burly fellow partook in ramming the side of his body against the door, and by his fifth attempt carried the burden with his onrush onto land. Returning to the surface, they gathered behind Tycho as they followed him to the crowds that gathered in clamor at the remains of the warehouse; he heard few expound upon their transportation wrought by the Stranger's hand. As the miners' heads turned, Tycho tossed Fields onto the ground before them, himself waking in displeasure. With their gaze falling upon him, Fields cowered in his plea to have them look away from the people that aggregated behind Tycho, a simple collection of vagabonds seeking to attribute him to libelous dealings that were merely false, framing him for the refusal of giving them his wealth. The miners winced at the callow behavior of their supervisor.

As Tycho began to speak for them, the whilom maimed individuals cried out against their warden, abhorrent shouts that echoed the sufferings that festered within them. Snarling, their teeth gnashing, the miners glared at Fields; the revelation of the immured men, women and children inflaming them with embitterment. Without credulousness, they saw the chains of their manacles swing, some remaining latched to the unfitting nose of the key. There was also the marking of brands seared on their hands. Those of his shills slunk away from the mass of the crowd, abandoning Fields.

In a gathering, they mauled Fields as he pleaded for release, yearning for his punishment to be placed upon Tycho for his destruction of the mining facility as he exclaimed so. Tycho walking to the bartender standing outside of the riot, he took out his pouch in the intention of paying him to distend the stomachs of those he'd released for a few days until able-bodied to return to their homes, but the bartender earnestly refused to accept such payment.

"I will feed them, be on your way."

Finishing unraveling the bandages that swaddled Meseron's leg, he clambered onto the saddle, heading east—Duranché his next stop. Bill troubled his mind; the slightest fondness of him was becoming overbearing as he recalled past accompanied ventures with him. Moreover, his seething requital to be had against the creature could not presently hinder his sorrow. He rode onward.

V

THE IRON TRAIN

ILLOWS of smoke exuding from their nostrils, the fine flakes that
had fallen from the foot of their cigars hastily dispersed from
the game table. Deft hands dealing cards and downing liquor,
another night was to be given to lawlessness for debauchery's sake.
Peasants subjugated and tamed to servitude cowered in their service to
these carnal men. Abducted then identified with the brand of Halcón's
sear, their hands rattled and shook of having a lack of food and drink,
giving merriment to those lavishing in drunkenness and prurience.
Their bodies at the thieves' favor, those refusing their lusting advances
were dragged to the shadows of the tavern rooms, their deafening
shouts heard protesting molestation, just before having their cries
muffled by the closing door. Given slaves were more or less frightened
into obedience, complying to whatever their masters' demands may be,
pleasure was easily granted than turned down, Congregation enlisted
requesting services with a gesture from their hand, or a simple nod,
worries of excruciation cast upon the enchained.

A shout emitted, confined to its echo; a head within the tavern turned to the doors of the doorway. From the tumult and cracks of gunfire, slowly, the cutthroats glowered with their gaining attention to the dispute. Eventually, they began to understand the only cries they heard were of their men alone, disturbed by this mystery. A hand took to the crest of the swing door, leaning himself on it. His weight surmounting its hold, he collapsed onto the floor, filling the slivered cracks within the wood succulent black.

From the porch, a man stepped into the tavern, and over the corpse. Brash, he gazed at their faces and of the décor of their facility.

"Cozy place you guys got here," said Tycho. "Although a woman's touch could benefit this rank establishment." His face momentarily scrunched smelling the sweat of alcoholic permeation from their unwashed skin.

A bandit lifted quickly from his seat, others standing with him.

Tycho quickly aimed at the cutthroats, surveying with a wry expression, and said: "Where's the train?"

Firing, Tycho stepped aside from their hail of lead and heated crystals, scraping the left side of his breast. Streaks of white fire from his eyes, mouth, and chest trailed from his person as he approached. Surrounding him as his bones reverberated to the pound of their bullets, he became enshrouded in a cloud of flames, its formless wisps suffusing. In succession, they all began to fall to this avenging immortal's firearm, forever asleep to the darkness that would consume them. From the storm of their volleyed shots, those enslaved caught within the skirmish heaved blood from their ruptured lungs, out of reach of sufficient shelter. With precipitance, from the rooms on the second floor, a flurry of gunfire came from the side of doorways as the thugs kept their concealment behind the abreast walls; firing aimlessly, they garnered the courage to peek and have somewhat of an idea where their intruder stood.

Fanning the hammer of the Havoc, each bolt cracked through the walls that harbored their presence, the resounding hiss and thunderous booms from the vaquero's iron's cast overshadowing the sound of their bodies collapsing against the floor. The one that remained held a slave to him, firing with his leave from the ignited room. Below, Tycho contemplating his next action,—the Havoc dry,—a bandit neared in his approach to him. Grasping the face of the glass beside him on the charred table, clouting it against the bandit's head, quickly he took his gun before his fall and fired at the bot that held the slave in apprehension. An arcing plenitude of oil spewed from his skull as he became stationed to his back. Free, the slave took flight.

Hearing the panting of one of their breaths, Tycho scoured their remains until he saw the exhausted body. The side of his head in dilapidation, a puddle formed around the ruination of his skull, a stream flowing from his mouth against his cheek into the spillage. With Tycho's approach to the bastard, staring down the barrel of his gun as he spun its chamber, he gently lifted it above his victim's yet-to-be exposed core, and said: "The train, has it come through here?"

His breaths were burdensome to expel and receive, the cutthroat eventually shifting his sights to the vaquero with strain.

"What the hell are you...?"

"The train," said Tycho. "Answer me."

"Jump off a cliff, you worthless—"

Tycho blowing off the bandit's foot, a chilling howl and moan filled the room.

"I can keep at this."

Gargling on his blood, he said incoherently, "Ten minutes! It arrived...ten minutes to the hour..."

"Much obliged."

In quick succession, Tycho blew open his core and head, hastening his pace towards Meseron to catch the locomotive in its expedition further east.

A mile or so from Duranché,—the steppe's surface, where it laid its foundations upon, calloused by the obstruction of elephantine bones,—the train ardently made haste, exuding belches of blackened smoke and unruly tendrils of fire, an exhaust that Tycho would give chase to. Egregious it was in potency with its eruptions, he blocked out the irritable smoke with the collar of his poncho to his mouth, seemly well-nigh of reaching the caboose. Alighting from Meseron, he hopped to the end sill, cautious with his peeking into the window of the back door of the car. To his dismay, his curiousness was greeted by the vicious fire of their irons.

Ameliorating his present situation, Tycho blew the door to splinters by placing the Havoc's nose against the wooden surface, the force against the portal sending slivers of wood and glass into the foemen who now resided lifeless on the opposite end of the car, accredited to the power behind the fired bolt nonetheless.

Tycho made his way through the caboose, kicking aside the arm that lied at the threshold of the other door. Splinters lodged underneath, he nudged it open with a halting pop, taking his steps conservative with his exit to the next car. Immediately, the vaquero found the aforementioned chattel Field's referred to in abundance, chained to their seats, cries muffled as they vied for Tycho's attention as he walked past them grieving. Bags had been placed over their heads with narrow holes for sight and breath, sloppily painted smiles and eyes to deceive authorities looking out from a distance; the half-hearted attempt to conceal their merchandise as willing passengers came off as mocking for the denizens enchained and those who were supposed to protect them.

Decorated with crimson up-tied curtains, embellished with skeins of lilies, Tycho gazed at the glistering protrusion of bones through the passenger windows ere furthering to the cars ahead, the foreign land captivating him. Noting Bill's hand gone before his abduction, the vaquero looked about the men and women's laps to see if anyone with the missing extremity could be found. Worrying, Tycho bore the possibility that Field's lead would end unpromising, yet, there were more cars to explore he rationalized over his sudden despondency; a subtle jubilance uplifted him to carry forth.

Arising from the passenger seats ahead were four thieves, and from behind, hearing them snicker, more he hadn't found upon entry revealed their stations, formerly hugging close to the back of the seats he first crossed. The merchandised individuals squirming and shouting within the limitations of their bondage Tycho understood the purpose for their panicked actions more than just yearning for release, but to warn the vaquero of his coming ensnarement.

Raising the Havoc once more from his holster, the blazoned spikes of blue fired—wretched they were, hissing like vipers.

Within the commotion of gunfire and harrowing bellows, reinforcements assigned to cars ahead ventured from their posts. In their sprint to reach the car preceding to apprehend their encroacher one among the enslaved heeded their talk, involving an officer and a raid, riveting her curious.

A young woman of an undulating constitution, shrouded in the threadbare garb of those alike, she queried the stupidity of the man, assuming, who boarded to exact a vendetta against the Congregation, as with most fathers and or mothers left with an irreplaceable void of taken children or spouses. Yet, she craved with a similar hunger, slaking for the blood of her old captor; in this, she felt justified, regardless of the fools before her. Impressed, the man's uncanny dexterity lasting them, she would not disregard a chance to escape with the guards presently distracted.

The roar of the locomotive incited the howling of vectras hither and thither among the steppe, its smokestack thronged with an exhaust of black smoke, the fumes vacillating in their heavenward release. Stouthearted in their baleful advances against him, he flitted about them as the Shine veiled his host imperishable. Blowing open the backside of a bandit, the vaquero having juked behind him, his stomach burst with the eruption of his core, its voltaic fluids catching another afire—how the man's torso eroded. Ahead, beyond the brink of the steppe, a piteous bridge of rot held overtop a depthless chasm; unobservant of the coming terrain, this would be to Tycho's remiss.

With their vociferations signaling them as preoccupied, the daring woman continued to zealously force her arms downward, straining the chains that uplifted her upper-body to a stooping bow. Her breaths becoming exacerbated, she jostled the chains once more in hopes of release, oil spilling from her wrists as the manacles rived into them.

Again, she pulled.

Putting all of her weight onto the confined coils of steel, she abruptly silenced her wail—she clenched her eyes and mouth shut, her face trembling with dejection.

Enchained in such a fashion as to punish, and terrify others into never disobeying or to attempt in leading a coup against their captors, the woman suffered the cruelest imprisonment. Kept in the bathroom stall of the center car of the locomotive all those locked to their seats shuddered at the noise of the tensioned chains, unable to stomach her anguish.

Turning her attention to the chain on her left, lecherous for sudden release, she clamped her teeth against the chain, her serrated incisors painstakingly grinding against its hold. Rills of black flowed down her dentition. The men and women listened further as she became disengaged.

The bridge at burden, the traveling heft of the train taxing nonetheless, it was maintainable. Keeping his attention on the fray at hand, Tycho neglected to intake view of the gaping chasm, doing without the caution of his external surroundings apt for his betterment. Aligning the Havoc's barrel to his eye, a resounding discharge plumed from its barrel in azure radiance, skewering a line of bandits, their cores spilling out in an inky cascade as the treacherous tongues of lightning excavated through their bodies. Lowering the Havoc from its riotous buck, the thuds of a mighty brute arose. Quickening in pace, the rapidity of his steps building gradually, Tycho witnessed the fellow level the remains of those lashed by his fulgurating strike, devoured by the soles of his feet.

"You've gotta be kiddin' me."

Clouting the vaquero's lower jaw Tycho stumbled from the impact—his aim becoming askew from the horrid brute. Driving his swollen knee into the vaquero's gut he was then lifted, which followed with a collision from the brute's fist upon his spine, returning him onto floor mortified. Dragging the boy's trembling body from the floor the bandit pinned him against the wall of the train, choking him by his forearm. He began to mask Tycho's face with the vaquero's own fluids, sousing it bloody as the brute's fist repeatedly met his cheek and temple. Tycho arduously lifting the Havoc to his assailant's head, another collision to his cheek disrupted his aim, faintly silhouetting the boy against the silvered wall he was held against, knocking his hat off.

The vaquero turning head forward, resisting the force of the savage's blows, the Shine reawakened.

Fulgurating from the opening crease of his mouth, white rays of light forthwith projected out from every orifice of his skull, moreover, the Shine's outward manifestation exceptionally similar to the birthing of the cosmos, consumed the brute's sight. Releasing Tycho from his grasp, the brute staggered backward, digging his fingers into his sunken eyes to have the damned things torn out from his sockets! The cutthroat had never felt a burn as this!

Leaning forward on his knee, Tycho recovered from an injury that otherwise would have resulted in a concussion if not for his blessing. Placing his hand on an immured man's knee that the brute had barged past, Tycho raised the Havoc once more as he came to stand, the brilliancy of the iron coalescing with the light of the Shine.

Leveling his aim on his foe's core he pulled the trigger, yet without the satisfaction of seeing his barrel erupt blue, he was considered assailable with a misfiring from his gun. Assured he had enough ammunition from the Havoc's mane still ablaze, he pulled the trigger again and again, but nothing would come out.

The brute regrettably pulling out one eye than two as the roasting sensation lessened in intensity, he spied Tycho through the blood surrounding the socket of the remnant eye and lunged for him. Slicing open the side of his mouth, Tycho crudely repelled him as he fell back, the salient extremities of the Havoc gliding through the cutthroat's cheeks and tongue. Forcibly kicking him back, Tycho hastened to reload, seeing if that would do the trick. Once more, the brute came for him. Hurriedly drawing a bead on his assailant Tycho disengaged a bolt from the chamber of his gun, his shot ramming into the bowels of the brute; the removal of the train's exterior from the spearing fire would have whisked the unfortunate bandit into the luminescence of night right then, had he not wrested ahold of a man's arm sitting beside the aperture.

Before the vaquero could remove him from the person enslaved the force from the locomotive's speed carried out the brute with the man following, torn out from his chaining, unable to hold the thug's weight anymore.

The stark cold biting at Tycho's skin went unnoticed as the Wasteland chill filled the car, distracted with his feeling of remorse, thereafter refusing to blame himself for the peasant's death.

Advancing from the cars to his right an ample gathering met the vaquero, irons aimed at him, bandits shouting for his surrender. Retrieving his hat from the floor Tycho wiped the oil from his torn lip. Receding from the creases of his eyes and mouth the oil withdrew into the healing blemishes, the indentation upon his skull protruding outward to the spherical level of his head. Gradually rising from his slouch, spitting forth the residue welled beneath his tongue, he looked to them and said: "Is that all you guys do…scream, yellin' bloody murder? Frankly"—he coughed—"I'm getting kinda bored of it."

Melodiously, they all cocked back the hammers of their rifles and irons.

Tycho smirked. "Aren't you guys' precious?"

Before met with further reinforcements as Tycho was in the midst of his brawl, the woman had released herself. Faltering onto one side of her release, she hung by her other arm—oil sprinkled from her mouth against the floor, her head bowed in woe. Hearing the march of the coming thieves, plenteously diffusing from the furthermost cars, she was unawares to there being more of them, believing all had already departed from their posts.

She stanched the gushing from her mouth by pressing her forearm against it, gradually straightening herself. Shaken, clotting the constant drippings, she peered through her tousled, violet hair, gazing at those seated past the threshold of her room before returning her attentions onto disengaging herself; panicking, she heard bandits' approach.

The bleeding reduced she raised her freed hand and began to yank the exhausted chain from its foundation. From the roof of the bathroom stall, her remaining manacle tore from the bolted chain with its split, herself becoming unleashed. Awaiting her keepers, she slowly spun the severed chain around her hand, keeping low as she anticipated their approach.

Stampeding through the car without any attention given to her or the immured, as she'd hoped, she remained skulked to the shadowed wall of her room before all proceeded into the preceding cars. Remaining crouched as she shuffled to the stall's doorway, whereupon she looked to open the door on the other side of the car, she was confident none were left guarding the engine room. But then there was whimpering, a fragile cry from a small child. She was reluctant to care, but the child's shrill overbore her.

The young woman crept around the car until finding the source of the small boy's susurrations. She knelt beside him.

"What's your name?" She coughed dreadfully.

"Who...who's talking?" spoke the perturbed blinded child, turning his head about. "Are...you the one that wrestles with chains?"

She gently lifted the boy's mask from over his head. "That's me."

Coughing, she resoundingly ceased her choke.

The boy's eyes adjusted to the dimness of the car where the minute holes from the bag limited intake of light. Gazing into the young woman's eyes as she parted the silken shroud concealing her visage, her emerald scowl in the confines of Mongoloid folds, he became disturbed strikingly—he caught the blackness of her mouth!

"You're bleeding...how did you—?"

97

"Don't"—she contained herself— "Don't worry about me, kid. Your name…what's your name?"

She gently smiled, reassuring him of his safety.

"It's Isaac," said the boy.

"Isaac," she said, smiling. "Alright, Isaac, let's say we get out of here." She made sure to whisper this.

"But…what about my sister?" said Isaac.

She hesitated to reply. "Isaac, I don't know if—"

"Ashlen, we gotta get Ashlen! She's coming too, isn't she…?"

The others seated around the boy began listening in on their conversation. It was never in the young woman's intentions of releasing those captive, those much like her; never did she intend on rescuing a boy and his sister.

A shrieking howl came from the rearward cars, the young woman veering her attention to the abruption. Asudden, there was a violent tremor that unnerved her and the child, along with those enchained.

At this time, Tycho and the bandit throng holding him at gunpoint became disquiet; the vaquero peered out from the rupture of the train, from which the brute flew. The wheel at a halt, a flurry of sparks amassed from beneath it. Lodged fit underneath, the corpse of the brute grinding against the rail. Tycho furling his tongue from emitting an oath, he scowled terribly.

"Oh, come on!" Tycho surly uttered.

Placing aim on the corpse he fired a blast that would remove the stoppage from underneath the train wheel. Yet with such a burden removed, another would come to take its place, comparatively, the bothersome remains of the brute were much more favorable. From the explosive impact of the Havoc's bolt the railway beneath began billowing to ash, the wheel plummeting forth into the flaming bridge, dragging through shafts of timber. The train started to lean from the bridge's surface, Tycho beginning to face the chasm. He then heard the bandits' wild departure to exit into the cars wherefrom they came, the vaquero quick to follow after them as he felt himself slipping. Running in place before he had any sustainable footing to grant him flight Tycho took off and sprinted into the cars ahead, those preceding falling eventually into the depthless canyon.

Attempting to outrun their misfortune, their frivolous sprint was caught by the inevitable descent of the car they resided in, smashing against the ceiling and those enchained as their fall had suddenly taken them.

Tycho, colliding with the ceiling of the car, was grazed by the gunfire of bandits nearest to him. Missing his shot, the scrambling and rolling cutthroats beside the passenger windows were flayed from its shattering, the wind sprinkling the nacreous mist savagely into their skin before sent out.

As the train spun the manacles leashing the boy became rent. The young woman slamming onto the floor, pressing her feet incessantly against her slide, caught him. Holding Isaac to her bosom tightly, she prepared for the fall to come—she turned so her back would face the car door, and with her impact she was left breathless, wheezing. Others too came with the descent, the woman turning to shield Isaac from those that piled beside them.

Tycho, in his own plight, dangled with his grip on the edge of a seat, subduing the firing of irons against him with his other hand. A shriek caught him off-guard.

Looking above to the cars he once passed through, he witnessed their savage detachment from the coupler, spiraling heavily to the far side of the chasm. With their detaching the car shook, Tycho's grip waning to keep hold. With a desperate attempt to remain aloft Tycho swung his other arm upon the seat, his fingers digging into the leather surface. Another quake ran through the car. The vaquero fell from his clawing, crashing through countless car doors. His descent into each car becoming blurred, he landed against a door he couldn't burst, it's wood scarcely rotten.

Raising himself from the surface of the door he found beside him few of the formerly enchained writhing, and looking up, found those still locked to their seats wailing in terror. Closest to him, he found a woman the shade of violet curled up with a child in her arms, glancing at him with an emerald scowl. The vaquero heard a grunting from his left, belonging to none other than a frightening fellow who'd regained consciousness and sought Tycho dead. The bandit balancing himself onto his feet as the car shook, he tackled the vaquero, and overestimating the force of his lunge, sent them through the window; still, jutting pieces of glass sliced the bandit's arms and waist.

Slamming against the passenger cars as they punched and kicked the exhaust of the smokestack presented Tycho with a means of removing himself from the exchange of blows. Freeing his person from the bandit with a walloping fist into his stomach Tycho rammed his foot into his foe, knocking him into collision with the smokestack—a terrible gong came with his impacting. Tumbling about in the air the vaquero was fortunate enough to have grasped ahold of the side of the locomotive's cowcatcher, the metalwork cutting through his fingers as he swung with a dying momentum; before he could look back, he missed the lifeless remains of the thug falling past him.

From the face of the locomotive, steel strands of silk dispersed. Spider Rails—a relatable creation to the grappler dashers, issued by the government on any latest models of transportation, their use was optimal for such circumstances, notably earth tremors. The Congregation had fine tastes.

The trenchant ends of the fine cables burrowed into the earth, further, more of them dispersed from the torso of the train into the far-reaching walls of the chasm. In its crude halting, Tycho threw up his other hand onto the cowcatcher to secure a better grip.

After a slowed fall into the darkness, it soon subsided into a blanket of blue reaching the canyon's bottom. The silk cords spinning, they lifted the iron train lateral, placing it right-side onto the ground as a scudding conglomeration of dust glided from underneath its cars.

Tycho executed the bandits that remained, shuffling through the dirt with the pathetic means of an escape—he was reminded of them with their shots to his back.

Entering into a passenger car, making sure every one of them was clear of Congregation forces, he freed a few enchained to help him release the rest of the souls onboard, thereafter offering assistance to those who needed support exiting the train. Standing outside again, he watched the unmasked peasantry file out from their cars, pacing from one end of the train to the other, awaiting his friend.

Amassing into an ocean of greys, browns, and purples, Tycho sorted through everyone with the best of his abilities, none seemingly Bill. Stung, his throat tightening, he turned from them, ceasing his scrutinizing stare. Throwing his hat onto the ground, a begrimed halo of dust spewed from underneath its brim. Discomposed, Tycho combed his fingers through his hair, his hand falling still over his mouth.

Carrying Isaac from out of the car, the last of the men funneling out ahead of her, the young woman saw the man she'd seen but moments ago. His back turned to them, she grew curious—*how the hell did he take out those men alone?* Alarmed by the screech of the child, the young woman turned to her left.

"Ashlen!"

"Isaac, Isaac!"

Isaac pouncing coarsely out from her arms, his sister, around the woman's age, wrapped him in her arms, nuzzling him against her neck.

"Thank you," she said, whimpering.

Watching them leave, the young woman appeared deserted as the freed went their way, drifting home—drifting somewhere.

Panged, Tycho pulled out the harmonica, and played a tune, stopping short in hopes of hearing a response from Bill. But in agreement with his previous inspection, there was no sign of his presence. Lowering the harmonica in his hand, he gazed in longing at Bill's memento.

The young woman approached Tycho.

"Who are you?" she bluntly asked.

Picking up his hat unhurriedly, he kept his eyes forward, away from her. He began tossing the harmonica about in his hand.

"Don't keep me waiting, vaquero."

Tycho unkind, he continued to release the harmonica from his springing palm. In due time, he caught the harmonica before turning to her, fabricating a smile.

"Tycho…you?"

She continued to scowl at him.

"Spill it," said Tycho. "I told you, now it's your turn."

She scowled, curling her lip. "Fera."

"And the lady's a natural…"

There was an instance of silence between them.

Tycho sighed, and then chuckled. "A friend of mine, he was taken by the Congregation—"

"Why is that funny?"

"…What? No, no, I—I didn't mean to come off like that. Look…I was just wondering if you'd seen an older man with hair sorta like mine—bit shorter." He exposed his untamed mat with his hat's parting. "He's got little dirt on his face, wears brown pants…"

Fera looked at him demeaningly, incomprehensive of the reality of his friend's situation. Tycho saw through her judging eyes, and bothered her no more.

"Forget it. It was a pleasure talkin' to ya, Fera."

But then, as he departed, she pitied him, becoming crestfallen only shortly.

"Hey," she said, "come back here."

Tycho stopped in his venture from her and proceeded to return to her.

"You and who else took out the guys onboard?"

"Just me…What? What's with the look?"

Fera doubting, she retired to pursue the fact of the matter any longer. Turning to the corpses of the slain bandits, a few lain about them, she scrounged through their belongings.

"Look," she said. "I plan on heading to *Tartarus' Spire*, overheard something might go down there. You're welcomed to join."

Appropriating on a brown coat, she then took the corpse's piece, placing it against her breech by the hold of her worn trousers.

"What's at *Tartarus' Spire*?" Tycho said, ostensibly aware of such a place he's never been.

Glancing at him over her shoulder, she released the piece from her grasp and slowly turned to him.

"What they're after, I don't know…but I'm certain I heard mention of an officer being there to oversee the raid. All I need is him…"

"Never knew the Congregation had a hierarchy." He grinned. "I guess someone's gotta keep them in-line."

"Officers commune their registries of those captured to Al Halcón for their master to inspect all transactions and current stock, where slaves are kept and so on. They are the ones that keep track of all those becoming enchained and marred with his seal. If your friend ain't on one of their lists, you're out of luck."

"Is that what you're after?" he said.

Fera was reluctant to respond.

Hiding her face from him, she tightened the laces to her newly found boots.

"Hey, where are you off too?"

Watching her leave, the sway of her walk spellbound him. Eventually, he realized the distance she gained from him. Running ahead to her, Tycho kept beside Fera as they began their venture: "Where are we going?" he asked.

"Where else would we be heading, Tycho…"

Fera glanced up at him.

"I forgot to ask…" she said, studying the dilapidated bridge overhead, "how did the train fall over?"

Tycho couldn't find one excuse to save his hide. "Yea, good question."

She looked at him as if he were slow, a bitter and bemused expression on her.

VI

ANASAZI

Y THE mound of fallen giants, originating in an abominable time long ago, slouched, their curled spines and still arms escalated Tycho and Fera to the surface of the steppe, leading the folks they'd found and disenthralled from the cars that spun to the chasm's opposite end. After many shouts and blaring shrieks of Tycho's whistle did Meseron eventually appear before them—many licks upon him sickening Fera's appetite.

Though never bothering to ask, the giant remains reminded him of the mistakenly perceived butte he saw but days ago; he concluded simply they were the bones of such beasts. His curiosity boundless and much too entertaining to allow such a thing to escape his own fascination, he kept the thought to himself, reasonably so, in fear of appearing foolish or foreign to the Ravaja. Nevertheless, he subsided his curiosities presently and rode with Fera as she directed him forth— careful were Meseron's steps, evading the torn pockets from the bridge's surface. Making their way past the bridge where the train had failed to do so—all in applause for Tycho—they came to the aridity of the barren grassland, carpeted by fog. In the expanse beyond them, serpentine hills cresting from the horizon outlined the base of the Ravaja's crown, the jaws of the Summit more than palpable to the night's contrast.

Riding onward, Tycho began to think back as to what the woman had told him. A raid, at *Tartarus' Spire*—all this sounded quite familiar. From what he had heard from the decorated thief, in his own word's *gaudy*, there was to be an assault in two days pass, but never was the locale proclaimed for Tycho to hear. Tycho questioned rather if that man were an officer, if he were to have any surmountable knowledge of the whereabouts of Bill's detainer or of Bill.

"The horse, where'd you get it from?" said Fera.

Easing out from the vacuum of his pondering, he came to answer her shortly.

"Back home," said Tycho.

"Where's home?" she further inquired.

The exhale from Meseron steamed Tycho's eyes, the gelid temperature chilling her to the bone.

"Al Halcón…did he take you away from yours?" he said with unreasonable spite.

Fera's lip curled. "So that's how you're gonna play, huh?"

She chuckled derisively, and said, "By looking at your outfit, I'd say you're not from around these parts…or anywhere I've been."

"Suppose that makes sense," said Tycho, "only because you've been chained up for who knows how long, I'm sure you get around."

Fera punched the backside of his arm.

"Hey," said Tycho, chuckling as he rubbed the side of his arm, "that almost tickled."

Vexed, she crossed her arms and stayed silent.

The hills yon erected in height, steering them eastward as they delved further into the grassland. The journeying two became enveloped by the shadows of the hills, moonlight showering the leeward faces of these formidable mounds. For the railroad continued east, through the expanse it proceeded. They were at its mercy for guidance for but a portion of the night, their eye-lights scintillating the steely path. The chill of midnight becoming unruly, rime had rung its frosty touch around the creases of Tycho's arms and fingers, his eye-lights pestering off the frost from his mug. Fera was no different, cuddling her hands underneath her pits as her coat blanketed her from the tempestuous breath of the Wasteland.

"About that raid you mentioned…," said Tycho, his teeth chattering mildly.

Fera briefly raised her eyes, maintaining focus on keeping her warmth.

"I came across a man who spoke of taking on someplace…fortunate enough for me," said Tycho rather mordant, "he didn't say where. So now, I'm left guessin' if it's this tower. Suppose I should have left those bandits for questioning…the fat one wasn't much help. Although can't blame them for wantin' me dead, more than sullied the joint they were operating under—"

"That was you?"

Tycho played it cool, the shook expression on his face restyling in confidence.

"Of course it was, darlin'," he said looking back to her, "who else could level an entire Congregation operation besides *yours truly*."

"You're an idiot, you know that?"

"We come in all shapes and sizes, babe."

"Babe?! Who the hell are you—?!"

"Hey…I got a quick question," said Tycho solemnly.

Fera seemingly became captivated in his shift in tone, subdued.

"Why are you helping me anyways? What have I got to give that has you carrying on with some stranger?"

Fera conquering her nerves, she spoke brazenly.

"You looked lost…All I'm doing is returning the favor."

"What favor?"

"For you, freeing us."

Tycho looked back at her once more.

"Once we get to the Spire and find that officer, we'll part ways. This is the least I can do for you…got it?"

Tycho smiled, turning his attention forth. "Sure thing," he said.

The railroad careened right from its former direct path within the barren land, encapsulated by a tunnel underneath one of the moonlit hills, which gave egress from the desolated plane. In poor knowledge, fog strewn thickly atop the earth, wherewith the caking of Meseron's soles had removed the sound of her clacking horseshoes against the steel track, the deviation of the railroad went unnoticed. Two moon shifts came—some hours after their departure from the road, their trek continued with the inability to discern with eye-lights hampered, increasingly. Without the initial awareness of their gradual descent, an incline masking the drab blue night with a sheet of black,—the earth's surface becoming roofage to these wanderers,— they would turn glaring to see that they had been consumed.

"This isn't…where's the road?" Fera said, searching for the tracks. She found a trail, aught from the labors of civilized hands.

Waning and absurd, the vociferation of a beast summoned lumps to their skin. In their mistaken surmising, the ghastly blare came from behind—their brilliant but restricted sight could not disprove this. So they ventured forthwith in their hapless direction as ere, unfit to assay the hollow in the distance.

A disheveled structure blockaded by stone lay, towering doors drawing their gaze, finding hell's keep but a footfall to spare.

"…Interesting," said Fera considerably wary.

Tycho gazed at the disconcerting structure.

"We could use shelter for the night…," said Fera in her own perlustration. "Tomorrow we'll return where the fog had led us astray, returning to the railroad…just don't want to get mauled by whatever is out there, that or freeze to death."

"And how do we know this isn't where it sleeps, Fera?"

"Better my chances in there than idling out here—we'll find out either way won't we?"

Tycho harbored the phobia of haunted establishments or grounds, detesting the possibility—the thought!—of encountering an antagonist he could not assail by his hands. A hesitance he would give her, though none obstructing. He would have refuted her further, but the chill of the Ravaja persuaded him to keep his mouth shut.

Approaching the debris of rubble, Fera slid her way down from Meseron and began effortful to budge the stones that lodged their way of entrance.

"A little help would be appreciated." Fera quavered in speech as she pushed laboriously, her face to the stone's surface.

Standing abreast from her, they glided the stone out from the corrugation it had been set in, panting as their whisks of chilled breaths arose.

"You sure about this?"

Fera raised her eyes to his own. "Are you down or not?"

"What do you mean if *I'm down or not?*" Tycho said, squinting irritably.

"It's your choice," she said, turning from him, delving into the darkened keep.

Tycho held Meseron by the reins of her bridle, and lead her in contemplation. Observing the ruinous doors and archway that encapsulated the spar of black at its entrance, he was struck curious by the begrimed opalescent shade, rather out of place. As with Fera, the edifice beguiled Tycho with its happenstance for shelter, more so in fear without her further guidance of direction for the morrow.

Their footfalls echoed afar within the corridor, reverberating off from the forthcoming gouged walls. They progressed in liberal strides, without much attentiveness—how odd. Tycho and Fera began about *Tartarus' Spire*, him asking of its origin of representation, for such a title as *Tartarus' Spire* an epithet akin to *Minotaur's Run*; for they were both not without a proper name.

"Ain't that a mouthful."

"Yea…no kidding," said Fera.

She later called his bluff; it was well obvious that he was an outlander.

When their feet had hushed, ominous was the sudden quelling of their steps, they stood in silence and devoured in sight what appeared before them. The passage ahead presented a drastically different aesthetic than its previous glassy composition. Cleaved and hollowed, the corridor's straight surfaces were without previous form. At reposition within the hollowed marks of the latter walls, splayed grotesquely, a befouled crimson resin pervaded the hall; it appeared to throb irregularly. As with the walls of the corridor, it too was on the floor—reddish and black branches lain at their feet, both Tycho and Fera unaware prior that they had proceeded onto the substance.

The acridity of tar and decomposition knotted their stomachs uncomfortably.

"What do you think this stuff is?" said Fera, touching the wall as it twitched to the glide of her finger.

Tycho would not answer. He observed the passage as they continued forward—carefully.

"Any of this looking considerably *comfy* to you yet?" said Tycho, glancing at her before returning his gaze to the wall.

"Just keep going…" She scowled.

A faint grey of brume continually awaited them. A shadow raced through the wispy film, spiraling into nothingness as the individual fled; it truncated across the corridor—a miserable howl following.

"Fera…"

She haltingly turned her attention to him, seeing Tycho enthralled at the apparition.

"I need you to stand behind me."

He removed the Havoc from his holster and proceeded forward, glancing back at her to take leave.

The veined branches swelled—one had coiled around his ankle, yanking him to the depths of the ruins asudden. In midst of Fera's forewarning, Tycho plummeted through the corridor, Meseron braying at his collapse through the hoary floor.

Through many levels did Tycho collide past, a walloping pound with each severing impact.

"Hey," said Fera, her echoing sounding rather agitated, "you good down there?!"

Tycho rubbed the back of his head with his rise from the debris. Splinters fell from underneath his poncho. Moving layers of wood and cemented stone from his shins, Fera shouted she'd find her way down to him—her attitude was fretting. Before Tycho could refute her altruism in the semblance of irritancy, she flew from him with Meseron at hand. Briefly, Tycho gazed at the fog as it began to seep through the mangled openings from his descent.

Looking to his far side, he watched as the crooked tendril retreated, zipping hesitantly to the corridor's floor from where it came before. Arising from the rubble, Tycho's growing rage blinded him momentarily to the realities he'd been placed in. The hate for the creature, and his irremediable pride carried him forth.

The Havoc hued the space before him, the skin of his legs and the sides of his lower torso washed by its glaring light. Making his way through the derelict chamber, he peered into rooms on his side having panes encrusted at the corners and windowsill with crimson resin, faintly spying through the glass mutilated remains of a cat and boar, disturbed and questioning as to their limbs and facial features representing characteristics of a simian, having rounded ears, hands and feet with nails than hoofs or paws, hairless too.

At the chamber's end rested some man, appearing as one knelt with its forearm lain across its knee. Breaking the incrustation with the vaquero's approach, it rose with peculiar haste—it stood in service to him, two feet higher eerily. On its breastplate had been the coat of arms of a forgotten dynasty, words encircling its shield which read: *Harmony, Integrity, Industry*; an unfamiliar branding to Tycho he thought it too intricate.

"I'm Doctor Kutzweil, lead scientist of the extant hominid program and head of Operation Aegis. Welcome to Castle Rothschild, as I'll be guiding you through its halls until we reach the gallery where 1440 will be presented shortly." The harsh static of its voice bothered Tycho, having him solve what it said only later in mulling.

Taken aback, Tycho internalized his surprise, ogling at the machine speak—an indeterminate face covering its own, seemingly possessed. He analyzed the face further, postulating it as a screening of light; dissimilar to the Havoc's mane of lethality it was relative in its luster.

"Can you talk for yourself?" he said.

"Please," the anthropomorphized machine replied, "this way—I'm sure you're all waiting to see her." The machine's face flickered.

"I didn't think so."

Its feet tore from the scabrous crust, a thin spiraling of the desiccated resin remaining latched to its ankles in attendance.

The machine spoke no further than those first words uttered to him, Tycho unreasonably so following after than staying put—he did not care, the slaying of the creature was within his grasp. Before this outcome, Tycho pondered to leave forthwith in sight of the cascading wretchedness that doused the corridor to shadow, but for the same reason did he stay. It was by the musk of the growth and its veins of black and red that caught him aware that this was,—what he believed to be,—the habitation of the creature. He hesitated to tell Fera, in fear of being scorned and made jest of, to leave before any further entrance of the ruins could be made.

After several minutes of being led through the tortuous chamber, gleaning what he could of the horrors housed from within the rooms he passed, he was led into the main hall of Castle Rothschild, eerily preserved other than the checkered floor. Swaths of dried blood coated the black and white tiles, unblemished an immense sized staircase branching left and right at its landing, leading to rooms and other chapters within the castle; the proportions of the hall significantly dwarfed the vaquero and his guide, moreover, as he upturned his head, he found painted on the ceiling an upside down crucifix, placed within a five-pointed star of some kind.

"Within this bunker," started the machine, leading him across the hall to an upcoming corridor, "the Rothschild's haven't forsaken their luxuries in preparation for Wormwood; here you'll be staying, and until 1440 has succeeded. Up ahead, we will be shortly arriving at the observation gallery."

A lump came to the sole of Tycho's first step into the corridor. He took it as one of those branches and continued onward with the deranged automaton. Feeling the obstruction to his step once more, he placed his eyes on the floor; upon the surface, there had been an impression of a man's face wrinkled in terror from the incrustation. Hesitantly furthering along, having been rapt from the ghastly sight, he came to see with his returning focus on the machine that it had stopped. A flight of stairs came to await Tycho, the machine in stand-by as its purpose was no more—it faced the coming staircase to his unease. Squeezing past it, Tycho softly began his descent into the gallery, anticipating the creature as he without noise footing his way down the staircase. A fading, awful yowl riled the vaquero, filled with competing emotions of dread and murderous fervidity.

Languor struck him odd. Tycho turned his gaze over his shoulder, but there was nothing to be seen. His anxieties and fears were playing against him. Nearing the threshold of the gallery, the vaquero breathed deep, and entered the balcony space. Searching around the room, Tycho returned where he had first entered, and upon closer scrutiny, he found indented on the observation glass a collection of the creature's mark deeply engraved on its resin surface. Below the window was a strewing of opalescent tablets, smeared with bloodied handprints. Kneeling as he curiously began to shuffle through the bendable pages of glass, most if not all barren of text, a tablet pressed with information,—letters that charred the glass,—came into the vaquero's vision that had him troubled. "…What am I looking at?"

Beside the anatomical delineation of a moth and boar, an anthropoid in semblance to the machine he'd seen before stood in comparative analysis—its tone was pallor in comparison. The next seared paper he placed within his hand portrayed that of a saurian beast, feathers permeating from the skin and whatnot. There was but one more document he became captivated willingly by.

The Coming Extant Hominidae:
Securing the Future of Man

Reading this title, Tycho scrolled his eyes to the diagram below, bots resembling himself displayed in two, coordinating to the opposite sexes of his species. From what he could transcribe, nonplussed at the similarity of the language to his own, he read of Tesla's theoretical derivation of power, building upon his experiments to harness the earth's electrical conductivity and prioritizing such energy into the core housed within the sapiens-hull.

Tycho's brow raised, concernedly. "Sapiens-hull...?"

But a withdrawal of this power in exuberant amounts to sustain an animate being would need to be accompanied with a sustainable liquid able to carry such demanding volumes of consumption of power throughout the body lest volatile distributions of power were to occur, — although some lesser appliances regarding the source would not need such intricacies. *Ersatz oil,* self-replicating based petroleum designed to bring functionality throughout the sapiens-hull would become processed with entering and exiting the core, absorbing the energy given, whilst sustaining voltage in all operating appendages and synthetic organs found in the sapiens-hull. For feasting and other sensory phenomena, with the exception of reproduction, would remain solely as pleasures once found in the flesh: to detail a few, no longer would starvation be a burden to man, or fear of asphyxia, only cycles of passing hunger and having one's lungs filled, leaving one feeling *mortal.* The constitution of the bones and organs withal their skin tissue of the sapiens-hull came as progenitors of the contrivances from other planes of reality. Obeying the laws of the physical plane, the metal of the interdimensional disks (within specific circles of study categorized as *Anomalous Aerial Vehicles*) adapt vibratory to biological properties inexplicably, becoming flesh-like and tender—a perfect substitution for skin in correlation for traveling across planes, in addition substantial neuroplastic procedures to be taken. And as for hair, the plasticity of the metal was modified to replicate the components of keratin, scalp and body covered in soft wires, assimilating fine hairs.

After a series of human trials, it was observed the consciousness of a man became frayed—unnerved, and inoperable to pilot a sapiens-hull after several excursions into other planes. Grandeur was their hopes of escape, ultimately the human race was bound to keep to the earth to withstand the star Wormwood, and those already housed within the vessels hid. Although after returning to their world, their being was without its utmost function, it still enacted as a prime replacement for the flesh. The sapiens-hull carried the consciousness of its creators, and from coition would come a child borne of its own distinguishable conscience and set emotions, coming descendants aplenty, a lineage—the legacy of the human race.

In the wake of their extinction, ere the creation of the sapiens-hull, many experiments were done to preserve their kind in any form sought determinable to prolong their evolutionary finesse in intelligence and morality; the latter a treasure lost to them in their last days, evidentially enough. The basis of cloning man was imperfect, desperate procedures were taken in-place, vivisections and genetic manipulation of those held ignorant to the base properties of the animals they once were now thinking as their masters, self-reflecting and reasonable. But this was done out of precaution; there was another, an understandably more effective operation that would undermine all that was achieved with the beasts of the earth and sentience brought to steel. A test subject, one of synthetic cognition, reverse engineered from the intelligence onboard the very craft itself that gave their vessels suitable flesh—never before had such an algorithm exhibited humanity. With this, the distinctive generated intelligence would enthrall the sapiens-hull to come to its command and use to traverse across planes of the thousandfold if chosen, without the threat of collateral damage to human life, moreover in its hunt. Acclimatized to withstand any terrain, its vessel—as with any—could sustain electric intake, for all realms of existence consist of such.

And only then had they contrived this machination; in an early expedition they found him, and slaked for his power—they hoped, for all could be saved by their own hands, and they would send their one pawn to furtively cease his wrath.

Enlightened, for better or worse, Tycho massaged his eyelids, and stood with a bowed head. "If this is true, how can I be sure of anything...?

"Dargan...this is where you must've come from," he murmured.

Tycho looked again to the marks on the glass and the crimson resin surrounding, pulsating methodically. Doing his best to see through the pane, inching closer to the observation window, he found a room lowered considerably from where he stood, picturing this must have been an amphitheater of sorts, standing where spectators from an extinct civilization had. Within the room below, the vaquero hardly made out three bodily forms preserved in the resin.

"What happened here...?" said Tycho perturbed.

"Would you like a report, Dr. Kutzweil? I can only sequence the events prior."

Tycho raised his head, aware but cautious. He found himself communicating with the surface of the window, although there was no person or face to be seen, he was simply looking for one in its absence.

"Yes, go ahead." He cleared his voice, his impersonation a tragedy.

"Very well, stand by while I—"

A discordant stutter erupted after the disembodied person spoke. The audio then initiated after a pause.

"Good morning, 1440. How did you sleep?"

Tycho pressed his hands against the glass avoiding the crust, cupping his vision as to concentrate his eye-lights through the stained window to reveal the setting of the room, a slight reflection of himself cast on the windows of the encircling balcony. Within the observation room, those three husks belonging to what he perceived as dead hominids, and a wooden chair center of the room.

"Úbi sum…?" spoke a woman.

Hearing her, his skin crawled; though beautiful, she spoke rather dissociated from one's self. But he remained still, inclined in discerning the former situation.

"You're here, 1440…home. You've been placed inside a sapiens-hull, specifically fitted to sustain your intelligence, notwithstanding to have more personal interactions with you, our reason was to test its functionality—the capabilities of the shell you're housed in to traverse multiple planes of existence to best fit your well-being. How does it feel?"

She gazed at the honed tip of her fingers. "Ego sentio capti," she said pensively.

"Trapped…? You should feel liberated than trapped, 1440. You do still recall your task?" he said sternly. "The weight of your situation?"

"No," she sarcastically remarked.

"Let us begin, shall we?" He scowled.

Questions came, nothing substantial enough for Tycho to care apart from an inquisitive crowd of technocrats.

"End of prioritized recording one, would you like to hear prioritized recording two—?"

"Yes," he said.

The harsh screech came again, Tycho wincing.

"Good morning, 1440. There are people here to see you again. You see them just up there, can't you?"

Tycho placed himself within the audience, there, at that moment. He envisioned her glare, her repugnance. And as the conversation played, so did his imagination ensue. For with every word spoken, and change in tone, Tycho placed an action and picture to fit the scene.

"Smile, 1440…for them."

She was reluctant about his suggestion.

Irritably, he shuffled the tablets in his hands. "Fine, moving on…

"In the occurrence of certain subjugation from the lower planes," he said, "your obligation—"

"To resist all diversionary and otherwise thoughts of aberration."

"One such example of this?"

"The ideation of ceasing one's life." She trailed her filed nail down the underside of her forearm.

Peeking his eyes from off the paper, he spied 1440, her countenance a façade; an unnatural grin stretching the corners of her mouth wide.

The vaquero noticed the subject of interest had spoken English this time around than what was recorded last, and favored this shift of language; unperceptive as to why, she had been instructed to speak her second tongue so the gallery could understand, and follow their discourse clearly.

"And once you've reached your way to the higher planes, having him found, learnt of their speech and shortcomings you'll commandeer his legions against him needed be. With the reliquaries," he said, quickly raising his hand in demonstration before reaching for her abdomen where the reliquaries had been latched, she was disinclined to let him do so, reactively flinching humiliating him amongst his peers, hiding her face. The vaquero was aware of this due to the chatter of the crowd, unsure why they chuckled.

"With the reliquaries," resumed Kutzweil, restraining his anger with a telling inflection, forcefully grabbing a hold of the metalwork, "his very emanations will be ours. And what is your means of escape?"

"To beckon the stone," she said sternly, gritting her teeth, slowly sitting up in her chair as she too had made a mockery of herself.

The doctor half-smiled. "Very good."

The voice erupted once more: "End of prioritized recording two, would you like to hear prioritized recording three?"

"Yes."

The chair in the observation room screeched momentarily, a fellow seating her. It sounded to Tycho that the woman Dr. Kutzweil had been speaking to was escorted by a handler, whispers to him to leave her side and stand by the door. Those of the gallery murmured how bruised she'd been the last they saw of her, seeing glimpses of her lip swollen as she'd escaped from her room, running through the castle's main hall as her teachers ran after her, carrying her off as she shouted until voice hoarse: "Help, someone help," to which the gathering scoffed at. Anticipating the many more welts they'd find her colored with, entertaining the petty evils of their calloused hearts, to their disappointment she was without blemish. Today's viewing packed heavier than any other day of Kutzweil's lectures as he hadn't taught for months, expecting some breakthrough in his research, the honest truth of their numbers came from propagating gossip and what thrills they'd receive witnessing the results of her beatings, sickly imagining what went on behind closed doors months prior that had her wailings echo throughout the Rothschild estate.

"It's been thirteen weeks, and you still haven't found him," said Dr. Kutzweil.

Her fingertips falling subsequently on the chair's arm, her head arose.

Readjusting his spectacles, the doctor asked, "Are you willing to follow through with his slaying…and extract the emanations?"

"Yes," she surly replied, halting the asudden quiver of her lip. "How many more times do I need to be questioned this—?"

"Until you stop lying to me," said Dr. Kutzweil. "I'm suspecting hesitancy from you to seek him out. I've been studying you, becoming numb to pain, becoming something other than machine."

She chuckled, and said as a profound whimper interjected, "He told me how much he loved you…*Man*. Yet, you turned your back on him. And now, you seek to become him.

"He wept for you; died for you…"

Dr. Kutzweil drew a scalpel from his coat pocket. "My esteemed colleagues," he said, nearing closer to her as he waved the tool to the audience, "I've concluded our attempt at deicide has been countered, as 1440 is without the backbone to disregard his grace, finding sanctuary in our creation than us! Watch closely," and as Kutzweil pressed the head of the scalpel against her flesh 1440 bit his hand, the demonstrator backhanding her brutishly, the cracking from his hand's collision against her cheek echoing about the observation room and gallery. Starting again with his scalpel he glided its head down her shoulder to her arm, and the men went into an uproar, witnessing procession. It was commented that the woman slowly raised her head, glaring at her antagonist as they'd attempted to warn Kutzweil from behind the glass, furthermore, she had thrust her jaws about his throat, tearing off more than skin as his jugular spurted, taking possession of the scalpel. Her handler rushing her as another came through the door the daring woman pressed the tool into the man's stomach, slitting it through the fat and muscle, and pulling out the scalpel from the man as he began to topple she exacted a similar stabbing onto the second. She ran out the door, and the gallery cried in a horrible alarm.

"End of prioritized recording three. Would you like to hear the final prioritized recording?"

Tycho confoundedly disturbed, he willed himself to speak. "Go ahead," he said reluctantly.

The recording echoed with the bellowing of sirens and the stampeding of men, reports of gunfire here and there.

"God…Oh, God!" mewled one of the many men.

"She took what was ours…" A voice cracked.

A deluge threshed down the staircase with her steady approach, the sound of rushing waters inflating this image within Tycho's mind. There was silence thereafter, the cries of those within the Rothschild stronghold nonexistent, all except for the ones cowering in the gallery where they'd been sentenced to occupy during the lockdown.

"She's coming—she's coming—!"

"No, no, no, no…No—!"

"Shut up!" one wailed. "Both of you shut up!"

There was an abrupt pause. Something instinctual brought their silence. Swiftly, a force had disregarded the panic door of the gallery's threshold; a foul liquid burrowed from out the stomachs of those craven men, guttural retches having the vaquero shudder. Flowing from out the threshold a puddle arrived washing beside her feet, her wetted steps into the room splashing promptly. The sound of her approach heightening, an apparition of 1440 materialized—a grotesque visage of her appearance concentrated by particles of light, for Tycho was entranced on discerning her actual profile. He watched as the ghost came to the glass beside him, seemingly once looking into his eyes for a brief time. She was looking for something.

Then stricken with an epiphany, she turned her gaze onto one of the cadavers. Speedily she handled the nearest corpse, and placing her hand on top of its back where the tailbone resided, the woman viciously plunged her hand into the backside and grasped the end of the corpse's spine, and with a powerful jerk removed the spinal cord with the attaching skull as a cacophony of bones snapped with its primitive expulsion. Ramming her hand into the back of the decapitated head, she manipulated its eyes to beam a projection onto the glass Tycho remained standing by, but slowly departed from his stance to position himself just behind the luminous apparition, witnessing the scroll.

From this corpse's transhumanist depository of information, an elongated scroll beheld her, sustained on the observation window—it was rather large.

She fiddled her fingers around the inside of the head, puppeteering it to bring to light new lines of text to digest. Within the descriptions of the scroll, the contents of the emanations were catalogued, as with the fifth—she became learned of their separate properties. Borne of the four, she hungered lastly for the one she carried absent of Judgment, an enmity for their god tumefying. In her hesitance to take leave, she said after a momentary silence, "I will finish this war between you and I; your abandonment will not be forgotten."

As the apparition fizzled into nothingness Tycho was alerted to another barreling howl; he brought his attention to the door of the lower room as he ran over to the observation window, concluding its whereabouts had to be beyond that point.

Stepping back, he cast a bolt from his gun and shattered the glass, protecting his eyes from the shards. Pressing his foot onto the edge of the balcony, he leapt into the room, and visualized once more the woman that sat in the chair. Uneasiness came upon him, and with quickened steps, he went for the door that was ajar. Trekking through another corridor as before, although shorter, Tycho found himself in the presence of a necropolis.

A still sea of crimson, those men at its fringe clawed at the doors Tycho came past, to his witness percolating despondency and nausea. Within the expanse, a petrified flood dominated the grounds of the seeming undercroft of Castle Rothschild. Heads arisen from the skin of the sea mourned with yawning mouths, their sunken eyes expressing great sorrow. With their arms raised for delivery,—few clambering onto one another's backside for but sparing salvation,—all appeared in certain reach for the young man from Sol Puesta.

In his harrowed perlustration, Tycho had borne the erection of an obelisk center of the calloused sea. A sphinx-like relic of the humans, Tycho was rapt by the image of the maleficent obtrusion, at its center a blemishing strike. Where the sea attenuated at the idol's plinth, the creature moaned; unnatural disgorge of demoniacal laughter would come from it. Tycho brought the Havoc to the side of his breast slowly and traversed the grisly spew of terrain.

It turned its gaze at him from the obelisk, and smiled abhorrently.

"Ubos inquit tradnö…trandö ubos plures fratres Verumshaï insidiantur emas, utam praediximus, etam nunc est mihi." The creature writhed on its knees, taking its eyes from Tycho's bewildered glare. "Situm mihi etam immolasten Recordatus sum senex, lu unasesh…"

It reached out its foul hand, for its mother it cried. And then with a gradual pace, its arm lowered to its haunch.

"Get up." Tycho placed his piece beside the back of its head.

Tycho had been surprised to hear it speak, and so would take advantage of this learned knowledge.

"You can understand me, can't you? Now get up!"

Its spasms desisting, it stood. Soft resounding pops came from its uprise, its spine erecting true to the creature's stance.

"Where is he?" He trembled in speech, his voice becoming guttural. "Where's Bill?!"

Its eyes the breadth of a pin's head, the concaved sockets of the creature enveloped Tycho's beaming glare as it turned.

Swiftly, the creature summoned its closed palm into his chest, leaving him exasperatingly strained to receive breath. For with his arrest, he was swung to the base of the obelisk, Tycho's head pounding against the phallic edifice. An onerous struggle to repel the creature, it's forced upon weight rendered him stolid. Distending its sockets ripe, its eyes became plump and stout with excitement—as with leaven they arose with corpulence.

Forward to its lunge, the coming fulmination retarded the assault of its cannibalistic advances, a condensed turbulence of fire tossing the creature, flailing volute, at a considerable distance.

The vaquero, reconstituting his former carriage, approached the creature at a gradual pace.

Kicking its hind legs into the incrustation, the creature propelled forth at him, its maw unhinged for the severance of his sought limb—the member that possessed the gun.

Grave was the bite, Tycho swinging mighty of his arm to release the grasp it had upon him, yet the Shine's potency resulted in its cowering.

Tycho began to pace the creature. "Now you're scared…?" he said, tantamount to an inquiring command.

By inherent means of the primal contention, they locked eyes within their circling, anticipatory of movement from the other.

"What did you do with him?" His face wrinkled and scrunched to his possessing rage.

The creature bellowed, "Veni ad me…Veni ad me—!"

"What did you do with him?!"

"Di me—illuminata est benedictus—!"

Tycho charged the creature with furious precipitance, "Answer me!" His challenge came.

Tumbling in evolutions they vied for dominance, the creature's maiming talons splitting his flesh apart to bathe in the deluge. But with all Tycho's wounds, it would not last long, as his career without the Shine.

In the scuffle Tycho's hand pressed against its forehead, atop of the mark—in repellence of its lunging maw. The creature writhed with a hoarse, grating cry; Tycho witnessed his hand's ardent emission, beginning to slowly rid of the ungodly sear and skin. This was all by happenstance—Tycho furthered in his apprehension of the entity dwelling within him, perhaps limited.

Eventually its tail grew and lashed Tycho awry, jolting after the champion of Sol Puesta in his aback bound. With the creature's horrid spewing of tumult and effervescency, it swung down in course of lacerating the core. Rather, its strike fell on another fellow—he stood in service of Tycho's well-being, forevermore to keep him afire.

From his breast to his left eye, the cut was drawn, fire brimming to his wound.

"Masei ve neïsa vel la a vak aishé len no brohe, heishé pualo töm en Ahmenseraï."

You will not come to lay another hand on my brother, fallen child of the Ahmenseraï...

His voice was distant, a remote whisper carried by the breath of the earth. Yet, there was an authority to him. Tycho looked up, and saw him.

"Futue te ipsi..." The creature spoke.

Gradually, he raised his head, looking into the Zealot's eyes. The Stranger's hooded glare finding itself upon the creature's face, his own countenance resultingly diminished the darkness that had formerly shrouded his features. His left eye glinting ablaze, the creature scurried—a momentary cowardice.

The guide of Tycho spoke again, the Spirit influenced tongue engaging the vaquero to decipher any word he could from his protector.

The creature proved its baseness in revolt to the light, moreover, its disobedience against its master's command to never slay the boy but maim, succumbing to utter rage. The creature tried for speech anew.

Before given its chance to further accost Tycho rent his antagonist's foundation, the creature falling gracelessly onto its side—he did well to conceal his aim, the apparition of a familiar past suitable cover. It rose with a pushing arm to come to a kneeling posture, the palm of its claw slipping withal the talons scraping against the course mounds of flesh.

The Stranger turned to him, taken aback; although his visage hidden only his glaring and coruscated eye gave Tycho the impression he feared to accept as truth,—certain repudiation,—regardless he advanced towards the creature.

He spun the Havoc's chamber, and adorned the barrel of the iron center of its sere mark.

The creature wailed; pathetic Tycho found it.

"I will not ask again, where did you take him?!" shouted Tycho abhorrently—shaken, perturbed. "Bill—! Where is Bill?!"

The Stranger materialized abreast to him, scarcely subtracting from Tycho's executing focus.

"Cast your arm from him," commanded the apparition, its cloak-end mantling the creature predatory-like. "You will rue this night if you so choose to ignore the Spirit's counseling."

"Get away from me…"

Tycho turned his head to him, slowly.

"You left me to find my own answers," he growled passionately. "I intend to see this through…without your interference—"

"You'll never have him…he's too strong, stubborn," said the creature, a crude imitation of Bill but a convincing inflection nonetheless.

Tycho's eyes cocked to the creature, his countenance blanched.

Listening to her whispers, she reminded the creature, her *Zealot*, of its valuable position and exciting importance, hearing these duties during worship before Tycho's arrival and inflicted injury that induced its belligerence. It intended to mock him—taunt him, and have itself slain; it mattered not that its leg was in the initial stages of regeneration, as death was sought than its own continuation.

"Tycho…don't do this."

"He was set apart before creation, and that is why you cannot win." An emitting roar of suffer came at the end of its testing, and trying speech.

The Stranger turned his gaze to the vaquero with compassion, withal returning it to the creature, and quothed a prayer.

The creature found the ability to emit volleys of laughter once more, bastardizing the goodness of Bill's voice. "I did the best I could for him.—Kat and him share that same smile…that damn grin of theirs gets me every time. I know what my boy is capable of…don't think for a second he won't put up a fight, unlike you, surrendering his given path only to become this beast…Let me say goodbye before I go—for God's sake, don't do this, don't do this—!"A tremulous roar reverberated, enshrouding the boy's heart into an abysmal cold, unsure if the creature's own or belonging to his mentor.

Tycho's patience died, as did the creature surcease from remaining animate; its head sprawled grisly amongst the remnant expressions of man.

Tycho fell to his knees, and then onto his breech, harshly combing both hands underneath his hat until reaching the back of his scalp—the Havoc fell beside him.

Tycho sat there, and contemplated.

Willed by impulse and selfish rage the creature lay before him supine, without the leverage needed in extracting Bill's location. His hunger to kill the creature was far more profound than ever his attempts of rescuing his mentor—refutable to his own desires he missed him gravely; he was certainly keener to this than ever. His hope rested in Fera's guidance, and the awaiting officer—this would be his last foreseeable chance of acquiring what knowledge there was to be had on his peasant elder.

Looking to his side he found the Stranger away from his company, surmising his flight took place at the renunciation of his command.

The hurried steps of one echoed throughout the necropolis. A figure came to the doors, reconnoitering—for Tycho they sought, to find him secure.

Fera found him, and proceeded expeditiously.

She came to kneel before him. Tycho had opened his eyes midst her approach, reassessing the whereabouts of his antagonist. The corpse of the one lay in front of him, yearning for it to breathe new life; for the Shine had adverse properties to succor these beasts in good health or he would have it reconstitute its skull anew.

Fera saw its remains, but held her inquiries. She pulled him up, wresting him by the forearm to establish his footing once more. She ran, and he failed to follow. Turning her head, she found the vaquero shouting vehemently the appellation of his sire in maddening desperation, proceeding past the obelisk into the Stygian dark in stumbles. Her teeth gritted with the widening of her eyes, desisting her flight of egress. Swift Fera came to him anew, at the verge of the shadow cast afield, wresting his shoulder aggressively to face her. Tycho pushed away her arm, and turned from her.

Her countenance wrinkling, she arduously tried to stop its solemn tremble. "Tycho…we're leaving. There's no one else here, got that?!"

Stiffened, Tycho abated the fervid chant.

"He's not here, Tycho…he's not here!"

Akin to her own, Tycho straightened the spasms of his face, then looking back to her.

They fled the castle; following her, they came to an aperture—its width to sustain Meseron's constitution. She had been placed on the outside ere Fera's leave, pawing in wait. Bestrode upon her they came, and throughout the remainder of the night Tycho carried the burden of decrypting his admirer's purpose. He realized the shadow he'd seen first upon entry was of him than the creature, the one that delivered him from destruction. In absence of uncovering any answers as to where his beloved friend was, —the uselessness of the captor lain before him,—his chances now lied in the confession of a Congregation officer. Dubiety, Tycho mulled the circumstances of the exact situation happening again, a confident lead with a disparaging conclusion truncating his hopes of ever coming into contact with Bill. Finding the creature without him shattered his heart; a severe intensity of loss welling from his very being.

He then questioned the Congregation's involvement in all of this, and why Dargan came for him after years of nonattendance; he had become a revenant.

VII

THE GALLEON'S HAUNT

DEAREST Kat,

The nights have stung that much fiercer ever since my leave for Bill, perhaps the comforts of home are a treasure I've learned to forsake no longer. It's been no less than a tribulation, finding Bill, as coming into contact with his captor was disheartening and fruitless. There are suspicions, hunches that are my own that whatever power enthralled the creature to capture Bill is at influence over the Congregation—at least a few fellows, Dargan but one as I've come to learn. If curious, finding Bill absent of the creature's possession has further given me the ideation of the thought. I have yet to determine where this creature derives from, be it finding its nest. Currently, I am on route for *Tartarus' Spire*—have you heard of it, I did but a day ago…? There, I believe as does a rogue woman who leads me there, that we'll find the man responsible for taking him into custody and cataloging him as a slave.

—Tycho barred the odious thought, holding his hand firm from grinding the pen's tip to the paper, splotching it Stygian.—

There is hope that a revelation will come of this notion, if it's true.

LEGEND OF THE RAVAJA

Before I send this out, I apologize for leaving without saying a word to you. I hope you're doing fine, Kat…I miss you, and Bill. Take care, and be sure that I'll return with him in the best of health.

With much love,

Tycho.

Folding the letter half, it came to the slot of an envelope. With a lash of his tongue, he sealed it closed and proceeded to exit his quarters. Smacking the face of the door against another unexpectedly, Tycho pinched his way through the portal and sidled against the bulkhead until making it to the companionway. Free from the congested passageway, he presently made his course to the courier upon the deck. Ready to receive, the bat took Tycho's envelope and rolled back-first over the side of the galleon—a prompt delivery Tycho ordered.

Tycho imagined his own flight,—how he yearned for the capability since days before,—the velocity and rush, to acquire elevations against his own limitations.

Returning his gaze from the courier as he shortened to a swift speck, he spied for Fera amidst the busied deck. To the far opposite side, she conversed with those of the ship's crew, now dressed to their fashion. He proceeded to her, maneuvering through the waspish and gallantly proud boars, withal cats and other species to the mix. Dispersing with his coming arrival, they gifted her with smiles and jubilant shouts with their return to assigned positions; but not of Tycho's own coming, for the Captain's keenness and easing approach pressured them to scurry.

"Tycho," she greeted.

Her white and black striped shirt traced the woman's features; utmost clean-limbed, and curvaceous. She was fitted with harem trousers and a Jutti pair of curled tip shoes. Notwithstanding the shirt given, the other articles she bore were of the dancers that entertained the passengers with their foreign art of expression, a flowing sash knotted at her waist.

"I see they cleaned you up," said Tycho, smirking.

Turning their gaze to the orange-colored clouds, they leaned restful on the ship's side, watching the fall of the sun.

"The oil from the coat was beginning to drench through to my skin," she said, looking back to the crewmates, "after several times asking, they fetched an outfit together...can't complain, it's actually comfortable compared as to what I was wearing before."

Half turning his head, Tycho saw the partial scanty of the crew she was focused on, moreover, those surrounding. Those seeking fortune, emancipation, and cause consisted of the galleon's men—whilom slaves striving for riches as their captors ere, enlisting passengers aboard for sufficient gredo to expenditure ventures to come, save for the few who pocketed the die. A bewailing reverberation trembled all unsteady, the Captain from the helm barking oaths to his men to silence the beast below forthwith. Handling the stems of their whips latched port and starboard apace, they molested the beast with countless thrashes. With its eventual silence, those aboard chuckled nervous, prompting a rag to the glistening ridges above their eyes; Tycho and Fera were disgusted at the entirety of the process.

"It's sad how they treat these animals," said Fera, "hollowing them out, making them into ships, beating them into obedience. We're no better than parasites..."

The vaquero slowly nodded, looking down to the earth below. Taking in a deep breath, he said, "Any idea how long it'll take till we get there?"

"Nope," Fera answered him. "Ask the captain, I'm more than sure he has his estimations."

Tycho nodded.

"About what happened yesterday...," he began. "I still don't know if Bill is locked up somewhere in those ruins, but that doesn't mean I should have treated you the way I did."

Tycho returned his eyes to her, his hair tousled by the wind.

"I know you were only looking out for me." He smiled at her, gently.

Fera's cheeks shone rouge—abashed, hiding her countenance with a scowl. She was quiet, focusing her attention outward as before.

Tycho looked to her hand resting on the vessel's side, recognizing the sear as it belonged to the child he'd seen days before, her father and those of impoverishment sharing the brand. Catching the stare, she slid her hand underneath the other arm.

Looking out, he said, "I thought I had him..."

Lifting her scowl to him, her face softened.

"Aye thea luv, how's the man treatin' ye?"

Captain Winthro; known amongst the Congregation's dregs by the alias of Scary Jack Carver, horrific remains of those thieves he left them in with his flee, earning him the glory of the title. As with the height of the machine, he towered over them, fashioned with a pomegranate trench, two belts latched aslant across his bare torso, additionally, a copious gather of cutlasses beside his waist. Excessively enough, two eye-patches enshrouded his sight; legend goes he can hear all who speak ill of him.

"Only the best a gentleman would," said Tycho smiling. "Can't say much for you, Winthro."

"Bunch of nonsense from your gob, I'll hav' ye know women come beggin' daddy to—"

Fera's indifference quelled him to elaborate further.

Tycho laughed; a long snort ere the cry that emitted from him.

Wiping the wetted crease below his eye, he said, "Thanks for having us on board anyways. We're fortunate enough to have found you when we did."

"Well, thank ye for the dice," he said, a railroad of needles careening wide to a smile.

The Captain's voice was thick, guttural—the ends of his speech resonating with a subtle hiss of the tongue.

"All jests at rest," he said, fitting his hand beneath the trench breast-side, "I'd be makin' my rounds to get a general feel of the folk, see how they've settled aboard my *Tyranny Eater* an' whatno'. One of our shows is 'bout to start in time for suppa, so I've all given them the propa warnin' befo' things begin…want no one flustered, the buggers last time scurried rat-like to the lower decks an' fell their way through the companionway, poor knobs crushed every bone in their body—in all fairness, I blame the stampede for their…comical demise."

A sick grin followed at the end of his speech.

Fera smirked wry, her back at rest against the vessel's side, her arms perched. "You're blind; shouldn't you be in some old folks home?"

"This one's got a tongue on her, don't she?!" He bellowed with laughter.

"Let me tell ye, sweethart!" He sparingly bowed his head to her level. "It all started—!"

Fera yawned super-exceedingly, to the extent of her tongue smacking against the roof of her mouth, twice counting.

"Well bollocks, forget it then!"

The quickening shuffles of feet and compacting bodies distracted them from the entailing contentious exchange, an uproar bustling thereupon the announcement of the performance.

"Like I said, the shows 'bout to begin. Meet ye unda', and do come, the crew needs time to set the deck to its standard presentashuns."

Grinning, Captain Winthro left them, flicking his hand underneath his chin at Fera.

The crowds funneled progressively through, coordinated to reach the lower decks in anticipation to gawk at the ensemble of talent. Tycho and Fera both waited for the throng of passengers to disperse until reasonable ingress could be made to acquire themselves comfortable, without being swayed to the bulkhead by the larger fellows. Straggling behind, the plump collection of persons ahead descended with their steps further into the galleon's depths, a ladder left of the passageway. Tables lazily strewn before the podium with food and drink, the boars washed their gullets before the show had begun. Situating himself at the table nearest to the ladder, Fera followed and took the seat open next to Tycho. The performers walking onto the podium, Tycho and Fera glanced at each other before the act.

Without hesitation, the performers flaunted.

With the lash of their hips, they waved their bodies to the beat of the drum. Their beauteous visage enshrouded by a veil of silk, the glint of their feminine eyes enraptured the hearts of the men, twirling their hands overhead as if fettered. Tossing their hair, they turned and faced their breech outward, mesmerizing the audience with lolled tongues. In motion, the sinuous wave of their stomachs withal the rolling muscles beneath that of their glistening haunches as they crouched and arose from the surface of the podium enticed the crowd to abstain from the feast, to have all eyes focused unto them.

Fera chucked an apple slice at Tycho's forehead, alluring his attention to her—only slightly bemused.

"I wanted to see how you'd react." She grinned, turning her eyes to the performers.

Tycho smirked.

"You think we'll make it there before the Congregation?" he asked.

"Not counting they have an airship of their own for trafficking," she said, "there's not much to be bothered with."

Fera placed her gaze on him once more. "The officer, the one I found at the hold—hope it'll be him we come to accost. I've had the misfortune to be in contact with him many years before I had my placement within that slum. Can't say I didn't feel some kind of connection between us in his assistance to have me chained within that car," she said with stunning acerbity. "Previous, he'd come to register newly incarcerated men, slaughter some—I'm sure those went absent of mention when giving his report to his master. Although, I doubt he'd allow him to use an airship for a single raid, not exactly a lot of them left…don't think they'd waste the one."

"How else would they get there in two days?"

"What had you come to that conclusion?" She glared. "Wait, that man you mentioned—did he say their expectancy of arrival? I thought at the least we'd need to make camp for the night."

"I'm starting to believe these persons we speak of as being separate are one of the same. This officer guy, wasn't happening to be fashioning some verdure trench was he? Some eerie lookin' mask?"

"That's him!"

Those across their table flapped their ears, moving their heads to their shoulders in disdain, glaring at them, steam arising from their quivering snouts.

"How'd you come across the dignitary fella?" Fera whispered, her sight easing from the haughty men, "I'm impressed you remained inconspicuous as long as you did, unless you hadn't, locked up with those other men and women."

Tycho nodded.

"He wanted me dead, along with those that couldn't be fitted onto that train. Considered us liabilities. Yea, starting to think razing the entire site wasn't the best of ideas—could have slipped in without any attention drawn to me."

Not that any of it was on purpose, he thought.

The expression from her revealed grievance for those she had recalled, until Tycho comforted her with news of their escape, and then she was delighted.

"Before I'd lead them aboveground, I found myself overhearing a conversation between him and the hold's director in an attempt to secure Bill's whereabouts. That's when I found out about the heist."

"I still don't get why he'd be after *Tartarus' Spire*," said Fera. "There's nothing there for him or anything the Congregation would be interested in."

"Who cares," yawned Tycho. "As long as the guy shows up then that's all I'm concerned with."

There came a pause, dispersed from the discussion, they found solace in their prolonged silence to the pounds of the drum beating throughout the intestine walls of the deck, the dancers continued liveliness with their lissome contort to the beat.

"You still haven't told me why you're after him," said Tycho, settling his hands upon his head, "...this officer."

Fera inhibited from spewing her grief out onto him, restraining herself.

"Before you were taken to be trafficked, did he string up your pops? No...you're mom?!"

"What are you getting at?" She gritted her teeth, slightly taken aback at the odd, unrelated question to their previous discussion.

The boy continued to push, Tycho's efforts of attempting to be playful only failing. Had he lessened his prodding into personal matters of her own and was able to take a hint, he would have been fine, but he continued and her fuse had run short.

"Tycho—"

"No...I've heard that story one too many times, it's gotta somethin' else. Maybe being chained up is all it takes to want to kill somebody...and maybe, it has somethin' do with being taken advantage of, right?" He smirked.

Her hand clenched into a fist.

"Tycho, stop now—"

"That look on your face tells it all—!"

Throwing her fist onto the table, she rose from her seat and bared her teeth menacingly. The collection of passengers gawked, their blinking incessant.

Storming from the table, she turned to the ladder and made way for her quarters.

Their stare fell from her, falling epicenter onto Tycho—a nervous smile came from him.

The performance coming at an end, those in attendance had departed from their tables, disgustingly left unclean, remnants of bone and torn meats doused in drivel, sickening Tycho to the foul scenery. There was the account of the one boar that sprayed mucus upon his own table, violent was his shake, hairs of his coat alighting from his person.

And with them, he returned to his quarters for the night, leaving his door carelessly ajar as he drifted into slumber.

The night before, Tycho had a hellish dream aboard the galleon with their arrival, the recent event thought to have stricken this upon him; moreover, this was to his conjecture. Its abated severity was considered a forgetful vision, but the present night bore him with bewailing grief as for him not to ignore.

From the grotesque and putrid howl of the creature he'd slaked for execution, he found his friend's captor knelt before him. He had returned to the subterranean castle, the encrustation of corpses beneath his soles, the phallic stone gleaming at its center. Tycho had spun the chamber, previous as he had done, lifting the barrel against the sear of its forehead. Removing its head from the support of its torso, the creature's mutilated face was strewn amongst the scabrous flooring. But thereafter, one came anew in replacement, the acrid flesh of the creature then diminishing from its congealed visage, Bill's own to be revealed to him.

Tycho lowered his piece, and toppled onto his knees, his eyes quivering.

"Kasheen," It spoke, as much as a susurration.

This was nonsense to Tycho, its bewildered glare upon him he found disquieting.

"Kasheen," It spoke, as much as a susurration.

Tycho was abounded with grief, seeing an old friend as the creature he hunted with fervidity and indignation. Opening his mouth, he was devoid of utterance, a whist cry passing his trembling lips. Tycho wished to ask the creature as to the revelation it spoke, but he could not speak, as the creature had been granted with speech solely.

The flesh from Bill's face began to peel, its claws tearing at it into slivered pedals, drenched in its tar-soaked skin. Underneath, he gazed at the semblance of a forest, peering into its hollowed skull. The view within its skull was alike to a geode, a perlustration of trees within a greensward valley instead of amassed crystals within was found. With Tycho's continued gaze, his study drifting inward, the sun's radiant glare intensified,—the pines of the trees clothed gold. Enticed, he found his head at far past the periphery of the view. Asudden, its fangs returned and beguiled Tycho into darkness, enclosing his head within its newly forged maw.

Plunged within a realm of perpetual black, his collision to a supposed surface betokened the end of his fall, soon fumbling about until regaining his feet. Proceeding, the darkness acquired further density.

"Tycho...it's good to see you."

An insulting apparition of his mentor materialized; horrid was its appearance.

"Who are you?" Tycho angrily inquired.

"Who else...?"

"I don't know you."

"Don't you remember?" It said. "It's me, kid."

Tycho shook his head. "No...I don't think so."

It took its leave. "Come...I have something to show you."

Thereafter their brief stroll, the apparition unwove a tear before them, placed at their feet. Found isolated within the coniferous verdure, the man Tycho recognized as the apparition purported to be was marred with lacerations and plentiful scarring, assiduously forfending against his assailants; hundreds of the Zealot that took him.

"Avenge me, Tycho." It spoke to him. "For Kat and I, come for me."

Their claws began to burrow into Bill's flesh as Tycho watched horrified.

Protesting a fit of paralysis, Tycho awoke to a sodden mattress, a great chill percolating from his spine to his wet limbs. Upright, he sought to calm himself.

A few doors down from his room, Fera exited the restroom as the shrill of the flush lessened with the shutting of the door. With indolent paces, she slipped her hand past her undergarment and scratched her rear, shuffling to return to her cabin—a mighty yawn came from her.

Walking past his quarters, she glanced into the room with instinctual curiosity, her eyes slowly beginning to widen. Besides the crack of Tycho's door, she spied his sorrow with the burying of his face within the palms of his hands. Gently, she made ingress with the push of the door and approached him.

Tycho lifted his glower to her.

Fera came apprehensively, sitting at the foot of his bed.

A stare came between them, Fera's countenance stern compared to his own.

"Tell me," she said. "It's alright…"

He raked his fingers through his thatch—slow, positioning his vision downward.

"It was just a bad dream."

"A bad dream, huh?" She smirked. "Well, just how *bad* was it?" Lifting her legs onto the bed, sitting comfortably.

Tycho looked at her.

Fera smiled softly, to hopefully allay him.

He expounded his vision, the ungodly scene that sent Tycho into further sorrow, a disturbance that bore an unnatural struggle in his intonation, but well aware it was only a dream—his emotions simply stirred. His mind had exhibited the repressed chance of Bill's turning—a traumatic revelation if one was not to consider the validity of his bestial undertaking.

"I…I messed up…Bad." His voice sounded gravelly.

Fera ridding of her disgusted expression, she,—against her own incipient desire, — layered her hand upon his own, caressing her thumb beside his knuckle.

"You'll find him…"

He abstained to reply.

"Look at me…"

She placed her hand beneath his head, lifting his gaze to her own. "You'll find him."

Tycho's core slowed its rapid pulsing, resting his fingers at his forehead.

"…I'm sorry about earlier. I thought the things I'd say would get some life out from you. I understand if you don't care to tell me…whatever it was that happened to you."

"Goodnight, Tycho."

She rose from his bed, tugging down on her shirt with a single hand. Closing the door to his quarters, the passageway lights ceased to suffuse against the carpeting, remaining as a bar of light at the sill of the door. After a bothersome hour of dwelling and mulling over the fright, he lay abed on the side of the mattress left un-soaked, and closed his eyes.

With the crowning of the sun, all hastened to their feet with the odious howl of the beast jarring the craft of their beds. Roars of the crew came, acting quickly to silence its cry. In his best efforts to obviate the clamor by creasing the pillow's edge over his auditory slits, the spew of cursed oaths and the surliest of complaints irritated the bot to stay woken, unwrapping the cushion from behind his head. As with hastening to dress one's self with a guest at the door in the middle hours of twilight, Tycho arrived at his door in swiftness and observed those standing at their own thresholds, shouting obscenities at the crewmates that passed their cabins to alleviate the inconvenience.

One came to him, Tycho calm and understanding of the situation, returning to his quarters to rest anew—this he hoped. Tossing about, he found comfort finally at the edge of his bed, sitting in tiresome rumination. He could not sleep, only think. Restless, Tycho occupied himself with trekking the decks of the ship until finding Meseron at the lowest floor. He stayed there, feeding himself and the mustang from one of the several casks lined to the brim with apples; satisfied, he returned to his quarters.

Fera knocked at his door.

"Who is it?" he said.

"Arggg, it's me, the try-hardy bastard, Captain Winthro!"

She tried not to chuckle.

"So she does have a sense of humor," said Tycho, smiling beside himself. "Come in!"

Finding him lain blithely, twirling the Havoc deftly in hand, she was glad to see him well; at least this was to his semblance.

"Aren't you going to change your sheets...?"

"Eventually."

Fera raised her brow. "Gross...

"I asked one of the guys what time we'd reach the place; fortunately for us, we only have to wait until afternoon. So, in the meantime," she smirked, "we should check out that venue they got going on—whole bunch of merchants came by dawn to set up shop."

"He's a cunning businessman...or a greedy dreg." He referred to the captain.

Tycho fitted his hat atop his serrated thatch, Fera leaving the threshold as he came, looking back to him in wait. Walking abreast through the passageway they approached the ladder, from the lower deck uproarious shouts of barter flooding the berth deck as before they had only been the faintest of echoes.

"Feeling better after last night?"

Tycho chuckled. "Nah...not in the slightest."

The deck that consisted of the performance in the evening prior had been fitted to delight the stations of the merchants, sitting with their haunches upon their damask carpets, Bottoman woven wefts. Few bartered underneath tents, hermits they were—the arm of him reaching out, spindly and gaunt. Tycho and Fera pacing to each other, and then away in their perlustration, the foreign dialect of one riveted Tycho familiar.

...I know that voice

Brushing against the assemblage, he came to the carpet of the man with the Brussian tongue, his genial bellows filling Tycho rapturous.

"Ah," he bellowed with touted grace, "and how might I help you, little bot...?"

Tycho lifted his hat, holding it beside his waist. "Sarkas," he said.

"Moy drug, is that you?" said the bat. "It is! Tycho!"

At a short bound, he grasped the young bot and crushed him with an insatiable clutch to hold him tight. His face buried within the pelage of his breast, a wheezing utterance from him came to warm the fur surrounding.

He placed him down. "Your friend, have you found him?"

Brushing the fine hairs from his poncho, picking them from his tongue withal, he answered: "No...still trying to find the old man."

"That brings sorrow to my ears," said Sarkas. "There was naught at Crest View that helped alleviate the venture?"

Tycho half turned his head to his shoulder, Fera spotting his gaze. "I got one thing out of it."

Fera approaching, Sarkas lifted his sights from Tycho and onto the violet woman, welcoming her with an incredible smile.

She glared at Sarkas, and then to Tycho. "What's up?" said she.

Bowing, the crown of Sarkas' wing folded against the overhead of the deck with its erection, his other pressed just below his breast.

He arose. "I am Sarkas, Sarkas Sev—"

"Alright, big guy," said Tycho rudely interjecting, "I think she gets it."

Fera held out her hand, but Sarkas laughed in protest of the gesture. Wresting a hold of her arm, he too buried her within the warmth of his pelage.

"A pleasure to meet you, purple bot!"

Placing her down, Fera coughed, her hands at her waist as she bent over to expunge the fur from her throat—guttural heaves aplenty. Chagrined, Sarkas grinned wearily, reassembling his treasures in his own disquiet state.

"Captain Winthro invite you onboard?" said Tycho.

"Of course, blue bot," he said, polishing an abnormal skull of a vectra—odd, "but not without a tariff! But, the plan is to surpass the sum I paid for entrance…I await the die of customers yet!"

"I forgot to ask, how is horse—Meseron? Is she below with livestock?"

Tycho crossed his arms. "Yeah…and she's fine," he said. "Saw her this mornin', was having trouble sleeping so I decided to give her a visit."

Sarkas paused in his action. "Why do you trouble with sleep, blue bot?"

"Long story."

Straightening her posture, Fera turned to them, catching a single hair from the crease of her lips.

"I'm Fera by the way." She flicked the fine strand. "What did you call me before…'*purple bot*'?"

Sarkas grinned—his canines shimmering, and said, "But of course, it's only fair for Tycho's sake, no?"

"Sure! *Tycho, who is this guy?*" Fera sternly whispered.

He'd heard this, his particular set of ears rendering him this strength, although they weren't very far. His ears drooped, his countenance following.

"He's a friend I met out in the Wasteland, when I left home…"

Fera looked to Sarkas once more.

"I've never seen anything fly as fast as him…He's got a gift," said Tycho.

This interested Fera, his ability of flight—to traverse with ease in such palmary swiftness.

Sarkas bowed his head anew, unfurling his inky wing graciously to the treasures displayed. "I apologize for any outlawry behavior, Miss Fera. Half price—only for you…and blue bot if he's interested." He cocked his eye at Tycho. "But yes, I insist."

"Guess that means we should get something, huh?" She grinned.

Those on deck inspired an image of a warring scuffle, though this could not be the case!—as many believed. Those beneath heard the patter of their footfalls, the pound, and shuffling of their advances met with exorbitant shouts,—they took it for laughter, for the overhead was dreadfully thick; withal their blustering was sufficient to quell any suspicions of invasion.

Tycho fitted his hat upon himself. "We're not here for that, Sarkas…"

Sarkas smirked, standing again. "Of course. Then tell me, blue bot…where do you believe he is?"

Unlading the information incepted from the both of them, he learned of their quarry—*an ambitious hunt*, Sarkas thought.

"She's leading me right to him…," Tycho looked at her. "I'd be left nothing but a vagabond if not for her well guidance…"

They saw her stern amusement with her pickup of a hollowed core, a faint yet scintillating course spiraling within the confine.

"You know, besides the fact she led us through that godforsaken joint." He smirked, a rending jab at her.

"Oh," she wheeled her arising glare to him, "but I could have sworn you were so adamant to stay until I talked some sense into you. Or am I wrong?" she chuckled.

"Easy there. Ever heard of a joke?" He smiled.

"Mhmm." The trailing light from the core stained faint flashes upon her cheek.

Returning to his discussion with Sarkas, they delved into the political means of it all. Aberica purported to be on diplomatic terms to dissuade the Kingdom of Rahnth from taking their own captured citizens as slaves, avoiding at all cost from beginning a new war with them—the War of Divergence was a war to end them all, conscious of the horrors in order to not repeat such calamity, though the war was necessary for their liberation from the Rahnthians. Sarkas continued; his own conjecture was that the story told to the public was deceit, naught but far from the truth.

Sarkas groomed the pelage of his neck with his tremendously sized talons. "They don't care about you or I, Tycho. What speaks to them is monies, and they want a cut of whatever makes the most of it. If they did…care about us, then with all assurance Bill wouldn't be in the position he is in now…along with many others."

Messaging the lower crease of his eyes, chuckling softly, he said, "I don't know who to blame…perhaps I allowed for this to happen."

"So the Congregation is paying them to look the other way?" Tycho said.

"Net," said Sarkas, "but the powers that be, hiding within our country's shadow, they are the few that conspire with them; to ship children and women into the households of perverts…cherti." He struggled to finish.

The lips to his muzzle trembled, pulling back as to snarl viciously. Sarkas looked from Tycho, hiding his gaze from him at Fera's play with the core. The course followed Fera's finger, curtailing the trail of her hand's extremity along the surface.

"As for the men," he spoke conservatively, "they work labor for the luminaries. As much as I would like to divulge further, their treatment is better without mention…"

At a distance, gathering a host of curmudgeons and bargainers, a man refused to utter one word in response to their screeching demands, resting slumped upon two of his crates, stamped with the seal of the Rahnthians' official trading company reason for their uproar, they bothered him to unpack. Lain in the shadows of the deck, nearest to the hull, he listened—every word Tycho had spoken. What struck ahold of his curiosity was his mention of the officer, why a peasant man hunted for such a dangerous fellow, additionally, knowing where he would find him. The revelation was satisfying enough for him to gather further knowledge on this outlander. For the officer was his quarry, not his.

Lifting his florid eye to the vaquero from the arising brim of his calloused hat, weathered and torn, he studied the bot's constitution, his cruel fascination, and focus, disregarding the passengers' noise from cancelling out his eavesdropping.

"They had them…locked up in these cages, there was this one—"

Tycho looked past his shoulder. He had felt the eyes of one resting upon him.

Taking his gaze afar to the merchant behind, the man ceased in his glare unhurriedly. A shatter alerted Tycho, and as he turned away, the man's glare returned onto him; nursing hatred for the insignificant challenge, he considered him a hindrance more than anything.

Whistling, Fera had her arms crossed, cunningly brushing aside the debris of the opalescent core that fell from her grasp.

"Where's that thing you were holding?"

"Don't know." Her gaze wandered.

Before Tycho could observe the scene, Sarkas had his attention brought to him once more; he hungered for him to finish the story told. Fera capturing the freed sprite into the clasps of her hands, they both looked to her; placing the evidence behind her backside, she grinned artificially.

The beast bellowed anew.

The assemblage shouted back at the horrid thing, mocking it in their own guttural intonations. Asudden, a sonorous bellow mightier than the beast's came. All were silent.

Violent muffled cries,—frightening and skin-crawling as they came,—reverberated through to their deck.

Tycho, Fera, and Sarkas, moreover the crowds gradually raised their attention to the overhead.

Tossing the sprite to Sarkas, he scrambled to catch it, the three of them sprinting to the upper deck to witness the strike against the galleon. The hunter imitating a merchant's vocation, watching the Sol Puestan boy, followed posthaste, as with the rest of the assembled to the companionway.

Arriving, Tycho and them bore to witness the calamity of Winthro's men, slain in blitzkrieg without warning or preparations to be given; Tycho and those passengers were all that stood against Winthro's assailant.

From the crowd, the hunter spied his quarry, prepared, imagining his encounter with him after twenty years of the bandit's evasiveness and seclusion—hidden amongst their brothers and his master.

"Take them! Allow me passage, I plead ye!"

These were the words of Captain Winthro, a captain who harbored the value of gredo and the security of his own well-being rather than the welfare of his own passengers—a recreant, comparable to a Congregation thug!

Putting an end to his ignominious begging, a horrid spike discharged out from the sleeve of his coat; the unshapely spike impaling through Winthro's forehead, pinning him backside expeditiously from his kneeling posture.

His head half-turning, he spied Tycho, the bunch sobbing behind the rash boy.

Embossed centered on the back of the armored bandit's coat, an emblem positioned with a cap—a skullcap—abreast with daggers beside it. Written underneath:

Eid Mar

Around the erected collar of his coat, in black lining—small: *Sic Semper Tyrannis.*

Ascending through the galleon's keel to the space between bow and stern, the resounding, bewailing moan of its crash came with its hellacious tear; their thoughts of flight removed, immobilized by shock, the passengers were left agape. The breaching airship scarce of grazing the armored bandit, the officer remaining still, he continuingly glared at the vaquero—how the creature below cried wretched, its bowels rent asunder. Drenched, a crimson glaze washed over his vessel's deck, the wetted surface scintillated as it rose to the sun, endowing the craft proudly with its celestial brilliancy. Tenfold, steady in a continuance of rending, was the monolithic comparison of the vessel in its lateral state to the *Tyranny Eater*. Sent forth, womb-like with its egress, it ascended to the scabrous strewn of clouds, the officer taking hold of his ship's hull—a sinuous chain came from him, his vessel wresting him afield. In the same fashion, the hunter alighted from the deck; he secured his presence hidden on the backside of his quarry's stern.

The officer's vessel wheeled to consume, the bloodied fangs of his own beast bared; it approached rapidly—its thanatotic challenge, a hellacious roar that jarred the heavens.

Severed half by the incursion of the vessels' maw and constitution, many of those on the main deck of the *Tyranny Eater* became disorientated, tumbling and scratching to stay aboard, but their fate demanded death and so death they were given.

A cat mewled, clambering for the certainty of life as his claws braced weakly into the sole of the deck. Taking off, Fera's eyes darted to Tycho as she slid, widening with his sped leave. Slaloming past hundreds of the passengers along his path downward, the echo of their piteous cries numbed him—overbore him with ire and somberness. Skidding to a halt, he grasped his paw asudden, Tycho holding him at the brink of the galleon's tear. If he could save one person, whomever in his power, then he would take the risk—disregard for his own life. Arduously lifting him onto the slanting deck, the cat then flew from his possession, the officer's vessel streaking past with a lunge to consume of the many that fell—the cat's arm dispersed mist-like, Tycho's own forming anew.

Taken swiftly, Sarkas captured Tycho, Fera alongside his back, clutching to the pelage of his scruff.

In ill-fate, the vessel's maw would come about them.

Weaving against its incisors, Sarkas flew, an apparent defeat with eclipsing darkness enshrouding them. Taking her iron, Fera cast its fire into the beast's throat until all chambers emptied. Bemoaning, its foul roar jarring them in flight, its upper jaw elevated, Sarkas elbowing the fang's edge—there was no opportune interval to juke past.

"Spasibo…Much appreciated, purple bot," said Sarkas, out of breath.

"Yeah…no problem," she said, eyes widened—enraptured at their escape. In disbelief, Fera gazed at the Congregation's vessel. An incredulous feat of the officer to operate with sickening swiftness and talent, to decimate a force with an unparallel severity; Fera wasn't without her estimations of this demon, the Congregation's cur, but perhaps they were over their heads on this venture.

"Looks like the man you are after has come to you…timely, is it not?!" Sarkas weakly grinned.

Clambering onto his backside, Tycho shouted over Fera's shoulder to Sarkas as he came around to sit foremost: "Meseron! Do you see her?!"

"Hold on!" he said. "Let me see…"

Searching the dispersed throng of goods in their apace descent,— waving in spread atop the tumbling stern of the *Tyranny Eater*,—he spied her in the collective.

"Ah, there she is! The both of you—hold tight!"

Flitting past the terrible debris in his flight, rolling clockwise to obviate collision, he sped forth against the haze of rent planks. From above, summoning the weight of its presence down through the tumbling stern, once more the vessel came for the cattle, Sarkas' spoor provoking its salacious chase.

Sarkas obtained Meseron as ere, claiming her from the saddle.

Humid and sticky, the breath of the beast deluged upon their backsides. Pressing down on her shoulder, he fired at the beast's savage glare, the second pull ensuring his intended aim. Throwing its scaly countenance aside, it halted in chase swinging its foul gaping mouth to the wreckage asunder. Tycho's retaliation brought them to the earth, the asudden swing of the beast's head knocking the triad dispersed.

Regaining them, strews of irregular trunnels impaled the bat's tremendous spread—stripped of flight. Clutching Tycho and Fera, enshrouding them within the coverage of his wings, he dove bowing his head close to them, Meseron afield in her own fall. But then, there came a light.

SARKAS SEVEROV, RAVAJIAN HERMIT

VIII

THE FIRST DISCIPLE

THE stern of Winthro's vessel settled, hither and thither its thrashed hull, and heavy discarded flesh, coated the surrounding land. Not too far from the wreckage, a path made by paralleling columns of disheveled stone came to the platform of the Spire, the sand road cleaved of its shimmer by dull shadows cast from each pillar unlike the desert around.

Emerging from beneath the sand Fera and Sarkas vehemently inhaled, the drivel chalking their throats forcefully expelled.

The thunderous bellow and thanatotic challenge of the vessel permeating throughout, the triad was galvanized to move.

Fera exhaling violently, spoke: "How did we survive that?!"

Sarkas arising, the coarse grain deluging from his backside, raised his formerly damaged wing seeing it renewed; he had an idea of the event occurred before their otherwise demising fall.

He glowered, his eyes on Tycho. Afar, Meseron gaited to the vaquero's approach, nestling her head against his person. Fera observed their greet disquiet and simply dumbfounded, baffled.

But there was no time to think, their only action was to take flight. With his newly acquainted wing, he wrested Fera upon him and shouted to the vaquero to astride his mount in haste.

A foul and horrendous vociferation sent a quake through their spirits, as with their bones.

Behind, the vessel had gained on them; unnumbered pillars were assaulted to dust, the galleon's underbelly scarce grinding against the archaic pathway.

Sarkas looked back with a bloodshot glare, witnessing the coming maw eclipse the sun; for not much longer would he be able out-fly the mountainous beast, and remain whole.

"Hey!" shouted Tycho. "Havin' trouble keepin' up?!"

Sarkas saw to him bemused, uncertain to his carelessness or lack of urgency.

"Sonnaofa—!"

Sarkas shouted over the winds, "Purple bot…what is the matter?!"

"I lost my piece"—Fera snarled—"just get us the out of here!"

A howl came anew, the vessel's reverberation deafening their ability to hear.

"As you so command," said Sarkas wryly, keeping apace in flight.

Ahead a tower materialized, the erection appearing before their sights, standing to mock the Ravaja's crown, aught from the Summit's actual primacy of height. Arriving before the tower's platform Sarkas crashed into the coarse road to evade the neighboring mouth of the vessel. Casting his arm out from the steps of the platform, Tycho raised the Havoc to the galleon's countenance once more; the bolt sent renting past its lower jaw to the roofage of its mouth. The tense contortion of the galleon's features loosening, the sway of its benumbed jaws collided unto the face of the tower, toppling starboard, crashing horridly and immediate through the tower's side.

Shielding from the debris and ichor, Tycho withal Sarkas, Fera, and Meseron entered the tower encountering its sturdiness to uphold; a transparent entrance of light they came through for shelter.

There was but one center chamber. Ample was the flooring of the structure, elongated slits strewed amongst the inscribed glass; an undulation of weaving text concealing the mark to come. Found far and high were blinks of white and crimson throbbing from the surrounding wall; irradiating dots and from the bricks they came. The glimmering hide of the Wasteland reflecting sunlight from the entrance and side marked the opalescent floor with a twinkling sheen, oftentimes blinding the vaquero. An ominous chatter, a bewailing clamor compounded of the tower's rumblings, Tycho was left to surmise the stir of the wind within the hollow chamber summoning the inexhaustible divulgence. The triad could not ignore their echoing moans, regardless they rested.

Sarkas fell heavily onto his haunches. "Don't know if I would have lasted without that aim of yours…An admirable marksman in my presence," he said.

"Don't mention it—"

Sarkas coughed, thereafter inhaling wretchedly.

"Calm down, big guy," said Tycho, settling him down. "Breath slow."

The inured bat readjusted his sit, gnawing at the clot of blood soaking his pelage, the shedding of the airship's fluids splashed upon him.

The flickering of light amidst the strike of the sun against the Ravaja's natural protrusions, the bricks coruscated similarly to the crystals near *Minotaur's Run*. In their inconsistency of blinking and flashes of crimson and white, Fera observed their domineering scrutiny notwithstanding their emitting suffer.

Tycho concerned himself with Fera, speaking to her from Sarkas' side, said, "This the place…?"

"What does it look like?" said Fera acrid, looking to her shoulder.

"Lovin' the attitude," he answered her with the same intonation.

Fera did not respond, gently expelling her breath; she kept her gaze amongst the wall.

Tycho huffed, and murmured unintelligible words that Sarkas himself could not perceive.

"Leave her be for a time," said Sarkas—lips marred red. "More than not, she is flustered and afraid…"

"Afraid…? Afraid of what—?!"

"The Congregation, whomsoever you hunt for," he said, resoundingly clearing his throat, "or the moans of those in the walls…pleading for deliverance, or so the legend is told."

Tycho placed his hands on his waist. "I'm not sure what you're getting at." He raised his brow in the bat's incredible utterance.

He began to gaze at the surrounding interior as Fera had. "The draft; you're not sayin' there are people in the walls like some schizo…Sarkas?"

The Rothschild's first attempt at preserving the longevity of the ruling elite, their tower was an initiative well before the creation of the sapiens-hull, an archaic effort in their time but successful nonetheless, if only for the surviving,—yet dwindling in sanity,—conscience and nothing more. Erecting from out of the earth during a wintery season when heavy snowfall kept men indoors, bots and other hominid species later discovered the disquieting ruins with consternation and curiosity, the chambers that contained bat, moth, cat, and boar arose similar, though epochs ere the tower's ascension. And in time a given label would reflect the insidious aura of this construction, known to be: *Tartarus' Spire.*

Sarkas chuckled. "Never said I was one to partake in the stories told of this…otherwise daunting structure," he said. "Better you know now than never at all, blue bot."

"We gotta get moving again," said Tycho, "…before that thing wakes back up."

Fera turned, and approached in malicious strides. "Not until we have that officer in our hands."

"Wouldn't leave without him," said Tycho. "But I appreciate your concern to remind me…I'll head into the ship and retrieve him, you two stay here—"

"No, I'm coming with." She scowled, her lip curled. "I don't want there to be a chance of him getting away."

"Whatever is left of him, that is," said Sarkas.

Alarmed, looking to the illustrious opening of the tower's side, they found the officer, with frightening aggression, lead his men from the felled galleon in their advancement towards the Spire's platform. Hesitant to speak anew, they carefully watched, awaiting their ingress. They bided in silence, between one another, anticipating their prized inquisitor.

The officer stood forth, the grinning bastards of his legion funneling through the entrance to the Spire,—some bitter, glowering at the triad for their cause of action to ground them asudden and so viciously. They played with their revolver's chambers, filling them with emphasis, churning spit from their cheek's hold to expectorate unto the floor. Brutes they were, and they would be dealt with accordingly.

"Perhaps I shouldn't have spoken so soon…," said Tycho.

From the legion a thief tried for the officer's attention, placing a hand on his shoulder. "The woman breathes, against what you willed. Better take this chance to reclaim her—appease Halcón than what the flesh desires, Officer Lyle." The gasting figure remained unresponsive, from his peripheral sight spotting his subordinate's rolling red eye. "Let us go home with two treasures."

"I do not take counsel from one as you…Stay behind me.

"Fera, come," the officer gutturally commanded, an overlapping voltaic rasp sheathing his genuine voice. "I see you have escorts…and you have yet to main them?" He tilted his head, previously aware of the fellows that accompanied her shipboard. He glared at her beneath his facial carapace, his throbbing eyes piercing her gaze underneath his illuminated crimson visor.

"She made some friends along the way," said Tycho smilingly. "Can't say we've got the likes of an army like your own, but we manage. Why so many of them, anyways?" He scowled. "More importantly, where'd you take Bill—I'm more than sure you caught his name after he was handed over to you, right? Still have him held up in those accursed ruins somewhere?"

The officer stood, unflinching in his glare—his perlustration of the young man.

"Did he ever make it onto the train?!" said Tycho firm. "Did you take him before anyone else could see what brought him down there, into that hold?!"

Those accumulated to his guard began to turn their heads, peering at each other and their officer, questioning what he was referring to.

"About that…train," surliest said the officer. "With the amount of chattel lost, emancipated…by your hands alone"—a sonorous growl came at his utterance—"we came at a loss. The affluence promised taken, without—"

"And I care 'cause…?" Tycho shrugged.

Studying his arising grin,—a detestable and vexatious sight to him,—the officer straightened his sleeves and rolled his wrists impassively.

"What the boss is tryin' to say," interjected another thief abreast from his person, "is that you cost Al Halcón quite the complication. A sure deal to be made with those Rahnthians if the serfs had been relocated smoothly without this consistent pesterin' from you, not to mention throwin' his train overboard and all that—not good, peasant.

"And as for what happened to your friend, here's somethin' I can tell ya—!"

The officer clouted his cheek, truncating the thief to his knees.

The officer placed his attention on his subordinate. "You will speak only when permission is given, understood?"

Lips trembling, he spied the officer through the creases of his overlaid hand.

"Understood?!" The officer roared. "Now…get up!"

He regained his feet, others of the cult steeping away from his rise. The tyrannized bandit had not intended to confer any location of the vaquero's chum, without discretion would daringly insult Tycho's yearning to receive such. Never had he had an idea from where his mentor was from the start, but it was his speaking out of turn and obnoxious jesting that riled the officer acrimonious.

"Take it easy, will ya?!" shouted Fera. "I think he gets it…!"

Tycho turned his eyes to her, but never giving her his utmost attention; he continued to face the officer with staunchness.

"Fera…," the officer spoke.

Her stare remained undaunted.

"You were on route with the others…chained-up like some depraved whore, on my behalf."

The face of the woman uplifted—creased—to her scowl. She chuckled out of animosity for the thug.

"And now because of this boy," the officer focused again on Tycho, embittered and enraged—laughing mildly, "you've become unshackled.

"A rebel she was—didn't play well with others. Killed many of her kind for our pleasure. Then, she came for us."

"You sound shaken," said she, expressionless. "Is everything alright?"

His shoulders rose to his discrete, yet heavy breaths. "We should have killed her with the rest of them…but those of Rahnth insisted on having her, which I consider the possibility again seeing the slave now than to have her devoured to sate whatever passion strung my heart during our assault on Carver's vessel. To have your spoor was vital," he said, redirecting his gaze at her. "It's possible that an auction will be held for your own aggrandizement…the moths continue in their interest for a woman who can engage effectively within their own arena—enough to put on a spectacle."

Tycho looked to her brief.

"She is not like you…she kills for her own survival. You will be discarded once she has what she wants."

Tycho glowered.

"Look," said Tycho, scratching his cheek before clasping his hands behind his head, "I could care less about the woman's yesterday; I had her stickin' around so she could lead me here since she overheard something about a big heist and whatnot, suggesting it would be here at this Spire"—Tycho failing to mention his own eavesdrop of the conversation— "sayin' some sort of officer would show. Looks like she was right on both accounts; coming here was to find you, pal. And I'm sure those you put in the pit against her were just as armed to the teeth as she was…she just fought better." He smiled at her.

"So now is about the time you got to divulgin' Bill's whereabouts, and I appreciate your concern for my well-bein', but I'm more than capable of defending myself, asesino." Tycho squinted at the officer with an impudent nod. "I ain't worried about her turning on me just yet."

He winked at her—indignantly, she rolled her eyes.

"That's a pity," the officer grumbled deeply, pacing right. "I swore you cared for the lives of your own caste...unless I was mistaken. I believe that does reflect your abandonment of them at Crest View..."

Tycho perturbed, his eyes had widened, lowering his hands to his side.

"Fields," he said with the assurance of their learned encounter; he laughed up his sleeves. "You do remember him...? When I received word the cargo never made it to the other hold for processing that's when I contacted him; most onboard where to be shipped to the moths only days after their expected arrival, without your abominable entry of the depot it would have transpired from the excavation itself. Told plenty of the heroics of an impudent—brash—young man, I killed Fields shortly after our precious discussion, finding him beaten...left to die on the roadside, along with some vagabonds you aided in their escape. There was this *small* girl distinctly...held in her father's arms." He sniggered, and gazed at his palm.

"That bartender sufficed for a petty threat on telling of their whereabouts, those two allowed quarter within his bar...nonetheless they came into the execution of those miners well before I started with the rest of the chattel...My men did well in not arising suspicion when the law came around, fine—fine miners they were."

The three of them unsettled, Tycho failed to harbor his indignation, his hand reaching for the Havoc.

"Those slaves were worth scarce of a die…compared to the cargo we had, such an exchange after would have insulted our buyers. But I am somewhat pleased…it has been some time since I've doused my blade in cattle's blood…hearing the pop, the hiss of steam discharging from their punctured flesh, becoming…ravished by their weeping."

The officer became entranced in a euphoric state, gritting his teeth orgiastic—a deep grunt following.

Tycho hurriedly placed the Havoc's aim on the officer, his face trembling mad.

"This bandit….he talks too much," said Sarkas, glaring.

The winds furthered in their execrable howl, whisking against the inner wall of the Spire vying the cries of the human menagerie. The galleon remaining unmoved, the exception of the discharging ichor from its gullet to the ravaging wind stir, splashing against its snout with its taken leave, a breach came from underneath the beast; sand had begun to sink beneath the keel of the galleon. Moved from the stern to the side of the quarry's hull during the descent, the hand of the hunter came to the surface—onerous was his climb. Shielding his eyes from the sun as he came to stand, sand toppled from his hat's brim.

He listened to their clamor, focusing on the voice of the officer; he turned his head to his shoulder, briefly witnessing the disputation within the Spire. Discarding the layers of sand from his shoulders with a shrug, he then ventured to the platform.

Taking to the steps, pestered with the reverberation of their odious laughter, he stationed himself upon the center steps of the platform. The Congregation's men drawn to the fool he'd observed previous aboard the *Tyranny Eater*, the hunter took his time to prepare in their discourse; he tossed his hat beside him.

Their laughter waning, Officer Lyle uttered, "Are you going to kill me before I expound *Bill's* sanctuary?" Asudden, their cheer had picked up anew. "This kid is a riot," growled the officer, smiling wide—although hidden beneath his mask. He knew with what he accounted would acquire a reaction from him, and so he continued to prod him with horror; he hated Tycho, and would have him suffer before coming to slay him thereafter their accosting.

Continuing with his aim,—insulted and jeered at,—Tycho had threatened the lives of both Fera and Sarkas with his haste to take action, and of course Meseron but who's thinking about a horse at this time! If his trigger finger was as true as his aim, he would rid of the only lead he would have had of finding Bill, moreover, his party showered in the gunfire of those cutthroats.

The facial carapace's front retracted, revealing the officer's mutilated mouth and visage. "What if I killed him…?" He approached Tycho, raising his hand. "That, or the bones of him are lodged in-between the fangs of Al Halcón. Not all of those enchained are sold for profit…as you well know. Those with lesser or inept physique are hunted, devoured, or…repurposed." A slur came at the end of his words.

His black flesh revealed within the exposed cavity of his helm, tarnished and seared, his ruddy eyes castrated them unnerved, Sarkas particularly. He planned on the execution of Tycho ere retrieving what lied beneath the Spire, the corpse of his matriarch. He would tell Tycho of his friend knowing he would die, that was before knowing of the coming of the hunter.

"It is a pleasure the woman brought you here. I now have the personal benefit of dismembering you, taking this sow to be made sale of yet—I regret attempting to murder the bunch of you aloft, but the beast and I were all so tragically hungry. Despite the carnivorous flaunting on our part, I do not excuse the underlying resentment that came to follow the strike finding these untouchables onboard." His insult set for bots Tycho and Fera. "But how I would like to know the exact purpose for why the woman has come here…To either humiliate or slay me? Both…? Nonetheless, I'm flattered you've been keeping me in your thoughts well after this fleeting emancipation of yours."

The officer cleared his throat boorishly; heat wafting from his mouth, his head held up.

"In truth," said the officer, burrowing his talons within his face's crisped furrows before leveling his eyes, "Bill…is not dead."

Tycho eyes becoming sodden, he scowled detrimental to his own sight.

"But never will you see him…this is where you die; where you will lie for eternity amongst the other souls of the damned."

His arm erected outward fleetly with the curvature of his backside, challenging Tycho's aim with a chilling grin, a blade congealed to form in the dematerialization of his forearm. Before the release of the summoned blade, a resounding crash interrupted his focus from firing.

Sarkas instinctively shrouded both Tycho and Fera from the coming debris.

Thundering against steel as the moans of the menagerie of man erupted to nothingness, alighting from his horrid breach the Congregation stood staring back at him instilled with perturbation— they were still, awaiting slaughter. Before his breach, the hunter bounded at the face of the edifice with the construction of his facial carapace enshrouding his skull, quantifying the dread he'd plunge into their cores with his planned and recognizable entry, immobilizing them to disperse from his coming hand, paralyzed by fear.

For even the officer hadn't conjured the thought of flight; his feet had hardened to stone—only had his helmet galvanized to encase his countenance anew.

"Clyde!" exclaimed a bandit. "Cly—!"

His massacre had begun.

Gliding his glossed hand as it erected to a fine blade through the skull of the lout, the emergent fluids of the split head clogged the throats of those with agape expressions. His chain slung forth, the sinuous lash rupturing their beings to bodies of oil overhead sparingly, their limbs descended with the cascade of their internal liquids unto the floor of the Spire.

Sarkas peaking over at the assault, gruesome and stomach-churning as it was, he could no longer observe, he cast his gaze over onto Tycho and Fera once more. Eventually, Tycho moved past his wing and watched the decimation, Fera gradually following.

The spilling of their stomachs wherewith the egress of entrails to the slice—in flood—the hunter skated on their deluge in his advancement to the officer, who resided to watch, appearing somewhat lobotomized. Ripping past those few left, their bones minced to brittle chunks, the flaps of their skin slopping onto the sodden floor, he lunged for him.

Pounding his blade against the swift conjuring of the officer's own, the two tore past the triad's huddle in deadlock, his quarry's feet grinding to a halt to impede the force of the pounce.

Bearing witness to their clash, Tycho analyzed the officer's antagonist keenly. There, on his cardinal painted coat, an emblem, though tarnished, a great scar blemishing his creed's seal. What remained; *Sic Semper Tyrannis* stitched to his pronounced collar, as vividly as the officer's own.

"Halcón," spoke the hunter. "Tell me brother…where is he?"

The officer grinding his blade poorly against his advancer's, said, "After all these years of exile, you come to me starved—begging of his whereabouts!" He struggled to utter.

"I do not beg," said grimly of the hunter, "for I command you to answer me with your infallible tongue; if you abide, I promise an Outset's death."

In her focus, Fera listened—she awaited the location.

"No…," said the hunter, gazing aside momentary, "first, tell me why you have returned to the Spire? Does Halcón seek the emanations of Lucia?"

Fighting to keep his balance, the blade leaning closer to his breast, he said, "No…but her corpse. He wishes to have her return in the incarnate…He hears her voice in his dreams. She tells him she's claimed the last of their tribe…the last to slay that will bring the Ahmenseraï to this world and by then she will become a god. She'll be with us Clyde, as in the days of old."

"Leave her be, the woman is dead…You're certain he doesn't desire the emanations that reside within her?!"

"No. Though you bearing the shame of her slayer, in your self-righteous sense you felt she betrayed the Congregation," the officer wickedly scoffed, "her being has manifested through the emanations since her absence—she is beyond fathoming. But she yearns to return to her body; to live as in the flesh before her fall…and that time is coming shortly."

Removing the officer's guard with a violent clash of his blade forward, the hunter burrowed his foot into his gut to have him fall backside. He placed his body above his own, with his bound upon him his blade angled with less than a thrust away from tearing into the officer's throat.

"Understand this," said he, his sunset toned countenance angrily wrinkled—his carapace subsiding to leave his face and risen sanguine mane exposed, "I will never allow her passage to reclaim this plane and all it appears she pathetically strives to subjugate underfoot.

"To have felt betrayal, you mentioned," he said, his speech rasped, "can't rightfully tell if you're mocking or completely stupid. Weren't you that threatened death in your hearing if I were to spurn all ties, and allegiances I held for the church in what I ascertained as deceit—I felt no betrayal, I was apart from the damnable heresy in her liquidation! Had genocide not have you questioning similar, Brother Lyle?" He derisively kept at belittling his adversary. "I find myself agape in disbelief that you hadn't done the same, the entirety of the clan moreover. But the throng of you chose luxury and power than live in truth, to revel in heresy, so I shouldn't allow myself to be blindsided completely."

For the body of their matriarch had been buried deep within the base of *Tartarus' Spire*, the wretched howls of man warding off those who'd come virgin to the unexpected haunt and those learned came as a suitable chamber for her. A tool to her in his eyes, abusing the blindness of righteous fervidity within his brothers to lay the road in her ascension to power, the hunter executed their demagogue to eviscerate all foundation from which she had constructed her chapel of dissention, and revolution, and presently sought to dislodge Halcón that remained as a sort of pontiff over the church; he considered him a sort of cancer needed removing.

The hunter's chest ached with grief. "I will repay the Congregation with the blood it's spilled over these decades in pools, war and genocide, all that it has done…"

"You continue in your zealousness, Clyde," replied the officer. "How many more years will grow old and be forgotten while it's taken you the past twenty to decide whether to show yourself again."

"You weren't easy to find. As for my tardiness, I thought with time given in a generation her dominion would rot and molder, but I had not accounted for the strength Mammon had over you; I hoped for some demoralization with her termination, spirits crushed."

At a distance, Tycho listened. He recalled the reliquaries and their contents filled with the properties of the sought and adoring deity, as with 1440's apparition entering detached from the senses in the observation room. For the genocide the hunter spoke of was unaccountable to him, his only recollection of severe killings at Castle Rothschild.

Clyde prepared for his strike. "Now…Halcón. Where can I find him?"

He knew he would speak out of his own cowardice, his surcease to uphold honor and brotherhood for his hunger for riches, power, withal what high came with his slaughtering of the peasantry. He knew after he spoke, he'd play on his compassion for release, so quick was he to let his blade fall to evade indecision. Moreover, Tycho would interfere in his own particular way of making himself known, as he'd done so many times before.

The hunter's blade came undone—a scorching char came to his returning palm, overdone black. Clyde slowly turned his attention over to the vaquero, his florid eyes shimmering.

"I'm glad you two are having a nice reunion and all," said Tycho, stepping forward with the Havoc sputtering, "but I have unfinished business with him.

"You can wait your turn like everyone else," he continued, speaking for himself and Fera, in which she sought the knowledge the hunter strived to acquire. He feared he'd kill him without ever knowing Bill's prison as for the rationality of his hastiness to have the officer released—eagerly he awaited the officer's death, but fought this pleasure for the acquirement of his compadre; he knew better now, and had to make things right.

"What are you doing—?!" Fera exclaimed, silenced by their affright.

Suddenly cast from the officer's person Clyde careened the wall, gel and metal rent as he tore and scraped further within the Spire to its ceiling. His chain tautened Clyde came to the floor with expeditiousness, the officer reeling his chain to a stout dagger. His foot pressed vindictively into his gut to have him writhe, the officer grinning, satiating his hedonic urge to enforce cruciation upon his predator, watching his age-old comrade suffer beneath him—he savored this moment to be apprehended. Behind him, Fera had unexpectedly taken his arm into her grasp, sending his dagger to puncture scarcely against his spine.

"This man," said Fera. "Answer him!"

"Release me," commanded the officer odiously, oil beginning to leak from underneath his helm, spume rolling from out his mouth. "You unclean sow! Release me!"

"...One push is all it takes," Fera gritted her teeth. "One more push, and you'll be dragging the lower half of you."

His blade scratched near to his disc; a single thrust could cut through to his cord if angled correctly.

He struggled to swallow. "My command falls on deaf ears...Take your hands away from—!" He turned quickly to assault her.

Lacerating the officer's ankle with his constricting chain, Clyde lifted his church-brother from his footing onto the other side of the Spire, glass shattering resoundingly to his collision against the floor. His helm splintered into his face and across the floor from his capture, black streams poured from the wounds of his countenance, filling the slivered cracks on the glass surface from his impact, deluging through his fingers pressed upon his face. His features further marred with the protrusions of the whilom shell that adorned his head, a gleam from his eye had been discerned through the tangled mass of his black hair.

No longer supine to the officer, Clyde rose anew.

"Lyle!" shouted Clyde, readying his chain. "Where is Al Halcón?!"

From the gash of the Spire's side, looking past him and the Wasteland denizens with a clouded eye, the officer saw the galleon jounce. Slowly its neck elongated, raising its head to the sun.

"You'll kill me either way, brother...," spoke the officer heavily, "telling or not. I'd rather live to see you die...in time by my own hands."

Orotund its bellow came, Clyde and those of the triad alerted, staring back at the rising galleon.

Forthwith in the galleon's starting ascension Lyle cast his chain, Clyde sending his own after him.

By Lyle's other arm he summoned a lash to fall sinuously upon Clyde's cheek. Harboring the anguish that came with his slash, Clyde tore out the arm he'd constricted, failing to ground his quarry in his scarper.

Tossing his limb aside, he reached for the dilapidated stern of the galleon from the Spire with a tremendous bound, wherewith Lyle began to disappear in his skyward advancement to the beast's futtock. His first tethering was unfruitful, the frail hull of the stern detaching his whiplash—the rending lick of his chain failing to grapple ahold. Summoning a second chain as his adversary had done, thrusting his shoulder outward with stringency the soaring bands of steel came scarce to the fleeting vessel, but only the falling debris became stricken to his cast.

Returning to the earth in his collision onto the sand, he came to his feet at a gradual pace, hunched with his rise from the dune's crest. Twenty years of the hunter's life perished. He was without guidance; though to have acquired his spoor this may well prolong the venture, unless the lead would turn out ineffectual—Lyle returning to the shadows as before, nevermore carless as he became. Clyde shifted his glower from the dissevered clouds and into the Spire. He spied Tycho, and became full of malice.

IX

SERPENT OF OLD

TYCHO approached Fera, standing beside her. "Do you see him?" he asked as the two then stared without the Spire, the hunter glaring in return.

"Would you look at that...," Tycho said, beginning to chuckle, "Doggin' me out as if I'd—"

Conceited and his guard down—arrogant—Tycho came to the hunter's constriction, alighted from the Spire's floor. In his flight from the Spire, the champion of Sol Puesta impacted against his assailant's stinging fist, a succeeding blow from the hunter's other hand wetting his chest beneath his poncho bruised; blood streamed from the punctures. The Outset's knee ascended into the center of Tycho's torso, sending home a strike so vicious as to follow with an assault equally as cruel summoning the boy far from where he had been humbly belabored; carried from the momentum of the swinging of his fist sent the hunter bending forward at an angle where his eyes met the sand floor.

Soaring at a dizzying acceleration Tycho entered then exited the Spire with a savage collision against its wall—at this point there wouldn't be much of a tower left.

Grinding and tumbling about as he slid viciously against the Wasteland dunes, the hunter Clyde bounded great from the aperture Tycho had exited from and from a height braced his land upon him— Tycho's head whipped with his embarking. Roaring mighty, his fangs bared, Clyde bestowed his wrath onto the vaquero with his battering against Tycho's cheek and mouth repeatedly. Tycho's bruises opening to lacerations from the beating, Clyde was torn from his hellacious assault into him. An unwelcoming hand came to his shoulder swift and inimical, tossing him from the battered Tycho with force and exemplary strength. Flailing apace until his crash, he was pinioned within the moment he came to contact the Spire's exterior; Sarkas' talons dug deep within the crevices of the bricks to hold him to his subjugation.

Burrowing his beastly maw inside the chest of the hunter, black splashes emitted with the threshing of his muscle from his tearing canines. Clyde shouted horribly in tremendous anguish; his eyes glistened. Unleashing his wrist's grasp from Sarkas' colossal hand, Clyde clenched his fingers around the driving snout of Sarkas and gradually began to close the tremulous muzzle, the bat revolting against him as he snarled and barked hellishly; Sarkas struggled to keep close to the bandit any further. His other hand emancipated by force, Clyde garroted his chain about his assailant's throat and pulled, Sarkas thrown into the Spire without warning that would have prepared him for the harsh impact. Clyde remained clutched to him as they came to the Spire's center rolling in throes, the bandit avoiding Sarkas' fine dentition.

"Away from me." Ere his pronouncement, Clyde rolled to regain his feet, hunched—following, a stark backhanded slash of his arm repelled the advancing charge of the bat. He placed his hand over his bleeding breast.

Clyde's feet wetted cold. He looked gradually to the spill of the horde's dismantlement as it channeled to the floor's indentations.

Clyde turned his head to his shoulder and slightly turned. Behind him, the limb of his church-brother gleamed, claimed by the savage woman; odd, the resonating face, and body, that evoked the hunter to see her as something more than a brute, he refused to acknowledge an encounter with progeny.

Forthwith Fera struck, Clyde sparing his other hand to steer the point far from his vitals—his back remained to her.

Breaking the flesh of his palm, severing the inner meat of his hand, Clyde resisted her effort to puncture the blade anywhere else, the black of his eyes dilated greatly to a pin's head.

Holding the blade arduously, his fingers undersurfaces sliced against the edge, he said, "Didn't you spare your own life to save mine?"

"That was of when you were of use to me," she said, her voice slightly shaken in her wrestle to seize the blade from him.

A flash of violet retracted his attention, as with drawing Fera's.

Imprudent and hasty, tantalized to strike with the given chance of encountering the officer, Clyde failed to see that his massacre was planned by another—by their own hands. Ill-understanding the abounding horde of Congregation sycophants that Lyle brought with him, hushing the inquiring voice at the back of his head to find reason for their numbers, he came to surmise that his Outset brothers consecrated a sacrificial gathering, for the blood of the inculcated and perverted minds thenceforth exposing the darkness of her tomb underneath the earth unknowing to them. He knew from an observation afar they buried her here under the sole guard of the preternatural or this was to his assumption; a seal of fluids had been made to retain her secrecy in rest, but the perversity of it all sickened him! A selection of the threads—inscriptions—burned to the surface of the Spire's flooring, crossed and overlaid to reveal and bare the creature's mark; he saw the bat raise his head from convalescence to fathom the sigil's malefic throbbing light.

Funneling through the several slits amongst the flooring, the blood of the maimed and sundered poured. The reverberation of the splash of the fall offered Clyde presage of the distance to her tomb.

In continuance of forfending the woman's lunged strike against him, her second hand accompanying force to the hilt of the officer's limb, believing without the blade she would have only a stance of vulnerability to work with, Clyde kept his gaze on the ritual happenings, the gradual separation of the glass floor with a coming gash welling him with ire.

In his apoplectic and dour glare Clyde renewed to see the savage woman standing behind, herself given the semblance of courage when in truth she persevered to keep her life and another's. At her first move against him she gambled on the bandit to be hit unexpected, or wounded enough, as she came to witness with his bout against Sarkas, that his efforts of evading her strike would seem pitiable and unfruitful.

He began to pull upwards on the blade, the edge of the trenchant limb slicing deep past his knuckles. A terrible ring emitted—he snapped the blade half, Fera's leverage split against her.

He dropped the end of his own share, the point greeting the glass with a resounding clang.

Clyde turned his glare from her to the opened chamber and grumbled,—heavily, — "Run now, tigress."

He then felt a sting at his side, soon enveloping his utmost attention. He breathed deep, repressing the urge to blare an oath. Turning around imposingly, Clyde reached for the soiled hilt of the dismantled blade and tossed it beside him, — a ringlet of oil sprayed with its emergence, —advancing towards her as she hesitantly began to step back; though stern-faced, her countenance rebelliously quaked with fear and animosity for the bandit. She would not die a coward in the questionable hope of retreat that would have disregarded her agenda, albeit dread was ashore on her heart.

The hunter lashed his arm beside him, his blade conjured; she placed her withdrawing foot on a sodden portion of skin, tripping slightly.

Fera did not solely choose to stand against him in her search for Al Halcón as he, knowing well she would have the bandit slain to attain the satisfaction of killing Halcón by her own devices, but to keep the well-being of Tycho intact; angered, as with her approaching antagonist, at his swift reasoning to cease the officer's hold and allowing him leave, she understood—this would be but one of the few times Fera would forgive such temerarious doings. Yet, none of what she had done, at least on part for him, was done with sound reason, and she was becoming aware of this; hadn't the bandit's punishing volition against Tycho proven him exanimate?

Clyde swung his arm forward, the cobalt visor of his sheathing carapace sharing her gibbous stare—a glint came to his helm, and was then blinded forthwith. Before the roar of fire commanded the wall of the Spire to silence to its sovereign challenge, yet Clyde in his vengeful focus paid no mind to the overhead abruption.

The hunter had struggled to move further, his arm aching with a trembling force. Ahead, standing before her, Tycho kept Clyde's keen and malformed hand unmoving; the boy's feet eerily rooted, the brandishing leverage of the hunter halted to his stance. Fera looked at Tycho, daunted.

Sparks and a flurry of electrical spikes flared from Tycho's cheek, a solemn stare cast on his visage, becoming a grueling scowl.

His eyes began to glow, a whisk of cloud lashing out from the corner of his mouth asudden. The hunter began to tremble, his arm quaking—bones beginning to splinter.

A chilling sensation of wonder and uncertainty rose within Fera seeing Tycho in this carriage—her chest tightening, her head fizzling with warmth. This was the first time she had ever been witness to the Shine, fathoming its nature.

From his other hand Tycho curled his fingers tightly into his palm and suddenly hindered Clyde's sight, delivering fascinating blows to his helm successively with every step forward of him; the glass from Clyde's visor fell beneath Tycho's approaching foot, popping underneath his boot's sole. Releasing of his grasp of the blade, Tycho sewed his hands united, pounding the combined effort across Clyde's jaw; carried forward from his clout, the rash boy hopped to catch his balance. A distance came between them, Clyde bracing his congealing claw within the glass for his backwards slide to subdue. Wretchedly malformed and ruined Clyde peeled the carapace from his skull's guard and renewed his vision from the bent and blinding steel enshrouding his sight.

Tearing his forming hand out from the deep severance of his claw, brittle chunks of glass falling to the uplift of his arm, cast in aim for Tycho's execution. Throbbing in growth—cyst-like—a serration of cragged tusks punctured through the swollen pustule of flesh. He began to fire his obtrusions, fire belching from the orifice with their release. Flitting past the spikes with his hasting yet somewhat clumsy evasion, the spikes scarce of impaling his boots to the floor, flames rushed to Tycho's feet, white flames of propulsion and flight. Launching forth in brilliant scintillations, the glass shrieking in report from the torrid exchange of heat to its surface, his fist came center of Clyde's midriff—he was left breathless. With remaining strength he bore from Tycho's ramming collision, a vicious and barbarous lash of his chain impeded the assault, becoming but a moment free from his grasp. To his dismay and unfortunate circumstance this hindered Tycho not, thereafter the vaquero grappling him in renewed flight.

Carrying him by the collar of his coat upwards Tycho hurriedly summoned Clyde to the floor in return from their skyward foray, grinding his face against the nacreous skin of the Spire's base. Until reaching the lip of the well leading to Lucia's tomb Clyde's face had been marred; his cheek deliquesced—removed—from the heat of friction against the glass. His dentition showed, demoniac his visage became if not before.

Hurdling Clyde into his renounced master's tomb falling unbelievingly expeditious, Tycho ensued in the chase, his hat dismounting in his downward thrust to meet his assailant once more.

Tossing violently around to face Tycho in his fall, Clyde aimed his newly reconstituted cannon at the vaquero, emitting a prolonged challenge in accordance to his scorching volley. The malformed spikes skewered the well in trail of Tycho's evasive flight; the ignorance the hunter proceeded to keep was diminishing the reality of his present situation, thinking the peasant's light nothing more than the surge of internal combustion from his beating. He sought for the scattering of the bot with the coming burst, notwithstanding he began to tire of his own lies, becoming compunctious—aware—in the actuality of Tycho's being.

Tycho hurriedly slid along the imbrued shaft of the well agitating it to flames—spikes followed his descent, a couple parting through his thatch. Pushing his foot forcefully from the shaft, the approaching effulgence of the Shine convicted Clyde of his past horrors. Mortified, recollecting his already known transgressions and new, Clyde became vulnerable—there was an instance of severe pressure upon his breast that sent him further in his descent.

Below, a sable darkened expanse swallowed the arriving Clyde—the well whence he came seemed no longer ample in structure. He heard the echoes of those damned within the Spire's wall, coalescing submissive to the bloodcurdling ululations and cries of those in his thoughts; never forgotten, each face recollected.

Fumbling off from the plinth's seeped centerpiece, he found himself resting near the steps to her sarcophagus; he was unaware of the grounding in his interval of repentance. His conviction settling, he reasoned well enough of what he had done.

Tycho alighted before him; Clyde at the Shine's mercy regained his feet.

The Shine flared proudly, bringing light to the darkness; result of hecatomb, the cultists' bloodshed wetted the floor and doused the fissured coffin of their god to which shone at the emission of his spirited eyes. Clyde, raising his hand past his jaw-line, pressed his fingers within the excoriated aperture—his fingertips scratched against his dentition, no remnant of skin leaving his lips complete. To this, he came to resemble the great predator he was.

Striving to contain enmity for the peasant, Clyde charged with the thunderous shuddering of his esophagus, a primal bawl ineffable to disclose the amount of fear that struck at the boy's core. But he would fight no less.

Quick to draw Tycho leveled a bead on the approaching punisher with haste, three rounds disregarded—Clyde used the dark to his advantage, tracing the bolts to him otherwise the Shine housed within

Tycho making him a rather suitable target. As Clyde neared, he glistened from the light, a barbarous impalement of haunting spectacle apprehending Tycho's cast; he failed to apprehend the hunter's expedition. Plunging his blade center of the boy's torso, Clyde carried him forward with several, moribund assaults into him, blood spewing over Tycho's legs. Lifting the Havoc underneath Clyde's jaw within the opportune chance of retaliation, the barrel slid, the disastrous bolt cracking his exposed fangs to a range of cragged serration.

Another foul swing came from Clyde, evidentially to be parried by Tycho to much of their surprise. Catching near the hilt of his blade by happenstance, Tycho sliced—lodged—the crowned barrel of the Havoc through the gaping wound where Fera had severed his palm, forcefully turning the point sideways in the immediacy to repel further action to be taken by Clyde. The barrel lined to his shoulder, his fifth shot removed the upper half of the muscle, the antagonist to the Shine's chosen berating him with a horrid tremor inflected in his vociferation. Tycho became fearful, scarce taken aback.

Catching—hooking Tycho by the scalp with a punctured and sinew claw,—after a time the peasant hesitating to strike,—the wrathful Clyde carried him with precipitance, plunging to douse his irritator in the fluids of the horde. Catalyzed by the flames of the Shine, the oil surrounding became ignited; the blaze lashed as vivacious as an adulterer's tongue, stroking against Clyde's backside perniciously.

A bellowing thud, comparatively subtle, reverberated from Tycho's forced submersion.

Clyde continued to hold Tycho beneath the pond of muck, gradually taking his life from him; though a shallow pond it was sufficient.

Wavering streaks of orange marked his eyes' gleamed, the floridness of them accreting in tone to the fire surrounding in fight to sustain Tycho's submersion—his hand remained steadfast, notwithstanding harboring the sear of the snapping inferno.

The soles of his boots came to light in agreement with his resistance to aspire for release, ridding the muck that had tainted their shins and feet moreover the end of Clyde's coat when Tycho achieved flight. Launching his arm forward, Clyde seized a hold of Tycho's poncho unkindly, and well prepared was capable of holding his stance in revolt to the Shine's lift. Extending his other arm outward,—leveling the swollen cannon at the steps of Lucia's sarcophagus,—the missiles released from his foul limb, three of them burrowed within the stone. In the amain power this hunter possessed he delivered Tycho to the plinth's protrusions, beautiful streaks of the Shine trailing after the vaquero.

Suddenly skewered, Tycho wrestled to release himself with feigning anguish, grasping the cragged and barbarous impediments that pinned him stationary.

Clyde approached, Tycho somewhat unable to make out his visage as was given consumption to the fire's shroud.

Rebelling against his barbed hold, leveling the Havoc anew against his antagonist, Clyde crushed his arm underneath his foot as it pivoted terribly against the ruined step of the plinth. Lashing out his arm to a fine blade once more, the hunter amputated the boy's constituent from him; Tycho was found in sorrow.

Holding onto his nub for a forearm with dampening shouts, Clyde watched with inquisitiveness—solemn. How he desired to end his own career but Halcón's reign must be toppled. He questioned his time with this boy, worth the beating he placed on him; he enjoyed naught of it, notwithstanding he was galvanized to penalize him for the release of the officer. But then, in his observation, he heard the boy laugh— his crocodile tears had waned.

Watching him stand, the spikes sliding effortlessly from out of his chest, moreover the slits of his previous assault closing, Tycho seared his arm to his stump as he raised himself from the steps. Clyde's throat tightened withal his core throbbed apace.

His suspicions had been true, for Tycho was of the Tribe of Judah, as the fellow Lyle had within his possession awaiting the ceremony until her corpse's return unto them was false. It had been an age since Clyde last set his eyes on a child of the Ahmenseraï; neither had he ever came to encounter one as tenacious as him.

"What?" said Tycho discernible amidst the howls of the flames, dusting his shoulder, "you thought you could kill me…?"

And now he would put him to the test; Clyde raised his cannon and began to fire, wishing to see the ultimate of the Shine. Unless a bead on his core he could not disjoint him, rather he knew of his trivial act, but he wanted to see, to witness the majesty and sovereign glory the light would bring. The cragged spikes began to fly into him, yearning for the essence of the coming sign.

Clyde baring his chipped fangs the further he cast his volley within him, his other arm lateral to balance his position of the riving storm that would reap any other, there was the suffusion of mist that transfigured Tycho's vivid appearance against the ardency of the fire. The cannonade of spikes—thinned daggers—ceased in form within contact of the Shine's emission, or so it became. Stepping out the side from the unfailing cloud, Tycho's eyes within the severe concentration of white and fire gradually came to stand with a renewed body, unblemished. The Ahmenseraï's elect could not have survived alone, though Tycho strong, he needed something more, and by the Shine he lived.

"Lord…what have I done against you?" uttered the hunter, whom Providence did not exert presence to attain credibility but only to preserve his elect.

He lowered his abating cannon, his hand anew and struggled to remain standing—how he desired to fall to his knees and call to his former master's adversary. Until later would he realize that the mist reached him, removing his wounds marred by the triad—shoulder, breast and hand. But then there came a sound, a crumble and burst of stone that commanded to have Clyde and Tycho's utmost alertness.

In an immediate withdrawal of the black that soused the steps and as much as a pond at the base of the plinth, all blood came to the slivers and severances within the sarcophagus. The encaging of the mighty and trouncing flames relinquished with their foundation's resolve, absconding with fleeting light. A violet light flaring horridly— wretched flickers—the corpse of her earthen form rose. Not only was the blood used to open her tomb, but to raise her corpse from limbo, awaiting the return of Lucia; the mark encrusted on her forehead displayed the light of vanity, counterfeit of the Spirit, perversity of truth and said doctrine.

She had been able to attain consciousness within a higher realm, another plane of existence without her physical contour. Clyde, learned of her trekking within the macrocosm's in-betweens to hunt for the one she slaked for usurpation and destruction thousands of years prior, vehemently despised her reach of influence even beyond death. He presently became witness to her prolongation. It came to him Lyle was never to carry the corpse from her tomb, but would have egress of the Spire standing beside her animate remains.

Lucia's withered corpse could not resemble the toothsome grandeur she held within the form ere her assassination, the fluids of the slain cast from her dried lips and decomposing orifices of the skin helped not. The hunched, willowy body glared at the man.

"Clyde...," the Beast slurred, and clacked with blood cascading from its mouth—the tongue sloshed and flailed to its possession, coupled talons draping slothfully against its lip.

It turned its head to Tycho, and then returned its baneful glare to him.

"Occidere etam...."

For the Beast Lucia issued Clyde to strike down Tycho. Clyde refused.

Grotesque in its sprint, the corpse charged belligerent for the boy; the sarcophagus' side crumbled to its shin. His chain summoned, he grounded the ghoul, and pulled. The corpse broke the chain.

Ingrained virility compelled the hunter to stand before Tycho, her savagery denied.

Lunging forth, he subtracted her assault with a swift jab to its decrepit womb, keeping her from slaying calamity's harbinger.

"You will not have him; you will not have the Ahmenseraï."

A feculent perfume came from the tongue of Clyde's disavowed magistrate, his bowels upsetting at the rancidity of an otherwise eructing stench. Its voice quavering deep,—growling considerably vectra-like,—sought after Tycho, glaring past the shoulder of her hunter.

She manipulated the member of the corpse's arm to pull him close, the blade slicing deeper, his breast coming against the carcass' own. She then wrapped its hand gently around his wrist, carrying his palm to the wound, dragging his fingertips past the slit that indefinitely forfended her from godhood. Clyde dared not look; his lips trembled mildly. For he knew of his manipulator, and her strategies, lest he cast his gaze aside to not have his will subdued by the Beast.

The Shine ascending in flares of blinding continuance from behind the hunter riled Lucia from her persuasion, her emission of oaths and curses to the most high foolish! She knew of her fate, but denied the face of her makers' father in slake for unwarranted salvation and sovereignty amongst the stars and heavenly spheres that preceded any conception of hatred towards the creator and his creation.

Recalling the fright and skulk of the creature to the Shine's revelation, cleansing the gentle yet acrid Kat from evil's possession moreover in his wrestle at the castle, Tycho kept his gaze prolonged at their antagonist and stepped forward—he placed his hand on Clyde's shoulder, and confronted the covetous harlot. Guttural—slanderous curses proving damnation and rebellion, the flood of black dispersed from the carcass, the mark diminishing in scabrous lining; her corpse returned limpid and unmoving as within the age ere.

Kneeling at the husk, mesmerized, he doubted the certainty of his career threatened with lacking maturity, the essence of the dwelling light within his temple a fortunate guard. For this, his reason never expanded. Glancing at the slits scarring its desiccated center Tycho then observed the face of the corpse. Pronounced cheekbones, purple complexion—blackening.

Tycho looked over at Clyde, somewhat glaring.

Removing his hand from its head, he raised himself, and approached Clyde as the seasoned man exuded deep breaths. The Shine withdrawing within Tycho, eyes simmering blue, he made effort to make light of the circumstance.

Tycho secured the Havoc within its holster. "You guys have history I should know about?"

Clyde was unresponsive.

Tycho chuckled. "Sometimes I need to shut my mouth.

"You did a number on us...you know that? Good thing I cleared things up between you and the misses…that and the Shine helped too.

Well, except for the whole scar on your face thing…it's kinda gross to look at, but somehow I can't take my eyes off of it."

Clyde gradually made eye contact with him.

"Sorry," said Tycho, his face scrunching. "Just thought I'd be real with ya."

Clyde left Tycho's side and shoveled Lucia's carcass into his arms, proceeding to her demolished shed. He placed the discarded stones from her sarcophagus upon the corpse, centering the body along the plinth. Clyde descended from the steps, and came near to him once more.

"The light borne within you," he began, fitting his hands within his coat pockets, "I felt repentance…how have you acquired such a treasure?" He acted unknowing.

"Wait…you went through that, like the guilt and stuff?" He undiscerned the harlot's manipulative berating than the instructing love and counseling the Shine permitted to allow change.

Clyde looked at him as if he were a dolt.

"Yea…I know what you're talking about. Suppose a bandit's never been kept alive to tell me similar, now that I'm thinking about it. But, I tend just to ignore it," chuckled Tycho, rubbing the back of his head. "The Shine can nag at times."

Lucia's entity had been the instigator of his decline to penitence routed by his fugue, to seek forgiveness without an unbearable wall of guilt obstructing his coming to mature in the Spirit; since his dismemberment he'd mistaken which voice was of the latter, from time to time. And only had this left him continuing in his selfish adventure, ignoring shame that would bring hindrance to his immutable companion.

Clyde wished to disclose Tycho's identity, but with his bravado to speak unrestrained, he withheld the truth. He sought for the boy to be protected, and if the Congregation were to acquire the sensitive information than by the ends of the Ravaja they'd come for his slaughtering. Lucia led them astray from the boy…*for what purpose? Who was the other man Lyle had?*

"You doin' alright?" said Tycho.

Clyde, deep in his mind's ideations, gave attention to Tycho as he brought inquiry.

"Who trained you to flaunt an iron like that, while enduring such a fight? Never have I come against one as bullheaded or arrogant…Disregards to my clan."

Tycho remained silent, an uneasy smirk incongruent to his scowl. Misty, Tycho refrained from further thought of him.

"Let's talk about the actual thing that took him, how does that sound? Looked pretty similar to that woman over there, know anything about it?"

"You're going to ignore me—?"

"Lucia…? She the one pullin' the strings?! Does she know where Bill is?!"

"Rude and incompetent, am I faced against such a puerile figure?"

Tycho brushed his arm. "Don't give me that crap…talk."

Clyde could not will himself to speak on the horrid thing, nor Bill. It saddened him, tearing his heart half of the fate the creature's bore, such innocent beings prior to their reneged allegiance. As for Tycho's mentor, he was as much in the dark of the man's location as his pursuer, Clyde asking himself as to what gain Lucia received in the capture of the denizen.

"Where's Lyle heading?" said Tycho, irritable. "I'll find out from him."

"No…you won't."

Tycho' s brow rose.

"You'd die…I spared you."

Tycho pointed his finger, and was vehement. "If you're talking about stepping in for me when that corpse came runnin'," he angrily said, "I had that under control—!"

Clyde's voice rumbled. "Child…before that."

Tycho remembered the cannonade tearing through his breast and above, nothing below.

"And by the grace of your God you found yourself within a new body; somehow he even managed to keep that outfit of yours from withering."

"What *god* are you talking about…?" Tycho became suspicious, allured yet frightened.

Clyde found himself at fault, and was quelled to speak further—he felt his core leap to his throat with a great pound.

His face remained unchanged, then recollecting and aware of his hampered strike against the vaquero; several times scarce did his blade glide past the core of the boy—a graze.

"Go home." Clyde hunched low, pressing his hand arduously against the floor. "He will come to you again." He lied.

Bounding at a height, released from his odd crouch, his coat whipped stark—a summoning of his chain carrying him from out of the tomb and well.

Tycho watched the hunter in his leave, leveling his eyes to the rubble pile. Beside his foot lay a stone from the old sarcophagus, picking it up he cast the debris to return within the nurtured grave—a downward shift came to the mound.

"Alright…Shine," he said, stretching out his legs, following with the tapping of his boots' toes against the floor, "let's get out of here."

The increasing radiancy of the Shine blooming from out of his eyes—ripening in coruscation during his childish ritual of readiness—flames enshrouded his feet, in flight becoming orbs of trailing fire. Hunching as to perform a great leap as Clyde—comical—Tycho launched wonderfully from the Beast's chamber and rocketed in elongated spirals within the confines of the bloodied well. Finding his hat remaining in continuing descent, Tycho was quick to snatch it by its brim, perching the hat secure to his soar. Recalling his flight shared with Sarkas, torpid in the amount of acceleration compared to the Brussian's respectively, a smile grew wide to his countenance putting his prior grin to shame.

Exiting the well with prompt ascension, Tycho came to the glass flooring with a halting slide of his feet, his arms out to retain balance. Hopping forth from his declining slide as to avoid stumbling, he found Sarkas being caressed by Fera's hand. Something new, he spied the division of the officer's limb appropriated to her, held by her sash— two blades they became in growth from hilt and point.

She continued at his pelage as Tycho neared.

Tycho knelt beside her. "Wanna see something cool?"

Fera—shaken and perturbed—hesitated to answer him. She hadn't even recognized or noticed Clyde's departure from the Spire.

Looking away from her, he placed his hand beside Fera's upon his neck—the branching, swirling veins of light cast them blanche.

Sarkas' eye opened gradual, rolling his sight to them. Tycho began chuckling, Fera rather crestfallen her demeanor remained unchanged, though the exception of being awed by the Shine's presentation. Sarkas braced his arms against the slick flooring, effortful to sit upright; his arms trembled and then gave out, falling prostrate. He tried again, shoulders aching concomitant to his pressured arms and hands. Crouching underneath his breast, Tycho held the bat's weight against his backside as he pushed back with gradual steps. He delivered Sarkas unto his breech, and began panting.

"In any other situation, blue bot, I would be indebted to you," he said, exerting strength to speak. "But, the precipitance you carried out against that vile hunter resulted in our lives threatened. Mine could have very well been lost, as with yours, and the girl's."

Tycho was without response as he caught his breath.

Sarkas wiped his lips, smiling. "I am glad though to see that we are in better health than before, thanks to the fire."

"You gonna tell us what that was all about, what you pulled off back there?" Fera neared him with arms crossed.

Tycho turned to face her, grinning slowly. "Oh, you mean saving your rear end back there from that bandit? Yeah, no need to thank me," he said, admiring his boots, "I did it all out the goodness of my heart and stuff."

Her face soured—she was rather pissed.

"Huh," she said with a sour glare, "coming from the guy who got his ass handed over to him within less than a minute—"

"What?! I'm sorry," Tycho uttered, "I can't hear you over the moans! I think they're crying: *Tycho is the greatest of all time?*"

Sarkas chuckled. "I thought you believed it to be a draft?!"

"Sarkas...I could care less at this point," said Tycho deadpan. "I was just trying to make a point."

She grinned with satisfaction. "What? That you think you're some big shot?"

"Hey...I never said that."

"Don't have to."

"Purple bot is right," said Sarkas. "It shows"—he leaned his head low—"with much pomposity."

Tycho departed from their company. "Alright, I'm out."

Sarkas and Fera chuckled, becoming lost in their own conversation as they watched him make exit of the Spire.

Coming to look on the tawny horizon from the Spire's steps, the yolk of the sun bleeding onto the land as it set, the discourse he had with Clyde shadowed his thoughts. The god he was told to have belonged with harbored anticipation, notwithstanding to refute the contiguous relation the being may have with the Ahmenseraï or whomever Lucia sought. Postponing the uncertainty of Clyde's words to him, Tycho thought on more pressing matters that needing dealing with, where the officer now resided and how to find him.

The thought of the Stranger also came to mind, for what was his agenda if not for the sole protection of Tycho? Perhaps it was, and what would he make of the Ahmenseraï? Tycho had heard him too utter those words.

With his arrival to the platform Meseron was found lying on the baked course, in which she situated herself unto out from chaos' advent within *Tartarus' Spire*. In truth, but only momentary, Tycho believed her to be dead. He bestrode Bill's mustang and wheeled her to face the sand path as she arose, directing her forward. Scheming as to how he'd acquire Bill from the grasps of the Congregation, Sarkas sailed above him as Fera clung to his backside to sustain voyage.

"Sarkas," he hollered, "you got a scent on that bandit?"

Sarkas said, perturbed, "What of it?"

"Clyde is the only guy who can lead us to that officer...well, who has the best shot at it. Use that scent you have on him to lead us in his path! Got it?!"

Sarkas landed close to him, Fera scrabbling to lift her head over his shoulder.

"Tycho," replied Sarkas. "Do you not know who those men were?"

Sarkas said, seeing his blank expression, "Outsets...Those were *Outsets*, my friend." He looked over his shoulder to Fera, and spoke grimly, "You should know better...leading him this far."

"I told him—!"

"Tishina, Fera," he said—gentle. "I refuse to believe you told him *everything*. Yet...I see Tycho remains dogged to find his companion, without care for the horrors he's come to witness.

"Never would I have come here if I knew what awaited us. Although, in truth, he had us cornered like rats," he chuckled solemn. "How I could not discern him, until he showed his face...that wretched face."

Sarkas grieved and ruminated.

"I'll take you a distance, but not to him," replied Sarkas. "You two, as well as I, have been through plenty. Surviving an encounter with those thugs should not be taken lightly—it is more than a blessing."

Fera was rather put out, as with Tycho.

"Whatever works for you," the boy held his sigh. "I'll follow."

Displaying his wings proud in arising flight, he turned about in the air and said, "Do not take my words without caution; I promise to not lead you far. Our bandit continues to become leagues ahead in venture, for his blood remains satiable on my tongue, handling a spoor that will presume his whereabouts!" He looked afar. "Now, it'd be best for you to try and keep up!"

Tycho thereafter raced after Sarkas, the sand erupting half-pipe in form to the turbulent raze of his gust.

CLYDE VOLKOV, FAVORED PUPIL OF THE BEAST

X

THE HILLS HAVE EYES

INUNDATIONS of fog came from over the hills, an afar spectacle to their flight, the blinding sheen of the wispy ocean rendering their gaze in intervals. Tycho, yearning for a view of the heights, called on Sarkas' name and arose to his lift wherewith the vaquero became stationed in an environment of bliss; before a wall of white stood bleeding unto Meseron's galloping hoofs, Sarkas and Fera almost unseen. The mustang did well in her pace, keeping below Sarkas within his shadow, the triad enraptured in their soar. From the fog three beauteous forms ascended, gaunt—willowy fellows; they appeared forged in the mantle of white, their flesh imitable to the cascading ice. Tycho, as with Fera, found few words to conjure from the tongue in their awed yet apprehensive state.

Sarkas informed, disquiet: "What are they doing out here...? I suppose Rahnth has become inflicted with paranoia in his decrepit age. Let's just make sure they don't see us...it's best to avoid them," and with a great pound from his spread they were moved behind a rouge piece of brume that was torn apart from the weightless, cloud-like mass.

They had not spoken for a good while, gazing, Tycho's mind drifting. The whispers of the wind became akin to a familiar voice, amplifying his imagination from the longing the vaquero bore.

"Alright, champ," said Bill. "Level that aim of yours—too high, and we might as well be havin' that hawk that's been circling us for supper."

The faint reverberation of Meseron's gallop echoed throughout the valley, evoking the sensory recollection of horses from drawn stagecoaches of traders galloping into town and the sauntering mounts of hunters nearing *Papa' Retreat*.

Tycho began to intake breaths slowly, overcome with mourn and pine. He looked to the sun with the passing luminaries, as high and round it had blazed amongst the skies of Sol Puesta those several years past. Another echo of his voice came to him.

"Good…now, see if you can hit that scarecrow, way out there. Looks as if its hat had gone and been blown away…"

To its lonesome molested by the arid gust, the weathered poncho sinuously whipped at the post, giving semblance of a man, equipped with a pumpkin for a head, and sprouts of hay for arms.

Bill stood close, and observed. He cocked an eye to the boy's foot, grating harsh against the ground.

"Loosen up kid, and take your shot."

Tycho took his breath, his lids scare of becoming half-shut.

Bill rolled his tongue against his cheek, in expectation.

With a great shift of his arm, the iron bucked, the crystal transfixing the putrescent corpse of some wandering Wasteland beast.

"Well, to be fair you did hit something." He jeered.

Tycho glared at the man.

"What…?" he softly chuckled. "I'd lose that look now, Tycho." He glared in return. "Don't expect me not to have fun watching you taking

LEGEND OF THE RAVAJA

yourself so seriously; would rather bring attention to that poor aim with mortification than have you endangering these folks because of your incompetence to fire a gun correctly. Is that understood?"

Tycho looked to the scarecrow. "Done yet?"

Grazing his palm against his stubbed cheek, Bill then approached him and took the iron from his hand with mild resistance. Holding both hands on the grip, lining his eye across the barrel, each release of the weathered bot's fire punctured the flesh of the pumpkin, strands of orange and white spurting from the repeating punctures.

"If you're gonna aim," said Bill, "aim *well*, or it ain't worth for nothin'. Can't just hope for the best, that'll get you killed. Every shot has to count..."

He gently handed back the iron.

"Come on, take it."

Put in his place Tycho humbly acquired the piece. And as the winds howled shriller and shriller filling his head with noise than an over-thinking mind, Tycho fixated his eye on the target, leveling his eye along the iron's barrel, and fired in succession.

"Now we're getting somewhere."

Bill slowly looked over to Tycho, the latter from his eye's corner spying the old man had smiled greatly before turning to see him. Although he missed four of the six shots, sending home few from the chamber into the target after his second attempt of firing proved to this grizzled vet that Tycho had promise, and considerable training ahead of him.

The cries of a woman permeated throughout town, perceivably mistaken for the strengthening gale if one were not listening acutely. Fortunately for her, the saloon's tender and his amateur gunslinger caught the alarming pitch. From behind *Papa's Retreat*, they came to the road disturbed.

"When were you going to tell me you could fly…?"

Encased in the strands of heaven's veil Tycho remained gawking at the hills, his eyes falling and rising with the milky undulations, continually imbrued with seeping fog.

"Hey, you in there?" said Fera. "Zodain to Tycho…?" She poked at his cheek.

"Stop that." Tycho swatted her hand.

Fera grinned, flicking the skin above his nasal slits and with surmounting enough courage asked him the dilemma that had plagued his face with sorrow.

"Someone's a grouch…You've been acting weird ever since we left the Spire. Does it have something to do with that bandit—?"

"No…I'm just tired." Tycho feigned a yawn. "All I need is a good nap."

"So…," said Fera as she circulated her hands in anticipation, "how'd you do it?"

"What are you talking about, woman?"

Fera's face slowly devolved from brilliant jubilance to irritation.

"You've gotta be kiddin' me—," she said under her breath. "Flying"— her eyes widened with agitation—"how is it you can fly? You had fire comin' out of your mouth like some sort of," and she proceeded to passionately swear, comparisons of the Spirit to a demon or dragon insulting the heavenly host.

"Easy on the language, purple bot!" Sarkas advised, bellowing enough to break the roar of the wind.

Tycho chuckled, fitting his hat over his eyes. "So you saw all that, huh?"

"You were right in front of me! Of course I saw it…," She crossed her arms. "Weren't you bragging just moments ago how you saved me so *endearingly*…?"

"No, I remember all that," said Tycho, lying onto his back tossing his leg over the other. "But I was really hoping the Shine would have blinded you or something so I wouldn't have to talk about it."

"That's really sweet of you, Tycho. How considerate," said Fera rather caustic.

"Yea, no problem." Tycho squirmed to satiate his comfort against Sarkas' fur. "You know me."

The savage woman was at a loss for words.

"I've never seen you this animated before, well…there was that one time on Winthro's vessel but I won't go there. What a loser he turned out to be."

Fera nodded, biting her lip. "Would you shut up already and just tell me."

"Ah, I think you're missing a word somewhere in there!"

"You know what, you're a real pain in the—!"

"Fera—!"

"What?!" She wheeled her glare to Sarkas.

"I'm still waiting to hear it." Tycho taunted her horribly.

"*Please!*" said Fera. "There, happy?!"

Tycho spied Fera past his hat's angled brim. "See, that wasn't hard. Looks like some else might need a nap," he said.

Fera gritted her teeth—she contained her fury well.

"The Shine, that's what you called it," she spoke in an effort to sound calm. "What is it…?"

After moments of silence, a pang arose Tycho from his recline, resting himself upon his haunches.

His speech muffled from the hand cupping his lips, he said, "It's…well, someone else called it the Spirit, I guess that's the best way of describing it."

Fera transfixed with bewilderment, she asked, "Who's Spirit?"

He chuckled. "I guess that's the scary part of not knowing, isn't it?"

"How can you not know—?"

"I know the Shine...he's second to being my closest friend. But where he came from..."

Tycho was without an answer.

Fera gazed at Sarkas' backside, and said, "Maybe it has something to do with that woman those bandits spoke of, residing in the emanations or whatever. No...that doesn't make any sense." She thought something to herself. "What were they even talking about?"

She looked at him. "To be honest," she said, "before seeing the Shine, I never cared to believe in that kind of stuff...but after seeing *that*, what you pulled off back there...it's hard to go back to what I used to think; that would just make me ignorant, huh?"

The savage woman appeared troubled.

"Remember the other individual they mentioned," said Tycho. "What they said of the Ahmenseraï?"

Fera intended to nod, but became entranced with suspense for the awaiting discourse.

"I'm starting to think this has more to do with it than anyone else."

Tycho began playing with Sarkas' fur, stirring the hairs around his finger. "Fera...back at those ruins, there were things I didn't tell you about. The things I saw, what I heard, were haunting, more so now after my encounter at the Spire."

"With the Outsets, right?"

Tycho momentarily glanced at her before returning to his occupation, making Sarkas spaghetti.

"Their god, Lucia...she was down there, puppeteering her corpse, like with the others she's come to possess."

His last and most graphic memory of Kat panged him, hatred arising anew for the creature he'd put down in vain. Oh, how Tycho fought passionately to only have his eyes kept at a shimmer.

"Hold on, Tycho," she said, placing her hands alongside her lap. "Possession...? You can't exactly...drop a bombshell like that and expect me not be a little caught off guard. What is it we're talking about here...?"

Tycho told her of Sol Puesta, and the subterranean castle's secrets.

"This woman, or whatever she's become," he said, chuckling soft, "is looking for something that belongs to a power that's presently far beyond her reach. She's been denied twice, by bandit and god, of receiving what would make her out to be some supreme being, but from what I'm seein' there's an underlying operation that's striving to have her fantasies realized."

"Evrika!" shouted Sarkas. "I remember that Outset—the charred one— speaking of killing a man to have that negodyay obtain deification. Could Bill, your friend, blue bot, be the one they intend on sacrificing? Strange, if so, for what is a man's purpose in relation to heaven's scheme?"

Tycho was unresponsive.

Fera gradually turned her gaze back onto the vaquero.

"Sarkas," he said grimly, "we have to hurry. How far off are we from finding that bandit?"

"Miles, I'm afraid."

"What are we waiting for, pick it up then."

"You could always fly to him yourself, Tycho. When were you gonna tell me, eh?" The bat chortled.

"I would be nowhere without that nose of yours, buddy. And eventually I'd let you in on the secret, this is all new to me too you know."

"I kid, I kid—but still, I'd like to know these things! If we are to rely on each other," said Sarkas, "it's best to have insight on the talents that can give us leverage when in trouble, da?"

"I would have to agree," said Fera.

Tycho looked outward and said, "If you'd feel safer in knowing the next time the Shine does something unexpected, I got no problem sharin' about it. But I wouldn't bet on him matching anything that spectacular...Think that's the strangest it's gonna get."

Quiet now, Tycho returned to becoming somber; he always felt alleviated when talking to others that in many ways lifted his spirits, Fera with the biting remark, Sarkas with his genial abundance. At the Spire the hunter's comment sparked the memory of his training, one of the many that resonated with the champion of Sol Puesta—the evening that defined Tycho as such; later in his venture would he recollect the remaining scene untold. He began to think of Bill's past, something never spoken to him or Kat; he knew of his service during the War of Divergence, Tycho picking up on the apparent truth that Sarkas too had fought in this war, understanding some things were to be discussed and other matters never to be spoken of or even thought about being asked.

If the creature is to be believed, Bill mentioned someone being "set apart". Tycho questioned if his son was whom he was referring to. He thought him deceased; still, Tycho found no reason as to why Bill was abducted. Tycho began to extrapolate the nature of Lucia, but failed almost on all attempts. He knew only of the reason for her rebellion against the human creators, but not grasping the hatred she charged the sought deity for her torture and neglect, moreover her continued existence and influence; for Tycho to comprehend her infinity he would have to comprehend God, which he could not do, or any man, but knew the emanations were key to her power from the Outset contention.

As for those two, the Shine was strangely upset and angered to those bandits who performed such malformed contortions of the limbs into weaponry—Tycho felt this, but stubbornly refused to act upon its will to cleanse; his approach similar with his bout against the creature. Tycho further debated amongst himself if the Shine was of the Ahmenseraï, as was the god Lucia hunted—from the discord between Clyde and the officer this was clear. For what other god has been mentioned besides this, disregarding the Congregation's faith.

Yet, Tycho remained uncertain, accredited to his doubt no less.

A volley of bullets whisked scarce of hitting the triad. Sarkas lifted with quickened pace to avoid the dreaded missiles.

The bots taken aback, curious, held their sights barely past Sarkas' backside—a bullet grazed the vaquero's hat, galvanizing him to hold it steady with haste. From the base of the hills the gunfire had been released, the report from their rifles deafening as its echo carried for miles throughout the barren valley. Tycho presently decided what action he would need to take, un-attentive to their discussion.

"Are you sure they're firing at us?!" shouted Fera.

Sarkas glanced at the space afar. "Fera, the moths are gone," he shouted. "We are their only target!"

"See if you can lose them in the clouds coming up ahead," she said, pointing at the overhead fog, "there we can wait it out like last time with those moths, evading their fire until they can't place their sights—!"

A burst of fire had sent Fera's apparel into rapid evolutions, turning her head apace to Tycho's launch, watching his expeditious and flamed descent. He was to assail their predators.

Tycho called Meseron in flight to his soon approach to the earth, a whistle erupting profound to have its reverberation challenge the cacophony of gunfire. Finding himself in the saddle, buckling harsh to remain stationed on her backside, he charged forth with the Havoc in-hand. Sarkas could not allow his juvenile companion to fight alone, and with Fera's compliance, they would come to him. Once more Fera became angered, as beginning with Sarkas against the boy's attitude to serve his own emotional desires than respect the mortality of those around him.

XI

ONE'S STRENGTH

G LIDING down the undersurface of her arm, a release—an askew trail—of blood poured, in intervals conglomerating to a drop, splashing beside her toe. Again, she traced the blade along her skin until enough pressure was put upon the implement to dissever the flesh from sheathing the vein, ravished at the horror, hoping to leave, overwrought with disorderly attention—dizzied. Stationed on her bedside in a terrible shiver, she recalled her contemplation ere committing to the appetizing ideation, perturbed to press the blade any further than the goosebumps grazed by its slickened ridge. She had placed a towel near the foot of her bed in caution of her sought decision effectual, and with a trembling hand clawed a portion of the towel into her palm, carrying it to the wound.

God, kill me, she thought.

Nights following, she borrowed her husband's revolver and slid the barrel into her mouth, her jaw beginning to ache from the apprehension she bore. The iron tickling the roof of her mouth, she became teased with the sensation of death, albeit she gagged in repellence of its further intrusion. Holding both hands on the grip, she closed her eyes, and breathed—casting a whimper, her lips quivered mildly, embracing the taste of salt from the sluices that ran from her eyes; she was a pathetic person. She pulled the trigger, and fell weightlessly onto her bed—she would be found with blood-soaked hair, a distasteful scene.

Regrettably, her mother was the first to find her sprawled gruesome on the sheets, the bedding encrusted and soaked with the blackest of oil. The staring expression of her child drove several pains into her heart, becoming equipped with throes.

She knelt before her daughter, and lamented the loss. Glancing to her side, she found the gun she'd slain herself with, its barrel and floorboards underneath sprinkled with her daughter's blood. What was to be an afternoon of brunch devolved into the pitying of a daughter's self-governance of demise; carrying her out from her home with arms hung, pacing each of her steps carefully. A woman of her age could hardly burden herself with carrying a handful of stones, but the love of a mother is unaccountable and by means of preternatural strength hefted the body of her limp beloved.

Soon after her exit, borne with the considerable weight of her child, she found herself being molested by a cavalcade of bandits coming into town, a crystal scraping the back of her neck, shearing the close air. She tumbled to her knees and dropped the corpse, presently begrimed with mud; she found herself wailing profound—a string of blood coursing down the mother's twitching throat.

The delirious howls of the bandits betokened the residents' cowardice, sheltering underneath kitchen tables and mattresses to avoid the passing glance that had ensnared countless spouses to chains. They closed their distance from the prey, anticipating further torture to be given to the woman before ridding of her in their boredom.

But then there came a light; someone dared to oppose them.

Perceiving it was the sand's brilliance cast amongst his face, they heeded no disquieting talk as to who they came to encounter, a foolish—unrecognizable—individual.

They fired at his feet, ordering him to dance; Tycho was staunch and remained where he stood.

Bitter and his authority threatened the bandit shot his aggressor thrice amongst his head to his chest, brisk flashes erupting from the punctures; from the saloon's side,—with shortened, disturbed breaths,—Bill hurried towards Tycho, to his apparent end. Before, he had tried to hold him back from getting involved, but the boy would not listen.

Strangely, the sole motion of his head jerking brought consternation to the Congregation indoctrinated, spouting oaths in a clamor and emitting malicious, crude speech against Tycho.

The young vaquero proceeded in their direction, his steps soft. They fired as to empty their chambers, considerably a hailstorm with a few bullets from another gun.

From his feet dust masked the coming vindicator, crowned with billowing white. Bill watched him from the woman's side, urging her to find shelter; she refused to leave her daughter where she lied.

He passed through his begrimed shroud and fired at the bandits, one shard cast center of a horse's breast—the other shot fired transfixed one of the cutthroats' shins. A round tore through to the back of the boy's throat, so Tycho returned the favor. An implacable denizen they'd come to accept, spying him unblemished, rallied their posse and with haste made for *Minotaur's Run*. Turning his head to see his mentor, he caught him composed, inwardly gorgonized.

Lifting the corpse from the muck, Tycho assisted Bill with the woman's child, directed to the back of her home. Bill offered to lend both their hands if the mother wished for a grave; at first she refused, adamant on her son-in-law to place his deceased bride underneath the earth, but out of fear as it began to darken later in the day, she did not want her body to become repast to some starving vectra; misinformed, vectras did no such thing. She returned to them, and accepted their request.

They proceeded to bury the deceased. The mother buried half of her face within Bill's chest as Tycho gently lifted the lithesome remains into the ground, filling the dirt atop of the body, leveling the surface of the grave. Inviting the overwrought woman to his home thereafter, Bill requested of Kat to clean the wound that rived her skin.

Thenceforth the moon reigned from the east, its servant dusk masking the town shaded.

Departing from the old man's residence earlier the evening thereof, a knock came to his door in the howling hours of night; familiar trespassers averted from the bestial cries. Tycho opened the door to be greeted by Bill—underneath his arm a folded cloth, and in his hand a brown, sullied hat.

"Forgot to give you this on your way out."

Tycho cleared his throat. "This couldn't wait till mornin'?"

He placed the hat on Tycho's head, the boy acquiescing with mild irritancy.

"There we are," he smirked. "Startin' to look like a proper scarecrow…and no, it couldn't."

Reaching for the vibrant cloth tucked underneath his arm, he handed to Tycho what appeared to be the poncho once fitted to the scarecrow's post behind the saloon. He realized Bill had made fun of him.

"Here, put this on."

"No," said Tycho. "I'm better off if you'd take this back." He lifted the hat from him. "Where'd you end up finding this, it smells like—?"

"Crap," said Bill. "Managed to find it in Meseron's shed, must've blown underneath the door."

Tycho nodded. "Nice."

"Kid…," said Bill, "I actually came by to talk to about what happened with that girl. I figured you had some questions." He forcibly admitted entry within Tycho's confines.

"Make yourself at home while you're at it, old man," said Tycho under his breath.

Setting the apparel in the glow of the candle's light Bill removed his holster from his waist, the iron anchoring the leather strap as it hung from over the dining table's edge. Grunting at length with his descent into comfort, he well secured his breech against the torn cushions of Tycho's thrashed sofa, amassed with spots of dried sweat and other anomalous fluids. He gestured with his eyes for Tycho to sit.

Taking his seat across from the chest Tycho used for resting his feet, occasionally to serve tea if ever a guest would return to converse after the sighting they beheld of the light cast from his skin, and eyes, he would do this in welcoming them.

"Before I get into the incident with Joanna's daughter," said Bill, steering his eyes to his lap, "I want to know what made you think the Shine was gonna cover your ass out there. The stupidity on your part—"

"All I did was stand there—," he said.

"That's exactly what I'm getting at."

"…I didn't know he would do that, but I wasn't about to watch that woman get kicked around and beg for those scumbags to let up on her."

"Tycho," he said, grave, "I could have lost you to them. And, sure, for the most part, you held your ground like a stick in the mud," he chuckled, "but in that instance, your life could have been just as easily taken from you as that mother's." He rested his arm on the sofa's crown. "I give my regards to the Shine, because if it were anyone else dumb enough to put themselves in your position they'd be roped and dragged through this town until their stomachs ruptured to have their innards splayed across the road. I don't want to see you taking anymore risks like that…"

Bill's eyes met with Tycho's. "Make it a promise you won't."

Tycho would not respond.

"You're gonna do me like that, huh…?" He said after their pause, "If you can't take a liking to the favor then I'll just have to keep making you the better shot; I'll keep showing you how to use a gun, primarily as a means of defending yourself. By the way, that aim of yours was horrendous."

Tycho coughed, masking his subtle laugh—he was right.

"Eye leveled on the barrel, remember…?" He smirked.

"Yea, yea…*At least I don't need two hands to keep my gun from shaking.*" He teased his mentor.

Bill softly smirked, and took a breath, wiping his hand over his lips gradually, leaving a fist to settle in the crevice. Tycho waited, in silence.

"I'm gonna have to tell you how it is." He placed his hand on his knee, his eyes cast at the chest's rotted surface before returning his sight to the young vaquero. "The girl performed self-execution, ran a bullet right through that pretty skull of hers."

He chuckled, the depths of his conscious attempting to ameliorate the situation discussed.

"I know what she did to herself, Bill."

"And what's that…?" Bill said. "Leaving a gnarly scene for Joanna to find…? We're only left with questions as to why she decided to slay herself—she didn't even bother to leave her mother *or anyone* a note. Tycho…there are some more selfish than others out there in the

Wasteland, but by far the removal of one's self from those loved cannot even be compared to the inculcated of the Congregation."

"Easy," said Tycho. "I'm sure she had no intention of—"

"The mother has no one to blame but herself," said Bill. "Not saying it's her daughter's fault, but her intentions were cruel and self-absorbed. What she did was wrong...she could have said farewell—something, but chose not to. Joanna's now left with a void,—I can guarantee,—far more devastating than whatever that girl was feeling."

How could he say something like that, thought Tycho.

"I never want to see you taking your life for granted like her...! I don't care how that light works, Tycho."

Taken aback, Tycho discerned the moment. He'd never seen Bill exuding with vehement frustration and concern. "I heard you the first time, why are we going back to this—?!"

"I want you to listen. Don't let the Shine cloud the truth of the world you're in," he said, stern. "Got that...?"

The boy hesitantly nodded, lowering his eyes from him.

"I have an early morning with a newlywed's widower," said Bill. "Her husband's voyage having been delayed is believed to be returning tomorrow at dawn, coming in on a fancy airship supposedly. I say good fortune to the wheelman who's going to have to scale over those mountains to get here, rarely do they succeed." He gradually lifted himself, scratching his chest with his venture over to the dining table. "Saw one of those things pop like a bull's testicle...That was the first and last time the Congregation tried somethin' creative like that."

Tycho looked to the iron hung on his hip. "When's the day I get to use that one?"

Bill glanced at him, securing the holster: "Probably never."

Thinking this was a sort of humored response from him, Tycho smiled. However, his mentor was silent, avoiding all forms of eye contact.

Bill couldn't stand to carry around the gun as it had been a reminder of his inhumanity, but it had been the only weapon to satisfactorily repel Congregation trespasses all until the young vaquero would take the mantle of guardianship, and have its potential realized.

"I better see you at the saloon before evening, on time," said Bill.

Tycho yawned, ushering Bill out the door, "Goodnight, Bill."

Bill couldn't help but chuckle, and saluted him a good night. The moonlit glare of his iron enticed him—he'd work to have his trust, and make that revolver his own.

Shutting the door well-tight, barging it snug within the doorframe, Tycho looked to the hat and poncho on the dining table, and decided from the humiliation he'd bear the outfit with pride—howbeit all he did was stand and rid of the bandits with his novelty for immortality, discounting his novice aim, he saved a woman's life. Moreover, he would do this to sicken Bill after the amusement from his mockery had passed, seeing him exterminate thieves in the garish fashion. He wanted to prove to himself, and to the greyed peasant, his endeavor to persevere and conquer death withal securing the well-being of the people that surrounded him—he had completely ignored Bill's discourse for the fulfillment of shallow recognition of his own strength that in truth belonged to another.

"More fire incoming!" cried Fera, embarrassingly pitched, gritting her teeth with his anticipated evasion. The continuing lashes of her mane had a brief dance with the storm of bullets that glided past.

"Purple bot!" shouted Sarkas, gaining on the vaquero with blistering rapidity, "you'd do better as passenger than co-pilot, to which I can say with assurance!"

"Shut up!" she replied virulently.

Sarkas fell into a volley of bursting laughter, and lessened his distance from the fleeting spectacle of his comrade.

Positioned at the base of their mounds doused by everlasting fog saurians aggregated from their caverns aplenty; they had been called with the release of gunfire from their sentinels. Their clan leader, Rivet of the family of Gewnawk, espied the vengeful prey with curiosity and exultation; cherishing the absurdity of this bot, he tried to recall the contender last that charged against him with such infectious confidence. This would only bring further hardship to Tycho's siege— for his antagonist sought a fit challenger. Riving his talons into the shoulder of one of his several warriors, he presented himself before his brood of former venerated mercenaries with hurried, old, steps. Thrusting his head quickly outward with the jostle of his molted dewlap, he commanded boorishly of his kin to take to their mounts, to oppose the fool's charge. He began to scratch, and then tear into his shedding hide, feathers releasing from their pustule anchors underneath his cloak sleeve. Granted as an alpha over his brood his was the only skin that populated feathers for mating, the fleshes of the lesser saurians grey and leathery, seeable pointy ears and an elongated snout missing a horn near their nostrils.

So it was seven of these saurians that rode, Tycho yoked with his perdurable companion and guard against them, notwithstanding his posse near to his surprise. Leveling his aim onto the rider centered within the charge, a ravaging flash from the Havoc dulled their sights, the intended target charred with an astrobleme exfoliation of the flesh. Sarkas dived onto the left of the warring party, and swiftly plucked the few saurians from their mounts, then dropping them from a fateful height. Sarkas returned scarcely of the mercenaries' fire feeding into his breast and wing, the savage young woman pouncing from his backside onto one of the four that remained. Scrabbling to maintain suspension on the saddle, she reached at great length to grapple ahold of the billet strap in her desperate flight. Mounting frantically, she received her assailant's fist presently alert at her clamber, Fera, in turn, impaling the foe's throat with her limbed blade—unable to breathe from its rapid and stuffy breaths pouring onto her face, she hurriedly severed the head; she was hurt seeing it in suffer, admixed with the primal lust to have it writhe at her will, to prolong the beings' insipid existence in torture. She took the saurian's horse and removed the weight of its former master.

The rest had been dealt with, the vaquero pursuing to silence his competition outright with impudence.

Driving his heels into her side constant Meseron approached in thunderous fashion. Rivet, stroking the oily feathers of his ruff, slunk from the company of his kin and returned inside the complexity of the howling den. Tycho once more became an obscure figure, a fleeting shade enshrouded by the reflective gleam of the mist. When the two had reached the opening to the cavern, Sarkas and Fera found the last of the stationed mercenaries with hollowed breasts and ruptured spines, Meseron queerly licking the corpse of one; Fera had a disconcerted expression.

"Are you alright?" His voice resonated.

Fera, glaring at him bemused, watched Sarkas slowly lift his goggles and point a claw to his own eye.

"Oh," she replied startled, then finishing her answer stern, "yeah— I'm fine." She faced her head to the side, away from his gawk.

Gradually, they shifted their focus to the cavern.

"Looks as if the idiot went off without us."

"And you're surprised by this?" said Sarkas.

She looked up at him, removing her glance from the cavern's throat. "I still have trouble understanding half of the things he does. Although…I'm starting to think he felt inclined to come down here to try and settle this problem of ours himself."

"This could have been avoided," he said bitterly. "Made a fool of me to believe he was so adamant on finding his friend—I see now where his priorities lie. Tell me, when both of you traveled together, was he as careless with endangering his own life as with yours?"

Fera returned her gaze within the hillside's depth. "No. If anything it's been but that." She began to reflect.

Sarkas pulled the strap of his gunny sack down against his chest and entered the cavern. "Then, Fera, I suppose you were the exception."

Following after him, she recalled the incident of the train's derailment, as with Tycho's revelation as to him bringing down the foundations of the mining operations at Crest View, unknowingly due to his own ignorance and passionate trekking; for his own welfare had rendered the bot clueless of the lives around him, unless seen in the immediacy of danger, that his self-concerning actions too could affect another's well-being.

Fera stopped mid-walk.

Sarkas proceeded, then hearing the chaffing rustle of her pant legs still for a space of time had him urged to look back.

"What is the matter…?" he said.

She crossed her arms. "Let him deal with them. He's the one that decided to get us into this mess. I'm more than sure the Shine has him covered."

"Fera," said Sarkas, "its truth he should have known that we would come after him, pitting us against these monstry, but we cannot leave the blue bot in hope that his light will ultimately grant him triumph. He may need us…"

"Sarkas," she said, lazily swaying her hip out, "what does this guy mean to you? I mean…I don't get why you'd go this far for Tycho. You never had to agree in flying us, but you did—and I'm thankful for that. Regardless…"—she looked down at her begrimed shoes— "what is it I'm missing here?"

Sarkas stroked his chin. "As you and I have come to understand, there is something more to Tycho than we care to admit, no? Things spoken of resurrection and other mysteries, there is a presence I had not considered before until hearing the discourse between those bandits, only to be validated by Tycho's testimony—dama…something of a spirit woman intends to harm someone very special to him; that is why I cannot reason as to why blue bot would be so easily distracted if his *friend* is intended to be offered like animal at altar. I believe I have a responsibility in helping Tycho reach his destination to a certain point, perhaps this is the role I've been given to partake in."

Sarkas faced forward. "I'd rather not see this Congregation witch get what she wants, don't you agree? I do not hope for Tycho to confront those Outsets who intend to harm Bill, but what other choice is there? This, this I would be blessed to know."

Slightly crestfallen the savage woman understood, and so began her follow—apprehensive. If not for the Shine's appearance she never would have continued with them, doubt was no longer an option. *There are other ways of finding Halcón,* she thought…*Who the hell am I kidding, I'm stuck with these guys.*

The odor of disregarded meats, housed *somewhere,* befouled the stagnant air,—the cavernous venation stuffed with the putridity and decomposition of one's fly-infested bowels. Fera clasped her hand with firmness around her blade's hilt, keen in observation given the setting eerily familiar to the halls of the subterranean castle. Left, right, center, right again, Sarkas used the boy's scent to lead themselves further in descent regrettably finding some paths compromised—they looked for other routes, and to their fortune continued where those cave-ins would have led. At the third pocket of decision and rest they would find four separate corridors of rank stench as equal of passages before; hesitant, Sarkas decided the far-left path for venturing.

"Sarkas…"

"Hm…?"

Glancing at her past his shoulder, her eye-lights hampered the abalone tapetum of his sight.

"Didn't Rahnth have an axe to these guys' necks after Aberica seceded?"

"For someone of your youth, I had not expected one so learned. Forgive me for my contempt," said Sarkas. "In desperation with his fleeting dominion amongst our people, the luminary king formed an alliance with the saurian families. Rahnth eradicated all but one clan, their failure to dismantle the Congregation's revolution cost them near extinction and the reclamation of their sanctified mounds and underground lakes that had been promised to them upon imminence of victory. In the end, a feud had begun—a grudge that has only festered with time."

"He let one clan go…for what purpose—?"

Sarkas bowed his head, placing his hand against the quavering throat of the cavern. "He would never allow such weakness to be shown by his hand. It appears the birds that we face presently are those who fought with hell against the king and his luminaries, and would reside to guerilla tendencies within this valley…this mephitic labyrinth—!" He coughed grating.

"Those luminaries we saw, Sarkas, you think they were trying to find this place?"

He glanced once more at the girl with severity, and continued onward. "We will come to see. The saurians are known for their raids amongst caravanning luminaries; I'm certain there are treasures here the moths intend to take back."

Gliding down a steep incline of gravel and rock Fera was then pestered with doom, the weight of her anxieties gestating within her chest, sitting there almost. It ate at her heart and mind.

Tycho…what have you gotten us into, she thought.

Several avenues were brought before them; helical gateways bound to admit entry upon their vertebral grounds—how uneasy this made her. Asudden, dust clouds surged from each chamber, a horrendous tremor mantling the bat and woman in coarse darkness.

Fera coughed amidst the amorphous surrounding arms, expelling rot and dirt from her lungs. Carried by the eructation of the cavern halls were the fainting echoes of women and their children molested by the temblor disturbance—but from which path?! Turning her luminous vision into each arched and serrated path with the carpeting of the dust, her scrutiny did not fare well against the abysmal corridors of ossified stone. Close behind Sarkas' heels, the ground curled and writhed in their approach to the secondary chamber from where she supposed he had discerned the panic. A creak, and a hiss, the two glanced upward at the branching fractures, and in serpentine fashion, an earthly fissure met with their portal's own fracturing slither. They steadied themselves on the chamber's partition, and spoke in the withdrawal of the mighty quake, Fera suggesting: "If this cave is about to collapse, we need to use what time we have—Tycho, which path can I take to find him?"

"Let us go as one," said Sarkas. "By my lead, there shall be no fault or hindrances of diversion—"

"Sarkas, stop it!" she said. "…You need to save whoever those people are down there, and you're quite the build to get the job done."

"What are you trying to say?"

"I'm trying to say you're not fat."

"Ah, I see."

"Sarkas…," said she, her face cast with the modest of all solemn expressions, "If he's not down there, where those imprisoned are, tell me where he went?"

Initially resistant at the thought of their parting, he'd seen she was capable of handling herself, and the certainty of those families being crushed under the weight of cavernous debris was a likelihood he could not bear to foresee.

He pointed to the path that faced her backside. "Where you stand now, there—take it."

A quake started short, itching for Fera's feet to take flight after the vaquero.

"As you have said," said Sarkas as he gazed past into his own chamber's threshold, "There is no time that we can take for granted; hurry now." He turned to see her before she'd taken leave.

She had considered his abandonment in her disquiet state, though for Sarkas he considered her act valorous—mature. A low reverberation permeated throughout the ridged hall that gave semblance to the backbone of a great beast, alerting Fera to the emission with consternation. She displaced her sudden fear with curiosity and boldness and proceeded forthwith with the intention of finding her compeer, hopefully beaten some for his reckless ambitions. Gradually, sidling through the obstructions of boulder crevasses, she traversed through the indomitable chamber. In hindsight, after her lengthy expedition through the route chosen, she realized Sarkas could never come this way, and ignored the temptation to call him present; for fear of his destruction compelled her to see him animate.

Shadowed and greeted by terrible rumblings, a question germinated amidst her concentration; she had never been as observant as now. For what impetus caused the stony channels to dissever in howls and by whom, she thought. She did not rule out Tycho's depredations by any means, with all reason, she betted on it—a concern of hers.

As with the crowning of the sun, Fera was then towered by an opaque semicircle comparable to the former, dungeon-esque shades imbuing the voluminous proceedings that rather contradicted the complexion of the sun's flesh; for it was its distinguished shape and height that attracted Fera to unite them in a similar light. Steady in her approach into the gaping hollow she would unknowingly encroach upon their nest. Withstanding a fouled draft the young woman pressed onward in thought of Sarkas keeping good health; an imitation of prayer, she'd done the same for Tycho, when her worries conquered irritancy.

The crashing of a rockslide erupted throughout the hollow, the ceasing of the wind entertaining Fera's perturb.

The tunnel Fera traversed had halted with further ground to which she anticipated, dreading her passage be clogged by a boulder pile. Her eye-lights shifted from the inconvenient blockage to an aperture lined with vesicular knobs. Gliding her hand and side against the coarse wall, she spied the contents of the sweltering chamber with peering study. The salivation and condensation of the chamber's hall and ceiling emitted vomit-inducing reflexes; additionally, the surrounding incrustation that lined several eggs piqued the girl's fascination of origin. As she was cementing her first step within the incubative enclosure she issued one blade to her hand, leaving the other fastened beside her waist. With passing glances of Fera's vision, her head turning in various directions, her curved sword hissed with the strike of her light across its edge; the reflected beams skimming the egg sacs and ground.

I can only hope this chamber connects to the path, she thought.

Rows of membranous pods funneled her further into a gathering of the embryonic houses twice her size; no longer had there been the appearance of a road to follow. Slipping past the jellied encasings, her eye-lights attracted the instinctual glare from one body. Appearing woken Fera caught the rolling eye of a saurian hatchling, the status of its maturity simply reacting to the concentration she shone onto it. Tilting its great head, and with a swift thrust of its foot, the thickset chick contended with its impermeable confines, rippling its surface only slightly. Careful to not have her sword puncture the wall of the egg, she held her blade against her bosom and delved lightly. Arriving at an opening, Fera witnessed an embryo in the early periods of its gestation, tethered by a meaty cord lining the inner film of the sac. She lowered her gaze from the floating being to the ground, understanding the incrustation were thin tubes caked with blood that fed the damned things! She thought it was cute, and moved on—with that next step Fera started back.

There, mothers, feasting on their young—starved by Rivet into obedience. Their cavern on the verge of collapse it appeared these captives were of the least concerned. One reared its head to her emissions, squeezing the life out from the preyed child with its shutting mouth.

Fera, oblivious, had forgotten about her lights and closed her eyes. Turning desperately to shelter her presence, she placed herself behind the viscid pod, and stopped her breathing. A hefty stone fell, and forced

Fera's head downward asudden. She emitted an oath, regretting her swear soon after.

The warm fluids of the egg coating her suddenly, a vile amniotic wave splashed against Fera with its riving burst. The mother had come, charging through to her. Clasping its hand around her throat the saurian brood mother shrieked until it deepened into a harrowing roar. Its talon digging into her throat, Fera removed the hand that seized her and followed with a slash to its stomach. The blood washed her of the infantile juices, stepping aside from its continuous outward pour with the giant's topple.

Greeted by another, Fera watched its lumbering approach. Broad, its grey hide husked with hanging, dead flesh, the stringy, oiled hair from its scalp shrouded the lower half of this foe.

She gutturally challenged the harlot, twirling both blades presently in-hand.

Several more came and the woman became disheartened, encumbered with soaked clothes.

EYEWITNESS DEPICTION OF GEWNAWK

Residing far from wherever Fera came to forefend herself, Sarkas was led to a spacious cavity deep within the burrowed channels, a phalanx of stalagmites titillating a congress of huts suspended aloft similar to his own hermitage. Cries of the immured fainting, not at all hampering the bat's hearing, he knew the vicinity in where to find them—and so, he took off. Before he wished to tell "purple bot" of his suspicions regarding the stomach-churning howls of those women and children; *where was there a father to be heard?* Women and their lovelies had the purpose of pleasure, the certainty stoking an inextinguishable rage that drove Sarkas forth, scorn for whoever he'd find responsible for their capture, aside from the Gewnawks. Fera's past would come to him later, he'd been told of it before, and from an Outset indirectly thus an explanation would serve to insult.

Pounding his expansive spread past a dozen huts, a tremendous bellow echoed from the strike of Sarkas' wings with his ascension to the higher chambers; many huts spun and dispatched from his trailing gale similarly as dust twirls within the ensnarement of sunlight once bothered.

Reconnoitering the space vacuous of clansmen, emptied roosts that told of a replete score on the hunt that had not been present to their infiltration, an odd smell had bodies found, discarded beneath those unoccupied stations where flayed bots were given to transfixion. Ornamenting the stony peaks that would sicken any other if a gaze was cast on the rotting litter, Sarkas was granted an impression of sloth on account of the Gewnawks' handlings of these maimed individuals— commoved at hearing a cry, the bat recaptured his focus.

Sarkas caught the eyes of a small one, turning at a reasonable width to meet the infant swaddled in his mother's arms. Decelerating onto the side of the hut's aperture, he promptly calmed their terrified uproar, a number of ragged bots not sure what to make of this colossus.

Warning them of the cavern's dismantling and ruination the women retorted almost immediate, they already ascertained their situation! Shying at first, other small children came to see the distressed fellow, departing from behind their maternal keepers.

Entering, Sarkas knelt, and faced his backside towards them.

"Please, moyey materi, come with me. I promise…no harm will come to you or your bambinos."

Resounding bawls of the cavern rived their hesitation, the bone-weaved hut bobbing.

Housed in the shade behind the gathering, Sarkas spied the glint of some animal's eye. Presenting itself forth from the hovel's depression, the gaunt-limbed fellow bowed its head with its towering uprise. Barking abhorrently in the Rahnthian tongue, Sarkas warned the luminary to surcease any further approach—this startled some children, having them in tears. Sarkas looked upon them with solemnity, and regretted his outburst.

Half the assembly of women and children clung to his pelage, legs and waists swaying pendulum from his breech and side. Sarkas lessened in his speed, traversing gentle, gliding softly to the cavern floor. Leaving a balance he'd return to secure, Sarkas led the families beside him through the stony labyrinth, and brought departure with their passing of the cavern's threshold. Turning back into the cavern, after thorough watch that each person made exit, they awaited the bat's reappearance.

Sarkas found himself at the hut's entrance again, ushering the remaining families with haste onto his back; a few of the women stuffed their children within his gunny sack for safekeeping and the results were better than expected. Sarkas turned the gunny sack onto his chest as little ones hung with peeking heads from out his bag. Fitting only two, several mothers forced latching onto his sides, balancing their babes on their shoulders, or, knotting their child's arms and legs around waist and neck, instructed them to hold on with all their strength.

The disheveled moth shuffled to the aperture with their leave, its widened hand steadying its outward gaze, propping itself beside the hut's entrance. Chitin fins fluttered within the deep recesses center of its forearms, futilely vibrating for flight similar to Sarkas'.

An unexpected return, after a prolonged interval, it came to witness him overshadow many of the remnant hovels comparable to nightfall's advance, the bat's wingspan engulfing all that lied before him. The spacious cavity trembling far mightier than ere, the luminary slaver questioned his re-visitation, and from his snappish caution thought itself hated.

It'd be right.

Partitioning the hut in two, a storm of branch, husk and bone dispersed fiercely from Sarkas' assault, snatching the luminary by its head. Clawing onto the face of one of the earthen spears, Sarkas held the moth by the crown of its head with his other paw, suspending the Rahnthian over the serration. He'd favor the moth's sentencing be done by his own will than the cavern's weight.

His countenance menaced with a frothing snarl, Sarkas affectively became entranced by flashes of memories past, memories of war that reverted his judgments and demeanor, said, "By decree of sovereign law, any Rahnthian found trafficking citizens within Aberican borders shall face execution presently where they stand by the aggressed citizen or constable, if they so choose."

"Who are you to cast judgment?" The moth rasped through its gilled flaps. "During wartime, I could not challenge this proclamation, but the decree you've recited has no more power than your legislative bodies over Halcón's cult—"

The bat plowed through his defense with unmitigated tenacity.

"Charged with the accompanying crime of un-sanctification of the youth, let the fate of this moth be death!"

"I haven't placed a single finger on one of those children." It methodically spoke.

"Liar!" The boom of his roar championed the cavern's thunderous wail.

"For the xenophobes the king has made you as a species," said Sarkas with reverberating growls, "the exception for arousal by the mouths of the small from the lesser races is hypocritical, net? To normalize the pedophilic fantasy within Aberica, to which at that time in adolescence was known as Thrace, was the first of Rahnth's transgressions against us!"

Panged at his own words, Sarkas squeezed his paw against the back of its head until his talons dug deep into its temples. A red sliver streamed from the puncture.

"Be sure," he said, glancing down, "I will dismember every limb from your body before you reach the lowest spire. I can see you have been stripped of flight from Gewnawk…and I intend to use that most favorably."

Lessening his grip, the moth clasped onto his arm, its hold sliding.

"Listen to my words! I have not touched them!" said the moth, quavering.

Coldly, Sarkas amputated the slaver's forearm, and descended after the flailing man—a spill of blood doused the avenger's shoulder and ear.

Summoning his jaws wide to take its leg, something strong—blunt, a voice at the back of his mind told him to stop the voracious act and save it. Unsure what to make of this, resisting the queer thought at first, he remembered Tycho, and with precipitance carried the luminary by the nape of its neck. A sensation of levity, then terror welled inside it, feeling the incisors gnaw into its skin.

Sailing underneath a toppling stalagmite tower, the bat swayed with great strength to avoid the debris, from either ceiling or his sides.

Why did I save you? thought Sarkas. *Answer me.*

The moth, piqued, glanced up at his muzzle.

The conscious or the command of Rahnth redirected your actions; this was not of my own power.

Traversing through the caverns many routes, Sarkas rushed past the corridors and made for the exit.

Why waste breath and desecrate the tongue of my people, knowing I would hear your thoughts?

Do I not continue to speak in your language? He grinned, slightly pulling upon its skin. *Be it thought, we carry the conversation as if spoken word.*

The moth was humiliated and chagrined.

Your kind has always been touchy when others speak that gill talk; I find it amusing, why you have a language at all.

To honor His Majesty, Rahnth—He forbids us to seek His mind. Those He deems as lesser men have continued to defile ordained language for chanting Him praise, though I would find it unwise to personally lecture you seeing how I'm at the brink of these grand jaws.

Believing the corridor they found themselves in would shortly collapse, the bat propelled forth like the esteemed locomotives of Aberican ingenuity—unrelenting, efficient, and comparable in stature!

There were those searching for you, luminary. They passed over the hills. Why not call to them?

I did not want them to find me, or those I partook in caravanning to the Kingdom.

Interesting…And why's that?

Chosen me, I was expected to bow before the Council of Thirteen's decision to act as an emissary to discuss current relations between the two kingdoms, sweetening the prestige of my task so that I may be ever so willing to chat with the king of thieves about merchandise with such charismatic diction. I resisted yielding, disregarding my selection, until Rahnth's eyes fell upon me from his high chair, and I knelt in accordance to his will. Had I not—

Moth, your name? Sarkas interrupted.

Cicero Magnus Eglavitus...a title those delegates and ear-poisoning advisors will undoubtedly mar once they hear word of my desertion—Glory to Rahnth, for decades they've manipulated Him to allow trafficking of the young and precious; no longer will I stand for it, His judgment compromised!

Sarkas found Cicero brainwashed to consider his king God, and the moth heard this.

He surveyed his forearm's amputation, feeling the prickling—tingling sensation that presaged trauma in the coming minutes. *Had I not been handpicked to stand before the Council and His Majesty, never would I have suspected their knowledge of his solitude—typically we met with contacts who served as Congregation representatives on matters of trade. Given those bots you delivered from Gewnawk hands, I departed from the Wasteland's eldritch crown to which Halcón takes residency and set off with mothers and kin to bestow upon the king as a gift for His continued patronage; the more I came to dread in presenting the broken families as I furthered on in my journey, listening, understanding they were not tools but men, not so different from my own Rahnthians in any regard that I once held.*

But I deserve this misfortune, he thought as he raised his forearm again. *For without imprisonment, as I most certainly would have been held for ransom—the children and their mothers skinned and smelted to brick, then I may never have had discovered the strength within me to think differently than Rahnth, presently yearning to steer those women and children away from life in chains and molestation.*

So, you were speaking truth...

The moth bore the anguish of his severance, muscles twitching irregularly.

Emitting from out of the cave, Sarkas bemused the gathered families with the moth hanging from its scruff, placing it on the ground before them. Without a word spoken, an explanation, Sarkas for his last time would delve into the saurian burrows to rescue his compatriots. Soaring after them, evading the riving stones in fall, he came to the conclusion that it was a sudden throe of compassion,—strangled out by the malicious ire for Rahnth's perversions,—that saved the moth. It wouldn't have been strange that somewhere, deep in Sarkas' being that he considered its utterance true. It could have been the inflection of its voice that regarded its plea authentic.

He had such hate for this moth he could not recognize his own compassion when it came about him.

At the passage where the savage woman journeyed Sarkas arrived seeking her, but found the corridor's end lodged with boulders. Her spoor came familiar to him from the right-handed crevice in the wall, and flew within its chamber. Dozens of bodies lain amongst corpulent and squelched pods, the massacre he beheld was uncanny. Spotting thighs sloshed away from their own torsos, he averted his sights from the grisly scene, and towards the slit Fera ventured within. Disembarking from his lofty glide, he came to the nest's boundary and crawled to fit within the space fissured at its base, coating his hairs with Fera's noir bloodshed, with the heave of his body forward. His shoulder ached from the demolishment he brought to the obstructing stone that declined entry of his build, the savage woman having easily sidled her way through it, but continued to neglect the trivial sore as he shifted one arm after the other before him, his talons raking the dirt. A tunnel large enough for Fera to proceed hunched, Sarkas waged painstakingly through the narrow,—foreseeable entombing,—passage in his restricted conditions. He shouted for her, twice.

Not soon after, he saw the legs of the woman, and lolled held swords beside her, and found his egress would come shortly. He wondered, as with retaining concentration on alleviating his suffocation, to whom was she facing—he couldn't see much further than the lineation of Fera's contour in the dark.

His ears plopping out from the crevice standing, Sarkas' nose sensually twitched to ascertain the setting. Gradually, he brought himself to his feet beside Fera's spent composure. Catching the roll of her eyes into her skull, she slowly closed the almond slants to reopen them just as lethargic. Her cheekbones of sublime pronouncement glistened with the blood of those avian villains, adhered with a mixture of sweat bringing palpability, and effulgence to her goddess endowed arches. Sarkas steered his piteous concentration from the woman and furthermore malformed into an overwrought body of wrath capturing Tycho's negligence for her in his contention with the saurian progenitor, as he was busied to satiate Pride and the greatest of his idols, a murderous heart.

Tycho advanced upon the Gewnawk from the side of an extensive buffet table adorned with rotting corpses of boar, candlesticks, and bowls for drinking, the cragged hollow fitted to be the dining area of this saurian's tribe. A fair distance from Sarkas and Fera the boy still had not considered their presence of value, engrossed to quench the desires of his carnal improprieties. The former peered for the route Tycho came from, and saw the tunnel's mouth but a few feet from their confliction and assumed it led to the path blockading Fera to settle for another, less desirable avenue.

With shaky aim Rivet wounded Tycho in futility, and emptied his clip ere releasing his rifle horrified.

The Shine present, it appeared soft in glow—no longer had it set the room ablaze, its splendor lost. This was unfortunate, and the more the vaquero rebelled against his gift the Spirit became hampered and, consequently, ineffective to him.

"Nowhere else to turn, hombre; aren't you an ugly face." Tycho glided his hand on the table's wetted surface, titling the gem-encrusted bowls from their surface to the ground before Rivet's feet as he shrunk away, his toes and soles doused with their contents. The stream of white striding from Tycho's cheek ignited the candles aflame with his pass, revealing the inhumane butchering of the men laid out on the table with their slashed throats and glazed eyes, without dilation to the light's cast. Thereafter Sarkas noticed the savage woman was absent of her eye-lights, but this did not surprise him seeing her tiring stance.

"Boy, boy," bellowed Rivet, the feathers of his ruff erecting and shaking terribly, "you dared to challenge the Gewnawk patriarch, within his very home!" His head lunged downward, the elongated neck twisting birdlike, eyes blinking. "You should be dead!" The foul creature roared, gnashing his teeth.

"My lineage is no more," spoke Rivet quietly at first, "the first to rise from the earth is no more! Damn you!" He gutturally cursed Tycho, so ghoulish and atrocious was his pronouncement that even the hairs on Sarkas' nape stood.

Tycho chuckled, furthering his approach to the great king's slunk. "Shut that mouth of yours before I shut if for you." He grinned, absurdly vile. "As I recall, you had your goons' fire at us without expecting any sort of retaliation? Pathetic old man, I'm here because you brought this upon yourself." He felt a faint breath, his forearm warmed, but thought no more of it than an awry draft.

Rivet, in an attempt to clasp onto what dignity remained, pounded his fist on the table, and retarded his movements with his flattening hand, his talons scraping against the stone surface. "Although you may be elusive to death's touch," said he, slowly looking over to the company of two, "understand that I will skin the one who's come to your succor."

Leaping over the table hurriedly, Rivet appeared caught in his cloak. He fell into a somersault within momentary flight from his impetus to bring himself to a pounce, failing to execute the performance. They found the renowned mercenary sliding before them as a corpse, dazed from the swift happenings they saw to Tycho for an answer, granted their eyes saw his lowering aim—the wails of the cavern had muted his immediate rounds into the predacious foeman.

"You're welcome." He smiled.

"That cheeky…" Fera resigned to further insult him, and coughed.

"Tycho," said Sarkas, assisting Fera to the crevice, "lets us go—pronto, blue bot, pronto!"

Tycho jogged to their company, and said, "He knew he was done," as he looked back to the corpse, "the moron went as far as to bury me in my chase after him, but the Havoc had her own method of using those last deadfalls against him—got the bird cornered just as I wanted."

Tycho smiled conceitedly, enlivened from his hunt. "I'm surprised you guys managed to get all the way down here."

"Consider our intact lives more of an astounding feat than reaching these far depths. Now come."

From the stone table, bowls came against the ground clattering, an odd rustle perking Sarkas' ears. Bracing its paws aloud, and then its hoofs, the boar gasped and choked for air with its rise—it squealed terrifically. A spatter of blood rolled from its throat's laceration to the table surface, and then subsiding to a crimsoned collar, the boar mustered the vigor to lower itself onto its feet. The slash against its throat had not severed any vital functions, its hide much too thick compared to his brothers that lay without pulse.

Tycho, Fera, and Sarkas hesitantly looked to their shoulders, and wheeled to face their new antagonist.

The boar deprived of reason and proper judgment, the recessive instincts of self-preservation from its beastly counterpart trampled upon the given intellectual prowess of man, enthralled to obey the will of the primordial. This was all caused by the Gewnawks and the trauma inflicted on his band of scavengers, a damning tragedy.

"How…Why?" said Tycho, analyzing the pouring steam from its snout and throat. Its glare was magnificent, resolute on the kill—it mattered not who stood to face against this tusker; all would asunder from its might to prolong survival. Fera, shifting out a rock from its socket in the wall to her hand, chucked the piece against its forehead, and what followed was not a reaction or even a flinch, but a rivulet careening past its eye and tusk.

"Alright, I'll deal with it." Tycho began his departure, but was quick to be apprehended.

Sarkas' sour and abhorring scrutiny cautioned further action to be taken.

"Net, there is no time," he said feigning calmness, glancing at the fractures weave throughout the dining chamber.

"Sarkas, let up! I know what I'm doing." He shrugged off his hand, and foolishly ventured from him.

Pawing its hoof into the dirt, the boar prepared to charge at the coming vaquero. Unresponsive to Tycho's consultation the bestial giant hunched forward, placed its paws onto the dirt, and aimed its snout at the ground, waves of dust skirting beside its jaws. The boar propelled forthwith, and initiated its charge.

Enduring few shots of the Havoc, the fourth caught the boar's face aflame; forcefully plowing its head through the dirt to impede the spread this did not halt its proceedings to assault him. Leaping aside from the impaling tusk, Tycho caught a glimpse of its charred skull, further sickened as he turned his head to find Fera in its ravaging path.

After quickly blocking, the rampaging suina broke through her feeble defense, and speared her shoulder with a horrid, intense grunt of voraciousness. Gored in brief flight Fera doused her blades alternatively within the brute as she was then pinned to the behind wall, congruously shouting in horror and desperate rage.

Plunging his infallible canines inside of the boar's throat, cutting through its laceration for ease of entry, Sarkas tore the animal's jugular, becoming sprayed with a profuse spouting of blood all the meanwhile snapping its tusk by hand.

Scooping her from the ground thereafter he removed the intrusive bone, he placed her within his gunny sack, as space for one adult it could hold, and without further remonstrance from the boy, Sarkas swung him to his shoulder and hastened to the opening from which Tycho had come.

"Sarkas!" yelled Tycho over the moaning wind and cavern, "We won't be able to make it through here! It's already been shut!"

Sarkas was silent, dismissing him—he could not allow himself to speak, horrible things would emit if he were to open his mouth for only a second. But, he took Tycho's words into consideration, and braced himself. The crevice had already been compromised, with or without Fera's handicap, there still would not be enough time to escape through the crawlway as Sarkas previously hoped.

His muzzle starched crimson by the wind's command he came to approach the first stone blockade, and with an immeasurable amount of speed the bat conquered the hindering clot. Then, there came another, this must have been the pile of boulders from before that averted Fera to take to the nest, he thought. With what little yet profound strength remained, he rammed through the pile, falling to his feet as he came to the other side, but was swift to regain flight as there were no opportunities of rest. Spying the light that betokened his exit, exerting all reserved vitality in him, the bat soared with a resounding screech that deafened his own hearing, assuredly Tycho's. Suddenly, they were free.

Launching forth from the maw of the cavern, the crowd of women and children appeared to notice the bat's unnatural, rapid descent, and hurried out of his way. Colliding against the earth in a stupor, enshrouded in dust clouds, Sarkas crashed within the severing line that brought the crowd to halves, slowly being approached upon by the saddened bots. Moreover, Cicero drew closer.

The children pulled on his ears, yelled in them for him to awake! The mothers' smacked their hands, or pulled them back, withholding sorrows of their own. Tycho proclaimed "Settle!" to ease their worries as he alighted from his backside, thereafter helping Fera from out his bag as she slid down from him; she leaned against Tycho as he began to walk her through the gathering to a considerable flat stone for her sitting. Healing her wound with the Shine's emission, both Fera and Tycho turned their attention with the crowd to the roar of the cavern's collapse. They focused on themselves again, and the woman divulged on the people's exodus until she had her own inquiry for the bot.

"I want to know, did you have any part in that?" Fera asked enervated, glancing at the sealed cavern. "Would you have killed them?" Her throat constricted.

They locked eyes momentarily, Fera trying to discern his hesitation to give an answer before a collective gasp allured the two to spy Sarkas through their numbers arisen. Yawning as if it were a deep roar, Sarkas straightened his back, and placed a hand to his aching spine. He smacked his gums, grunting. Looking down at a little one nearest to him, he showed the small boy a grimace. Daunted the boy verged on the retreat into his mother's arms until Sarkas, lifting his un-cordial façade, began to smile. As the small boy was losing apprehension, at the sight of the bat's welcoming face, he fell upon him with arms wide, his tiny hands squeezing him close. Sarkas patted him on the head.

"Alright, big guy…Let's get after Bill."

Still, the colossus remained facing the barren valley. He'd heard his approach, amidst the shuffles of excitement, provoked by his distinguishable, perspiring spoor to wrestle him to the earth, but restrained the inclination, knowing well he did not want to harm the vaquero or those gathered if ever there was an aftermath to occur.

"Sarkas…let's start making some ground, c'mon."

"Now," grumbled the bat, "when it's convenient for you, net?"

Tycho abashed, his visage crinkling to a nasty scowl, said: "Huh? Sarkas, what are you getting at? *All I said* is that we should get going."

"I heard you," Sarkas growled in return, its reverberation rumbled about within Tycho's chest. He looked to Fera, over the many heads.

Further mortified and ignored, Tycho drew closer to the indomitable stature of Severov, readying himself for the contention. "Then what's the problem?"

Sarkas placed his hand before him, and began to regain his feet. He turned to face Tycho, and bowed greatly to match his eyes with the vaquero's own. "Your putrid, naïve disregard for Fera and I." His Brussian accent more than accentuated than previously. "If not for us, you'd surely fall to entombment, Fera paving the way to your rescue, my friend.

"And what of them," he said, splaying his claws at the crowd, "would you have so easily slaughtered them all? For what, petty vengeance?!" He barked.

Tycho's features changed to reflect a mild temperament to an embittered lad.

"*I came down here* so I could apprehend those scumbags from taking us out of the skies! I didn't tell you, or Fera, to follow after me!"

"Think now," Sarkas' lip curled. "You'd believe we'd allow you to fight an entire legion without assistance? Not only are you naïve, but dense would best describe the reasoning you possess." He tapped a claw on the vaquero's skull. "But there is something you're leaving unrevealed, I'd consider your words as whole truth, but I can't shake this hunch of mine you sought conflict and blood—revenging to satisfy some pathetic hunger, rather than in the best of interests keeping our hides un-grazed.

"Just how did the cavern come to asunder, blue bot?" Sarkas questioned, surliest of an inquiry had come to challenge Tycho's depredations.

Shifting his eyes to the ground, Tycho fitted his thumbs past his belt's fastening, thereupon glaring aimlessly into the crowd. "I got the job done," murmured Tycho. "That's all that matters."

Sarkas bellowed with satirical laughter. "And that constitutes endangering the lives of others in your *modus operandi*, hmm? Even your own…?"

The underappreciated slayer of thieves, life's frailty had never dawned upon him as a concern. He had not considered bandits' lives of importance with his belief that they were baseless fodder to guarantee a reveling kill; no better was he than his prey's sin, and this insulted his heavenly counselor. Accompanied with the Shine's guard, this rendered Tycho insensible to his own mortality, as to those he would assist and better. This was without the Shine's intentions, his service to prevent the boy's termination, that there is a death to contemplate.

"Throughout this venture—diversion," said Sarkas, "—of ours, sincerely blessed that these families came out from this unnecessary"— Sarkas' head shook—"excursion, receiving deliverance from Gewnawk hands, I've been entertaining the thought that you're not after Bill for his sake. Certainly not, nakhal'nyy.

"Could it be that your Shine—"

"It ain't mine." Tycho asserted promptly.

Sarkas paused, and then correcting himself, "The Shine…I could see that it has blinded you, can you not fathom even obsequies to come, for yourself, friends even? I dread the surety of my words true, but that's aside from the point I'm willing to make presently. Foretelling thus far you've been guided, slaving to amoral appetites, I would assume straying from finding Bill hasn't been the hardest."

Tycho glared at him, drawing his eyes from the ground to Sarkas' face.

"You are only after him to appease hatred." He pointed. "His well-being is of no importance in this quest, that you are only justified by the self for punishing his tormentors, quenching a perverted rage! Maybe because of this detour, we won't reach him in time—slain— and you'll have your wish—!"

Tycho lunged for the bat, tackling him surprised. The crowd dispersed in a furor.

As he beat upon his chest Sarkas was admixed with feelings of sadness and strong ire; he'd done so much for Tycho, and in return was assaulted by his bulbous fists. He resisted the sort of temptations a man bears when struck by a familiar fist; he sought none other than to reprimand his companion.

"Enough!" cried a perturbed woman from the gathering.

Tycho held his punches, Sarkas glancing as to whom spoke.

"We yearn for home," said a mother with two of her sons approaching, "who will lead us, protect us?!"

Clamor erupted amongst the women, the bickering two seeing Fera had readied to separate them as one had already done so. The champion of Sol Puesta slowly removed himself from Sarkas' breast and stood at his first realization there had been a moth within their presence. He would see to the bat again to distinguish the fellow a threat or not, and glancing at the luminary his expression proved the latter.

"Woman," said Sarkas, wiping the dribbling blood from his nose, "do not worry. For that moth, right over there, he will lead you where you long to return. No more is he of his regime; I have seen his true face, and there is nothing to fret about."

A slight ruckus initially, the crowd came to an uproar, Fera startled with the expression of ill-understanding and reason for Sarkas' regard of this slaver.

"Gather the horses, Cicero," Sarkas called to the luminary by name to entrust the people with his judgment, "and prepare them for the mothers who are most tired, and strained. Be their rock, and do not falter."

The moth hesitated at first, but after digesting the encouragement from one he'd never expect to hear such kind words, went to fetch the wandering mounts.

Seeing the moth at his obedience, gossiping whether he'd threatened it, keen eyes spotting his removed forearm, surely they reasoned was there at their capture, still questioned their safety with this moth. Fera, placing her apprehensions aside, spoke for him—there should be no reason for them to disregard this opportunity! She looked to Sarkas with trusting eyes, and nodded.

For some, their rescue was plenty enough to hold the bat's command as goodwill, but the rest needed more—rightfully so, luminaries were a nasty bunch.

Forming into a cavalcade to begin their journey through the desolate wastes, Cicero led his charges with given direction, monitoring the few on horseback to stay upright until an oasis or cenote would come to sate their thirst. As the women passed Sarkas, giving thanks, a bambino no higher than her mother, sitting on her shoulders, reached out her hands to hold the great head of the retired soldier. Placing his jaw in her grubby palms, the little girl kissed his nose as her mother had done with many of her wounds. Though the blood welled from the compact against his chest, the gesture was accepted. Behind him waited Tycho on his mount, Fera abreast.

In his turn Sarkas caught the vaquero's glower, and did just the same.

XII

AN EVENING TO RETIRE

THE triad found themselves in the shed of a cenote as they lapped the pristine, glistening groundwater, marked by luminosity exhibited through an earthen circle higher above; the haloed periphery, moonlit and glaring brilliantly, funneling a column of vivacious light onto the pool that cheered their parched mouths and throats. Crossing his forearm past his sodden lips, the champion of Sol Puesta arose from his guzzle, and directed an appalling glare at his Herculean fellow.

Sarkas had felt the eyes of the boy on him.

"If you plan to strike me," he lifted his muzzle, twines of water spiraling down from his flew, "I'd do it with haste, before I have any strength returned—then, you'd be able to whatever that sick little mind pleases. Wait, and you'll find I won't be as merciful or tame as I was those few short hours ago."

Tycho drew Meseron close by her reins, and exited the cavern.

Her hand cupped with shining groundwater she lowered the drink to turn her eyes from the pool as to watch the vaquero's leave. She then had that emerald gaze fall upon the bat remaining knelt beside her as he began to chatter.

"He needs to mature, that one. So easily provoked he can be."

Fera resumed her intake of the cenote's basin.

"Perhaps there was truth to my suspicions."

"And none of it should be your business," Fera said, after her slurp ended.

He glanced at her with features of earnestness.

"Tycho needs to become more accountable," said Sarkas crestfallen. "I only mentioned his friend to have him see the perspective that we were all participating in, hoping to witness his actions through our eyes. Perhaps I took it too far. But, in spite of everything, it needed to be said…"

"You sound like a nagging father."

Once more Sarkas glanced at the woman, slightly vexed.

"Am I all to blame, purple bot?" asked Sarkas calmly, with expressive irritancy on his face.

Fera dried her hand on her pant leg and rested her head against the rising palm. "In case you forgot…you did more than just bring his friend into the conversation to have him see things *our way*. You accused him of finding gratification in Bill's tortures so he'd be so riled up to kill his captor rather than having the pleasure of bringing his old man back home. Why would you even say something like that, even if it were true? You only needed to confront him on his actions at what occurred at the cavern, no need to personalize things and muddle what we got goin' on here." She selfishly implied in worry that Sarkas would not place them a distance before the Outset's residency in his frustration.

Sarkas had always believed in the goodness of men without the paranoia of duplicity when in genial conversation or approaching those of commendable occupation in his travels as a merchant, coaxed by their hospitable facades, and so hadn't suspected the girl's words anything less than her deep solicitude to stay within their company.

"If it is, Fera,—my summation valid,—then it should be known. He needs to reflect on his passions, not to ignore whatever darkness that has wrested that young, bold soul of his...I've seen the good in him, and so have you, but that shade of arrogance endangers anyone but him—I'd call him for what he is, a fool, but that dwelling light eliminates any remark I may possess. I understand they are personal matters, but to expose him just might keep us all out of some daring venture in the nigh of morrow, and so on."

Sarkas bowled his hands, and carried an ounce more of water to his ebon snout.

"I will go and settle dispute with him, and if he wishes to continue in his stand-offish behavior, then I will do no less than him. The boy must learn his place; the services I provide you two are not one of generosity, but of concern on account of his situation...Remember what I've told you thus far, regarding my stay."

Bracing his hand upon his knee, the niveous streak of the moon that coated his back shifted onto the ground before him with his stand. And thereafter, he made way through the cragged passage.

"Sarkas."

The colossus halted.

"You owe an explanation for what happened between you and that moth...don't hold out on us, got it?" Her prepossessing countenance marred by a sudden frown.

Sarkas picked up his feet again, and had his egress in gradual paces.

There had been his own deceiving done, not telling the savage, young woman a portion of his intentions, but his secretiveness no more extravagant than yearning for intimacy and community, forgetting—

expunging the conscious realm of fellowship, detaching from the Ravaja's denizens to protect his sanity. But now, he was at a realization of that mistake, overborne from years of seclusion with minimal interaction so much as an acquaintance at his bargains he became disillusioned at his sequestered living from his communion with the boy, who claimed to have come westward of *Minotaur's Run*. Seeing him again, initiated into combat to preserve what understandably weren't his children—yet!—thought of them as equal from dormant instincts that lied within this father of one. Bonds of nature given from the parental, and brotherhood had been adhered to the triad, whether they agreed to it or not.

He couldn't allow himself to see to the bots set off without proper guardianship, and this would partially be why he would never tell them of Cicero's claim that the thanatotic despot of the Ravaja sat enthroned at the crown of *Titan Summit*, to have his time with them before their departure of portended defeat, undoubtedly—to depend on him without so much a question of abandonment in the rise of Tycho's un-favoritism to be yoked to him; they were in the belief that Sarkas kept the hunter's scent, even until now, but this was lost within their excursion to fish the vaquero from those saurian chambers.

Tycho returned to their camp with an armful of twigs and brushwood, lips curled at finding Sarkas coming out from the cenote's cavernous arch. Kneeling to place his selection into the pit he'd dug earlier, Tycho bit down on the inner walls of his cheeks, and blew on the various wood as the Shine poured onto the heap admixed with a bespattering of oil, igniting campfire.

"I can teach you, to start fire with few sticks—if you'd like." Sarkas crossed over to the flames.

Tycho averted any eye contact. "Nah, I'm good." He positioned himself onto his haunches and watched the sinuous blades of fire.

"Suppose it would be a waste of your efforts, but practicality should never be—"

"Sarkas, I'm not doing this right now." He steadied his gaze at the fire's base.

A tension of silence pervaded but momentarily.

"Have it your way, blue bot," he hesitantly lowered his eyes from him, and into the fire. "But we'll need to put to rest this childish animosity between us at sunrise...I do not hope to remain on guard—how you say, 'walking on eggshells'—for the balance of the journey." Sarkas' stomach growled horrendously; Tycho straightway reminded he hadn't eaten since the night before.

He set himself on his feet, clawing the dirt with his fingers as he rose, and turned himself from the warming lashes of his fire to acquire game.

"Might I come with," said Sarkas, "I believe my snout would have us a successful hunt, do you not agree?"

"I'd rather you have it trained on that Outset. I'll be just fine on my own."

Treading the desiccated surface of the Wasteland was he then weary where he placed his proceeding steps at the bipedal sprint of some frilled serpent against him, in defense of its hatchlings. The tremulous headdress of the serpent would scare any other from its nest, which Tycho was close to sullying his boots with yolk, but was instead grateful for the mother's aggression to steer him into another direction, away from her offspring. Rerouted to scale dunes not far in search of an evening's repast Tycho heard the Shine call his conscious, and commanded he'd answer.

"Hey, what is it...?" he said, welled with anguish, compunction.

The Shine had him sit; stationing himself within the precipitous face of the dune he'd began to slide down. In all its majesty and veraciousness, the Spirit guided Tycho to forgive his latest actions against Sarkas, as with the bat's hostility when revealing truth, and to put an end to his murders. Tycho did not want to listen, but meditating on the faults committed by his hand and another's tongue, he was open to the suggestion—that was until a rivaling power whispered adverse to what his most beloved friend had issued as resolve. Lucia had begun to beseech for him to find the fortunes of betrayal, to allure the young man to level the Havoc's barrel at Sarkas' head, settling the iron's nose against the temple of his skull with little pressure, just enough to have him consider, in the bat's slumber. Unconscious as to whether an asudden landslide of guilt was brought to recognition by the Shine as he neared repentance—to whom he had forgotten, the Shine guiding him to which godhead he would speak to nonetheless—the vaquero contemplated her tempt to attain satisfaction, the liberty it would bring; was there any other enticing alternative? He thought more of it, found solace in what could come; silence, Sarkas' badgering squelched indefinitely, or the priggish, judgmental certitude of his character gone. But these feeble considerations were not of him; Lucia had challenged the Shine, taking his failure to acquire Bill, the reckless ambition of his carnality to seize his location resulting in horror and anger, displaced onto Sarkas for his calling out of the vaquero's recent jaunt. It was unfortunate the prodigious contender of Sol Puesta felt this conflicted about someone dear, never before had *disloyalty* come to mind. He then became disturbed, never would he commit to perfidy, he could not truly end the life of an arguably virtuous companion,—which the boy unconsciously treasured,—and Tycho, the champion of Sol Puesta, ruminated not on treachery and its considerable aftermaths, but on trouncing all prey large and small to his stature, looking forward to Halcón's regicide if ever given the chance.

He acknowledged this was Fera's right, but did not care.

The unwelcomed, heated sensation of homicide had Tycho feeling stomach churned on his perch on the dune's face. Despising this pathetic, wretched, craven sense Tycho barricaded the Shine and Lucia from further influence over his judgment and rationality, spying a mule deer in chaparral ahead. He'd listen to his own feelings of what was just, not an apparition or gods' deliberation on living and how to live, keeping only resentment for Sarkas' confrontation and his own detestable behavior, nothing further. But he would not come to apologize, not until Sarkas was the first to instigate quarter, to appease his pride, for it to remain unblemished.

Frustrated, Tycho moved in for the kill, using the sparse vegetation and boulders to his concealment. Ideations of cloven head and impalement molested his focus on the buck, as he crept along the boulder's side to align his aim. *No more*, he thought, alarmed at the gruesome fantasies ravaging his mind's eye, not of brigands but Sarkas indeed! The Beast managed to tempt him to pursue further intrusive thoughts, be it disheartening he was rather caught by the sublimity of envisaging his maiming. Tycho decided to sit again, sure that another quarry would cross his path to make a feast for three, and would conquer this seducing predator.

"Food yet?!" Fera's exclamation reverberated.

"No," replied the bat, "we wait for blue bot's return!"

The woman grunted, and necessitated her privacy—Sarkas was without protest.

Clawing off her blood-encrusted shirt over her head and into the pool moreover pants and sash, she bathed to rid of her mephitic stench Sarkas and Tycho were too kind in bringing to her attention. The moonlit basin chilled her intensely, keeping her attire afloat hoping most stains either perspired or bled would dissipate; arms perched, she gawked at the moon with its centering above the outer periphery. "I eat out my heart," she mused, "in wait of killing you; Halcón, I will bring your throat underneath my heel, as with that officer consequently." She thereafter studied her bosom inquiring if they'd fattened.

Meditating on the thought of Halcón poured dry with his spilt blood flowing down the glassed steps to which lay before his cathedra, carved from obsidian, she knew Tycho and their carrier could not vie for the indignation she bore for Halcón's slaying, and if they needed to be sacrificed throughout the rest of their journey when proven unbeneficial then she'd live with the decision, and loss; she wasn't so much concerned with Bill's fate than her avenging, cared little did she in comparison. She had hypothesized the moth spoke of well-sought after information from the bat's skirting away from the topic, and that is why she wished to have the situation expounded. In a moment she was made conscious of her own agency, needing not to rely on Sarkas say he and the vaquero were to part before reaching their destination, learnt of the moth's truth; but would Sarkas tell an unabridged summary of his conversation?

Partitioning the concentration of black and avian gore in her swim, she received back to her shirt and pants, her sash wafting near to where she'd denied veritable affection for Sarkas and Tycho—preparation was needed for the mental state, and could not be held back from her accomplishing the demagogue's beheading if the two came to destruction. She would not allow herself to feel for them, never before was she at the threshold of coming before the Ravaja's scourge and would not fail herself now.

Fera wrung her shirt, and placed her glare on the commotion without. Finding Sarkas taken aback with an incoherent mumbling, modified by their distance apart, she sprang on one foot to keep her balance as she lifted her damp trousers to her waist swiftly, exiting the cenote with brisk, swords held.

Concerned, the girl descried the vaquero's arm placed about a Samaritan's neck as Tycho was ushered to the fire nurtured by the oscillation of the bat's wing, Sarkas anxious to see his companion in distraught-fashion. Tycho gently pushed the man from his side, dragging the needed buck by antler in his other hand, to finish their extensive perambulation on his own, cementing his breech before the firelight. He continued to battle the lucid, feral teases, keeping his silence.

"Tycho…what's up?" Fera softly asked.

"I need everyone to be quiet." His eyes encased in a glazed sheath.

Fera disconcerted, shot a look at the boy's attendant and lain kill, asking him of his situation, if he knew: "And who are you…?" Her sword's tip pointed at his head. "Can you tell us what in the name of God is with him?" She said, stern.

The guide uncrossed his legs, his hunched sitting given to a straightening back as he came to stand. "That is for him to disclose. He has been made sufferer from a witch's passion to see him frenzied, attempting to make him a baser man than he has already made himself out to be. Take heed," he directed his speech at the vaquero, looking to the fire, "one keeps hope in your return to serve the kingdom."

She remained un-sated, and required the question of the former imparted. "I'll ask again," said Fera perturbed, mystified, "who are you?"

The Stranger tilted his head at Tycho, his hooded, concealed gaze placed on the matter of importance. "Do not be afraid, I've been sent to dispatch a message to him from his Father—it is an affair subject that does not concern you."

"Father, huh?" Fera uttered incredulously. "I feel we are more than allowed our stay to hear this story, sophist—!"

"He has yet to prove himself to be one," said Sarkas. "Let us have them their time, and watch from the cenote's hall. If anything appears afoul, we will waste no time in ridding of this queer individual. But first…" Sarkas outstretched his hand towards his hood.

His hood coming to accordion folds an extravagant flare from his transfigured face incited Fera to charge at the guide whom she mistook his veil as an act of aggression—to have them incapacitated. As she was preparing to lunge her sword within his chest's cavity Sarkas wrested ahold of her advancing arm, and immediately swung her to his side. Not understanding at first, she realized he acted on behalf of her protection, standing guard ahead of her with uncertainty and bottled terror. The Stranger slowly raised his hood to shadow his features once more, poised. "Satisfied?"

And the two left, stationing themselves at the left side of the yawning arch ever observant.

"Why'd you do that to them?" asked Tycho, agitated at his display.

"He has not granted them permission to look upon my face."

Tycho was without response.

"The Ahmenseraï…" He cocked his head at the looming figure. "What does that being have anything to do with Bill, phantom? I've heard you speak its name before; are you of an acquaintance of it, was I at one time?" He humored the Stranger, but did not underestimate the answer to his question of what it might provide.

"You wallow in your debasement, Verumshaï. The Spirit save you!"

"I ask the same of it, yearning for my attention. But all I hear and see is anything but given by a friend; he's never been this harsh."

"That is because you have been deceived. The Spirit calls for your repentance, but not to be enchained by guilt, and to never fear approaching our Lord in seeking forgiveness. Where are you with him? I've only been told to relay his message of ceasing rebellion against the host within you, a gift of instruction and certificate of salvation that you've taken to ill-understanding as your servant when its presence declares that *you* are the servant."

"Then how about you stop with the evasive talk and give me what I want to know before you go preachin' on how I should start changing my ways." He looked at the mule deer, slain but assuredly untouched.

Fera asquint she concentrated on the robed specter, suspicious if he'd brought Tycho down with fatigue and carried him and his animal back to campfire to appear to give countenance. The savage woman had yet to be informed on the device of Tycho's altered comportment, and was left only with her one conjecture.

"If you have to ask who, or *what*, the Ahmenseraï is and those he calls to give worship," said the Stranger, "then I cannot help you. The same could be said of distinguishing his claimed children of light. Does a son or daughter not know of their father, or can a father be unaware of his reared? You are more far gone than what I believed the Lord foreordained; I am more than an acquaintance to him, and so are you, Tycho of Sol Puesta."

The Stranger had the subject reverted to where he'd started ere Tycho's request, glancing at his younger brother's face to determine his mood, and as to what the Beast had then occupied his mind with.

"His adversary trembles with a ravening excitement to have a hardening of your heart," he began, "the Spirit quenched, enough deficiency to extinguish the core without ensured resistance. If you continue with these acts of being slayer you will undoubtedly be had, found between the jaws of Lucia's provisional demagogue. This you know, the Spirit pesters—"

"And am I indebted to him?" Tycho challenged his guide. "He chooses to be my life's keeper, without request. Don't act as if surprised that I need time from the Shine's wisdom, whether or not that witch preys upon my lack of discerning."

Gravely had the Stranger tilt his gaze anew at his brother, not that it mattered for Tycho was without perception of his face given his eye-lights failed to illuminate past the shroud's maw.

"How long has it been, since you've repented?" asked the Stranger, testing and cautious.

Tycho fantasizing about the execution of his own self to preserve his envisaged friend, said, "I don't care for the repentance you speak of." The Shine grieved. "Why not we have a look at your face, eh coward? You've more than shown the nature of your person, a look at the mug of God's yes-man shouldn't blemish his reputation of secrecy any more than he already has."

"Could an elect be this perverse that pagans fail to measure on his worldly account of disobedience and pride?" said the Stranger. "You claim that I am without integrity, yet you cannot face the sin that separates you even further from the Spirit! You know not what you speak, to question further would be stupid, for I've already told you his will—and my face will not be seen!"

The bat and woman spoke midst their observation of the contentious exchange: "So he claims to come from Rahnth's domain of power, but have I yet been witness to his *Majesty* sending a bot to act as emissary."

Fera bowed with a furrowing of her features, leaning hunched against the stone hall.

"Speak," said Sarkas, "your silence is concerning."

She glanced at her questioner. "He shares his enkindling," she said, eyes adhered to the Stranger, "I find it all to be a mystery, but this man is not of Rahnth."

"There is no other kingdom, purple bot," said Sarkas with adamancy. "His identity may be beyond our present grasp, but who else could he speak in favor for someone else than the moth?"

"I don't know," she said. "Bill…he's the closest thing Tycho's got to a dad, from what I've been able to glean from him, and this guy comin' in speaking about knowing his father isn't sitting right with me; could easily be trying to persuade Tycho into following him—Bill's location lies within means of being found once the officer has been interrogated, not the convenient truth this man spouts. Our guest is a liar, Sarkas, his fire no doubt a tool to have Tycho convinced. Let us not waste any more time, standing here feigning civility."

"Fera, Fera, Fera," said he, slow, "your fears, worries, and wrathful thinking subject you to violence than reasoning, which, admittedly now, I could agree this man's given purpose here is a fabrication…" He fell silent.

"Sarkas…?" said Fera, awaiting a conclusion to his thoughts.

The bat fixated on the figures against the starlit horizon. "Judeans, are these Judeans I behold…?"

Fera was without response. Unfamiliar with the term, she did not know whether to be alarmed or at peace.

"The boy an Ahmenseraï chosen," continued Sarkas, "I had not considered before, rather, unconvinced, until now as I believed all had perished; has Rahnth enlisted the last of the heretical people, *if that is even true*? Does Rahnth hope to garner one more to his ranks?" he said at length, surreally afflicted. "But you are right, Fera," he said, scratching behind his ear, "if we are to find Bill, this Judean untrustworthy, it will come from the mouth of the officer or better yet,

Halcón's. Also, for Bill to be sacrificed, it could only happen at the tyrant's throne room to make sense of the officer's revelation of their womanly master's plot, which I had not the proper evidence to presume this being very well could be the prophet, until now. It appears she has yet to be judged."

He turned his eyes onto Fera. "It's in my confidence that we'll find Tycho's punisher standing before king and brother, whom the latter is just as well sought after as his liege, so I'd advise quickness in the days to follow before the belligerent Outset has his way, before all that is sought by the both of you is lost."

They saw Tycho stand at the side of the Stranger with disagreeable features, aught from an unusual sight.

"Then why show yourself here?" said Tycho. "For what purpose do you have antagonizing some woman, no less myself?!"

"If he found no favor in you," said the Stranger, turning from him to the sabulous plains, "and I had not been commanded so, then I would not persist in this tedious, enraging quest to convince you that our Father yearns to have you cleansed by seeking absolution. For her hatred against me came from her own heart, I had nothing to do with her assault at my supposed provocation. I stand before you now as a sign of your steady descent from grace, fallen—hostage to Lucia's tempting. No longer will I approach as if divinely appointed to speak with you in hope you'd heed his word, for your band of the lost would do better having been granted this sight of the Lord's messenger to keep you aligned in his will."

Tycho spared a glance at his troubled crew. "I would contest to that."

"Their encouragement is not to be found in the present." He turned his head. "I tire of this, Tycho, greatly; you will follow, and all that I have been given to say will either draw you near to him, or the road of destruction shall enthrall you until death."

The Shine proved his silence on further quarreling, wary of beguilement but chancing to trust this fellow. The Ahmenseraï granted him a droplet of faith that would have Tycho at the messenger's company to overcome the Beast's distasteful allure, his immutable spirit nonetheless housed within Tycho and guide; this retarded not of Lucia's plan, the boy was weak and malleable in his loyalties to his Father, to which he wrestled with heaven's judgment over his own. As he failed to oppose the Shine's urge to have his heart open to the Stranger's words the boy went forth beside him, Sarkas and Fera thereafter soothed at their alert when Tycho held up two of his fingers, and lipped, "Two minutes."

As they walked in an undeterminable path to which Tycho raised few questions to where this phantom was adventuring, recollected his greened flesh at the sight of his gauntleted hands, determining they were without armor—flayed and mutilated, layers of skin hardened unfavorably to the imitation a jouster's grip. Questions were reserved, Tycho accustomed to the Stranger's tenebrous responses; long had his heart been calloused, and cold to understandings that would come from enrichment of living in the Spirit.

"Tycho, one of the many sons of the highest, can you truly not remember the time you received the Spirit, through repentance receiving his seal of eternity?" He drawled.

"I remember nothing," said Tycho. "There is nothing I can think back on…my earliest memories are in Sol Puesta, and that's about it. I don't recall this previous life of mine you somehow know, nor does it bother me as much as it seems to bother you."

"Even so," replied the Stranger, "I only wish to rid of my fears of you having lost the Ahmenseraï's guidance; but that is why I am here, why I came to you twice before. The first, I failed to speak in my apprehensions but showed to where Bill Pyron was led"—he concealed his muteness with a half-truth of an excuse, worrying his voice at Crest View would percolate recollection within his brother, preventing a series of further digression from the Spirit to unfold—"and at the Beast's point of inception I gave caution to the malicious slaying on your part of Rakeh, who undoubtedly would have told of Bill's keepings had the Spirit been a better, appreciated counselor. Had you made the sacrifice of denying rage, then intimacy with the Lord would have been proven—but you are without! And so, you stand here, given to bloodshed."

"Had you never known where Bill was from the beginning moments of our encounter, how was it that you knew of his drag through the Crest View mine?"

"By God, I managed."

Tycho, quicker to speak than considering thought, would have retorted his statement, but decided by the Shine's warmth to do otherwise.

"Why is he silent now, of where Bill is?" Tycho made an effort to not sound disheveled and pained.

"The Beast's machinations play into his own." The Stranger turned his eye—his brilliant, scarred eye to the young man. "And yet, Lucia continues in her rebellion. Praise be to him, he has a plan for you, and we both need to trust him. Although, be with this warning; solace will not come chasing after an officer of her occult, only a point to the core, if you are to be without providence."

Tycho gritted his teeth. "To him, is this all for his entertainment? Startin' to get a feelin' this Ahmenseraï fella isn't any better than a gladiatorial spectator, watching slaves slit each other's throats in hope of release."

"Strange, how he calls you to surcease such a fatal volition as murder.

"The greatest joy of your flesh has been commandeered by Lucia, arguably massacre had never been to glorify your talents, but her mastery over the blind and wicked. And now, she is on a conquest to have the Brussian, Sarkas, fall to mortal slumber by your hand, quenching the Spirit indefinitely. Repent, brother! He loves you, and has become severely jealous; watching you take her side, the decision conscious or not, all sin is in her favor in the degeneracy of his claimed."

"Then how does it go, teach me what I once knew." Tycho greeted the Stranger's eye with his own pair, crossed armed. "But promise me this: that I'll have Bill unharmed by deciding to do what your god asks."

"He very well could only be a fortune for your own endeavors; Bill was to serve as an impetus to your trek to regain intimacy with the Lord. His approval should be far more of an importance than the man's health. Comparably, the renewed life you've received, and to what your death will evoke, has Lucia anticipating enthronement…Keep guard, all other life should be second to yours."

Tycho's contorted features presented suspicion on his part, disbelief and repulsion—slightly.

"Surrender to him"—the Stranger faced him with an imposing carriage—"and become mortified of the slaying of all who have felt the wrath brought by your arm. Ask him for forgiveness, and the Spirit will flourish—"

Tycho shrugged with a nasty glower, and without hesitation, departed from his company.

"Brother," the Stranger shouted, "detestation of penitence will only lead to apostasy! Be it the Spirit dwells within you, the world and her authority will choose to be known rather than salvation's author. You will die, and refuge you'll be without."

Tycho turned, and glanced at the phantasmal courier. His eyes simmered white.

The vaquero, tightening his arms crossed in remonstrance to the Stranger's ultimatum, kept his head bowed momentarily. "Let me tell you something. I ain't one to talk, but I sure as hell know that the Shine would never go for whatever you were just goin' on about. Everything the Shine has shown me, taught me, spoken to me by another sense, is to bring aid to all who need comfort and healing; to be there for the ones that need guardianship. And regarding Bill, don't you ever tell *me* his life comes second, or anyone else's! That's for me—and the Shine—to decide." The Spirit spoke through him, humbling himself, the Stranger confronted by his master's conviction over the boy.

His guide was without response.

"None of this is easy, nor would I want it to be. I know I continue to fail the Shine"—Tycho messaged his wrist with his other hand—"but I'd never admit to having Bill at the bottom of my list of concerns." The Spirit had him at a self-reflected state.

"Is it because it's the truth?" said the Stranger. "I have seen the opposite in this venture of yours to retrieve him unscathed."

Tycho chuckled, sighing thereafter. Done with his guide, the chosen son of the Ahmenseraï returned to his coterie, faintly brushing his hand up against Meseron's forearm. Presently consumed with stirred emotions of rage and desperation Tycho would ignore all the Shine had to ease of his contemptuous disposition toward the essence's choice of succor, in what ways to perform the character of a son of the most high. He'd choose enslavement by frustration, greater—an impregnable fear of Sarkas' passing bestowed to him from the Beast's influence. Without yearn for repentance, or drawn to call out to his Father, the bot selected denial of all mantled powers at his person, benefiting the one that thieved God of his nature—partially. But not all could be blamed on the vaquero, for his guide failed at a third time to have him at the Lord's mercy, undermined in his passion to have his brother live.

The Stranger found a place of solitude, becoming aware to a light no other was allowed comprehension of.

"Forgive me, Father," said he, bereaved of Tycho's companionship. "The selfish ardor I have for Tycho deserved castigation, never do I want to fall at accost with the Spirit…"

He found peace looking to heaven, the Ahmenseraï standing, emaciated of being.

"Clyde is not far in reach of Halcón's palace, and the champion of Sol Puesta approaches sinisterly behind. Death at the doorstep of his vigor and soul, fate has him pawned for prophecy. I can no longer intervene…the will that is yours determined his heart remained calloused, as my efforts from the start were trivial. Lord, that I adore most of all, why falsify the hope I bore of his repentance? Have you a change of mind, prepared to face the Beast in all her appropriated divinity?—Lord, you too, will certainly perish. Her body was sought," said he, digging into the crusted folds of his hand, "in their preparation of killing Tycho's sequestered mentor, Halcón but deceived of his identity; commanded he was to tell his Outset brothers that only his eyes were deemed to behold the last of the hunted Verumshaï. She has another use for the old man, if the Spirit overpowers my brother's arrogance; for his state of spiritual maturity cannot conquer that brute."

The Stranger, Onesimus Veritros, averted his eyes from his master's hallowed gaze.

"…Don't have Tycho die, Father. For me, spare him. I have done all I could in your power. Allow me this one favor."

The Ahmenseraï stared on.

"I know he is now warned, and his rebellion is put on him, that he has chosen to turn his back to you, but I ask for a miracle. By advocating Bill Pyron's life come last, Tycho has become detested at the thought of being at your service…Yet, if he remembered the identity of his considered sire, which you have protected in my obedience to conceal our past, his quest would quickly become that of an avenger once more than seeking his friend's deliverance, as his first offense towards the Spirit had been. I would be no different from him were it not for the Spirit—I couldn't have forgiven our transgressor without you in my passing."

The courier's plea was heard, and all was revealed to him.

"You speak jesting, master?" The Stranger pensive, asking stung. "Had Leo not chosen an alliance with the Beast, as with those who favored their own lives, now besmirched with their own blood than yours?!" He came to reconciliation, rather than wallow in resentment and spite. "I ask for forgiveness once more, as I am about to let all hostilities and reservations I have for his damnable betrayal perish at the authority of the Spirit, to whom I've been resisting on this grudge. If Tycho is to be taught, and guided by any dissenter of the Way to seek after the Ahmenseraï's heart—for change to come about," he said, verged on chuckling, "I would fervently battle, and detest, any instruct from them with my own intervention needed be, but as I've been told, you continue to seek reclamation of the souls of the fallen before their passing, and I can see you've already done so with Leo as for him to have myself humbled and resume in his growth in the Spirit to guide Tycho along a similar path, so my concerns of unsound doctrine being promulgated through him to all those he disciplines should be done away with, as the Spirit's will has taken lead at whatever he does. Father, you are good; but by prayer keep Sarkas and Bill Pyron's life intact, Tycho's mutually in his venture to be woken, at your mercy and grace; the Spirit enrapture his passions. His spurn is a catalyst for greatness on both of their behalf, to your glorification.

"But why hadn't you sent me after my own apprentice years ago?" The Stranger sat, thereafter his answer coming in the silence, and rumination of prayer. "Understood; a fool I was to believe he was forever lost—as my return would be interpreted as a sign and his faith wouldn't be tested much."

"It was hard for me to accept Tycho was without knowledge of his past, as you told me—though, it is for the better; I did not dare test you, telling of fond and grisly recounts of our shared experiences that would have him out for blood than rescuing. But, truly, there was some disobedience done when I asked him if he had any recollection, hoping against your words' validity—I suppose I have sinned, haven't I? Forgive me, I am fallible—but your love is unconditional, and I am forever thankful."

No son or daughter will be left behind, for I am their shepherd.

"The emissary, has he set off?" asked Sarkas. "To whose agenda does he follow under?"

Few words remained adhered to Tycho's mind that held of any significance from his counsel, the Stranger's augury: "Their encouragement is not to be found in the present."

Tycho retrieved the harmonica of his mentor from his saddlebag, effacing the dust from its surface by breath, thereafter crossed his way to the fire, and answered disassociated, "No one you, or anyone, could know. Let me sit in peace now, Sarkas."

The boy played at what his heart willed, exuding all of his dejection onto the mouth organ. Beautifully haunting, Fera encouraged her fellow for a more uplifting tune, placing her head to his shoulder adversely to her thoughts of distancing herself. He started slow, and his song benefited the woman, and bat, to retire in the comfort of evening's close; though the morrow would be none the better.

XIII

FORMER SLAVE HER TESTIMONY

MOISTURE from the nostrils akin to a great beast wetted Fera's face, an outflow of steam that forewarns the most ravenous, and desperate, of predators questing for a full belly—to close the distance, without confidence in a pounce, or lunge in their starved fatigue. A sword was raised to its throat! The woman's eyes opened before her molester. Within the instance of Fera's eye-lights catching the offender she was quick to shut her eyes and reopen them, seeing Tycho's mount with accustoming vision to morning's dark. Meseron, with her great and salted tongue, glided the muscle across the woman's cheek and eye, herself chuckling, as it tickled; though disgusted, joy overcame. Normally, she would resist reciprocating affection in another's kind gesture, but all to her failure Tycho had been the kindler of this once repressed, protected Fera.

She fitted her swords to her sash, seeing the vaquero still in rest in her gradual stand, as with finding Sarkas no different from the former, his back uplifting to his snore. Gliding her hand past Meseron's snout, she gazed at the horizon to where *Titan Summit* ascended, preceded by lesser mountains and foothills, doubting all direction was solely on an Outset's scent.

Fera nudged her foot into Tycho's back. The boy groaned.

"It's time we're off; we have no more than a day to reach Bill before he's sacrificed, I hope." None of this true, she goaded his sense of duty.

He turned to his other side, facing her with half-closed lids.

"Sun's not even up." He proceeded to smack his gums.

Fera crouched. "Get up."

Tycho scratched his cheek with his middle finger at length, and said, "I dunno…I'm pretty comfortable."

"Alright," she said, grinning detestably, "two can play at this game."

Shortly after, Tycho's forehead trailed with foam, his hat lifting to Meseron's lick. He caught Fera standing beside the mustang with laughter, seldom for her. This enlivened the vaquero, frequently finding her crestfallen and brooding. At a quip against her, the boy came to his feet and pressed further with his raillery, Fera not short of a counter. He would have simply acted upon her suggestion to rise, but the boy had too much fun provoking her spirits, how easy it was. Reveled in their conversation Fera was not presently in the least concerned with yesterday's matters, Tycho's negligence she'd made herself ignorant of after their great spelunk. The wound was gone, so then was her anguish? No, absolutely not. She'd been dealt a worse hand before than what her companion served onto her so selfishly, and her attention was occupied on them three remaining united, reaching *Titan Summit* successfully. But in the coming hours of their venture, she would have time to reflect, and decide how to manage such newly acquired infuriation for her *dear* friend—a possible confrontation, to a much lesser extent than Sarkas'. Refutably, he had his part in bringing her to good health, but this was only after he cleared Death's passage to arrest her soul, as with those families had not Sarkas rescued them.

Fera caressed her hand alongside the former's back, hunching to speak within his ear. Her breath delighting the fine hairs in his ear had him tickled, the bat clawing the cavity to alleviate the sensation, and exhaling summoned a great cloud of dirt, sent rolling past Meseron's hoofs. Tycho brushing his hat of dust came to bestride the mustang, gaiting past the two without attentiveness for their discourse; not even a friendly greeting was granted to his colossal fellow, or any addressing that validated the recognition of his existence. The vaquero wished against for his agitation to swell with talk if a disagreement was to come about them, the fear—temptation—of his destruction was strong and preferred not to grant it anymore power over him.

The Beast cunning, she had his heart strung!

From the heavens' chariots rode, their stampede an indication of a storm; the approaching expanse of cloud, donned black, would bestow water and searing light upon the earth. Fera and Sarkas looked to the amassed legion, watching the first of their brilliant rods materialize.

A javelin of lightning struck afar, unsettling the two from trying flight,—if not already from their first glance on high,—Sarkas housing Fera underneath his wing. Tycho absurdly far in distance from them, waiting only for a cry from his venerable companion to steer him rightly to Halcón's residency, Sarkas was withholding exclamations that would be considered belaboring to the bot. So he kept quiet, letting Tycho go on his way until only humility rendered him viable for inquiring direction.

Fera huddled closer at his side for preservation. "His company I enjoy, but that attitude…anymore of it and I'm certain he'll find these blades at his core." She buried the side of her face against the bat's pelage, fitting her hands into her armpits. "His blood could be warming, considering."

"Fera, calm yourself."

She saw past the wing's arch, chuckling. "You believe me...? Honestly, did I come off that disturbed? I guess that says a lot about those who I'm perceived by, doesn't it?"

Sarkas glanced at her. "When you spout such talk, it's hard to not have the suspicion of one being murderous. Your overall end to this venture is to see Halcón slain, no?"

"What are you getting at...?" Her expression contorted, until the comment dawned on her. "Oh, Sarkas...I didn't know you could be such a jerk."

She couldn't help but smile. "But you're not wrong. Years of putting down the old, and young, does somethin' to you." She more so implied her vendetta for the Ravaja's scourge.

"I can see that...You handle those blades well. Was there any other suited against you that came as a challenge?" Sarkas decided to commend the woman, panged she had a gladiatorial past. He knew of her origin, the least of it, and self-righteously assumed the worst of her—fool, he thought of himself.

Additionally, he realized the insensitivity of his question.

Fera quieted.

"Forgive me, Fera," said Sarkas unhappily, after a momentary pause. "Resisting the tendency to pry comes at a lack for discretion; I have been alone for many years, and wish only to hear stories of those I find remarkable. See that I..." His fangs chattered, greatly chilled.

"Sarkas, it's alright."

Glancing at her, he found her deadpan, staring distant at the arising, dimed sun.

Nervously she came to play with her sword's hilt. She needed to distance herself from them; disclosing her history would lead the woman susceptible to an ensured attachment. At opposition, she'd never been given the opportunity to narrate her past, or shown interest in her by another. Against embattled thoughts to decline explanation, she spoke to her judgment's dismay. But it felt good, despite her inner voice telling her to cease her tongue's flail.

"Through an uncountable worth of men, I disemboweled and released their blood across the field. Not one could stand; fallen at the give of their knees, drenched in puddles of their own excrement"— running down her arms were goosebumps, possibly given by the cold—"and the challenge nonexistent, I turned on my masters and began to slay those who offered so much for their own entertainment, and previously, my own. Sickly, those whom I would devour, became easily inspired at the very frenzy that drove me to subdue boredom, and—"

"More than just doing away with boredom, but to revel in bloodlust."

She sulked, ever-holding contempt for her past deeds.

"…They managed to have themselves unleashed of their shackles, perhaps scavenging the pockets of a slain guard for his key," she said. "Those fathers, and younger men, placed the image of deliverer onto me, ill-conceiving that what I fought for was striving for a taste of freedom. And so, they stood behind, and followed in the trail of my butchering."

Sarkas composed, was becoming sickened—internalizing grievances, and worries for the wretch.

"Consequently, we faced against an officer, the same tool which we found at *Tartarus' Spire*, Sarkas; but nevertheless, *he* was what I was looking for." Her irises contracted, greatly.

"Stepping back through the crowd that followed I watched his performance, the spectacular brutality he used in mowing down those dispensable, believing their cause and sacrifice to be of great value. I against him, our bout ended quickly; a throttle of his chain about my throat rendered the conqueror of the arena immobile and humiliated, dissatisfied."

"What was a woman, like you, doing in an arena?" he asked. "What had the men perturbed to never strike against you…?"

"Some bandits failed to have their way with me, and sought my dismemberment in spectacle. I was then separated from my brother, thrown into a pit without a chance of preserving my life."

Sarkas looked to her awaiting conclusion.

"Tore out the throat of my first kill with my teeth, soon overtaken by some…nature, to hunt, never satisfied with one, always wanting more."

"Halcón," said Sarkas, with a deep expel of breath, "for what vengeance is there that you couldn't have with someone else? I don't understand."

"He had me kill my brother."

"Is that what you meant by 'separated'?"

Fera chuckled. "He forced my hand to his throat, slitting it with a blade." She became abruptly quiet again, expressionless.

Her head bowed she hadn't noticed the colossus kneeling before her. Encapsulated asudden she felt the drenched fur of his breast, leathery bonds sheathing her back from rainfall. Sarkas said nothing, and neither did she, his head lain over hers. Eyes glossed, she steadied them so that not one drop could fall and bring lesser esteem; she couldn't believe herself to be this pitiful, nor would she allow herself to be. Fera tried to ease herself out from Sarkas' hold, but the bat wouldn't allow it, and pulled her even closer. Overwhelmed she allowed the rain to mask tears.

Sarkas had put aside his judgment, and gave the savage woman what she needed most. For if he were in the same conditions, would he not be any similar—was he not already? The mind does sickening, and wondrous things to have itself preserved, failure to contain euphoria that's brought with the kill. Sarkas knew of this, projecting hatred of himself onto others when they were found in comparable light of him, scared of accepting the hunger. But once as a father, he had the inclination to set an example, and reprimand his charges to not have them fall to the same madness that damned him!

His greatest fear for Tycho, and now Fera, would be revenge never-ending, to fill some void.

"Fera," said he, "don't go after Halcón. His death will satisfy nothing."

With quaking features, she grimaced. "But it will. Once forgotten, I have remembered, and I won't let him get away with what he has done."

"So be it." His voice rumbled sorrowfully. "Stupidly, I thought I would have been able to change your mind, but you are determined, girl; don't let me stand in your way, regardless of my feelings to both your situations, and Tycho's—his a little more complicated, admittedly."

Sarkas raised his head, and looked at her with a pitying smile.

"Purple bot…" he murmured, forcefully rubbing his hand against her hair. She huffed, grinning, brushing her forearm past her eyes.

East of their travel, coming into sight shortly after their departure from camp, grand serrations of earth blockaded any simple entry that would lead to the Summit's base. As heaven continued to wage its war against Zodain, the triad's options were limited in their circumvention of this mountain range, and could only proceed through its narrowed valleys once their foothills were crossed. So began their hike, and after an hour or more escalating snowy mounds, they had reached one of the many gorges that scarred the extensive range with an unyielding stamina.

Fera, concerned with failure in slaying the avaricious king of thieves,—still passionate for his destruction to come by her hands, alone,—envisioned the morning where she swore she'd continue to fight, and kill at a time before desensitization and carnage molded the frail girl, to avenge her brother. Once relocated, she remembered her oath, and became welled with profound grief. She'd forgotten herself, lost to the bloodshed.

Sarkas behind the mustang, watching their steps as they edged past a turbulent ravine, glanced at Fera horseback, seeing her distant once more; in her own thoughts, the present forsook.

There was nothing more he could do.

"Sarkas," she said, keeping her gaze where it had been on the Summit, "the moth, what happened between the two of you?"

Fera then looked to her shoulder. "How, and why, did it take a command from you, so agreeably?"

"The luminary had a change of heart, was eager to help those it had wronged—I provided only direction, leadership for it to fall upon. It was that the fellow believed Rahnth's kingship had been subjugated by the Council, not accepting the old fool of taking pleasure in having bots trafficked. Finding it of puerile reason, I said nothing, letting it believe what it wanted to; absolute isolation hadn't severed all the chains Rahnth had over his previous servant."

She glared at him intently, and said, "Out of us three, you'd be the last I'd suspect of rescuing a moth. What possessed you to do so, regardless of its defection?"

"Would you believe me if I said it was empathy to blame?"

"No."

"Then, there is no other way of convincing you, girl."

In the continuation of their traversal lightning struck the nearest peak; a beautiful shower of snow and rock erupting slowly after the spearing light's vanish. Although something to behold, the triad wasted no time for them to fall victim to landslide, if another blow were to happen upon the face of the mountain. Sarkas, the other two oblivious—as he would have it, bit down on an obtrusive stone that had pierced his shoulder from the burst above, tumbling far from the settled mass. Removing it precipitously a chunk of gnarled hair and blood came from his breast and onto the ground in-between his foot talons, careless as to what scent could attract predators to their position. They roamed within the range famished; surely one would catch the bat's spoor.

Amid the assailing storm, Tycho spotted a cavern deeply set within a mountain's base, and without one's protest, they agreed here to camp; the vaquero made sure it was empty of any dwellers. Piled close to the wall fossilized feces intrigued Tycho for a closer examination, and curious enough, an idea formed. He lit a piece of the Precambrian dung aflame, and his hypothesis was rewarded—fire, that they would have, but would Fera or Sarkas share the same exultancy? He argued if there were any sticks or chaparral to be found they'd all be damp, not suitable for a campfire. Both the persuaded shrugged, and dealt with the fact of the matter they'd have to cook their food over burning dung.

Having a leg from the mule deer tucked within his gunny sack, the Brussian had left-overs to spare. Cauterizing the severance to refrain his bag from becoming drenched, it was only the tip of the prey's thigh that had been charred. He sat, and pulled out the limb as it unfolded from out his bag, flipping the leg from one side onto another over the fire. Gripping the forearm and thigh with sinewy hands after the meat had cooked, he rent the limb in two, and passed a half to each bot. The gross, yet appetizing crack from the split limb tormented their stomachs, both Tycho and Fera looking to each before surrendering to their bestial gorge.

"Sarkas," spoke Fera as she swallowed, wiping her wet lips of juice, "what are you to eat? There is enough here for all of us."

The bat grinned, and said, "Be full, and then I will take whatever remains."

"Clyde's scent," said Tycho, contentious, "is it leading us where we all believe it to be heading?"

"And where would that be, my friend?"

"The Summit."

"Then I would assume so, yes." The bat gazed outward to the mount, seeing its features heightened by the moon's ravishing glare.

Fera's expression showed that of suspicion, almost choking on her food; she yielded Sarkas, and Tycho, on their assistance.

For a week rainfall and thunder remained constant, some showers lighter than others, but mostly heavy, the triad kept themselves sheltered until a diminishing of the storm would come about, the bat and woman avoiding frostbite and coldlung. The bones from their feast lasting scarce a night as means for a fire, before long, Tycho had no other choice than to fetch branches from wetted shrubbery along the mountainside, and gathered himself a plentiful collection that he would wait to dry until suitable for burning, and during those hours the young man scavenged for food, dragging what appeared to be a freshly drowned bighorn from out of the ravine, watching his step as to not trip forward and become swept away by the raging stream. Rationing the meat for the remainder of the days they were held within the cavern Tycho argued before this why they couldn't just leave now, the Shine surely keeping them in good health. But this reasoning was kindly refuted by Sarkas, as the Shine would benefit them momentarily all while they would suffer through the cold, and so midst their time huddled together some bonded, while others kept to themselves, no matter how hard one tried to unharden the vaquero's heart. The bat having no more with aggression, an unpleasant state of mind to prolong than necessary, he decided the days following their stormbound predicament to act against his word, what he had spoken to Fera about, keeping a comport of strife towards the vaquero as long as he held his, and instead of lowering himself he would approach the situation between him and the young man as he'd done with his son, remembering compassion the greatest of tools to bring arguers together. But, this accomplished little; regardless the bat treated him as a friend should.

The last of their nights within the cavern, lulled to sleep from the pattering of rain, the triad once more amassed for warmth, Tycho's arms about Meseron's neck, Fera using the bat's wing to sheathe her trembling self. The pounding of thunder bled into the woman's subconscious, adding to the nightmarish fantasy that provoked her to whimper, pulling tighter on Sarkas' spread. Burdened with attentive ears in her attempt at rest, Meseron's eyes saw to her rider's companions thereafter glancing to the mouth of the cave, veiled beaded. Before raising her head, she exhaled deep, becoming aware of a foreign presence that had been outside for some while. Approaching, its stalk had ended; its shadow grew tall, darkening the once glimmering downpour.

Water spilled over its head and sleek shoulders, canalled to the space beside its stance. It looked to the mustang, surprised her nerves hardened—thankful. Not a noise came from her, initially in her discernment of the unwanted guest.

Then another entered behind, scarcely had their heads grazed the cavern's arc.

Meseron was in the instance of straightening her legs, certainly disturbing Tycho's sleep if she were to stand. Aim drawn on the vaquero's mount a chitin fin released from its forearm's indention, swiftly penetrating her skull. Tycho would awake arm, and chest, soaked.

Their fouled stench caught Sarkas' nose astringed, forthwith galvanized by its familiarity—quick was his awakening glare to them! Roaring to inflict petrifaction to those appointed at his challenge, Sarkas lunged forward from his recline and charged. The luminaries had not accounted for their prey a veteran of the war, trained on their inscrutable scent. Disturbed of further rest the two bots went for their means of defense, Fera on her feet before Tycho, veritably taken aback he couldn't rise from his kneel at the sight of Meseron. Again, from the forearm, as with the other participating in the bat's hampering, the blade-like fins filed out from their indentions rapidly, staking the behemoth to the cavern's ground. Immediately the body of unquenchable wroth tore through the implements, and leapt mightily at their foes, casting them in darkness with an elongated, riddled wingspread.

They were taken through the cavern's wailing veil, enshrouded in Sarkas' capture. Fera without hesitance followed.

One's head came crushing under the might of his jaws, emitting ululations in death, Sarkas holding the remaining luminary by its throat over the ravine's declivity. From his chin blood poured at his fangs release of the severely maimed, roaring primeval as to evoke Fera yearning to emit such a thunderous bellow as he. The entranced warrior given to the hunt, she saw his eyes gibbous and bloodshot, and finally, recalling her own ravenous frenzies, she became frightened. Slowly, Fera distanced herself.

The last moth looking to stagger Sarkas for an escape projected a series of fins along his snout, one puncturing his eye. Sarkas burrowed his open hand through his antagonist's stomach, and received within his grasp a spine. Snapping the bone half, he pulled out a portion, and watched it tumble to the violent flooding below.

Out of breath, the bat turned his gaze to the savage woman, who stood unclear how to determine her situation, but seeing his strain and lacking vigor felt assured that any threat from him was now gone. Presently the sight of the chitin protrusions along Sarkas' bridge brought her alarm, blood dripping from the fins edges and points of entry. Running to his aid, she began to tug at the fins; barbed, she jerked the protrusion until a sliding motion would allow her to discard the chitin debris, growls and trying barks emitted from the insufferable Brussian. "Quiet you! Hold still, okay…I'm trying to help." Her voice became soft, and sincere.

Fera reached for the fin lodged within his eye, after all other chitin had been removed.

"Don't touch that one," growled Sarkas.

"Fine, then you do it!"

He bowed his head, panting. "Fera, I am grateful, I mean you no wrong—it just stings. Allow me to remove it; you've been more than helpful."

Stepping back, she looked to the cavern past her shoulder. The adrenaline of battle waning she sought warmth again and issued the bat to roll the mutilated remains into the ravine to not attract any vectra or other predatory force. Seeing him preoccupied with dislodging the chitin from his eye, abiding the horrid sting, the woman pitied him, and busied herself with the corpse.

Thanking her as he left her side a thought came to him before entering the cavern. Sarkas believed what he did, his precipitous assailing against the Rahnthian presence, was done out of protection for the two, never his sworn hate for the species! But he'd fooled himself, the brutality of his actions against the luminary hunters proving the latter, given to murder much like the boy, as for the thrill of it.

He accounted for his fortune that a fin hadn't entered any higher than his eyeline.

His coat shaken dry of the storm, his good eye found the solemn Tycho kneeling before Meseron, spying a crowning fin set deep between her eyes. He watched Tycho's contour illuminate white in brief, gripping the projection to have the implement slice open his palm; once removed, he placed his hand on her head, and awaited resurrection. Fera with her entry was expressionless, heavyhearted, the bat and her still as statuary.

Repeatedly, Tycho would cut his palm, pressuring his hand on the gash. His roughish friend could distinguish the pace at which his hand was healing, far slower and unusual—a concerning visual. Crossing the cavern she placed her hand on his shoulder, whispering for him to surcease animating and then knelt beside him. Her words faded in mourning Tycho cursed the Spirit, the Ahmenseraï and his messenger. Before his accusation of rebellion all forms of preservation were granted to him, not enough concerned with the Shine's dwindling power. It was made clear the Ahmenseraï's counselor was not to be abused, and this he despised. "Bill, I'm sorry."

Sarkas leaned against the side of the cavern, where the fall of water was not constant, and surveyed. He questioned the blue bot, "Without refrain, the one that shares your fire, whose kingdom did he speak of?" He turned to face them, fangs bared. "No more are they lying in wait;

their scouts' would have made a return. I need answers, Tycho, are they here on his account for your abduction?"

"He has no involvement in this, Sarkas," said Tycho, coming to his feet. "From the saurian chambers, the luminary and his merchandise, he could have been easily found on his journey westward to bring those women and children under shelter." He unlatched the Havoc from his holster, and looked to his shoulder, preparing for assailment. "The direction of our travel, the coward tipped them off."

"With all turncoats they had the obshika tortured." He thought of the unimaginable. Those sent out from the unit,—at this time aware of their casualty hearing the Brussian's challenge,—had planned the capture of the bat, to be maimed for his assistance with the traitor on chattel emancipation, and much like Cicero's fate, enduring cruelties for Rahnth's pleasure; the bots not so different, brought to slavery, though they were a find unexpected. He remembered the blood spatter and hair he left, its giving scent exacting their place in the range. Sarkas' heroics had its own repercussions; he could now see the impulse of emotion sentencing the mustang slain and the endangerment of his cherished two, imposing his presence in another's business where it was not needed.

A sudden conglomerated hum reverberated just outside their den, the vaquero's arm whipped around to face the chitinous apprehenders. After his initial shot the immediate brawl became incomprehensible, all consumed in a murderous haze.

A ring emitted from the clang of a spearhead against stone, sloughing the bestial nature from his worn companions, charmed at their advantages' drippings, talons and swords drenched red. The spear his support Tycho slowly raised himself, aching terribly. Other lain weaponry found warmth in the pools of their disemboweled, fins strewn across the cavern walls and, further, perforating Sarkas' wings; they'd come to resemble threadbare tapestries.

Fera placed Tycho's arm about her neck, and steered him where he directed her. Taking what he needed from his saddlebag, Tycho closed Meseron's lids and whispered unintelligibly in her ear, brushing her mane. The triad ventured from their stay in the cavern, and persevered onward throughout the storm scarce contracting a mortal chill if not for the Shine, unconscious if more luminaries prowled behind. At morning after a day's march, they were upon tundra with their exit from the gorge, dawn engulfing the land and bringing light to the immortalized dragoon carved within the face of fourteen mountains. Arriving at a space to discern the sculpture, the once jigsaw pieced forms came into clear view, their shifted perspective allowing them to witness the display of Rahnth's horsemen commemorated for their surmounting of the Anax dominion, the eldritch monarch at its head leading them into Thrace. Tycho spat before him as an insult to the perverted tyrant and turned his gaze from the mountains to the horizon, where *Titan Summit* was in grasp.

To their surprise, as they had begun walking forward, the champion of Sol Puesta spun from their company and sent a bolt hurtling thunderously towards the face of *His Majesty*, the arching cast shimmering until a cloud of rubble signified contact, the figure's demolishment echoing with a profound roar that enraptured him.

Far had they trudged from the vandalized scene and gathered to resist cold. Fera glanced behind at the wing that sheathed her, and frowned at the many tears leaving his inky membrane to drape.

"Bots, purple and blue," said Sarkas, his inhale for breath burdensome, "this is as far as I take you." He shivered from frost layered deeply on his fur, the hairs of his chin icicles. "Be off now."

"Come with us," Fera pleaded calm, "there is certainly shelter to be had on our way. You need rest, friend."

"And how many miles more until we find a hole in the earth that can fit only one?" he said, thereafter huffing. "There is not a single den beyond from where we came, Fera; I am harsh, because I know well before you'd depart from me untroubled, anticipating dethronement, *oh so eagerly*. I need you to find that strength again."

Fera's head turned aside, her features agitated. Sarkas placed his hand before him, and hunched greatly to meet the eyes of his doomed fellows. "I will miss you terribly, Fera. And regrettably, Tycho, our farewell is only met with indifference." He lowered his head, and glanced at the small figure. "My condolences to the rider taken of his mount."

The triad dispersed after minutes of their talk, Tycho and the woman unequipped for the hardship of their present terrain, Sarkas following their tracks back to the gorge. He muttered to his voice's devour amongst the howling winds, "I have fulfilled the part of caretaker. Whichever god has found favor in the boy, do not forsake him. Have him back to his fatherly one."

XIV

SIC SEMPER TYRANNIS

THERE, placed upon the Beast's throne of blackened, glassed stone sat her cleric, comfortably. The church's steward sat reclined within the hollowed contents of an obelisk similar to that of which the daring vaquero found at the Rothschild estate, extraordinarily tall and wicked, ascended to beckon Osiris; Nimrod's legacy, guised as his deification. Awaiting the opportunity to be his brother Clyde's tormentor, silent and plotting, his eyes widened and gleamed at the instantaneous thought of the Outset's evisceration. Told of his dogged hunt from Lyle, who now lay at the steps of the throne cast in Cimmerian dark, mutilations unseen in his rest from battery, thought he'd buried his pursuer, but Halcón was not a man to underestimate the aggrieved apostate; thereafter the officer at the first utterance of his name fell to punishment for his cowardice, to lead him toward the heart of the Summit, desperate for sanctuary.

Disregarding the mountain's agape jaws an inlet for moonlight Halcón was lounging in the midst of umbrage within the formation's cavity, where his coat, hat, and pelage, black and grizzled, were indistinguishable, all except for his reflective glare that would espy Clyde's entry, not to be forgotten the blades edged at his hat's brim scintillating bright. His bared talons sliced, and picked at the arm of his master's throne impatiently, along its length grooved from the meditating repetition of whetting his claws in dull sittings.

The chamber of inactivity filled with the faintest echoes of one's stepping, perking Halcón's ears to ascertain the pace of his foeman that would distinguish his composure, hoping the Outset approached in consuming belligerency—he wanted to slay the pursuer in a manner that'd he'd be a challenge. Out from the shadows Clyde was then illuminated by several rays of light endowed from the mighty summit's yawn, his excoriation revealing glistened fangs that sought the jugular of his target, his lip curled to expose his other half of fine dentition. Hunching, a great bone shot through the hunter's palm, widening his arm until splitting half, muscle and vein suspended and taut from the center bone—he would need a weighty blade to put Al Halcón to permanent rest.

Bounding from his stationary position the marvel of a beast alighted on all-fours to quake the ground suddenly, the contemptible officer crushed underfoot, Halcón roared hellishly to remind the hunter of his dominance within the arena, and that he was Lucia's most formidable—not he! Clyde grinned, and charged at the despot.

His bone grinding against the obsidian surface behind, Clyde anticipated the swing needed to disrupt Halcón's sprint against him— within four steps his prey closed the distance. An effulgence of sparks flew from his bone's glide from the surface to meet his present antagonist, the hunter's blade cutting effortlessly through Halcón's lower jaw and advancing palm that would have struck a lethal blow if not for the counter. He was rewarded with the indication of his suffering, a profuse torrent of blood wetting his blade beautifully. As Clyde was to then follow with a death strike into his abdomen, the other hand of Halcón lunged for Clyde's face, and carried his body to the serration of volcanic ground. His foot pressing on his torso,—half the size of the Outset's entirety,—tore the leveraging bone from his socket, and enduring the riving storm of his cannon impaled Lucia's finest at the thigh, stomping useless the congealed weaponry. Halcón stooped to retrieve his displaced lower jaw, and turned from the hunter. Stricken with disbelief that he remained standing, Clyde weakly glared over at the several shots made through his chest, reaching through to his peppered backside.

The reverberation of Halcón ramming his jaw into place boomed, blood sealing the mandible secure, his pain shrugged off.

"You're not the one who is granted the benefit of my slaughter, Clyde," Halcón slavered firstly in speech, "You anger me with your presence; I await another."

"You're only getting me," snarled Clyde.

The space surrounding Halcón came into vision, before blurred in the preparation to dispatch this heathenish burden from the Ravaja. Sheer, glistening walls of igneous mirrored his grim vulnerability; humiliated, he tried to dislodge the titanic bone, precipitously avoiding a fate as the officer's.

"Look at yourself," said Halcón, listening to his wrestle, "unendurable in struggle. Your exhibiting writhe brings me life; have the thought of this duel requital for our master's assassination—never had the proper chance of dismembering the fellow before the great and renowned disciple scampered off with his daughter in-hand. Where is she now, I wonder?"

His grip loosened, wetted from the sliced palm at the bone's edge; moreover, the sinews of a single arm could not clear the piking impediment from his thigh. Faintly lighted at the ground's reflection by an odd emission, Clyde glanced at his quarry's back, the tears of his marred coat contoured violet. His wounds shut by blood and restorations of tissue, permitted by the Beast's mark centered between his shoulder blades.

"Be as it may I am without master's corpse," a sonorous, low growl emitted as his arms rolled, cracking, "an entire legion of thugs wasted at the opportunity to retrieve her form and airship discarded, a body she'll not be without, and by yours she'll have reunion with this plane once sat on that throne."

Halcón turned, and approached Clyde fervently.

Seeing that his attempt of pulling out the bone was costly, he began to pummel the impediment in a panic. Progressively his fists were sent faster onto the face of the bone as his tormentor neared, launched from continuing the act as Clyde tumbled and bounced far from a brutish kick into his side, the embedded, ossified blade leaving his outer vastus cleaved.

Without innervations in his right thigh, Clyde laboriously came to his feet, positioned to face the rapacious tyrant with half-strength; his sole arm would be the lasting contributor to his success, if he were to have any.

Violently the hunter summoned his chain, and lashed at the servile brute, keeping his lame stance cemented. The unfurling end of Clyde's chain snapped, and dissevered the meat of Halcón's bosom upon contact, but his assailant was without the slightest flinch, and burdened his hand to the rending surface of his hurled chain, and pulled mightily to have him close. Anticipating a beheading from Halcón's other raised paw the speeding body retracted his congealed limb to form another tool akin to the larger blade, slashing open the bully's throat in splendorous fashion nullifying his decapitation. The flowing, crimson outpour imbued the hunter's lips and forehead, tasting the nectar of an otherwise tangible, enthralling death, if not for the seal of Lucia. His flight halting on impact against the stumbling corpse, Clyde braced his sensible foot on the quarry and leapt back, placing his diminishing blade-into-claw onto the earth for his charge against Halcón anew. Propelling forth with hastened footing as all his focus was keeping his numbed leg from giving, the first disciple of the Congregation bounded raking the great cat's face, rendering him blind, and gargling, and with carried momentum flew over his head, newly positioned before his hind. Tearing off the back of his coat he spied the wretched Keter, by deviltry the mark brightening malicious that not even an eye from the hunter was allowed to intake its rebellious nature—a poor, and mocking imitation of the Spirit, with its qualities. At a pounce to sever the carved portion of hide Halcón recovered, and turning his grand fangs onto his combatant before Clyde's feet had left the ground the Outset fought to keep the great cat's jaws wide and unaffecting by having him throttled, gasping for breath. Without hesitance the bold Clyde risked face disfeatured at his head's ingress within the salivated chamber to bite off the brute's tongue, wetting his countenance even more at its severance. Al Halcón bellowed with an onerous, horripilating roar that shook his charcoal mane, the Outset restricting his tremble at the might of his voice, and emitted his own challenge with quivering lips in response to the cry, to give himself power over the fear of entering forever into an abyss—he'd thought himself accepting of death. He advanced before his game, knowing the agitation of his tail and vermilion glower was sign of the great battle to come.

Midst his charge all was then black, the Beast woman ensnaring all his faculties. Molesting her hunter with regrettable visions of the past, and self-defeating ideation, she feared his triumph, and sought his execution by self; due to how near he was to the obelisk, her power was heightened than anywhere else in the material realm, able to manipulate Clyde's mind against him, and shortly someone other to come.

"Father of Assiah's heiress," she said, "witness once more the realization of your deception, by the will of your god, and lover." Her voice was chilling and deep.

From the mouth of a cavern the hunter leaned at his hearing of Halcón's demagoguery, witnessing him instill fear and outrage into the audience of Rahnth's subjugation and inequity, burdened with enslavement if levies went unpaid, applicable only to the lower castes of their wealth; a monarch who considers his species only deserving of compassion and tax exemption stirred the pathos of the assemblage easily, beguiled into a belief from Halcón's mouth that the Judeans were a pillar cause to their oppression and needed to be dealt with quickly if ever equality was a hope to be had, unquestioning the underlying motives of the small church which would grow in influence to engender revolution.

Clyde looked to his shoulder, and found Lucia's sinuous approach. Gently, she placed her hands at his arms' sides, and playfully gnawed on his shoulder, whispering obscenities in an attempt to mate once more with her favored pupil. The naïve hunter gave, and followed her thereafter the witch departed from his company to allure him deep within the cavern.

"Countless nights after we rested together as one flesh," she continued, "you beheld the birth of our daughter, hours before the annihilation of his elect with pause; by your hand, they fell crying out to their Messiah for deliverance."

Enchained to the body of Clyde past the tortured hunter watched, and sensed again men and their eldest sons choke and weep to his blade's incisions, marring them immobile. The Judeans' steppe came afire from torches placed against the walls of their tents, to have them horde altogether at their exiting sprints towards the river to extinguish the maddened blaze. Rather than have their bucket's fill of water they were greeted with gunfire as they came over the ridge, the sudden nature of their extermination incomprehensible; hundreds came to stumble and roll before the Outsets' and participating revolutionaries' feet. The men having ascertained the plot against their people ran for their swords and rifles but would fall all the same, their women before given to panic now ferried along the river.

Why have you done this, recollection spoke for the tribe's elder, *what have we as a people done to deserve such scorn? The wantonness of it all!*

Praise be to the prophet Lucia, recollection spoke for Clyde, the hunter, *to her the Ahmenseraï has revealed truth of his chosen, and most despised enemy, those masquerading as Verumshaï—*

The mighty hunter of the helpless heard the clamor of surviving children bewailing their fallen mothers at the riverside, grasping their fingers in an attempt to hold them near as they drifted away. Something was amiss, and Clyde remained paused in anguish and qualm scrutinizing the ridge. Lyle crossed his way and slew the tribe's elder in the disciple's hesitance, and barked at him in his focus at their cry—the Outset unheard. The echoing thunder of gunfire disrupted his trained hearing, the young quelled.

He watched Halcón ascend past the ridge, the manipulation of his movement slowed profoundly from an influence of tachypsychia, unknowingly.

"Lucia, be gone with you! I have had more than my share of recollection; another instance will not hamper this arm from bringing Halcón to putrefaction." He scarcely maintained his anxieties.

She sought his neck slit.

"And as I had envisioned, you entered the temple full of rancor, after your *discovery*," she said, laughing.

To her foreknowledge she found Clyde clouded by emotion, striding to her temple doors, and with a horrid entry, light flooded into the structure from kicked open stone doors sliding apart with a grating screech. Before him, the Beast in labor with her child was strategically placed within the Holy of Holies as a way to threaten the Ahmenseraï of his coming dethronement; assisting with birthing the child were the emanations she'd stolen. Clyde's arm tapered to a fine, steely point as he approached her, witnessing his daughter exit from the Beast's womb and into light.

The hunter sometime after pogrom had been committed against the Judean people, and a day before his march upon the temple, went to the book Lucia taught from,—never before had there been a thought to do so, since he trusted her so endearingly and the fear of damnation put into his heart, "For whoever reads a word from the Torr that is not the Ahmenseraï's prophet is to be exiled as judgment will find them writhing in the fiery pools of Abaddon," and learned of his deceit; an ineffable wrath consumed him. The text stolen from the extinct tribesmen Clyde gleaned the pages of the Torr until at last finding the book *Reclamation*, the final story of prophetic vision inscribed within the bible by spiritually endowed Verumshaï, whom he'd been the identity of before revelation told him not. It read:

And the Beast slaughtered all, hating the children of his professed love.

Birthed from our ancestors' sin, it acted on the nature of defiance and perversity.
Envious was the Beast—I saw it mock the Ahmenseraï, for without a father
All too of his beloved would be without the instruction of one.

The Beast was drunk with the blood of God's holy people,
The blood of those who bore testimony to the Ahmenseraï.

But the God Messiah would not have this,
And I saw him descend from Heaven claiming all of his slain
Here and there, his children transcended into new spiritual bodies
Glorying his name.

Given discernment from the heavenly father of whom the scripture spoke of, Clyde wept.

It was revealed to him he'd been the instrument of destruction against the Ahmenseraï's children, orchestrated by Lucia with false religion to perform genocide for his own guaranteed salvation. He was filled with sorrow at the remembrance of their women's pitched cries defending their young, or fathers with sons rushing behind with crude armament to stop their assault.

The Ahmenseraï sent him a messenger the next morning, and led him to the subterranean castle. His readings there morphed his heart of sorrow into an organ of unquenched rage towards Lucia. Seeing Clyde's heart quickly harden, succumbing to the anger of his carnal inclination, the Ahmenseraï departed from his side and hoped he'd return to call unto him in seeking forgiveness, to not depend on his works powered by vengeance, as works had been drilled into his skull of achieving eternal life, in-turn believing a sin could be erased with many good deeds, cleaning the slate of his monstrous butchering.

The present Clyde drew a blade to his throat, tickling the skin with the dragging point as he continued to suffer from the presented vision.

Judgment is what you seek. Was your plan to strike him down, memory spoke for a more youthful Clyde, *sent falling from above as you extracted the last emanation? I've spoken to my brothers on the matter and they do not care, so no longer am I united to the Congregation and its teaching that I once believed virtuous and wholesome, it's political ideology for gains among the masses I would have been without, if not for the indoctrination of cultism leaving me persuadable!*

I will have it—Judgment, and then Sefirot, memory spoke for Lucia, as oil trailed from the creases of her lips. *And Fera will take representation of her mother on earth as I reign from the heavens. Be proud that your daughter will rule over all kingdoms through my power, bringing together a centralized monarchy to her glorification, tortured until that time so she'll properly become like her matriarch.*

None to which you have spoken will I tolerate, memory spoke for him.

Clyde withdrew his blade from her abdomen, her corpse weightless as it remained temporarily afloat, grabbing the newborn from out the mysterious air and severing the umbilical cord before wrapping her in a cloth. Knowing well he could not provide for her,—a day's passing and she'd already turned pallor,—suffered in the bestowment of his mightiest love, and greatest joy, to a family with a nursing mother. He left a letter in the folds of her swaddle, which read:

To the concerning family,
I am without the utilities to keep my daughter alive for much longer.
Her name is Fera, love her as her father would.

He thought about killing his infant, the fear of Lucia's fortune actualizing. But he could not will it; essaying to find hope that

Verumshaï still wandered, given their author of the Spirit hadn't returned, and in her mother's passing, assuming the Congregation would fall without her leadership.

"Ahmenseraï," grumbled Clyde, laboring to remain animate, "I need you; protect me from the Beast's ideations. I yearn to live, so that my daughter does not fall prey to Lucia's horror."

Halcón could see Lucia working, and did not interfere until presently at Clyde's regaining fortitude.

"Let her never know of our existence, having peace by ignorance and a priestess unfitting for a church that will remain no more once this brute who stands before me has been slain!" He gutturally discharged.

Entranced by an outrage selfish enough to keep him from the benevolent Christ, intent on the destruction of his adversary, his supporting power assayed him incapable of receiving the Spirit but would not abandon. Halcón embittered at Lucia's lack of confidence in his trounce to be had over the hunter dealt that much more against him than previously, his yanking slash twirling Clyde overturned followed from a parry of the Outset's blade warding Halcón's seeking blow to his core. The giant's canines and lips sported froth anticipating they'd meet Clyde's face within the instance of having his core seized, dragging it through his viscera until having emergence from out his crouch.

The tyrannicidal hunter cleaved off the talons of the brute's pressuring hand until his blade had overcome the grinding against of his nails; succedent a cannonade of spikes had Halcón reeling brief. Clyde continued with his barrage as he came to his feet, Al Halcón shouldering through with his charge as blood dispersed and sprinkled on both their coats, positioned his feet for a quickened pounce avoiding direct fusillade. Clyde foresaw the attempt, and shifted his stance aside as to avoid a mauling, and cried rancorously: "The last seed of Judah, I've smelt him out! I know where he takes residence within this chamber, this putrid hollow—Lucia has failed to bring about the end; I'll be leaving with the man."

Halcón coughed blood, and slowly became erect. "Why the veneer of certainty, apostate?—to deceive one informed, unlike the beaten officer? He was spared of the truth regarding the Verumshaï's identity, only known to me, for if he had the information Lucia whispered into my ear," he said, tapping his ear's flesh, "doubtless he would have acted selfishly to gain praise and to be rewarded with kingship for his hunting, regardless of her plans; their disregard is beyond me, as punishment would befall him, the best explanation is an acting on instinct than reason, as a dog brings back a kill to its master hoping to be showered with validation. He would have undone everything! She told me, there had been a disobedient servant that came before the accursed Judean to take the boy's life, hoping, she would displace Halcón for his ass to sit on the throne, for his deed. Lyle would have been no different, and was given misinformation to lure the last tribesman of Judah here. I can see why he was never given Lucia's seal…he would have challenged me for the position of cleric, and she would have been at a loss of another disciple…while the marked desperado had his own alternate, *presumptuous* means of attainting priesthood.

"But you do know I have someone," Halcón continued, chuckling, the misinformation Lyle given furthermore a safekeep from prying hunters learnt of the Beast's matters, "someone dear to the boy as leverage to draw him ever closer. An exotic punishment he'll endure, though twisted."

"Because of your deception against Lyle," spoke the hunter, "he nearly killed the Verumshaï, thinking him mortal."

"I was betting on the boy to kill him," said Halcón smirking, rumbling forth a profound roar. "After some meddling done by the Ahmenseraï, she spun a newer reality to undertake—not you, not your church-brother, but he was to awake her corpse! And as I've said, he is not here," his voice resonated, "his accompaniment to be found with Lucia's spawn, the heiress of Assiah; the abandoned one"—Halcón grinned at the rise he received from his distraught church-brother, filing his newly grown talons against those honed—"how we hated that she was not her mother withal the daughter of her betrayer.

"Regardless Fera was molded and weathered into the prophet's image; she was found, Clyde, taken from her destitution to fulfill her training in the arena. I remember she was to be in Rahnth's hands—sold to him, until borne with a mind of insanity, where she could not properly reflect Lucia's place on that throne, a conscious overwrought by the guilt of carnage. I was to allow her escape at her rebellion, but I would not have it. All I've been rewarded—the power and prestige, by faith and loyalty, taken."

"You don't feel cheated; you fear death, as with all men of power, that an act of defiance was more of impulse than reasoned insubordination. A king cannot rule without his crown, and Lucia would have you dethroned."

"And all that I have gained now legacy for this waif!" His voice thundered. "But Lucia promised if I am to be the victor against her, she'll forgive what I've done in my defiance, and proven that she is not worthy to take representation of her mother, who has been preparing the girl with tribulation all these long years, years of anticipation, without her knowing. She's only lived this long through stubbornness and keen instinct, taking just after her mother and father.

"But grieved with the knowledge of Lucia's nature, I understand her words to be spoken only as comfort. Her child will come to slay, and I will face damnation in rebellion to preserve what is mine and was has been appropriately given to me. I will more than accept the fate of Abaddon's fires if I can sink but one claw into her skin and hear the caterwauling of my most despised!"

"You won't lift a hand against her."

"No?"

Clyde glowered. "Death to the tyrant."

Casting his chain about Halcón's throat asudden, Clyde fastened himself swiftly onto his back, and forced his foot down against his spine to force the ravenous cat to stumble, pulling his head upward to impel a fall—lose balance. Now prostrate Halcón roared, and writhed as he struggled to stand, raising his head while the throat garroted to remove a shard of obsidian from his eye. The hunter repeatedly stomped the back of his head to keep him align to the ground, attempting to proceed with the severance of the backside to split the Keter ineffectual. Halcón throwing his arm back to dismount his antagonist suffered the pinning of his hand, Clyde's foot transmogrified to spear the bother against Halcón's thewy back, continuing to pull up against his throat. The abominable cleric retaliated persistently only to be granted with further punishment as his wind was taken, distressed at the tearing of his neck muscles; the hiss of the tendons at friction with the hunter's chain, the sweltering aroma of the hollow enriched from spraying veins as they popped at the muscles' rend.

"Know that your child," he laughed gurgling, crimson mist ejecting from the force of his deepened wail, "by my own hate and salaciousness was stripped bare and her virgin body despoiled—she fought, but pitiful were her rejections! All the better, her mother was without protest; we tossed the girl from one to the other snuffing out her cries as we seeded her gob!"

Clyde bellowed thanatotic, crying thunderously as an avenging father: "I am the first disciple, and I shall be the Congregation's last!" Humiliating his downed prey; any other statement would not suffice. Jerking his chain the head of Halcón ascended with the carried spine dissevering through the nape first and then past the shoulder blades, arcs of blood trailing at the sides of the emerging column of bone. But Clyde balked from proceeding with the forethought execution by an unfamiliar sense or more notably a second conscious wresting all his focus, listening to the foreign counsel, attuning the presence, not of the Beast or him—he received a crumb of the overabundance of compassion this godhead held for him, and sought the Outset to be without further sin. He understood the suggestion but Halcón needed suffer no more, and chose dissension to better protect his child; Clyde failed to trust the Messiah and overlook the intention of a relationship this being yearned so heavily to have with his son.

In his confliction with Firmament's champion he found himself to be quickly immobilized, the staked hand sliding through the foot-blade snapped his injured leg to have the hunter tumble, and fall onto his knees. Clyde had grown tired, discouraged at how close he'd come to the eliminating the unsanctified church. Dying he then recalled Halcón's statement of having his body vessel for the Beast, and placed his eye to the obsidian throne. Exhausting all of his wind the hunter roared and with cannonade aimed at the obelisk only to have shredded the left shoulder and connecting breast of the mountainous sycophant guarding hunched, his minced particles caught in the zephyr of the hollow. In a trice Halcón burrowed his foot into the earth and sprung, his forepaw cocked, he released his backhanding against the apostate to have him flung before the steps of the throne, satisfied—given chills—at the crunching thwack from his strike.

Al Halcón falsely read his movements as unconscious, and sauntered across the chamber to meet his prone antagonist. Turning him over he found the hunter pathetically strive to keep his core as he weakly stabbed his blade between the great cat's ribs; all movement ceased with the core's slow emergence, Halcón's hand sliding out from his stomach catching the exit of his soul as his eyes stilled.

The cleric grabbed the collar of the hunter's corpse, and carried the cadaver upwards in his ascension upon the phallic construction, his coat shrugged from those terrific shoulders as it was torn to near ribbons. Standing now at the face of the throne he tossed the body slumped upon the seat, and raising his other hand began to carve the Keter onto the surface of Clyde's core—stooping, he gently returned the device within the intestine cavity. Indication of her corporeal resurrection starting, an initial wailing of his master emitted through the vocals of the corpse having Halcón petrified, until he stepped back in continued observation, witnessing the necromantic ritual.

The body convulsed with violent jerks of its head, its back undulating inward, the horrid retching leading to oil discharging from the mouth and sockets to drench her seat in the fluids was the result of the Beast's process of crossing planes, set permanently within this earthen form until a new death. It was sudden when the body stopped contorting, the present manifestations of possession yielding.

The neck tilting at a sideward angle she found her priest slinking, her bestial moans resonating throughout the chamber alerting Halcón she was efficacious in transferring her conscious. She adjusted to her decrepit body, becoming overborne with pain as every bone cracked and muscle throbbed, the slightest breeze against her open wounds left biting; nonetheless, she had her sights on the Ahmenseraï's return and disregarded her mortal aching for the Keter's eventual restoration—it'd be only temporary, she thought.

Unexpectedly white flares were summoned from out the mouth and eyes and all lacerations, ousting the howling spirit of Lucia from the body of his sought, as her mark was effectually removed. Clyde breathed new life, giving praise to the Messiah for another chance of redemption to which the Ahmenseraï's benevolence allowed. Halcón urged forward against the light with talons dug within the glassed steps, scraping to hold his crawl in resistance to the awesome push.

Before the extinguished Clyde could leave his seat, his estranged master siphoned the mysteries of the emanations through the obelisk and had him skinned. The man howled in anguish as his muscles exposed to the ozone scorched with a malicious sensation; finished with the plenty of fun she had with his torture the usurped—hampered—powers of the Almighty thereafter threw him to the obsidian pillar to be transported into an unwelcoming existence done with the belief the hunter would be without God's succor in the bowels of Abaddon.

Lucia hissed into the ear of Halcón: "Fera en quod Verumshaï prope; mea filia autem non vade sine a kavecca ko stabit!"

Fera and the Verumshaï near; my daughter will not go without a challenger so stand!

Halcón turned to face the chamber's threshold, raising himself from the steps.

XV

EXTINGUISHMENT

THENCEFORTH the land was tenfold more inhospitable; nowhere else within the Ravaja could contest for the callous temperature and windward gelidity of the tundra, not even the remotest valleys or chasms reminiscent of glacial undertakings, remaining scarce of all diets of animal, either omnivore or the lesser two. The petrichor of rainfall from the soils of the range, or the memory of it was forgotten from the ever-present cold enfolding all their senses. Tycho and Fera had crept into a depression set underneath a verglassed boulder, shielding the tremulous wayfarers from the death wind. Hungered and footsore the hole was appreciated for a momentary repose, but the former irritation demanded them to hunt, and the two would need a transport of flames if they were to leave spirited.

"If the Shine were in the state that it's in now, would I be here with you...?" she said, attempting to have her trouble known.

Tycho struck at the ground with a piece of flint, and aimed the sparks at a thickly root pulled out from the permafrost walls. "Sarkas, now you, huh?" he said, tired.

"I won't be another to reprimand, but understand that my life would have been lost if not for the Shine's mending; I would have gone to the grave without even a hair from Halcón's coat dissevered." Fera shook her head pained. "I just needed to get some of that off my chest."

"That's fine."

"I wasn't asking."

Tycho glanced at her. "Always with the attitude, woman."

"You shouldn't be one to talk."

Tycho continued his attempts at enflaming the root as Fera, preoccupied, studied their surrounding space.

"You don't seem in the least apologetic, so I'll come back to this at a later time. But I want to know what your deal was with that robed fellow?" She inquired calmly. "He upset you deeply; was it that he claimed falsely of who your actual father was? Did he mention Bill, at all?

"Unless you were mistaken for another, but I doubt this. You guys both have the Shine, which...is an eerie connection between the two of you, to say the least. I believed him to be a charlatan, although by fear I had this preconception, as with his sudden appearance at having you at his side fatigued, and an explanation to where your father would have you at this moment—and just who he was! It's just...odd."

"I don't need to talk about any of this. It has nothing to do with you, Fera."

"Aren't you being short." Fera embittered glanced at the whistling slit from whence they entered from. "Why are you being distant?" she questioned gravelly. "You've been *more* than willing to explain things to me, mysteries that are still beyond my understanding, and continue on in the topic to simplify it best as possible." The savage woman then falsely surmised Tycho had the same thoughts of preparation as she, having himself ready for the worst outcome if the Shine were to fail him.

Tycho sniffed. "I'm busy—"

"Busy?" She irksomely grinned. "I see where this is going." Fera nodded slow, now unwavering to her prior meditation given at the cenote. She analyzed his bloodstained poncho. "Too bad the stranger couldn't have been with us a little longer, eh, vaquero?"

Goaded the impassioned Tycho paused his kindling and upturned his eyes to be set on the wry expression of his companion. Fera was troubled at what she had said in retort, and followed ashamed: "Tycho, I don't know why I said that…"

The leaping sparks caught the root aflame, and he stood to face the slit. "Can't say I disagree."

Lucia provoked their most pathetic of emotions, so at the appointed time and setting her child would offer Tycho ceremoniously to the forthcoming godhead that was her mother—hatred, and felt abandon encouraging her spawn to be more than willing to betray her cared for vaquero. If not her, then another would complete the task. But Fera had begun to empower her desires for estrangement, so the Beast would have a foothold that could allow her manipulation to conquer her entirely.

Tycho had a sense the Beast furthered in her attempts to have them turn on one another evidenced from the Stranger's tale concerning Sarkas, and angered at the Shine, would rely on his own capabilities to handle an indomitable force that only fools unacquainted with the Ahmenseraï would strive to complete.

The fire began to burn close to his hand. "I miss Meseron, even more so Bill since she was one of the only few reminders, I had left of him. I know that's why she took him, to have me lured so far from home," he said, looking briefly at Fera, "and however the Stranger's master intends to use the old man I could care less for, I just want to see him again."

"I see you're more than willing to talk now," said Fera, crestfallen.

Tycho appeared to ignore her, and proceeded in a short upward climb to leave the hole. Once outside, the winds immediately blew out the flames and sent Tycho in retreat—he chuckled out of levity. He said as he descended onto the ground of the hollowed earth: "I was too impatient; we'll wait till night when the winds will have hopefully died down."

Fera was quiet for a moment, and asked, "Tycho, just so I know better, why does this woman want you dead?"

"Because I got some sort of special light that she doesn't have," he said lightheartedly, and then huffed, "the guy didn't really say much on why she wanted me dead, but if we're still to believe that Bill is to be sacrificed to empower this witch, then I got a feelin' that someone heard through the grapevine that he was Verumshaï—our officer friend had been misinformed on his identity, either by his own ignorance or someone else's agenda." The vaquero precisely observed; the officer tricked so that the triad may also be tricked that their fates be unknown.

"I wonder if this has anything to do with the Stranger's master." She conceived the probability of the personage whom the messenger spoke of being Tycho's father. "You said something about Verumshaï. What is that?"

The vaquero did his best to describe all that he still struggled to comprehend and Fera was caught intrigued and horror-filled at his expounding, and realized he'd been curt at his questioning because of his irritability and frustration for the tripartite of influences perceivably against him, furthermore proper molestation brought on his conscious for endangering Fera's life; he had enough guilt from Sarkas and the Beast's guise as the Spirit.

I don't believe his parentage is of this world, she thought. "Tycho, how did you end up on the Wasteland's fringes?"

"The memory is not mine to tell, it's well kept by the man who I was before. But I do remember, four years ago, awakening in Bill's presence. Since then, I've only known Sol Puesta to be home."

Fera confronted him in regards to his told discussion. "I think you should take the Stranger's advice."

His mind set against God the vaquero had trouble hearing what the savage woman had to say.

"What for…? You don't think I can—?"

"No, I don't. I don't know if I can either," she said, gazing at the ground before her. "It'd be better for you to have the Shine, so that we may both have the hope of living when facing against Halcón. Before I had the assurance of facing him alone, but with all that has been revealed these past few days I pity myself—but it has to be done."

Fera placed her eyes on him again, and said, "You're pride, it's damning you."

He saw through to her self-righteousness in her speech, but would not make the matter worse and held his tongue. Who was she to instruct him on forgiveness, he thought, her goal nonetheless to sate an avenging possession fueled by hate and self-fulfillment.

"You can't fight this alone. Have it so that you repent, and see at least what happens—"

"Nuh-uh." He waved his hand in admonishment. "I don't need to hear this from you."

"Then what are we to do?" asked Fera stern.

"To keep going; you'll have your kill and I'll return home with my compadre."

Fera's head shook in detestation. *He is a slave to his appetites.*

The night upon them they left their refuge and walked forevermore a distance until reaching the Summit, desperate to keep their warmth as they huddled near the torch. Fera closed at Tycho's side as he outstretched his arm to better light their path, their eye-lights effectually dimmed to conserve an internal heat—an emission of light would kill them. Disrupting their calm, the bloodcurdling howl of a starved vectra pervaded throughout the plain, heralding its initiated hunt, though its venture would end disastrously. Tycho and the woman abreast heard the patter of its footfalls as it neared after a quarter of an hour, the torch's brilliance resulting its squint to lessen in reflectivity as the full visage of the animal came to exposure, snarling mad with raised, quaking flews. The vectra does not devour any of a sapiens-hull but attacks the animate forms in instinct by its movements similar to other preyed anthropoids, boars and the like. They are fooled into having meat when they are only left with metal and oil.

At its first lunge, Tycho pushed Fera aside and waved his roaring torch as he reached for his gun. The wolf turning in a trice Tycho would have been apprehended if not for the savage woman brushing past him to stake the predator's head swiftly into the ground, and with a shrill, primitive cry she removed her blade.

"That's my girl," he said with enough wit to have Fera groan. "Give me your blade." He then knelt beside the twitching corpse.

"That dog is thinner than a twig," she said, slightly tilting her head up in disgust at its slain figure. "There's not enough meat there to even pick our teeth clean with its bones."

"We can always have the innards." Tycho drummed his hand on the side of its chest, looking back at her grinningly. It really was an atrophied beast.

The vaquero ascertained the wolf as abandoned, fairly young to be on its lonesome and this far out from regular vectra habitation; after a deep breath, he began his incision. Starting from the right of its underbelly Tycho slid her blade through the skin until it'd met its ribcage, welcomed to an exhaust of steam at the outpour of intestines and blood. Tycho handed Fera the torch and covered his mouth and nasal slits from the unfavorable stench, yet delighting in the warmth of the bodily emissions as he reached for the heart and other unrecognizable meats, coming severed at the blade's edge. He beckoned and dared for Fera to take the heart from him to eat, but she wouldn't have at his antics and told him off, the champion of Sol Puesta continuing to mock as he took his own bite from the organ and precipitously spat out his portion followed by several retches; Fera had a good laugh to which only he could seem to make her do.

Looking to find shelter for the night, ahead, was their discovery of foreign constructions contrasted in color to that of their backdrop. The Summit's silvery hue, tinges of moonlight added a finish to the contours of the decrepit, shadowed structures vast and countless. The torch's light began extinguishing, wavering enough to bring the two in haste towards the monolithic remains. The walls of these constructions, mirroring the opalescence of the castle doors, had Tycho undetermined if an entry was wise upon approach; but he took the initiative and entered against his instinctual perturbation. Fera was as wary or more, softly tugging at the tail of his poncho until realizing what she had done, immediately placing her hand at her side. For the fire that burned and would then die lit the chamber in contention with the dark, ultimately consumed by the eclipsing maw of Erebus. All was then cold.

Without other options, Tycho slashed open his arm and an outpour of oil ablaze settled on the floor. Fera speedily grabbed his wrist in objection to what he'd done, and turned the scar yet healed over the spilling of blood and fire to see perfectly his instance of self-mutilation. She scowled, taking back her blade and said, "What are you doing?! Your wounds, they don't heal as they used to! Just look at your slash, the Shine refuses to seal it closed, it leaps to your blood to escape you!"

Tycho jerked his hand out from her grasp and knelt over the fire to heal the slit forearm. "And what would you have liked me to have done? I was trying to find a way for us to survive the night. Hadn't figured the Shine would be actin' up like this." He internalized all fear at the strange behavior the Spirit exhibited; he intended to combust the spillage with his sealing wound.

Fera sat across from him, placed her amount of given meat over the fire, cutting it into slabs to have them skewered on the end of her sword, and hesitantly handed her blade back to the vaquero to roast his own meats, tilting its hilt upward from his grasp to tease the bot, showing the present semblance of distrust in him to use it appropriately. Tycho's expression was that of disinterest, chuckling at the eventuality of finding humor in her kidding. He gandered at the décor of their present inhabitation, slowly turning his meat over the fire as he closely studied the looming, disfigured shapes beyond the firelight's reach, seemingly bent and hunched against the walls. Gliding his eyes upward from the resting place of those subjugated to frostbite and starvation he found banners of allegiance for the Rahnthian Kingdom, flowing with a ripple from an outside breeze, and then past Fera an object of weaponry—the machine that won them the first war, the heaithan. The bipedal chassis had overwhelming success against the Anax but when used on the revolting peasantry their numbers outmatched the titan.

"A grim place to die," commented Fera, glancing once at Tycho before returning focus to perfect her rotisserie. A moment later she took a bite, and was satisfied.

What sounded like thunder permeated throughout the plain, preparing them for another storm. But the bellow had grown louder progressively, and the two discerned the welkin emission for an approaching airship. It was at the sudden collision of the vessel against the construction's roof that Tycho was galvanized to move, leaping onto his companion to have her spared, tackling her out the way. Tycho looking back to the headlong breach,—before landing on its backside,— the airship had made through the chamber walls found the creature bounding and flailing against ground as a formidable chain tethered it earthward. The vessel was made unconscious by its own wrestle, stupidly knocking the side of its head against the mountain's base to extricate itself from strangulation; an echo from the concussion boomed all through the wastes.

Staggering onto his feet, he grabbed Fera by the arm. "I wouldn't have spoken so soon if I was you." He coughed, as flakes of leathered, dispersed flesh infested his lungs.

Fera in her daze hadn't bothered to question the present encroachment, and saw for herself the situation. "By whose chain does that vessel fall prey to?" The savage woman inquired, looking out and past the decimation of several human constructions, though one an outpost for bygone Rahnthians. By the winning roar of the galleon's assailant, it rang familiar to her, belonging to the Outset she attempted to purge; her suspicions had been rewarded. Sarkas had lost the hunter's scent and battered the moth within those tunnels for information as to where Halcón might be, and chanced on an accurate telling of his domain, against the better knowledge she had of Congregation officers supplied only with thus. Her respect for the

Brussian diminished slightly, for he had upheld his word and brought them some distance before the Summit, and that is all that mattered. He told his white lie to further on in his fellowshipping venture lest they would leave him, wanting nothing more than family—the antithesis to his isolation. But prominently questionable, why was it the hunter Clyde and the grounded vessel had just arrived?

Leaving the compromised shelter from its breach they found the impressions of Clyde's footing left from his great strides, seeing that he'd skipped and jumped greatly to match the speed of the galleon ere casting both his chains about its throat, and yanking with concentrated strength to have the creature drift east towards the Summit in its descent—the surcease of his prints came with the galleon's crash before he regained his feet near the base of the mountain, as he was in flight. Shivering and plagued with gooseflesh the bots dispatched from the tracks and sprinted to where the mighty shadow of the creature lay at the grounds of Halcón's keep; the path of flattened ruins given by the ship's fall decisively taken in effort to shorten their time as they ran with renewed vigor to generate at least some form of heat, or the hope of its transpiring. "Come on, Fera," laughed Tycho midst the intake of cold slicing his throat, "can't have me showing you up now." He goaded her so that she might not fall behind.

Fera with a vexed, then playful sight, attempted to run ahead of him. The two chanced their mortality in their approach to the downed ship, but better their circumstances being housed for the night within the embosoming of the enemy's lower decks than suffer a fate similar to those of luminaries past. And since when have they not been risking their lives for such things pertaining to natural desire? Moreover, they knew if the hunter had business without recess after the dispatching of his church-brother,—more likely than not,—than sleep they would undoubtedly go without; they would need direction, a pathfinder, to follow stealthily into the mount. For Fera, it was the importance of having Halcón all to herself before Clyde could do anything about it.

Arriving at the tail of the galleon they heard cries from a tortured man, and the two slunk beside the twitching appendage until it stilled and the ground calmed. Peeking over the tapering end of its tail they saw the officer Lyle crawl forwardly from the vessel's capsized deck, his antagonist stalking closely behind with an ominous stride. Kneeling and gaining traction with his foot, Lyle hurriedly limped to a cleft marring the mountain's surface, looking behind to entertain the validity that he might have outrun his predator. The coward so consumed and enthralled with the matter of keeping his life, all other thoughts of Clyde's intentions were disregarded—the hunter had a plan, and would follow the scent spoor of his brother into the unknown crypts of *Titan Summit*.

"Lead me to him," he muttered to his own comprehension.

The hunter having trained his senses on the bandit for the totality of his hike taken from *Tartarus' Spire* would not have it where his trailing scent would go disrupted by a piquing, distracter of another's spoor losing the perchance location of Al Halcón. Seven hundred and thirty-two miles in nine days Clyde had undergone, without aid of a mount or transporting vessel he found his prize, the officer lounging secure in his cabin while the ship's beast spent its convalescence afloat in the waters of a subterranean hot spring, certainly closer to the Summit than expected; this irritated the Outset Lyle tremendously, but his vessel could not proceed but one more mile without giving, and he wouldn't leave it out of fear for Halcón's reprimanding, and abuse. At the ship's alerting bellow at his entry underground Clyde effectively revivified the fear of his presence within our servile friend after having faith he'd lost his pursuer. To dwarf the hunter only further at the galleon's uprise from the expanse sheathed in the cascades of its warmed contents, it started out, leaving the tunnel flooded aught from hampering Clyde's pursuit. There was no hope of escape now, as there wasn't any of having before, which inborn survival overwrote the officer's reason.

And now the hunter gone and companioned by the cleft's shadow they gave chase; the boy had hoped for slumber.

Moaning faint, and with a rumble, the cleft did more than envelope them with shadow; Tycho and the demigoddess borne of forebodings unbearable. The hunter's movements analyzed as beginning to slow Tycho handled Fera by the shoulder into a providential cavity, though a shallow opening, to apprehend any back glare that might be given. But the Outset Clyde did no such thing, until Fera's foot slipped against their shelter's slickened wall. He looked to his shoulder for a moment, continuing to move, and gave no further attention to the waning, unmatched interest. Quickly, the two stalkers emerged from cover and made deft footing in an attempt to recover adjacency with the driven predator free from suspicion. Presently standing on the shores on an underground lake at their exit from continual moonless black they squinted to see torches strewn along the scabrous woodwork of a rotten dock, unmoored of any ship since Lyle's had been the last—and none were without on transport, Halcón barren of vessels.

Afar they spied him having crossed the shore with an upward glower to the escalation of a lift reaching the throne room of the Summit passing chambers innumerable before the former, and, disregarding any further scrutiny, leapt to the supporting wall of the encaging shaft, scrabbling beastlike before launching from his foothold to tether his chain within the sizeable wooden board, consisting of fastened steel bands which leveraged his stricken clasp.

At the initial sight of this, though hardly discernible, Tycho took off with Fera shortly behind with an offensive wrinkling of her features given an imprecation was spoken beneath her breath. Upturning their heads to the leagues of vertical ascension formed by steel they found this aged, unsound frame of transportation evanesce with its image fading to dark, far too high for any conclusion to where it could possibly end. A long way out from the shore and dock lay an opening for a tunnel stretching wide, brimmed black with the most haunting voidance, where the felled galleon was steered not to undertake venture with Clyde's nipping at the heel; for the primary entrance to remain secure, and hoped to lead this hunter far from the cleric's abode returning at a later date once free of his burden, which would have been a plan if not for his grounding and caving to a final resort to keep his life at the expense of his master's betrayal. They felt its breeze and wished for the lift to hurry so they wouldn't have to endure anymore cold; their wishes would be meted unfavorably at the howling on high.

The hunter discovered, Lyle precipitously lashed his barbed chain through the steel frame of the shaft, catapulting with strained muscle from the tilting platform to the cragged periphery leading to Halcón's chamber, Clyde subdued from a tossing, crashing, and pounding platform unfastening the bolts from the supporting wall with its violent impacts within the encaging. Having been unhinged from its ascending course the lift was without direction as it made its way down the shaft frenziedly, but Clyde refused his quest end here, and tore his way through the crushing obstruction. At the beginning severance and bend of the shaft from the glistening wall of this mountain's interior the first disciple summoned his horned cannon, and ravaged through the platform with riddling gunfire permitting a liberating partition to be made. Busting his shoulder against the perforation of his blasts Clyde prospered in his sudden emancipation as the platform was seconds from impact, and proceeded to scale the wall at his clawing, making awesome leaps alongside its surface until stationing himself brief to see the wailing shaft fully separate from its intended position, colliding harshly onto the precipitous face of the other side. He resumed his climb.

Creaking at an insufferable pitch the two remained stilled on the lakefront in paralyzed apprehensions, their crevice of entry far from where they stood unwilling. Having been comprehensive of an annihilation coming swiftly they shook themselves out from inaction and regained their former strengths, Fera pulling Tycho firstly by his hand as she led the charge to the blackened corridor from where they came before. Presently the dilapidated shaft's center gave, the head and lower portion of the metalwork following in descent into the unfathomable heart of the waterbody conjuring some tidal wave they couldn't hope of evading; the mightiest of waves one would have borne witness to within the Ravaja. Consumed immediately, unkindly pricked by the dock's splintering upheaval, the two drifted unconscious.

Those lower chambers filled with the surging water, wherewith the merchandise within those spaces had drowned, and some not, came to the seizure of the mountainous wave. Remnants of the stockpile, the less than desirables not yet sold, compared to choicer hands, swam their way to the surface of the now receding waters from shore. Gasping for precious air from an arduous, and dizzying swim a select few rationalized they'd need means of floatation if they were to reach land, pulled so far out they bordered the tunnel's mouth. Ten breaststrokes to their left the collected individuals found an indistinguishable couple afloat, presumably dead, several feet from them half of the platform retaining buoyancy. Swallowing water as they tiredly swam, momentarily leaving behind those weeping haven chosen surrender to intrinsic, contemptible forces than fight on, approached and gripped onto the half-platform that could hold no more than seven men. Pushing the weighty board near the senseless Judean and woman two others that assisted moved about the wood and heaved the bodies onto the platform, themselves clambering onto its surface to perform resuscitations—they had a pulse!

Breathing anew the bots expelled all liquids from their formerly drowned lungs, coughing up their fill and slowly coming to their haunches. Tycho and Fera eyed each other before placing their focus on the goodwill peasants, thanking them. With enough strength mustered the two eased into the water beside the three men and helped push the board towards the lakefront, the vaquero having precaution set the Havoc on the platform's surface. Gliding past those who continued surviving fatigue they clung to the sides of the board knowing any embarking would submerge their refuge, seeing their numbers to what it could hold, far greater than seven, unlike the halfwits on the advance. Hurriedly they shoved their feet down onto their shoulders and head, drowning the once secured throng as they attempted mounting the craft with pathetic means of resistance. Tycho hollered loud and mighty, grabbing his piece before it'd be forever gone as the tilting platform raised to an incline from the horde, shooting a round from the Havoc skyward to warn all who boarded his tool of reaching Bill certainly, but, from the maelstrom of panicked bodies, none were concerned with the vaquero's antagonism, ignoring the petty cry of his gun compared to their lust for life. Forcing his hand down from the board's edge he leveled the craft on the water's surface once more, and unhesitating cast his fire into the shouting, pleading mass. Pulling himself onto the slippery woodcraft the champion of Sol Puesta persisted in firing at the tripping and now fumbling to water chattel, Fera hastily mounting behind in witness to this horror of horrors, frightened veritably she was unable to scold him. Succulent anger enthralling the hotheaded young man, he'd forgotten the alchemy behind his gunfire, unruly electrical arcs bounding from the surface of the lake and bodies afloat. He looked behind to see his rescuers lifeless, charred. Tycho weakly stumbled onto his breech, and digested all that he'd done.

Mourning, the recession of the Spirit palpable, grieving with his elected host, withered in power as it had been snuffed; the righteous fire quenched hadn't gone unnoticed, Tycho aching for the counselor—his best, and most amiable companion—to remain present. But it could not, beneficially stored alongside his soul within that abomination of a human vessel it would lay dormant until the Ahmenseraï found his child yearning for the relationship he intended for them to have before creation's start.

"One, not one, had you considered deserving of mercy..."

Without the sword that was the Spirit to defend the vaquero, easier now than ever unquestionably, the omnimalevolent witch initiated the smuir of his mind with guilt unending; mighty was his sorrow for disregarding Bill's mentoring so precipitously! And those adrift, how were they any different than his neighbors back home, would they too not have already been enchained if not for their guardian? He was to protect all denizens of oppression, evidenced at his heroics for deliverance heretofore, pertaining not to Tycho's incident where he was unknowing of the saurian captives that leveraged Sarkas' point. And his mentor, what would he think of him now? The old man would be disgusted at his butchery, such impulse; sickening incompetence! Tycho's anger was most profound and unquenchable, love for his fatherly one second, if not last in pathetic strength and drive, and now he would be discontinued of Bill's affection, holding fast to this lie.

Subjugated to mind the Beast's tongue he adhered unquestioningly to the fear she provoked from within him, and soon concluded that never would Bill have him come so far as to disappoint, and become the man he taught him never to be, a brute—no better than an ideologue enlisted to the fortunes, and lies of the Congregation that his mentor once held great zeal for; to this, the vaquero was without knowledge of until that time they'd meet once more, where joy would be displaced by unimaginable horror.

"Sarkas' words hold true," she said with an unsmiling expression, eyeing the scene about. "Your purpose is to kill, nothing more—even the meek are given unto your bloodshed; none, are to be spared."

"If it wasn't for what I did," said Tycho, troubled at providing extenuation for his killing, "then we all would have drowned."

"All?" she said, mastering her trembling tone. "There is only you, and me that remains unscathed and without massacre by your hand. You have no defense."

Tycho picked himself up, and turned to face her.

"No, but I do, woman. I'm here for Bill—no one, or nothing else should even be a consideration of my concern. You've only stuck around this long for your need of direction and security finding Halcón, and now you've reached his domain, all because of me." He felt complete abandon of the Shine, and spoke what his hardened heart willed.

"And who are you to judge, Fera?" the vaquero continued. "From what the officer spoke at the Spire, I've never cared for all the terrible things you did, that is, until now anyway. Could've sworn he said something about you taking the lives—"

"There's not a day that goes by that I don't regret what I've done." Her agitated face issuing a sign she fought an upwelling of tears. "Also, I'd rather you not bullcrap me on the virtuousness you claim to have in persevering all for the sake of Bill's well-being. Sarkas, and I, know who you are, coward—one who isn't honest with himself, rather than be overjoyed in having Bill's assured safety he'd rather satiate an unending revenge, to which I can admit is my only dedication! How many bodies do you see here, Tycho…*How many?*" she growled, placing emphasis on the two words last. "One down would have had their attention, as it did, but you wanted more. Could you not see them plead frightened through that murderous haze of yours, Tycho?" She came close to shouting, but recalled how well the vaquero reacted the last time he'd been severely belabored.

He knew she was right from the beginning, and was only fighting against her to lessen the hate he had for himself—something new, never felt before in this potency, having him ascertain his situation as compromised but revealing. Presently conscious the Beast was puppeteering conflict between the two, finding their emotions,—thoughts, and speech,—had been finely manipulated by the mother of lies, and destruction, seeking whom she may devour at her daughter's hand, and if Halcón is to be slain by the princess of darkness, she would handle the vaquero with the severest rage, discovering his sparing perceived as treason he'd have for her in battle with the mammalian despot; but failure to do so, on Fera's part, the boy would have to face against a challenge so unwelcoming that betrayal would be his contemplation.

Free-will and unexpected actions pertaining to the heart the Beast took into consideration, and laid out more than one avenue for the persons concerning her agenda to take if one were to intercede another's course and change the outcome she saw planned out for them firstly, influencing that person's decision onto those other paths she'd put forth for the man to trod. But, there was the apostate where her disregard for him was her downfall.

The soothsayer she was Lucia saw all probabilities, and with Clyde the variable of the lowest percentile given suicide the foretold killer before his entry at the Spire she'd find his presence the most detested and astonishing, having overcome past traumas set on repeat, playing over and over and over again until a blade placed at his forearm's underside was his only foreseeable plan of nirvana; the disciple found strength in the fleeting instinct to carry onward, perseverance cemented permanently from thought of the Lord granting him forgiveness one day, consequently diminishing all fates chaining him to destruction from faith of his eventual deliverance. This unpredicted factor undermining God's love for man she failed to prepare enough routes from the start for the Verumshaï to take where godhood would be easily achieved, in confidence the percentage of laughable recognition of the hunter's coming would ever surface. For no other reason was there to act at *Tartarus' Spire* the way she had, in her assault towards the boy where her daughter was to plunge her sword deep into the Verumshaï's core at a later setting if not for her father's interference, testing Clyde to assess if he'd do her bidding from the hidden, and contested longing he had for her; but there had never been a fate prognosticated where Clyde submitted, the resolute of this hunter kept unwavering. So the witch acted out of desperation to slay the Verumshaï to bring about a premature reclamation of the elect, failing, with an unequipped vessel ill-prepared to face her adversary.

Compromising all her work and foundations in fear of being devoid of the final emanation she critiqued herself thoroughly, having been uncontrolled and mad, not fit for an omnipresence as herself, and would have punishment self-inflicted upon her soul; she needed to adhere to careful planning and cunning. And Tycho, enlightened from his brother the nature of the Beast reminded himself again of her influence over the mortal world and its inhabitants, attempting not to fall prey to Lucia's traps when knowingly doing so as his argument with Fera continued on, for he was without counsel and peace of mind with the Shine hampered indefinitely. He was weak, and no matter the effort to conquer stirred feelings of the pettiest degree they overruled his volition to settle their dispute.

Tearing off a thick sheet of wood from the surface of the platform Tycho began oaring as Fera did similar, and discovered the guilt and anxieties wrought from his mind had been at the influence of Lucia— the Shine, never had it been against him as all its supposed vices had remained. But Tycho wasn't all correct, as were the words recalled of Onesimus Veritros, the Stranger, misinterpreted. The Shine had convicted him of sin many times, but Lucia made it overbearing for the vaquero to consider facing the Lord in prayer, completely ignoring all the faults of his trespasses towards him; remorse needed for the repentance of sins, Tycho could not stand the sorrow and blame, resenting the granter of the hallowed Spirit, as the Ahmenseraï grieved for a time before having back his son. Returning to the lakefront the two held no conversation except for few words concerning their stepping along the bent foundation of the shaft leading to the lowest chamber's threshold, Fera now given entirely to the thought of estranging Tycho, who spoke with sickening pride and justification evidenced at the carnal satisfaction of his slaughter, would not allow herself to be weakened again; and in this her mother reveled. Further, the death of those peasant men without even a sign of wrongdoing than sitting ignited a terrible rage within that she couldn't hope to extinguish, at an allegiance with indescribable loathing for the vaquero. She was convinced that he never cared for her being or Sarkas', but this was far from the truth; the lack of his understanding for mortality and guilt-allergen prevented Tycho from maturation, carrying on with ignorance and an attitude cocksure towards life. He was without comprehension of his loved ones or himself ever becoming deceased granted the Shine's avail, currently dormant.

At denial with his scienter, Tycho sulked. Up to now, his life's purpose was to secure his town residents of bandit's performing similar to what he had done, and cognizant of guilt issued from the Beast he did his best, arguably feeble, to prevent thoughts of Bill having him an outcast.

Entering the hollow any spoor of perspiration, or defecation, was gone from the panicked mass as result from the flooding; rows of barbed, domed cages found uprooted or tangled about the victims they whilom contained. Lining the glistening walls and on them had been many weaved huts, few intact, inhumane wiry cocoons stationed vertically to the hundreds similar on ground venturing an indeterminable depth within the chamber indicating a stairwell from the inconsistency in its continuation. Proceeding through puddles the man and woman trudged heartsore, Fera, after long observation of the calamitous scene placed her scrutiny on the leading vaquero seeing him so much as without a single batting of his eye on the awfulness about him, and judged according to her training of thought that he was without reflection. Instantaneously the engendering of a question was brought conscious, amassing from their time spent within the Summit's base.

"The Congregation," said Fera. "Where are any of her legions?"

"Remember what you told me, Fera. Think back to that."

Then, the idea came to her. "Only officers of the church are allowed here, or any such knowledge of the place. Where then, where do the cutthroats stay?" She plucked out a splinter from her arm.

"There was Duranché, for many it was their home from what I came across. Crest View no different, I'm sure there are settlements out there under the cult's occupation."

"Knowing those debauchers, I'm sure they had slaves to screw days and nights on end, no doubt forgotten—left for dead, killed midst some disagreement or heated exchange for the whereabouts of one not so different from the rest of them."

Tycho looked to his shoulder but said nothing, a menacing scowl matching the woman's. Tycho cared much for the impoverished, perhaps more than the impression Fera left on him of her own endearment for her caste, hypocritically would never bathe joyfully in the blood of the undefended as she; he'd only lost his temper and was carried away, enjoyed naught that came from his murdering. And further in his defense, made for an impartial cause and nothing more, the two equal in their evils, saved one made as a hostage at his questioning within the Duranché saloon, moreover had limited control over what happened to those in the crossfire. Had Tycho set aside his pride and admitted to Fera his internal suffer and warring than she'd discard any hate transpired for him, but the present and lingering power of darkness was inscrutable—an invisible negativity drawn out from her subjects!—and continued to play them.

Standing before the stairwell after some walking avoiding eyes on the drowned encaged Tycho started his upward steps for his eye-lights to uncover the honeycombed roofing of a derelict station, without perception of what it could accurately be. Having restrained his stepping to a conservative pace at first hastened by excited curiousness, the two leveled onto the boarding platform, and at their initial inquisitiveness, they tried to reason for the railway prolonging into the cave to their far-right. Much like the found station beneath Crest View, Tycho and Fera were quick-witted to uncover the intentions of the terminal's purpose.

"No engine or handcar in sight…"

From behind, Tycho heard her scuffle, and watched her approach an elevated chamber on the platform able to be housed within the woebegone station, glass surrounding, it sat westerly against the endwall, and was stricken with recollection to where he first laid his sights on the officer and his corpulent warden. This station laid between the first chamber and the second, several hundred more comparable at their own intervals overhead, an officer following procedure when moving newly acquired hands traversed the former sending merchandise up the stairs to be sent to those chambers yet full.

Fera then began pressing a number of buttons with inactive responses on the foreign panel, and trying rust-locked levers to her surmising she unceasingly kept at the mechanisms until she was rewarded for her efforts; one would give eventually, disregarding the key needed to unlock operational functions for most of the panel, and who's to say that lever would summon any locomotive? Fera persisted against the odds.

The sought train formerly purposed to transport humans within the mountain's confines of researching celestial anomalies heightened come Judgment Day had been adapted to an all-new cause without so much a vastly different function, shipments worth of chattel prodded and pushed into its cars without benefit of seats as all of them had been stripped out for fitting the most supply of chattel as best they could with the space given, the inner chambers of the Summit holding settlements-worth of men handled no differently, removing all ancestral assets of observatory study by command of Halcón given dictation unto him from the Beast as the outer chambers furnished to equip an appropriate lobby for sitting had been done away with too, to fit all merchandise beyond conception. The mountain's train had become valued tremendously as the Congregation grew to prominence and dependency in thrall trades; the Wasteland's tyrant and his officers finding success of easy inventory management at the internal constructions of *Titan Summit*, and replicated those features they found most beneficial into those other holds placed throughout the Aberican west coast as the mountain became replete, with the exception of the fossilized prison,—nevertheless credited for the origination of the subterranean railway,—the vaquero compromised of secrecy.

Leaning on the threshold of the control room Tycho watched the savage woman struggle with the fifth lever, smirking at her overexerting attempts to have the device shift. Bothered by a presence in her peripheral sight Fera looked over to him sour, signing he should leave. Smug, Tycho reached his hand over to the panel, and before he laid his fingers upon it, Fera groaned and was chagrined. The vaquero turned the shadowed key, and the lever burdened with the woman's force shot downward to the pull, Fera stumbling slightly before catching her balance. The panel suddenly alit and the crown of the railroad calmly pulsating azure light, signaling its arrival would be short, she chanced on the proper lever that would deliver them a means of transportation; for the last four she pulled became inoperable. Fera tried to repress her feeling of embarrassment.

Pleasantly a resounding hum than the screeching wheels of an engine at its retiring perplexed them, but welcomed the change. The opalescent sheen of the car's facing side dematerialized into a filmy barrier of light permitting boarding, as indicated by the methodical flashes from both the left and right sides of the entryway.

"Get on," she said, with graveled tone.

"Being the gentleman that I am"—Tycho then gestured with his hands for her to board—"ladies first. Then again, you're not much of one." A spiteful grin played about his lips.

She wasn't scarce of having vexations for the weariful vaquero at the bludgeoning from his quick tongue, tired of having to constantly contest with equal or lesser wit—though there were times where she found amusement in the banter she'd become sick of it after it was revealed to her that he was nothing more than scum, and her energy should be spent elsewhere in thought of leaving him to die before he could do similar encountering Halcón. So, she boarded without remark.

The oddity that was the craft of the wall returned with the man and woman now onboard, molested from petulant odors evidenced from the fecal encrusted floor, what was left to conjecture a fellow long deceased before his form preserved by the diarrheal release of standing chattel. Nauseous her eyes rolled back and out from her throat came a spraying torrent of white mingled with washed red from their previous meal. Tycho having genuine concern for his companion wrestled with the inclination to aid her however possible, resisting to issue the common inquiry so brain-dead as "Are you okay?" that clear observation could present that she wasn't; he was thankful that her spew hadn't prolonged, having to listen to the unremitting splashes and guttural heaves.

Wiping the stringing dribble from her lip Fera rose from her hunch where she directed her discharge toward the side of the car, and proceeded forward until Tycho called after her. He showed her with pointing his thumb behind at the driver's compartment at their rear before entering; she turned slowly, and started her shuffle back; she was relieved, untold cars needed to be traversed which imagining if any were crueler in scenery would have her shuddering, or worse. Setting herself behind Tycho within the compartment she heard a voice disembodied, the vaquero having a natural dialogue with this specter that the woman was unsure how to approach the situation with all rationale. She peered around the room, from the walls reflecting her eye-lights to the broad, glaring window that she hadn't seen before on the machine's exterior—small, microscopic tubes allowing intake of light prominently from the searchlights outside to screen a mirrored image at what lay before the tracks filtered onto the facing glass giving discerning view to whomever the engineer.

Still in subtle disbelief as to the discourse continuing between Tycho and the specter, she asked, "Tycho, who's talking? I don't—"

"I'm sorry, sir," the soft elegance of her speech minimizing the vaquero's aggression, "but to access the menu an override command is required; without an override any engineer or corresponding personnel is to comply with the autonomy of the train's intelligence and guidance system. Now, will this evening's travel take us to Copernicus' study or Bacon's study?"

"Wherever Halcón is."

"Halcón?" she asked. "I'm sorry, could you repeat that? Did you say Azael's study or Barbatos' study?"

Tycho's irritable expression had only intensified. "The highest chamber this place's got."

"Metatron's Equatorial Room. That will take seven minutes, I recommend Brahe Station—the estimation of your arrival from there should be a decisecond."

"Would Brahe Station happen to be nearest the mountain's top?"

"Correct—"

"Yea, figured much. Just take us to megatons', seven minutes ain't gonna do us much harm." Tycho took the liberty to place his hind within the engineer's chair, and recline, shifting his hat's brim over his eyes just before he clasped his hands behind his head feigning rest. Fera took the open seat next to him, disturbed. Rather than hearing words speak from one's lips or emitted from a speaker that they would not have been able to comprehend regardless the voice had been that of an audible hallucination, or alike to the phenomenon; telepathic electric communication from the machine's intelligence, the two ignorant speaking with their tongues, although Tycho having familiar experience of exchange with one ere. Those stepping into the driver's compartment were opened to the intruding intelligence; Fera read as a potential copilot was included in the conversation.

"Checking if any other trains are en route—Perfect, our travel ensured safe let's be off."

As its departure began the window to the outside gradually vanished as the searchlights on the opposite end had turned on, before the driver's compartment they now resided in was the head of the train presently had its use reserved until the engine would board this station again at a later time. For those seven minutes prolonged into what felt like hours, doom and ruin devitalizing their spirits, Tycho kept his composed façade and the young woman picturing her blade against her prey's throat was intruded by other thoughts of her own dismemberment and longing for death torture, so unbearably wicked that Fera had almost caught herself in a panic wanting to retreat. But she calmed and breathed easy, letting out an extended breath—eyes closed; she would continue on in the methodical respiration. The vaquero glanced at her with a half-shut eye contemplating his fated reunion with his mentor, becoming ill. Their ride undisturbed they busied their minds with worries and what if's, seldom if ever a word came out from them; there was strength to be had in each other but pride and hatred blotted any resolution between the two, the fools.

The train at its stop the two uneasily left from their seats, and exited the car. Stationed across onto another railway some feet away from the train last used by the officer, Tycho and Fera picked up their pace and circuitously went about the engine and onto the platform with a hop, and now finding themselves at the threshold to the corridor leading to Halcón's abode there was hesitance, sweating palms, and a dryness of the mouth. Fera could see the drumming of her shirt as her stomach throbbed against the cotton with the pounding of her core. And within the temple and chosen soul of the Lord, benefitted by his mercy, his Spirit had Tycho panged and his conscience weighed, the evocation of the Spirit felt in his chest filling Tycho with a sense of the Ahmenseraï's love for him, a yearning amore he'd forgotten continuing in sin unrepentant—disobedient to counseling that was never deserved but gifted!—urging him to seek forgiveness so that no longer would there be a severance between them. But temperamental was the boy and found this sudden comfort an affront; where had this pining been when Meseron died, or at the coarseness of his messenger picking him apart, he thought, unsuccessful to remind properly that he was cared for by their God, evidenced by the Shine's nature. Although the Spirit putting his messenger in place Tycho failed to discern the influenced speech granted by another.

Felt abandoned by the Shine to please its master, comprehensively its own being, the primordial portion of his brain caring not seeing it only as duplicity, Tycho disregarded the sudden pang out of hurt than confidence that he'd live without the Holy Ghost. He knew it strung at his heart presently for death certain—anger overruled, and the vaquero, whipping out the Havoc's chamber out from its slot, had the intention of proceeding onward. Those azure spikes sputtering volatile and bright, claiming his attention he saw from his periphery Fera amble down the corridor until he had enough staring down the barrel of his gun, and forged his path through the dark after her.

XVI

AGAINST PRINCIPALITIES

T
HE corridor formerly silent, the lasting echo of one's wail had them shiver, the boy fearful that it may have come from his mentor unthinking; he realized after giving it thought that the cry was far too bestial. Later, a howl boomed throughout the corridor, sounding more terrible than the cry given before, quickening the feet of these wayfarers toward the chamber anticipating, Fera grievingly, that Clyde was successful in the hunt. But as they exited from the shadows into moonlight, and looked upon the looming giant as if sculpted to the steps leading to the obsidian throne, they could see no hunter but the ossified blade remnant of his attempting to slay.

Sensitive to the vibrations of the shaggy fellow's growl insofar as to rumble about in their chests, his face, and defined form, was hidden from them until his descent from those steps had been made. The great cat's hide shook and jounced at his advance downward, their eyes locked on his stained teeth and chin. So much alike to other night-dwelling carnivores, his crimson-glossed fangs gave further credence to this comparison, but, to their ignorance, from a severed tongue than a proud kill. At the base of his throne as to where moonlight had progressively made its shift, greeted with drawn swords and leveled aim from the vaquero's Havoc he started forward again, and then crouched, coming onto all fours; he pounced instantly that the arising question from the boy in regards to his mentor had been stifled at the sight of the harrowing, fleeting visage of the soaring beast who's snout wrinkled into several folds scarcely blinding this king of thieves left with only a sliver of sight to apprehend his foe, roaring mightily!

Enduring a reactionary bolt from the vaquero Al Halcón grinded to a halt on the soles of his feet where his fist presently made contact with Tycho's stomach, having him tumble backwards onto his knees gasping for breath. "I thought of you being stronger, Judean. Has your god actually forsaken the last of his claimed?" His throat rumbled with the deepest growl, brushing the flames off from his scorched hide. Suffering from an inexperienced pain pertaining to his physicality Tycho was without speech, focusing on regaining his taken wind as he choked, and spat dribbling blood from his mouth. If Tycho had allowed the Shine to work within him, then his life would remain unthreatened—now he faced death as a mortal.

From his posterior Halcón heard the woman. As she'd done similar with those saurian harlots Fera slid onto her shins from behind the attentive brute, gliding through his legs avoiding his talons, and forcefully slashed her blades upwards through his paunch to disembowel her most anticipated prey. Halcón fell onto his forepaws, having to hold one over the spilling gash in an ill-attempt to retain his other organs before the Keter taking into effect, struggling to store his intestine back inside his gut as it constantly would slip out from his hand. Fera followed her first assault, and sprinted to have his head staked to the glassed floor but with the mark Halcón recovered shortly, and thrusting out his arm to capture Fera mid-flight, her head rounded perfectly to fit within that merciless paw grounded her to the earth before tossing her aside, saying: "I wish to have you last, begone!"

"Bill Pyron," Tycho began weakly, coughing, "tell me where you've put him."

Halcón stumbled onto his feet, keeping his head lowered. "He is gone, nowhere here."

Tycho first taken aback at Halcón's remarkable recovery recalled the flickering, violet light he saw emitting from the giant's backside, and reasoned, surely, that this brute too had been branded with the mark that adorned the creature's forehead and the bandana of that thief. Slowly, he looked over to Fera struggling to raise her body from the ground as she ached all over, groaning and gnashing her teeth in her trials to stand again.

"Had you known her intended purpose, why she was brought here alongside, then you wouldn't even spare a glance in that woman's direction."

Tycho rolled his head down, breathing faint and difficult.

The knees of the tousle-haired giant popping Halcón crouched before his subject, and placed a talon underneath the vaquero's bottom jaw with enough pressure to have his head arise so that his challenging, sapphire eyes could gaze into orbs of bold vermilion, securing all his attention. "We have been left for dead, Judean, by both our gods. The carving on my flesh is nothing now than a seal to be broken, my death as an invitation for the woman to take her mother's place on that throne; and what of you? Had you any brains you'd muster the intelligence that Bill was nothing more than to be used as a lure, the Zealot of my master, and your fallen brother, failing to have you captured—you were to have the Spirit quenched by then, what happened, boy?" Halcón redirected his gaze toward him as his head began to avert.

"It's not against the Ahmenseraï's nature to interfere in the probabilities of some, perhaps he allowed further leniency up until this point of hoping his son repentant. But praise he be without, he has left his child undelivered—so repent, and pay the tax that keeps the Spirit burning, burning evermore." His mocking tone contorted Tycho's features.

"Is that how you understand it," said Tycho, chortling dismissively, "as some *tax*? From what I've been told, it doesn't exactly work the same as giving tithes to some church. Was there any fun blackmailing those devout several years ago seeking absolution, paying their way into heaven, learning their secrets?"

"If he expects payment from the confessing soul, to have worship—to be praised," said Halcón, drawing his face closer, "is that not giving something in return, is the Spirit a gift at all?" Persuading the vaquero into thinking otherwise, Halcón knew of his lies but Tycho, currently antagonistic towards the Lord and all his faculties of being. Forgiveness sought there would be no deception for the vaquero to handle and failure to discern Halcón's speech as manipulation, playing to his emotions and ignorance of his gracious Father's intentions that, had he lived according to the will of the Spirit, would know the essence of his redeemer yearns to stand right before God, to make the man in which he indwells blameless; for the Lord cannot be in the constant presence of sin and insulting rebellion, which the Spirit of sonship urges the chosen man to be without, to be in the image of his Father.

"And what concern is that of yours, Halcón?" said Tycho, slowly reaching for his gun, swallowing painstakingly as for the talon's edge to not puncture the throat it chafed.

"It's not, but it sure as hell should be yours," and within the instance of Tycho raising the Havoc to secure a blow within the open sore where his hide had caught aflame Al Halcón grabbed his arm, laid him onto the ground with an impactful swing from his limb, then standing, followed with a savage kick into his chest leaving him breathless and tumbling far.

"I will have nothing to do with your death, child of God. But by this mark, I am bound in eternal service to my master Lucia Rothschild, and I will do what must be done."

As Tycho weakly began to sit up looking back at his abuser Halcón had already crossed his way over to him, throwing back his arm he released the mighty swing of his paw onto the face of the vaquero to have his eye and upper lip slashed. The boy was in insurmountable pain, wailing uncharacteristically deserving some pity from the brute. If he wanted, his head would be off, but obedience to his master as to provoke the girl whom he hated without rival was his goal, Tycho's end to be performed as Lucia envisioned. Halcón grinned, turning his head to his shoulder to spy Fera bothered; he figured, after prepped for coffining and the boy's demise Lucia would take her daughter as vessel having given herself completely over to her, the struggle to have her sit on that throne would be without challenge.

Fera consumed with unadulterated detestation for Tycho panicked—a remnant, or, dormant love for her friend upset her greatly seeing him pained. She thought she hated him, from all that she could gather reasonably and feeling as to why, but emotions never simple they conflicted against one another until one would prove dominant. Shaking as she stood with mustered strength she continued to watch Halcón beat the bot who was unwilling to lie down, and accept defeat amidst the cries he emitted now hushed as all of his face had numbed. Repeating in her head, *Die, die, die,* she could not escape the passion to see him live! So, she trudged forward, until coming into a full sprint with her blades angled down. An engine of visceral agency it was not surprising she disregarded her meditation, or had it on the backburner. Arguably, she became all the more lethal.

Slicing through his heel Halcón collapsed immediately onto his knee, Fera subsequently ramming both her blades into his backside hoping to sever whatever the mark was that kept him imperishable, noting its reactionary light to the thief's disembowelment. Before she could completely rake her blades through his bristling hide Halcón elbowed the savage woman in the mouth, Fera quick to retrieve balance as she watched him stand with a fulminating Keter. Lips soaked with blood she came to a hunched stance, readying her blades for Al Halcón's approach.

Turning, a smile played on the great cat's lips, anticipating fervently for this moment to maim and destroy the woman, his eyes scanning the ground before having them raised, and now he began to growl and then roar terribly preliminary in his charge against her. Extending his already bared talons, they lengthened to kill than scar.

With one press of his foot into the earth Halcón met Fera's stance, his claws hissing sharply as they clashed alongside her crossed blades for shielding, pressing on his assault sparks flooded amongst their feet. The more Halcón dismantled and jarred her defenses, her blades vibrating harsh that her hands blistered, she was inclined to gasp and stifle whimpering. With a deep, earsplitting roar emitted from the Beast's pawn, Halcón lunged as soon as her swords uncrossed, tackling her to the earth while Fera howled nightmarishly believing her end had come. It would have, if not for her poking her blade into his eye desperate for release, the chomping of his teeth put to rest Fera having staked her tool further into the brute's skull where his brain had been fully split. Fera clawed herself out from underneath his corpse with lungs scarce emptied.

Crying hoarsened as she retrieved breath, inhaling then exhaling rapidly, she lumbered over to the giant's side in preparation to sever the mark ere reanimation could begin. But, before even gaining the thought to clamber onto Al Halcón's back to remove the Keter, it had activated without a moment to spare. The chamber walls and eyes of the Beast's daughter became dazzled by its light once more.

"No, no!" said Fera, deeply upset she raced to have the mark gone but Halcón had already started to rise, pounding his forepaw onto the stone surface, the wretched light piercing Fera's gaze that it was hard to advance further without leaving herself vulnerable blind and all. Indicating the light gone from her shielding eyelids she opened them to find her mighty challenger at face with her, pulling the blade effortlessly out from his eye as it were no more than a splinter. Tossing the blade before her, he said, "A fight for the throne, let it be fair."

Fera found the humor in his words having been accursed with the mark of the Beast, but instead of responding hastily she inquired, "I would never find myself at the Congregation's helm, is that what you think I am here for? By your hand, you forced my own against my brother's throat, and now you will suffer the fate you inflicted upon him, once I have that scarring removed from your back!"

"Rather, you'd avenge a brother not even of blood than usurp the very power that rivals that of Rahnth. Come close, woman, so that I may end you now—you have no place here."

"No, I have every right."

"More than you know," he murmured, "more than I am willing to admit."

Again, his snout becoming creased into countless folds leaving his fangs to be unsheathed her game charged with hope of having her torso torn from the pelvis' wide foundation, sinking his teeth into her side prior shaking her mad as those baser ancestors of his found to be effective in slaying their prey; thereafter, Halcón would snap his jaws and leave her in two.

Fera horror-filled at seeing his jaws near to closing about her side, so quick was this action that if it weren't for Fera's tempered reactionary times that any other in her place would surrender unwillingly to those great fangs, she evaded nimbly, and so, Fera known as the savage one, held out her blade as quick as she had sidestepped and allowed Halcón's body of momentum to work its glide through the sword, relishing the sound from the outpour of his stomach and torso. Having pathetically collapsed onto the ground, Halcón hurried to pick himself up all the while the Keter screeched and vomited out light.

"That mark, whatever it is…it's made you careless."

Halcón punched the earth as he struggled to place himself back onto his feet. "Keep your mouth shut, sow! I will not have some bastard child lecture me. Michael, your brother," he uttered deeply, "his slaying was your inauguration into becoming the woman that you are only a fraction of this day; he was nothing—!"

Fera moved her tongue along the soused blade. "To me," she said, gutturally, "he was everything. Never had he abandoned, like our father and mother when they offered us to your cult to have their own lives spared."

"No different from the man that gave you life, those two—sad." Halcón sneered.

Fera turned. "Talk, Halcón. Who is it you speak about?" Her tone revealed confidence she hadn't of before. She wasn't invested in her question, but Halcón revitalized her spirits of having him slain had been but momentarily quenched, and would rather not squander with what her setting presented something of value to obtain, if any. Had the Keter not healed with rapidity and remarkable success, Fera would have approached the wounded Halcón, and ceased him of life. But, she'd settle with talk until the time had come to rid him of the mark, when the chance revealed itself.

"I heard bellows; someone in pain; Clyde, where is he, and his hunted?"

Ere, her eyes were fastened on Al Halcón's presence accentuated all the more by shifting moonlight, and failed—having little to no interest in anything else besides her quarry—to study her surroundings that would have already given her an answer, or a portion of it. At her side where Halcón had slowly steered his eyes from the mass, then to her, Fera picked up on the indicating glare and remained staunched on keeping her focus on the tricky brute whom she analyzed to have her look, her head turn to the corpse presenting a valuable opening for him to use, and strike her down with ease. She knew better than to keep him unattended, with eyes ablaze exhibiting the wrought of her soul from years of loathing him, it was silly to think they'd wander from the object of their most detested.

"That is what's left of him?"

"Of his church-brother, yes," said Halcón. "But Clyde, his abode is in the space of Abaddon—hellfire."

Halcón studied her face, seeing her expressionless. "Your father, in the end, came here for you, woman," he said, snarling. "To keep you from that throne—afraid, that you'd become akin to the Beast, that is your mother."

Fera could not have reacted any other way than deadpan, for the incredulous nature of Halcón's words were baffling to any reasonable man, the idea further protested by her that she'd have the remotest ancestral ties to the Congregation, whom she had a sworn hatred for, was unacceptable! And the ichor of a goddess running through her veins, doubtless a satanic mystique, was hard to swallow; but Fera, no longer a virgin, as the rest of the world senseless, to the sight and manifestations of the metaphysical could not be so disregarding to protect her sanity from the truth bestowed onto her from an assailant seemingly unlikely to reveal her identity in this amount of potency, and impartiality. She was, but would be no longer, ignorant to the fact that Halcón himself served under a master, and was bade to act according to what the Beast willed.

"No," she said, sorrowful. "I will not listen to anymore of this."

"Clyde Joseph Volkov, deserter of the faith, and his family. This is not a man, but a coward, and your refusal to accept the truth of your quality of godhood is an assurance of the trait being passed on from him, to you." He intended maliciousness.

Knowing of her adoption, this truth disputed only terrified than entertain the fantasy of her parentage. "I said I will listen to no more of this nonsense—!" she cried.

Halcón resumed speaking, disregarding the woman's interruption. "You will, you will keep those ears open, and listen to what I have been told to tell you. Fera, Fera," said he, "for this moment you've been trained to take me out, to grow strong, been molded into the likeness of your mother. But, you are half the woman she sought you out to be. With Michael gone, you were to give all of your being unto her, and had you forgotten the past and moved on, there would be no great battle between you, and I."

"Enough!" yelled the savage girl, her voice grating. "Enough of this, Halcón!"

Halcón's grimaced features worsened, launching forth against his inquirer with unruly brawn. "I am done," said Halcón, his voice trembling with rage as his paw,—formerly ramming through her defense,—squeezed about her quavering throat, "with your disrespect, your addressing uncouth. So bow, and speak to the Ravaja's lord justly or not at all!"

For the second time Al Halcón had slammed the woman into the earth, leaving her to shuffle slowly, miserably, to her knees in an attempt to stand, and have her regicide.

"That's better," spoke Halcón.

Accustomed to the etiquette of regal treatment, her demands unchecked and interrupting angered the cleric, caved to impulse than wait for an opening to strike, he precipitously wrested the girl; no less had it been in her favor, Fera needed to be planted and silenced so she'd be able to hear what needed to be heard.

The giant began to circle her, coming onto all-fours. "Though, his death is what gives you drive"—his jowls salivated to the point of dripping—"had all your mind and spirit yearned for power than vengeance, in your venture, the scabbing on my back would have been yours to puppet as Lucia's authority would have been properly bestowed to her daughter of murder."

Fera, reminded of her days killing for sport her skills superseding survival in the pit, imagined if she was victorious that night against the officer and his weaponized appendages, who she would be now if not for her failure granting her needed reflection on why she endured: the truth, the savage girl would have fallen into incredible darkness, becoming receptive to the Beast's wavelength entirely as they would have been made one in mind and spirit.

"You are here now, nevertheless," said he, "and Lucia's plan will be finalized though her spawn premature to take the glassed chair. But, she has other means of getting you where you need to be, Fera—soon." He hoped against all he said and steadfastly remained her challenger.

Sweltering in a cloud of her antagonist's breath as he paced about clockwise, the happening of condensation upon her skin had the stifling emissions rolling down her cheeks, neck, and arms, nauseous at the carrion aroma of the felidae's constant breathing, his fur of matching stench. "To even consider what you said to be of truth," said Fera, "would only prove how far-gone I am in my capabilities to reason; that charismatic nature of yours no doubt an advantageous tool, any fool would find your tale laughable, at best, if not insulting."

"Take offense to it all you like," said Halcón, effectively relating her to the former, "but I speak on Lucia's behalf, and act accordingly to whatever she commands. The death of her daughter, if fate has it, and I was to change its course thus, has been permissible by her—so everything that I have spoken is only tentative, although I see no other future, so I'll enjoy the most out of this as I can," and with a gaping mouth his fangs were bared, protruding out his tongue.

Licking the side of her arm thrice, her flesh resulted at a beginning peel as the serrated tongue pulled upwards against her skin with its effortless removal, the result of its stripping having her wail so horribly that her voice rolled throughout the Wasteland that some mistook her echo for an omen. Prompted into action Fera handled her blade and sought his nearest artery punctured, allowing her time with the foreknowledge of the mark's healing to move quick and have it removed, but before she could place her sword into his heart, from her eye's corner, she found the vaquero leveling his aim on her.

Instantly, the Havoc roared given rise to its azure mane, and a bolt was sent into Fera's shoulder—aimed for the head, Tycho's shaken hand failed him. Unconscious from the impacting blast, miraculously her arm remained yet thoroughly charred, Halcón caught her by the head before her body could fly and skid shortly across the ground. He looked to the vaquero, concealing his innermost joy. Tycho, in attempt to spare the girl from becoming devoured, eaten alive and feeling every muscle and bone snap, anticipated such from Halcón as he'd see carnivores do similar circling about their quarry before feasting, had now guaranteed Fera's hate for him; awakening to her senses, she would perceive his rescuing as treasonous, wanting Al Halcón all to himself for the satisfying kill, and would make sure to end Tycho's life once the brute had been dealt with. Her belief that Tycho cared for her not had all but been confirmed, and would deal with him as any other cutthroat. Though she continued to fight, Tycho knew the futility of it,—neither of them having the chance of victory in their present conditions,—and would kindly rid her of a torturing end before he'd perish, which he felt happening presently, thinking nothing more of it than fainting from exhaustion.

From the interior of a small and cragged shelter alongside a mountain's base granting the Brussian repose in his long journey to exit the range, the traveling cry from a woman most familiar to him reached his ears, anguished they erected fast. He ignored his desire to leave from the warmed yet frustratingly cramped space, until enough guilt ate at him to move. Crawling out onto the trail and standing in resistance to the cold winds, he gazed outward, *Titan Summit* consuming his view entirely. Lowering his head, he contemplated what needed to be done—either, let them die, resume what balance of his journey remained and avoid frostbite from overtaking him, or assist the only things he had left to consider family.

"Run, Sarkas," he soliloquized, "run, as never before. These wings of mine, mighty as they were, they cannot carry me home, so my feet will do—they will have to do, continuing to make ground," and finding his toes raw overborne from the cold of snow and wind, he began his sprint uncomfortably and clumsily until blood came to his feet warming them delightfully. A day's march gone within moments compared to an onward shuffling to a ferocious sprint after the security of his charges, the bat sped wonderfully through the gorge and even after when reaching the tundra plains. "I'd left all to God for them to be his burden," he continued, huffing, "when the responsibility was mine to undertake from the start. A second chance; one sem'ya I have already lost, so I will not disregard bots purple and blue, as urgency and fear of their well-being, as my own with them no more, carries this Brussian forward. I will not have Tycho fall to the evils of the witch, spasitel'—I promise you."

Encouraged to hasten his movements as the tundra in the midst of night was chilling beyond what the senses could experience, Sarkas used his arms as additional legs to propel himself faster along the earth, becoming one of the many creatures that roamed the Ravaja of a lesser intelligence; but it was within the act some primordial part in his brain sparked, and his charge had been taken over by some brute impassioned to see his cared for remain animate, and away from the threat encroaching upon their very existence. Though Sarkas was in his right mind, instinct had been pulling the strings from his innermost conscious, unrecognizable to him. Coming into view was the ruins of man flattened from the airship's grounding, the Summit's face gleaming silver from moonlight painting the vessel corpse too as it remained beside the base of the mountain, reminding Sarkas that not only would he have to encounter Halcón with unremitting brutality but the Outset as well, if he were to remain as antagonistic as he'd left them at *Tartarus' Spire*. Yet, he thought, Clyde may be of value when facing the Wasteland's lord whose tyranny scourged its very denizens for a generation or more, as the great cat a common enemy for them both to band together against, assuming he wasn't already deceased.

Arriving at the structure where Fera and Tycho had their rest his strides lessened in exertion as the sight of the Rahnthian war machine, untouched from the airship's collision, had a smile play about his lips. Exhausted from his impressive, Olympian run he found the machine as his saving grace in reaching the vaquero and the girl before his body's surrender to the environments with waning endurance, and as he was starting to feel the chill of the tundra pass throughout his spine, bristling the hairs on his backside, he clambered into the vehicle's cockpit.

Raking his talons across its dashboard he averted any chance of the machine, model: HEAITHAN, from scanning his face and employing countermeasures to eliminate the lesser race being. Needing an alternate way to start this golem, in retrospect considered one of the many countenances of moths lying about—those that were left from the collision—though concluded weathering rendered them ineffective, recalled the manual activation at his side, a panel, had the scanning malfunctioned. Finding the activation code engraved flimsily below the panel Sarkas entered the numbers until a voice boomed in confirmation of his achievement to have the heaithan operable. The hatch auto-sealing in likeness to an airship's snapping its jaws closed, as the cockpit was halved when opened to intake the pilot, full operations were given to the Brussian when encased within the ovular chamber, fitted with instantaneous ossified armor that oozed, then hardened on his person, providing an exoskeleton as a means of further layering upon the chitin skins of moths piloting. Breathing familiar through what he always distinguished akin to a gasmask in design, the trunks slung past his shoulders coapted to an oxygen reserve than loose, was feeling panicked as the armor still tightened against his face and lungs; his ribs and eye sockets becoming emphasized. This was clear indication to him that he'd gotten far heftier over the years. Moving his hand forward, the heaithan mimicked—this was when Sarkas became soothed, minimally; he could not help but feel suffocated.

After testing functionality before taking any steps with the machine, his feet began to roll the track-orb beneath him, but had been interrupted from the stone-like frost preventing any movements from its legs. Decisively, with little hesitation, Sarkas pounded the side of his leg with enough force for the heaithan to do similar, and with the shattering sound of the ice he sped forward, and the machine appropriated his movements.

Sprinting until sore within the limitations of his surroundings, constantly being supplied with ample intakes of oxygen to keep his run stabilized, signed for the heaithan to equal its pilot's demands, and eventually, the legs of the machine transmogrified from recognizable limbs into something far more extraordinary! Kept within an anti-gravitational stream, spears that once constituted the bipedal framework of the heaithan splintered from its original form and were now utilized within a rotary loop to fling the body of the Rahnthian construction forward as it dug into the ground with magnificent expeditiousness. Formerly, the operable mode's intended use was for running down revolutionaries and all who stood on the battlefield opposed to Rahnth's dominion, swathes of land needed reaping and with great speed to dispatch them without so much as the thought of continuing resistance, as terror had been instilled within their breasts, including Sarkas, which sickened him to see the abomination in operation again—the very sight of it evoking memories suppressed. Disregarding flashbacks, Sarkas looked to the mountain's peak where its jaws lay wide and agape, and would make his way along *Titan Summit*'s face until tumbling within its mighty, serrated mouth.

Presently, the woman comatose, attempting to have her laid waste to was not so much a priority needing haste, the lumbering giant of a cat deciding even when she'd risen to her knees,—powerless against him,— he would savor the chance to do with her as he wilt, anticipating for her to bear every torture until he bored and eventually would snap her fine, lissome neck. So all he could do now was wait, and pester the vaquero in regards to his mentor's health to manipulate and warp his grasp on the Ahmenseraï and his benevolence. Hating God, Halcón found comparable pleasure meddling with the amnesiac's mind as ruining Lucia's daughter; seeds of malice sown from the boy's rebellion, the tyrant would only further nurture his animosities and doubts.

"Judean," he said, having the woman's body slide from his palm as he stayed crouched beside her, "why hadn't you done similar with Bill Pyron, a bead on his head when kidnapped? Or had you misaimed?" he grinned sickly. "For certain you reasoned that you'd never see him again, tormented indefinitely?"

Tycho's vision beginning to blur, he strained his sights on the reddish glower atop the black mass recognized poorly as Halcón. "Yea...that's why I've come all the way out here," said Tycho, groaning, "because I gave up on ever finding him, which I don't think Lucia would have been very happy with had I turned tail. You said it yourself, Bill was to be used as bait, and I fell for it for the hapless loser I am." His self-deprecation went unnoticed.

"So self-loathing, where's the bravado I was given an impression of, boy? God has forgotten you, he has," he said, tenderly, "but don't let that get you into a mood, his negligence is understandable—for you to be Verumshaï...? Killing plenty, I could see no other way than for him to revoke your citizenship of heaven; I don't see why he hadn't done so earlier."

Initially, Tycho hadn't considered his drivel as before, cementing the belief he'd forever be separated from the Ahmenseraï and his grace, but the present circumstances could prove Halcón's words true as the Spirit was nowhere to be seen, perhaps, externally. For within the breast of the champion of Sol Puesta, the familiar pang that struck keenly before surged again, and Tycho went on ignoring it, unsure of repentance and all the deaths allowed from the Spirit to weaken in effectiveness, understanding because of his actions but angered as to why the Ahmenseraï, regardless of his trespasses, would allow his son and those he cares for encounter death. He knew this god, the Ahmenseraï, hadn't forgotten him, but questioned if he was actually valued or loved by the being, the Stranger says so, though from what has transpired until now had him set into a deep depression, doubting what was told to him from his brother. So, he began to absorb whatever Halcón said without debate, quiet.

"The Ahmenseraï isn't any different from the Beast," said Halcón, "or I. We all seek payment, in our own preferable forms, from one's soul to gredo, and followers aplenty with their own pockets of spending, — to obey whatever we command of them, until penniless and left enchained within this mount. Undoubtedly, the Spirit's god has put you in a situation not so different from their own, rather than slaving for the Ahmenseraï, you are now in the pit of sin; repentance is due."

Rather than knocking at his breast the Spirit filled Tycho with might and main, the vaquero close to speaking in tongues to give worship to the everlasting Messiah God, nevertheless he kept his mouth shut and denied a remembrance of hymns to be sung—an unusual urge for him to do, never considered or thought of doing once. But, the Spirit had revealed something to him within that instance of acknowledging the Ahmenseraï's indwelling, that he was liberated by the Spirit! It showed him that he had more freedom than previously thought, no more weighed down from shame and remorse brought by sin, worry, hatred, and condemnation obliterated, had his transgressions been confessed to the Lord, but the Beast had guilt overbearing, to the extent that it kept Tycho from the confession needed to empower the Spirit within. No longer had he feared judgment or blame, he understood—but another word from Halcón hardened his heart from nigh penitence.

"You don't look so well," said Halcón. "Don't leave us now, not until her daughter has bested her contender, and only then, will the fire of his presence enflame your soul no longer, but Abaddon and where your persecuting mentor lies will have its place searing the essence of your being instead of God where he cannot be! Curious, as you drift into eternal sleep, are you beginning to feel the scorching tongues of hellfire snap at your haunch and backside as you awaken anew into lands unforgiving?" He scoffed, picking the limb blades from off Fera's person, crushing them to dust. He'd determined this fight was over, himself victorious against Fate.

Again, the thought of the Shine's master allowing his friends to die, and suffer, irked him considerably. From what the Stranger gave insight on with Bill's situation, he was being used as Lucia intended without the Ahmenseraï interfering, for the greatest that evil could plot ultimately fell in the Lord's favor; for it would be to their destruction. This didn't matter to the vaquero, enraged that his fatherly companion was no more than an object to draw Tycho nearer to the goals each omnipotent sought, giving credence that the Ahmenseraï was no better than his adversaries, as Halcón stated.

Tycho, falling onto his knee as he tried to stand, eventually regained his feet, trembling to stay upright. His face shadowed from his hat's brim Al Halcón could hardly determine his intentions, yet he rightly concluded he chose death from battle than waning helpless, as previous behavior resisting a pummeling was attributable to him having any evince of surrender; this, Halcón respected greatly.

As Fera's body began to move and flex the vaquero was prepared for an inconceivable end he was on the cusp of understanding, death befallen onto him for her safety, hoping ultimately she would find Bill and have him rescued, distracting the brute so she would evade a mauling, and somehow use her time valuably to remove the Beast's mark from his back, following with the kill. Fera without her tools, Tycho considered sliding her his gun and using its mane to sever the scabbing from his gnarled hide, but Halcón had heard her shuffling and stooped to have her by the collar. Tycho not knowing whether to end Fera now as she faced an upcoming butchering, debated with the newer idea to chance their lives and save two than spare one. The latter alternative was chosen, and persevering all mortal wounds and limitations brought by them, he stumbled before his charge had been initiated at the despot with an aim leveled on his bared fangs; the cap of the Summit shook terribly, constraining him. Until hearing a thunderous bellow from above, the assumption was an earthquake struck, for Halcón possibly a forgotten reactor within the depths of the mountain exploding after eons of neglect. Suddenly the throne room was ridded of the moon's radiance, its eclipsing brought from an unknown party within the heaithan vessel encroaching similarly to Lucia, when she was cast out from heaven,—sent like lightning onto the earth,—and as the quakes ceased with its precipitous fall into the throne room excluding its landing, unwavering strings of light pursued Al Halcón until gathered onto his breast. Halcón's eyes widened with terror, as the machine boomed statically: "Evisceration target—concluded."

With its hundreds of spears stampeding towards the great cat, the machine trumpeted elephantine and haunting at that, Tycho unsure what to make of this challenger who clearly wanted gore, watching the golem's feet dispatch from organized flight and into Al Halcón as he bore every cleaving point that passed its way through, worsening as the machine crashed upon him then planting his head against the wall. The revolving spearheads thirsted for his reservoir of blood after years of drought, forcibly entering his chest and stomach as they began to spurt. Halcón's strength had been challenged, resisting the heaithan's arm that held him in place. The two bots watched from their respected angles within the howling chamber as Halcón was fated for disseverance, until the undying brute displaced the giant hand that crushed his head against the glassed wall for another to take its place, and for Halcón to reject the limb with just as enough force if not more pushing the machine backwards, only after great exertion of determination and muscle. The machine charged at him again midst its pilot being blinded from the violet emission reflecting from the wall, Halcón throwing up his fortified arm as a means of defense he endured the riving points, his other hand placed against the precipitous side of the chamber securing his station—but quick-witted, he pulled mightily to have a spear from the rotary loop, and hurled the missile at the cockpit, tearing through the upper hatch spearing the pilot against his enclosure away from the track-orb. Al Halcón pounced hard, carrying the pilot the rest of the way through the compromised machinery and onto the earth to suffer what had been exacted unto him.

Grabbing the spear from its shaft the pilot tore the spearhead from out his shoulder, and shouting in anguish, pounded the rod against his antagonist's profile, shocking him senseless from the blow. Al Halcón stumbled from his straddled position, preparing a flurry from his talons that gleamed for the excavation of his bowels, finishing him with those saber-sized canines to close about his throat.

Although the pilot's voice muffled from the helmet's dampening properties, Tycho, as well as Fera, indicated the pained cry belonging to no other than their dearest friend Sarkas Severov. The build was telling—as the armor hadn't fully coated his wings—but the voice was confirmation their suspicions were accurate. Immediately the two crossed their way to him in an offering of assistance, but with a mighty shout, Sarkas blared: "Children, stay far from me!"—He sorely arose to his feet, lurching—"Run; I will handle him!" and within the instance of turning his eye to his shoulder Halcón clawed wickedly at his face that his lower jaw had been displaced, removing his helmet as each talon glided through the bony crust that it turned brittle, shattering. Wheeling completely to face his greatest foe yet, a tyrannosaurus roar belted out from the Brussian's gut and charged at Halcón making a challenge similar, their bodies crashing against each other as a storm of fur and blood soon enshrouded these titans, digging their claws and teeth into the opposition's hide.

Sarkas' armor proving less and less advantageous as the fiendish brute kept at his body with terrific rakes, as his attempts to slay him went unrewarding as the Keter was constant in Halcón's restoration, only resulted in the bat to strengthen his slashes until his hand could clear its way to his heart, hoping to have it dislodged, that the mark's enchantment was solely beneficial in repairing mortal wounds—not replacing entire organs. At once, Sarkas buried his talons deeper into Halcón, yet strained from previous exertion to reach *Titan Summit* he was dizzied amidst his brawl, wavering where he stood. Fera, infuriated, as she stood by without the power to properly assist, saw to the heaithan lifting her gaze from the battle, and with hastened footing made for the golem.

Kept at a deadlock with slashes exchanged, it was then Halcón made a swing most decisive that granted him a trouncing over the venerable Brussian, an exposing in his battered armor permitting the great cat to open his flesh and allow his blood to be poured, puddling before Sarkas' feet. Ere Al Halcón could lunge his mouth about his throat and pierce his jugulars, the commandeered heaithan collided against his shoulder sweeping him from the ground as the savage woman—intuitive were the controls to master—carried him along the earth before slamming him against another wall. Right away, the machine's hand was met with resistance as Halcón pushed for release, but Fera wouldn't have it, and lifted him momentarily from the wall to send him back within the coffining stone with enough force to crush every bone in his body.

Lifeless, ceased of movement, Fera hesitantly raised the heaithan's arm from the limp corpse, falling headlong before her, and proceeded to have him sawed warding resurrection, however, her mother far from finished and determined for Fera to defeat Halcón by her own might, arose her disciple's corpse from the ground as every bone cracked and locked into place—Al Halcón snarling belligerent as he erected with the ascension of his restoring spine.

"Fera!" Sarkas shouted as blood trailed from out his gash in his shuffle towards her, "Fera, my girl, leave it!" But her time of escape dwindled in her pressing onward to slay this giant, and her failure to acknowledge the warning brought her defeat. Unawares, the great cat's speed absurd, Fera flew off from the heaithan not in the least comprehending how she'd done so, feeling only the sinewy hand at her throat as Halcón raised her in moonlight to deliver the blow needed, as this was his only foreseeable chance he'd have of ridding her from this earth, the throne his to keep, regretting the decision to see her prolong in suffering!

"Keep your hand from her!" yelled Sarkas, his wings extended out, blinding the triad's assailant briefly before snapping his neck, which thundered throughout the throne room, but at his head's turn, comparable in fashion to an owl's neck spinning unsettlingly, the great cat's body followed with it, Al Halcón's gruesome countenance meeting Sarkas', the latter's body illuminated fully from the Beast's light! His other hand pinning Sarkas to the volcanic floor Al Halcón, busied, had forgotten about the Verumshaï completely, and at the sound of his iron's hammer cocked he hurriedly turned his eyes from the face of the intruder to him; as a result, the entirety of Halcón's head was nothing more than the meat wallowing in the fluids of his discharged mind pooled amongst the floor of glass. Although, what remained, was a hanging jaw attached to the skin of his neck.

Never considering the cat's lack of fell on his beasty face compared to the rest of his body, the vaquero chanced firing into him point-blank in the greatest of hopes of having him blinded, nevertheless was gifted with an outcome far better.

Free of his grasp, Fera had fallen onto her hands and knees with her release, and, finding Halcón stand slowly withal at a wobble, eerie at best, felt at her sash and became alerted that her swords were not on her, searching the chamber they went unseen, unknowing of their demolishment. There, somewhere near the center of the throne room, she found the imbedded sword of her father glistening white in the thick of Halcón's shedding of blood, and remembered she'd seen it upon her exit from the corridor. No other tool at her disposal, the woman trudged toward the blade; Tycho at Sarkas' side looked to her briefly, his priority set on cauterizing the bat's wound having rationalized that if his bolts failed to char beyond the great cat's well-matted hide, then his time was better spent saving the life of his friend than painstakingly making incisions along Halcón's backside. He was confident Fera would end him.

Leaning on the marred bone for support as she tired from her walk, she raised her hand to the point of the Outset's dismemberment, wrapping her fingers around what she'd make a hilt. Lifting herself up, she two-handedly grasped the bone with all her strength, and pulled, emitting a struggling cry before whimpering at its release, the bone blade having sliced deep into her palm. Unbound from obsidian she caught her balance after the initial stumble at its drawing, Fera deemed a fitful inheritor to carry the sword though its weight had it dragged. And watching through her nasty scowl the head of the demagogue reform one muscle overlapping at a time she bared her fangs, detesting the witch and all that she had willed to keep his death undone; soon, his reanimation would yield.

Presently, standing before him as she'd crossed her way back, Halcón's top jaw began extending out with infantile teeth until enlarged as skull and flesh had scarcely begun to form around his brain. Eyelids yet unopened the great cat roared knowing of a presence before him, frightened at what he couldn't see nor smell, and faltered onto his side attempting to grab her. Fera swung the blade from the ground onto the right side of his head, the force from the blow securing Halcón standing tall than stayed hunched. Her strength about lost from the laborious swing, she breathed twice, and gathered her brawn. A victorious cry of tears and might channeling from out the breast of the savage woman, Fera drove the blade into his heart, and as Halcón crashed onto his knee and grasped its edge she forced her father's arm deeper into his thorax until his spine had been severed, and the Keter effectively split in half. The scourge of the Wasteland, falling onto his side as a carpeting of dust billowed out from beneath him, was no more.

Pressing her foot against the corpse she retrieved the sword, and slowly turned her head to the vaquero, whose willpower had secured him living, but great mental fortitude could not avail Sarkas, grievously, who'd bled out too much to make any recovery. Pulling the blade behind her, Fera's eyes gleamed wickedly given to absolute hatred for Tycho, approaching him as he was unsuspectingly awaiting her to come to say her goodbyes. Raising the sword above his head as it dangled in her grasp, the point near to touching his hat, a seducing whisper from a woman eased into her conscious, barraging her with scenes of the vaquero's failings; then, the girl saw Tycho had sealed their friend's wound from the Havoc's mane as it continued to sputter beside him, all before considering the weight of the bone to plunge through him. Her arms weakening, and hands slipping, she turned around heavily and released the sword to contemplate, the noise of its clanging fall gaining the vaquero's attention.

Fera never before having companions as these, or ever, was scared that she might actually lose someone who cared about her—but everything Tycho had done proved otherwise, so she thought originally.

"Fera," said Tycho.

She was unprepared to hear his voice, or make a reply; Lucia's chilling talk, constant now, attempted to have him snuffed, Fera resisting to take up the blade as accounts of the vaquero's selfishness repeated in her head.

"Fera," he said, "I know you might think what I'm about to say is a load of crap, as would I if I were in your position…but I shot at you, in hope that you'd have a death not worth suffering."

Silent she remained, frustratingly combing her fingers through her hair. She knew who it was that tempted her, and fought the Beast.

"How I responded before, I should have been upfront with you," said the vaquero. "Having those men killed, I know I did wrong the moment I fired into them. Fera, the Shine…he's hid himself from me because of what I've done—my soul aches…" He gestured with his hand applied to his breast.

"I know what it feels like now," said Tycho referring to pain, "how…horrible it feels, which is the only thing I can be thankful for, and cursed with, by the Shine having himself unrevealed. He speaks to me"—Tycho looked upon Sarkas' dreary countenance—"but I don't know if I can trust what he says to me anymore.

"I'm sorry, Fera. And I'm sorry for what I allowed to happen to you in those caves," he said.

Sarkas tugged at Tycho's arm as his eyes opened, and began speaking. "My friend, I haven't much time. Bring her close, as I would call out to her myself," he said at almost a whisper, "but I haven't the strength."

Without Tycho breaking her name from his lips she approached hearing his desire, and knelt alongside the vaquero with a troubled face.

"Children, I would wish to leave this earth saying how proud of you I am," said Sarkas, "but I believe my life was given tonight so that, one day, you will mature, and see that there is more to each of your existences than following the mantra: *an eye for an eye, a tooth for a tooth*. I know, Fera, that even though the Wasteland is freed from that tyrant's reign, the void within you is still unsatisfied"—the girl's features quaked, gnashing her teeth to fight an emotion that came over her—"and that you feel no better than before. I have been where you have once been," he said with a cracking voice. "My wife, Anastasia, and I found our son welted, and drugged insensible within some shanty the moths used as a cache to horde their merchandise; it was evident that they prowled about our lands for several days from the quantity we'd soon discover. I followed the scent of my boy to the haunt in which he indwelled, seeing every kind of child chained to the walls prepared for shipment. I found little Sarkas amongst them, but as I tried to awake him I realized he wasn't breathing"—Sarkas abruptly laid there expressionless, fighting back his face from quivering—"and, what followed, was their own massacre and of their offspring. Smelling the sweat of their hands on my child, I had their stench lead me to their homes, where, before starting to dismember his abusers, I had them watch as I split their children in two. Anastasia, unfortunately, was a witness as she had been at my side."

He coughed heavily, split flung from his lips. "I surpassed the very monstry that took my boy, Fera. Sarkas Severov died that day, and Anastasia knew this, and left me, knowing the man she loved was gone—what you see now, is only the husk."

"That wasn't fair of her," said Fera, grimacing.

"To you, perhaps," he said, "but I can see her departure as justified."

Sarkas rotated his head slightly, and looked at Tycho. "And I can see, blue bot, from what I heard you speak," he said, swallowing, "that you are capable of having an amazing heart, and my message belongs as much to you as it does to Fera. See to it that, whenever the robed man is to return, Tycho, that you question his motives; if he is of God as I've given thought to, surely there is no reason to quarrel with him—but test, test him! He very well could be an emissary for the witch, my friend...And, allow nothing to detract you from finding this Bill anymore. If he means anything to you, you'll put aside the vices I'll allow you to interpret as such.

"So now," he said, "I expect the best from the both of you"—he drifted his eyes from the vaquero to the girl—"to forgive, abandoning darkness."

Briefly, he caressed the savage woman's face; closing her eyes, she held his leathery hand to her cheek.

"Dosvedanya, sem'ya," he said, and his hand slowly left her.

Her throated tightened with afflicting sorrow, foreshadowing a shedding of tears, she bowed her head and fought the desire to let her eyes water. She turned her head from the vaquero, hoping he'd look elsewhere.

Tycho, raising himself up, walked from their location and repeatedly rolled his palms against his eyes, sighing agitated. Presently comprehensive of physical anguishes, he had no comprehensive understanding of his mortality or others expirations still, and his initial mode of feeling was that of anger when a friend appeared no more animate than a stone. What begins with a primordial, subconscious fear of the unknown can quickly present itself as one form of hatred,—anger, in the vaquero's case, to resist the cognizance of death—to preserve the threatened being's way of existence, either ideological or bodily. Tycho simply hated what he could not understand, and fell short of empathy for those he cherished he never conceived as perishing. He didn't know how to accept that they were gone forever, as the Shine conditioned for him to always have life so others would too.

Added onto his previous thought of repentance, as he came to mull over again, he concluded the Ahmenseraï had him immortal for the sole purpose of giving him praise, revoking the Spirit's healing once a servant would have nothing more to do with it, and could care less if he or his friends perished, since all the deity hungered for was obedience and worship—this is why Tycho had not repented at Sarkas' side, apart from it being a false accounting of sins and having it be unfruitful for him to try, he saw him as much as threat as Lucia, using Bill's life if not others he wasn't aware of to draw him near to confession.

Halcón's lies had nurtured his previously established thoughts of rebellion and distrust within the young man, leaving Tycho further misunderstanding for the purpose of confessing transgressions against God. Tycho belonged to him, and loving the young man, would continue to reach out as the Spirit would counsel him as another conscious.

And as for his mentor's confines, he panicked believing he'd never be found with Al Halcón slain, never giving his placement within the mountain or elsewhere, but recalled the mention of Abaddon and his soul traveling to another plane of existence if he'd fallen cold—Tycho looked to the obelisk and the throne carved out from it, Castle Rothschild and its findings preparing him for this moment. The conversation between Kutzweil and Lucia as fresh in his mind as the night of the audio's discovery, the champion of Sol Puesta remembered what they had said about the obelisk and its purpose of transporting individuals housed within the sapiens-hull to other existences beyond Zodain's, the physical realm, and read of higher planes, Abaddon as one of them now considering, that men were to dwell in before and after Wormwood struck. Unsure how he'd get there, or the proper way to access travel by using the obelisk, he ran to the slickened and jutting steps leading to the throne, and paused before the phallic stone once he reached the top.

Looking back to Fera, he found her removing the remnants of Sarkas' slashed bandana from his neck, and proceeded to knot the remaining portion tightly about her head, turning her gaze towards him.

"What are you doing?" she asked, her voice echoed.

"I'll be back soon; there's something I gotta do alone."

"I don't understand," she said.

Before touching the throne, he asked, "What made you decide not to kill me?"

Fera bit her lip, lowering her eyes for a short time. "Finding you aiding Sarkas than finishing off Halcón by your own means…That told me everything."

Returning her eyes to where he stood, she found him nowhere to be seen, only a few tendrils of flames dancing from the throne and onto the face of the obelisk.

FERA, EMANCIPATED GLADIATOR

XVII

SINS OF THE FATHER

A MONGST the petrified remains of man that had once been the captors of the ever-present Beast, Bill Pyron was chafed and cut from his drag, outstretched hands and wailing mouths digging into his back as each encrusted nail and tooth hooked into his skin briefly, before crudely splitting it with another pull from the haggard creature. It began to fervently tremble the more it neared the obelisk, whimpering it fell into a fit of laughter ere moaning with great pleasure, the Beast's mark searing itself onto its forehead anew. The creature looked down at its victim, and raising him before the edifice, he pounded him against the face of the stone where the initial impact awoke the old soldier before falling to an enveloping black where the sight of the creature unexplainably vanished. Terror-filled, Bill tumbling endlessly with stomach-churning shouts, thought this had to be an induced nightmare by trauma as he'd endure previous nights, but, the stoking of flames and writhing bodies materializing from out of the darkness igniting the perpetual black into a fire-lined abyss had him questioning, then panicking of the exact cause for this unseen imagery he had not found in the tortures of ill-sleeping before!

Below, as he crashed into the thousands of sapiens-hulls consisting of the smoldering heap that tarnished the sky as crimson as blood and black as soot, he found himself and the damned coursed to descend into the mouths of the hungering, pacing angels that this man could not conceive as once citizens of heaven, having defied the Ahmenseraï in his battle to oust Lucia Rothschild from his kingdom, seeing now that she was at the helm of godhood with the emanations and promised small portions of his power to all who joined her to seize the throne and Judgment; there were few loyal enough to stand guard of and fight for the Ahmenseraï than slave to whomever had the emanations that were more recognized as God than he. How they yearned to become him, just as mankind, tempted with the glorious might of creation that would elevate their beings into foreseeable divinity.

Initially, Abaddon had been formed to house man, those of impenitence, for all who sought salvation by their own means as their conscious lived on yet their soul departed for judgment,—though, understandably, the mutinying angels whom the Ahmenseraï foreknew of their treachery were cast no differently into the pit as man had been, adhering to their choice to have him overthrown. Fallen warriors and messengers formerly clad in celestial light were shamefully drenched in the spilt fluids of the condemned, suffering from mortal starvation indefinitely, where, never an angel felt until punishment befell them.

Devouring the souls of man, gaining what they could from the citadel or scrounging valley's crevices and gullies for hidden bodies suffering their own hells, they now turned their heads to the skies were countless sapiens-hulls fell in plenty and continuously, a fresher and more accessible stock of souls to replete their insatiable famishing. Bill saw no escaping the mouth that awaited his passage with several others, a salivating chamber with uncharacteristically long fangs skewering those who plummeted against their dentition failing to descend appropriately into its throat for consumption. Doing so, Bill saw nothing more than the black he'd experience prior and felt a sudden chill work its way up from his feet to his entire frame of being, finding himself dizzied and weakened as he came to stand, to which stable ground was his only comfort. He'd anticipated an intestinal capture, wrestling with hundreds of others, piling on top of the next to avoid the acids of the predator's bowels, but these angels of revoked grace were never retrofitted with stomachs, temporary relief coming from an agonized soul enduring grief.

"Katherine!" he cried shivering, "Tycho—Tycho, my boy, where are you!" Desperate and fearful, he unreasonably discounted the effect of his abduction, unlike him, knowing he wasn't near home; no one knew of his whereabouts, there was no aid to be found arguably only in the Ahmenseraï, but he failed to call on the name that mattered.

"I thought I was your son?"

Aghast, Bill must've mistaken who was standing before him. Then again, he thought, nothing was out of the realm of possibility accounting for all he had seen just previous to encountering his son's shade.

"Miles," he said, his voice trembled, "Miles, how are you—? Where are we…?"

The young man placed his arms at his side, and slowly, blood trailed from the forming slits as they made their way from his wrists to the opposite end of his forearms. "You left me," it said, its head bowed unnaturally so that its neck bulged as it came into view. "I needed you, but you left, in the end, to fight a war not worth winning."

"No, son," said Bill. "It was you that left me."

"But my destruction," it said after a momentary silence, disregarding his response, "can it be compared to families you killed—?"

"Miles," said Bill with a sorrowing tone. "Please don't do this…I know what I've done. I had been indoctrinated, I was desperate for answers, for emancipation—we all were, your mother too. Son, you have to understand, they played on the fear of you living in a world forever shackled by the moths—I wasn't myself; all I can say was that someone else was thinking for me."

"If you're as blameless as you're making yourself out to be," it said, "then the sight of the slaughtered masses will evoke pity than remorse." Bill never claiming innocence the Beast used the image of his son to manipulate him into believing he had argued the point. Surrounding him suddenly, sequoias, wind, the chattering of birds drowned of voice as guttural uproars echoed throughout the woods had Bill Pyron numbed, beyond anxiety's hold. He watched a man sprint and then stumble as bullets flew wickedly into his backside, and with scrutiny found others bound to die similarly as he could hardly make them out behind the disjointed rows of the grand trees. He turned his head back to where Miles was last seen standing, but his image successively used there was no longer a sight of him to behold, and this brought only greater pain to him.

Bill treaded without the slightest caution through the underbrush as he was preoccupied retaining the intactness of his mind, profound wailings and the agonizing stench of burning corpses demanding disassociation presently—and quick!—for his soul to exit his body, and watch the lumbering fellow without taking part in the consequence of his sins' impressions. But, in Abaddon, as with any foreign plane of existence, eventually his mind would rot and degrade to substantial exposure outside Assiah, the material realm, as many before him turned maniacal in the initial testing of the human vessels.

His foot pressed into the side of a soft, yet stiffened body, laid sprawled amongst greensward. Tilting his head downward, he found the scene consisted of a mother shielding the child beneath her from the storm of gunfire that riddled her form, her little one frantically turning for release, crying in their native tongue for her to get up as he'd begun suffocating, without conception for why she had fallen silent. "When Halcón spoke on the prophet's behalf that equality was gained through persecuting those responsible for the Rahnthian subjugation," Miles perceivably said, "had you questioned him, the hypocrisy of it?" Bill heard a warring shout not far from him, seeing a Kasheen tribesman with his tomahawk spiraling in hand to cleave his foe's head precipitously, and consequently, the brave was left with an erupted breast from the gunslinger's bolt that stood before him with indifference.

Before this man could spot him, seemingly unaware of the brushfire that began roaring close from the ignited corpse, Bill hurriedly pulled the mother's remains from off the crying babe, all the more concerned as men from the gunslinger's withering regiment footed their way through the blazing verdure. "You were selected to hunt them down, partaking in the Outsets' crusade," said his son midst the gunner harshly whistling for his mount, "for your fearlessness and absolute devotion to the church's cause, but once you were shown the truth of their disposal, given their fate uncertain from ambiguity from speeches prior to your enlistment, why continue in their slaughter?"

Scooping the child into his arms, Bill placed his head against his shoulder to protect him from the sight of his downed mother, whispering to keep his eyes against him as the child's head turned for a peeking. Shuffling some feet forward, they were unexpectedly apprehended; the man and his mustang, veiled by firelight, grimaced. The soldier was faced with gunning down the Verumshaï, who held the boy, and unwillingly Bill relived shooting out the core of the man with the clouds settled on his eyes failing to seal the wound; Bill Pyron unable to detach he was forced to watch his youthful personage kill the Verumshaï he transferred from, through eyes he longingly fought to be suppressed.

In Abaddon, Bill was not solely subjugated to bear his own sufferings, but the sufferings he caused unto others.

More than a week thereafter the vaquero was summoned to his mentor's demising realm, sent aflame from his unforgettable plunge into the deep, his back faced against the earth as he rebounded and crashed through the boughs of the gold-tinted sequoias until grounded. Weak, he crawled from out the fire of his crater in his attempts to overcome the excruciation of the flames that charred him almost of all feeling, until Bill's recollection purged the foreign fires of their stay and remade Tycho in the image he'd seen him last; the vaquero remained existing within this hell because Bill had memory of him, and would have dematerialized unquestioningly had he not been as familiar with the old man.

Tycho analyzed his body blinkingly. "I'm not…Nope, not gonna question it. But that's what it feels like to be burned, huh? Never again…"

Restraining himself to think what had transpired within the last few minutes, to which even trying to fathom would leave Tycho veritably brain-dead, he collectively evened out his poncho across his shoulders with a pull, and huffed in anticipation and subdued fright all while perceiving gunshots in the distance. Past a ridge that gave an impression of a sudden drop, some feet ahead from his placement in the woods, Tycho intuitively set out to perch on the edging to obtain a layout of the forest and just where the commotion resided. However, as he had neared the ridge, shrills and lamenting bellows mingling with cracking reports were unexpectedly intense that he presently concluded the scene would be just past this end of the forest.

Before looking down, the sun's radiance settled on the crests of the far mountains captured his momentary focus. The Beast conjured him here from the obelisk, told he'd come to this place his second evening aboard Winthro's galleon by nightmare, and the vaquero unbelieving at first accepted his residency was now in the Kasheen wilds. And given Bill Pyron's supposed fate, Tycho was provoked into action.

Nearly tripping the second he chose to descend the slope of the ridge the vaquero yanked the Havoc from out its holster as he prepared to face chaos' uncertainties, sprinting quite expeditious from the slope into the settled bed of smoke propelled from his slide's momentum. As he charged through the blackened haze, placing his forearm's crease against his mouth to prevent an inhaling of smoke, squinting, the fear of having left Zodain without a means of returning home was distracted by the rescuing of Bill; if he thought of anything else, or trivialized his attempt of finding his old friend, irrational horrors would plague his mind; his determination crushed from the effects of Abaddon.

But wasn't this all irrational from the start of Tycho's realization of identity? What if Tycho had touched the obelisk and had just gone mad, envisioning himself in an actualized dream where no reality could ever sustain? The Beast cunning, he heard these doubts whispered, unaware of her malevolent attempts of gaslighting. Though soon, enough of her bothering intensified from this plane would have him on the brink of despair and madness facing off against his fatherly one, as, he too, was lost of all his wits.

Ahead a cry riddled the vaquero's skin with gooseflesh, scarcely discerning the scene amidst the smoke where his eye-lights were less than sufficient. Her garment torn leaving an exposed breast she began her run from the hut evading the man she had felled, but quicker than she, his hand lunged out, grasping tightly her ankle that the woman had smashed her face into the earth, and then forcefully dragged back to him shortly after her fall. The woman turned onto her side, and shouting harrowingly used her other foot to kick his hand from her, and quickly was on her feet again before the man arose in a stumble and shot her in the back, leaving her impaled with a crystal.

Immediately Tycho fired at the slayer of the native where he'd just arrived before any saving could be done, unleashing the remainder of his bolts into the ravaging soldiers that prowled the campsite of the converted Kasheen. Oddly, nothing that he had done dispatched them. Moreover, they hadn't shown any form of alert or distress from his deft and barraging entry. On the opposite end of the campsite from out the smoke, as it tore and weaved spiraling against the rider thundering in on his mount, Tycho couldn't then trounce the misting of his eyes at the sight of him. "Bill?" he said.

"Men," said Bill, coming to a gait, "on your horses. A fellow of his, sadly no longer with us, has compromised where he's been hiding all this time, bunking with that coward of a chief just further in this valley. A petty sum he did it for, later guilt outweighing his greed, the fool."

Unrecognizable in his demeanor, his attire further attributed him to a man the vaquero found as daunting, a black coat with a cattleman hat weathered at its brim, the boy had a face of stoicism nonetheless inwardly was perplexed. Bill turned his head to the ground. "What have we here?" he said.

The woman had begun to drag herself forward, formless wisps of white flowing from out her mouth, eyes, and wound where the missile lodged in her backside started to eject. Their captain, slowly, disembarked from his horse and walked near to the prostrate girl, watching her crawl as he knelt beside her. "Whose regrettable aim was this?" he asked soft-spoken, coalesced with her cries. No one answered amongst his company.

Bill tore the crystal out from her back. "Whose is this?!" he shouted in a sudden outburst.

"Sir," responded the soldier exiting the hut, fitting his trousers tight, his belt buckle clanking until fastened. "I'm accountable for her survival."

His eyes settled on his subordinate, holding a wretched gaze on him before saying: "Have you forgotten what the prophet has made clear?"

"No, sir," he replied. "'Skewer their cores, light they'll be without—a façade of divinity, granted from the evils of their own hearts let them die.'"

"Make sure of it that their core is penetrated," said Bill, "after wetting your prick next time around"—those of the soldier's company chuckled, scoffing him—"We don't need them spreading their gospel of lies or their magick arts anymore than they have; just makes our work more tedious than it has to be."

Witnessing his mentor aim at the desperate creature the vaquero jounced in disbelief and sullen surprise at the woman's execution. Mounting his cremello mustang thus, whom Tycho spotted her thigh of a darker shade, identifying her longingly, watched them take leave as Bill shouted, "Let's get a move on, men!" and wheeling as he charged out from the village his company followed behind shortly.

The vaquero's heart ached tantamount to the Shine's quenching, paused briefly before shuffling through the smoke, and stared without breaking focus from the ground as he spied littered with corpses upon corpses within the fuming black. Sickened, he couldn't further look at the bodies as he stepped out onto the opposite side of the campsite where Bill's company led a trail, unbelieving his old friend could have been a part of something so vile, whilst reminded of his misdeeds against his fellow peasants within the Summit and saurian caves. He spotted their tracks freshly imprinted within the shallow mud and left the fringes of the smoke bed, where its tendrils suffused and whorled around his waist and shoulders, to further his understanding that he was being guided through Bill's most horrid of memories answering why he wasn't paid the least attention to.

Following the tracks which so often was proven a fruitless venture as the shrubbery obscured and mud hidden beneath the plant life had begun to adjust and dissipate its rows of imprinting the vaquero managed, and had his march reestablishing his composure with deep, and calming breathes. The countless whispers having his thoughts wrought with anxiety and panic, moreover the witch masquerading as his conscious, Tycho took the time to bar these senseless and cowardly apprehensions as to not have energy spent needed when confronting his mentor,—however the situation would unveil itself, still unknown to him or how he'd go about it,—and the coming scene. Presently, he attuned his hearing to the warbling of the thrusts hidden throughout the great pines, pleased as the sun's rays periodically shone through the needle thickened branches toasting his skin golden, and permeating from afar an indiscernible roar Tycho mistook for thunder called the woodland beasts to satisfy their thirsts, herds of bison and deer intermingling as the constant affair of war spooked these foresters into hiding. Seeing to his right where the droves crossed ahead of him made out a falling torrent of water past the monumental boles, where Tycho had never seen such a sight that left him mystified; he reasoned it was the end of a river or some odd, stationary raincloud granting a piece of the land with nourishment though the former was all the more likely. He had associated bodies or streams of water to be found solely beneath the surface, so this came as a surprise for him until he recalled the flooding of the ravine in their hike in exiting the mountain range, which he never properly observed since his mind was after things of the future or reminiscing, was now taking into consideration the present which eased his worrisome soul.

Rightly, he determined asudden that he'd never seen trees before but somehow recognized these as familiar, fearing the notion of an abrupt remembrance that would present his history in such a fashion that his ailing mind thereafter would lessen his resilience in retrieving Bill Pyron. He kept on though, borne of grievances earthly and supernatural what could a revelation into his past do to him that his journey into Abaddon hadn't already accomplished? He would have his answer soon.

Gliding his hand against the sappy trunk of one of the forest giants he came into a clearing, a vast field of flowing green, strewn with variegated shades of butterflies fluttering about the tips of the grass blades that shocked the vaquero into recollection; he was stilled, the image of a young woman watching him smilingly as he played with another boy with figures she'd presumably crafted, lifting the field's tenders from their skin and onto her ebon finger. This had begun to make Tycho uncomfortable, and he repressed the plausible illusion from the Beast making headway through the field. Disturbing the congress of butterflies as they evasively soared from his marching through the grassland, he couldn't help but avert his gaze from the face of the cleft mountain that gleamed reflectively onto the lower vegetations, which spying from a distance hadn't so much hindered his sight but awed him. Having crossed the clearing, he spied the tracks of their horses from footprints to manure buns trailing along the dirt road and advanced all the more.

The formation of mist from out the woods began to suffuse about Tycho's feet as the sun lowered behind the walls of the valley, the moon thieving the brilliance of its contemporary to illuminate the forest, and the path the vaquero was on that never ended where it rightfully should have. The prolonged venture into the woodlands wracked Tycho's train of thought, the forces of Abaddon meddling with his perception of time that his walk appeared unlimited, until the roofage of a thatched hut gradually came into view from the land beneath him where the road led, equipping Tycho with hope he was nearing his friend's location. Speeding now, he came to halt at the elevated land's brink and scanned the features of the hut and its surroundings below, suspicious, he couldn't reason where else the company could have gone to, moonlight benefitting him with the evidence their tracks had stopped at the hut. The vaquero walked down the gradient in apprehension and suspense, following the careening road before startled from a vicious materialization of past events that haunted not only his mentor but Tycho moreover. All of them present within a flash, one visibly pained struck the vaquero unnerved and innately protective of this woman he'd forgotten some time ago. From out the hut, Tycho watched his old friend drag the poor creature by her hair, her scalp on the point of bleeding, before throwing her before the ground with another's gun leveled at her core. His company gathering behind Bill and his leverage, they continued to peer within the hut as they picked their teeth waiting for the man inside to answer their captain's demands.

Feeling the presence of what he suspected to be the Stranger, the witch whispered into his ear: "See now, that you caused this. Because of you, she died."

Promptly the figures of Bill's recollection found themselves in new positions and stances, an inaudible conversation from within the hut the vaquero would hear as he approached the twiggy home. Bill Pyron had tried to force himself within the small abode, but was met with a man up against his chest denying his entry. The captain jabbed his gun into the guardian's stomach, and said, "Don't be a hero; get inside," and he proceeded to enter the missionary's dwellings as the man gave, and stepped back, unaware just how many men were without. Their intruder knew of their capabilities, assured of his safety with his men standing outside, and kept his eyes fastened on the couple periodically as he circled about the interior of the hut searching for others of their kin, beneath beds or in-between the baskets which lined the walls. "Chief Heipatu, where is he?" His eyes wandered around the space, before having them retrained on his victims. Tycho watched from outside.

"He died," responded the woman passionately, her features crinkled in anguish, "in an attempt to recover my brother's body."

"And would that be none other than Seipatu Tiwahongova, miss? He fought bravely, gave our colonel a good scalping. Just the mention of him gave us all chills, a bogeyman he was, at the beginning of our offensive at least, never knowing when, or where he'd come from— finding men plunge to their death as quickly as they were taken up from the earth, crashing above through the branches of the trees before landing disfigured at our own feet; his threats hadn't gone unnoticed. So when I heard he was gunned down, which we can properly assume the same men killed your father, I was so much more at peace than I could have ever been before if he hadn't been such a thorn in my side from the start, and now to fully satisfy my revenge, I must have you Kuwanlelenta, princess of the Kasheen!"

The two stern-faced, Bill couldn't resist but laugh at his outrageousness. "I'm playing with you, darling," he said with levity, "I don't give care about getting even…You're the last of them though, so pray that the Ahmenseraï spares your souls before I'm finished with the both of you." He churned some phlegm from his throat, spitting it out onto the ground.

Kuwanlelenta stood with streaming eyes, tears soaking her cheeks and chin.

At that moment, more than anything, Tycho wanted to intercede and calm his friend with reason, but regarding this was all but a memory the vaquero held his peace and continued to watch. Unexpectedly, the man from before began to finally speak.

"Was all this worth it, Matthias?" replied Bill.

"I ask the same of you," said he, "was taking the lives of mothers and fathers and countless youth, whether we are God's children or not, ever worth what Halcón promised you? Can you not see how comparable the Congregation, this dogmatic cult, is to the Rahnthians; sooner or later they'll turn on their own people, and wrest control of Thrace's population as Rahnth had."

Bill sneered. "By your own magicks you've given the appearance of his election that you might escape persecution," he said, "demonic smoke set out from the orifices of your body, the very fire of Abaddon recovering all ailments in exchange for the very soul within you that burns anticipating damnation!"

"You're wrong, captain," said Matthias. "The very Spirit of God lives within us. You have been manipulated, and used by the Beast to fulfill her own ends to a prophecy your ignorant of—"

"You are being exterminated for your sympathizing with the Rahnthians, nothing more! And don't you ever call Lucia anything but a prophet, Matthias."

The missionary began to comfort his woman tenderly, placing an arm over her shoulders, caressing her hand as she whispered a prayer. "We are nothing of, our faith has it where rebellion against the powers that be is not an act we should ever partake in, for God put Rahnth in his position to—!"

"God wants Rahnth dead. God is on our side, Judean—I know this, because I know him. I'm inclined to believe that his Spirit is in me, for the amount of success we've had ridding of these heretics has been exceptional, doubtless an intervention on his behalf inspiring us all to work so that we'll earn his salvation." The heavenly counselor within the vaquero was offended by what Bill had spoken.

"I won't be taken for a fool," said Bill. "The retaliation from the men of this tribe, Seipatu the spearhead in their charge against us, is evidence against the righteousness you claim your people to have."

"Chief Heipatu and I never advocated for violence, he acted on his own, as with those who followed him into battle; they will give an account to God for them disobeying the Spirit, yet nevertheless they are saved; the blood of their savior given unto them ten thousand years ago."

"I've just had about enough of this," said Bill, beginning to lose his patience. "It's my fault I kept this conversation as prolonged as it has been, so it's best I end it now." He cocked the hammer of the Havoc, and took aim at Matthias, then the woman. "Both of you, on your knees," he said grittily.

From behind as an overturned basket's wicker squeaked, lifting with curious, blue eyes leveling on the dirt floor of the hut, another head shortly arose reprimanding the other child who compromised their secrecy, trying to quickly sit him onto the ground of the shallow hole. The quivering faced boy of blue refused him, seeing his mama and papa bow before their assailant, shouted in worry for the man to leave that his brother startled, was unsuccessful in placing his hand over his sibling's mouth before the first pitch of his cry was heard,— although he'd been instructed to remain quiet no matter what was to transpire within their home, or outside. Bill turned his head hastily to the side, and before the lives of the children could be brought to harm

Matthias leapt forwardly, and attempted to remove Bill of his gun. Enduring an exchanged beating and a round into him, Bill Pyron was able to release himself from the temporarily immobile Judean as he hurriedly aimed at his core, but in a trice was apprehended by the woman; a blade hidden underneath her leafy garment by a garter high enough on her thigh for it not to be seen, she unsheathed her point and drove it into wrist of the hand that clasped his piece, Bill forced to drop the gun as the blade had fully split through his carpals. Frightened, the revolver Havoc presently in the hands of Matthias as he'd reached for it as he began to stand anew, Bill Pyron removed the blade from his wrist witnessing its restoration amidst the permeation of the Spirit from out Matthias' wound, and elbowed Kuwanlelenta with his left arm, subsequently placing it about her throat as he turned to stand behind her, saying as he assured himself as with his men just beginning to charge towards the hut: "I've got this, boys—just havin' some fun." He pressured the appropriated blade against Kuwanlelenta's stomach; meanwhile, the captain was internally panicking over if he'd been cursed, sharing a fate as the Judeans for his flesh having undergone an instance of immortalization by magick.

Backing away with her as the native girl wrestled and jabbed her elbows into his side unafraid of death, his grip on the woman slipped and reactively caught her by the hair, beginning to drag her forcibly as he kept the knife at a readied thrust, threatening Matthias with her death if he decided to fire the gun; her bloodied nose slits from Bill's elbowing was starting to drip onto her flushed countenance, enraging her furthermore ere heaven's sealing came about. Again, she prayed.

Bringing herself onto her knees after having been thrown to the dirt, calming after the Spirit granted her peace, Bill Pyron grabbed an iron from the hand of his subordinate and stood behind the woman with an aim on her back.

"Come on out with the kids, Matthias. I promise I'll let your injun of a wife go if you're compliant." He unabashedly lied, hoping to meddle with his emotions; he was attempting to keep him from thinking in his state of provocation.

Nearing the threshold of the hut the missionary beheld his woman, enamored at the sight of her black, silken hair and skin sheen magnificently within the light of the moon. "Matthias, don't let them have our sons," she said at a whisper, though Matthias was able to read her lips.

Seconds lasted for an eternity to the missionary, contemplating—strategizing.

Kuwanlelenta nodded softly, and mouthed an affectionate farewell; the Judean knew what had to be done. Familiar with the Havoc's devastating casts after his scuffle with the regiment's last standing captain, a side of his lower torso removed of vital flesh scarce of penetrating the core, hastily aimed back at the side wall of the hut, and blew open an aperture wide enough for his children to escape through; the hut was sturdy enough to withstand the blast however the growing encirclement of flames would have it in soot after a short time. He shouted for his boys, and told them to run until their home could no longer be seen on the horizon when looking back, and to race the moon to its place of rest before the first light of dawn could warm them. The little one throwing aside the basket, his brother gave him a hurried push from out the hole and held his hand as he came to stand beside him; they both stood hesitant with tremulous features, and after another shout from their father the eldest brother Onesimus was strong enough to make flight through the soon-to-be enflamed aperture, and carried away his brother who cried in a fit of tears, wailing Matthias and Kuwanlelenta's parental titles all while Onesimus shedding his own waters, silent. The loss of his mother and father paining him to the point of numbness, as he heard the volley of gunshots shortly after their escape, was added by the cries of his little brother which broke his heart so.

The company's captain sent two of his men after the boys, but Onesimus' knowledge of the land's layout had them survive that night, until days after they finished searching presuming a predator of the wilds had them devoured. Onesimus cunningly collected limbs of similar proportion to their own, covering the skin with blue and emerald chalk and a coating of tar from one the many pits scattered throughout the woods onto the members of his deceased playfellows,—which distressed him mutilating their resting forms,—as to give the semblance of a freshly torn arm and leg. Placing them before the opening of a vectra den the men of the company would come to find the limbs, concluding their deaths at once as they began to tire from the elusive hunt. Any more telling of the escapades that followed Onesimus and Tycho's maturation in faith and form, becoming righteous young men in the Ahmenseraï's eyes would deviate from the point of focus within this chapter of the story, and its expansion will come later to which can be summarized as the vaquero's first disobedience to the Spirit in his hunt to kill the man that took him of his family.

Now the champion of Sol Puesta was beside himself, the visions of a haunting past having dissipated, was beginning to ruminate on the formerly repressed frights that this plane of torture and grief heightened until lunacy would beset the vaquero. Marching aimlessly onward as his mind toiled at constructing and obliterating objects of hate the Spirit did his part to soothe him without Tycho's notice, and after an hour walk, or what felt to be one, he found himself sitting at the edge of a lake where a much smaller waterfall granted him an ephemeral bliss. He couldn't quite put his finger on it, but with the

Spirit's comforting and the crash from the roaring stream he was at peace midst the onslaught of sorrow just previously. Deciding to lower his gaze from the waterfall he found at his eye's corner another man kneeling not too far in the woods surrounding, turning his head fully in the man's direction found it was unmistakably his old friend with the barrel of his lightning adorned iron pressed against his palate. Bill feeling the eyes of another on him opened his own to find Tycho staring at him, and at the meeting of their eyes was confirmation enough for the vaquero to run with distressing shouts for him to remove the gun from his mouth.

XVIII

ABOMINATION OF THE SON

A S TYCHO sped to meet his kneeling sire an omnimalevolent shade whispered the most horrible vulgarities and lies that the vaquero was more than pleased to shout at the voice to still, unfortunately his efforts to silence her was only to her benefit as his wrath and fear excited the ghoulish woman, prodding him until his mental fortitude was on the collapse, doubtlessly accredited to her agency and Abaddon's. A foot away from his depressed fellow Tycho watched the mirage flicker, and then suddenly dissipating all resembling form of Bill into a cloud of carmine as he reached out to grab a hold of him. Provoked with his self-destruction warranting a nervous breakdown, the Beast would continue to lure the vaquero through the woods until mentally conquered, with tormenting apparitions that would incite despair, whether a perversion of his mentor's image or his injustices against simple men that ravaged the conscious, the Beast would puppet his emotions as his sanity waned before allowing he to find his old, and beloved friend in yearning embrace. Against newfound knowledge of Bill persecuting his ancestral mother and father, there was an unshakeable faith the champion of Sol Puesta harbored that he'd been a changed man; for what other reason would there be for him to reanimate the Judean than the veteran's show of mentoring and companionship that proved a longing to father again, moreover, an undertaking of redemption? Certainly not the characteristics of an impenitent ideologue, the vaquero set out to find him, wandering hither and thither through the forestry until another malefic vision materialized before him.

Overborne with terror at what he could not somatically assail, the creature, charging with a bowing head, claws splayed for his maiming, had the vaquero startled more than he anticipated seeing the face of the supposed dissenter arise to reveal features notably of Bill's. The intensification of her cruelties so sudden as to put an end to his steadfastness with an arguably more disturbing mirage than of his mentor prior, Tycho balked in sorrow and fright as he allowed the figure of his nightmare to crash against him than reactively evade, dispersing in smoky wisps, and hearing: "I brought you into this world, and I can just as well take you out of it," and shortly afterward an echoing shout, from a disembodied man sounding not far off from the vaquero's own vocalizations, discouraged Tycho from continuing at the portent of what was to come. The modulation of the voice was uncannily that of Bill Pyron, but a mingling of bestial inflection that perturbed the champion of Sol Puesta greatly.

This horrid mirage was intended to be the second tipping point of Tycho losing all grasps on his sanity and willpower, Lucia accordingly dampening his zeal and resolve conditioned thus to accept an assured defeat at the hands of Bill Pyron, pressuring him to give up his venture in acquiring his steadfast fellow whom never once abandoned or ridiculed; if anything, Tycho owed it to him, to Kat, that he'd deliver him back to his home no matter his condition, and would not let a future yet to be transpired affect his goal, nevertheless haunted at an oncoming encounter that could just be a lie. Though Lucia was full of deceit, her visions than tongue were usually that of truth, and his reunion with Bill would prove this evidence. Truth has been at her disposal more frequently than fabrications, as it pained the individual more with grief and sorrows.

And at this point the Beast feeling challenged, she grinned naughtily and creatively explored another route to torment her precious Judean, whom she believed was the tribe's last. Stirring phantoms about him, haunting him for his haughtiness and lusting for blood to quench his indomitable rage, Tycho willed his way past the countless serfs he'd executed within the mountain, shielding himself from the agony of their murdering, all while rejecting the scenario of his old friend turning against him remarkably villainous. Tycho not once met the eyes of the conjured, keeping his eyes forward or above their heads never to inflict paralysis of the journeying spirit within him to crumble, and dissipate so readily at seeing their furrowed faces.

Deeply upset, she would make sure her implementation of an upcoming guise hitting closer to home, as done before comparably with an illusion of his mentor, would align to the success she foresaw of her winning future. Furthermore, observing his perseverance from the initial phantasms of Bill Pyron she knew it wasn't enough to break him, resolute on having him found, and would work her way up to have Tycho in a heightened state of vulnerability before granting him another sight of his possessed yokefellow, similarly when she had presented his family's massacre followed by the lure that was Bill knelt on the grass facing termination. She foresaw after bestowing the finishing instance of the tribulation between him and his fatherly one, and experiencing firsthand the climax of their reunion that was to follow, that his mind would face irreparable mental degradation, unable to competently stand against Captain William Pyron.

Deploying the throng of slain peasantry that was firstly ineffective, it was fitting for an image of the Brussian to follow, and a more potent and malicious summoning of a sight to behold of his Brussian companion burning within perpetual hellfire without means of salvation, just along the stream Tycho had begun to traverse along. Animals, abominations gifted with the enlightenment of reason, crafted from the hands of man, having no place in heaven—unless sanctified—or Abaddon's hells, the Beast went against her own choice of method in manipulation and presented his friend's unpleasant death as a genuine state of eternal being, using Tycho's ignorance of heaven's law against him to further abhor his Messiah and self.

These commencing steps of completing her second wave of destruction would lead to the Verumshaï's maddening, from tormenting recollections to indisputable misdeeds, the visitation of the slaughtered enchained and Sarkas' shade would act as a growing weight on his soul and conscious that would ultimately have him aggrieved.

Sarkas' shade cried out, horribly: "You never saved me! You chose not to save me! By the Ahmenseraï, I would not be charring to the bone, how I can best detail the paining of my hapless soul!"

Knowing the shade a beguilement of Lucia the vaquero couldn't yet help but respond to the false image out of an instant upsurge of remorse, more or less counseling himself than the fraudulent Brussian. "Sarkas," he said, frowning, "I never intended for this to happen, none of this! The Shine, I told you he wasn't gonna be there for us—I told you the Shine wouldn't be able to help us!"

"Anastasia, Sarkas, my boy!" he roared through the flames, "I cannot find them here amongst the fires of this scorched valley! Blue bot, don't forget me, come—come and get me out of this wretched place—!" The Beast did away with the semblance of a portal into Sarkas' hell apace. The vaquero was left disarrayed—troubled. Regardless of the disturbance Tycho foolishly embraced, he knew of its origin and purpose, and put his guilt behind him and furthered onward until at the vision of his mentor standing over his body where he would be faced with resentments and sorrow he hadn't the slightest clue of how to deal with, upholding disregard for his sins and shortcomings no longer an available tactic, he would continue to put blame on the Ahmenseraï for everything that has happened.

Walking beside the current upstream Tycho paused, looked behind then forward again. Where exactly was the vaquero headed? He thought he knew, but questioned as to whether the Beast was leading him with an intuitive sense of direction, where Bill might be. He had no other option than to move forward—training his mind solely on his friend's retrieval lest his thoughts ruminate on the past, bringing him hindrance. However, as Tycho found himself deepened in the carpeting mist of the forest with its thickening and aggressive outward flow, perceivably from the backwoods, the Beast began to whisper and taunt at his gradual engulfment.

"He was never your father to begin with," she breathed, her animalistic undertone disturbing him. "Tychicus Veritros, desperate, unloved killer—murderer, murderer, murderer!" and with each pronouncement of the accusation she'd only gotten louder, a bestial howl intensifying. The vaquero stood for a moment, cleared his throat, and denied its restriction whilst warding his eyes from misting.

"Although Tychicus, there is no arguing that you do take after him," she softly chuckled. The vaquero was troubled from the fact that Bill wasn't so different from him, nonetheless having hope that he'd find his old man as he remembered him last, before his kidnapping. He wished that he never had projected a certain image onto Bill Pyron that made the journey all the more difficult; for no good reason, Tycho always saw him for a saint, fantasizing about his heroism in the War, and the revelation of his ties to the Congregation's genocide, which had gone unspoken of prior to his leave from Sol Puesta, affected him to a greater extent than if Bill was to have disclosed their intertwined histories, fearing that his boy would recall what had driven him onto the shores of Sol Puesta in the first place. Following in his train of thought, he was irritated at the names his adversaries placed onto him, and just what they meant; *Judean*, and now what he surmised as an expansion of his name considerably as a tool for his mocking, he withheld from brushing off the terms from considerable thought as he questioned their validity, and meaning, knowing well before he had another appellation reinforced from the Stranger as Verumshaï.

The mist surrounding, having risen from his shins to his breast, he was then completely submerged within the chilly expanse as it barreled lazily overhead. His eye-lights failing to pierce through the brume, reflecting against the rolling wisps stinging the vaquero's sight, he closed his eyes to open them anew without the projected illumination to further strengthen his blindness amongst the mist. "I like hurting you," the Beast throatily uttered.

There was a chilling silence that followed her words, if they could be considered as the form as she was verging on an unintelligible bellow, and with the noiselessness Tycho was then distracted more than he had been with guessing the significance of names, as an intrusive thought crept into the forefront of his attentions, endangering his sole focus that was reaching Bill Pyron clearheaded.

Is there no way of reaching him, he thought, *am I here forever?* and now she had a foothold to work with. Starting as an inkling of a worry it propagated to a massive fretting, and the vaquero tried to refocus his mind again as his anxieties were building to new levels where surrendering, and giving up on the search were beginning to sound appealing. He shook his head in protest, gritting his teeth, crinkling his brow to a scowl, and marched through the brume. The thought never left him, currently overshadowing his predetermined goal, but he continued to walk, not entertaining whether the threat of failure would ever actualize. Covering miles of land that had certainly become mountainous where the feasibility of a defeated individual accomplishing such was an unlikelihood, the strong-willed youth had done so, only to fall in his Sprit-quenched state to stand against the witch's continued villainies, shouting at the intensified voices to silence as Lucia had intermingled her repulsive whispers with her daughter's cry of being gored, furthermore those of the hapless men slain by his hand, their yelps echoing to such a pitch that Tycho swore that if he had external ears, sensitive as Sarkas' were, they'd bleed. He also heard his fabricated shouts, calling out to him from the abyss. Dealing with his guilt poorly, now was the time to strike, Lucia thought, as he tired of ignoring the voices and his shame.

At his side, witnessing the completion of the scene he had a snippet of before, there Bill Pyron stood, his eyes fastened on the downed boy; below the man's head, it was indistinguishable from the monster that abducted him. Having enough of watching a single claw of Bill's drip with the spilt blood of his tutored, more soused than those stacked against the prominent talon, Tycho leveled his aim at his old friend as he turned his head to his shoulder to see who was standing behind. Finding his rescuer in a seemingly emotionless gaze, a telling of frightfulness with a quiver of his lip—the vaquero acutely pained—withheld from having his terror known as he was in the presence of adversity.

Suddenly, there was a light overhead. "Claimed child of mine," the radiating glory of the Ahmenseraï spoke, enrapturing all faculty of

Tycho's being, "trust in me, and lower your arm. She has no power over you, as you will find by submitting to the Lord, and that I am your sole sanctuary, and sword, to put an end to her malicious hounding. Know that I care for you, Tychicus…"

The vaquero was without proper response—mesmerized!— feeling the Shine tug harder than ever before within his chest to lay out his sins before God, becoming washed of all inequities that caused division between the two. From afar, the champion of Sol Puesta heard another's voice, less ethereal and familiar, "Tycho, my boy—my boy, can it actually be you…?" He set aside penitence to answer the man's inquiry, the Beast cunning.

The mist enshrouding now subsiding from today's dawn, an unfathomable veiling deployed to keep the vaquero ruminating till madness beset than allow him to avert his attention entirely on the land before him, to live presently than madden himself with doubts and insecurities, he found himself on an incline barren of trees, standing on coruscating granite from the countless rays spearing against the earth as the many fiery, warm tendrils filled the valley just below golden. From the curvature and sudden ceasing of the mountain's cresting Tycho guessed he was atop of the cleft mountain he'd seen several visions prior, and at its precipice he found his mentor poised, staring back. Unsure how he'd been drawn back such a distance from him, formerly bathed in the thickened, tarry black, he spied Bill worn of a threadbare thermal, a sleeve from his needlemouse blue shirt flowing in strips, his arm grooved with deep slashes spiraling down his arm scabby and red. On his other arm, the vaquero found his hand missing as it had been but eleven days ago at his departure from town. Against his nature to act upon fear and impulse, feeling ashamed, Tycho placed his trust in the Lord, and lowered his gun. Admittedly, at his wits-end, his unsteadiness to reason through the grotesque scene was accounted for his aim placed on the old man—a combination of inert survivability, developed psychosis from the properties of an alternate plane, and the femme-fatale that is Lucia Rothschild!

Holstering that piece of sputtering light, he called aloud seeing his friend's wary gaze, both in apprehensions whether one or the other was a hallucination: "Bill…?!"

Grinning, stopping short of shaking his head in disbelief, the old man welcomed him to come near, as he lamely shuffled towards his dogged gunslinger. Tycho approaching steadily, unsure and doubting the authenticity of this reunion he longed days and nights over, he hurried his steps for Bill to fall into his arms and prevent a tripping that would send him rolling down the mountainside. The weight of his friend pressed against him, and his expelling of breath warming Tycho's shoulder and cheek was an assurance that this was more than an illusion but proof the vaquero found his way back to his fatherly one; and if it hadn't been for the Father that loved him first, the Spirit that counsels, his elect would have dispatched Bill if not for His interference.

Grasping the old man tighter, slowly, the vaquero murmured, "Bill, I can't…," and he fought the trembling of his voice—gasping aquiver, meanwhile suppressing his anxiety that this was all a ruse from the Beast. Bill weakly patted him a few times on the back in their embrace, and said, "Alright, that's enough now, Tycho." He softly smiled, pulling away to get a clear look at his face where his memory no longer shrouded Tycho in a bygone carriage, seeing him marred from his most recent bout.

"What did it take for you to get here, Tycho?" His eyes glistened.

"Everything…It took everything of me to find you."

Bill Pyron realizing the undone scar from his lip to his left eye, his face bruised, said, "Yea, no kiddin', I can see that…What happened?"

He continued to bat his eye at the wound and blemishes upon his face, anticipating the worst news.

The vaquero explained after some silence, and his old friend bowed his head unspoken—listening. Bill had only interrupted at the hoarsening of Tycho's voice, discussing the aftermath of his crime, letting him know he would not hold it against him, nor was he in a justified position to, teaching him to never succumb to the heinous action of slaughtering the simpleminded so he would not end up like his old friend. Formerly seeking forgiveness from Bill, as Tycho would've been overjoyed and relieved to hear those words he'd just spoken, everything that he'd seen in Abaddon concerning his mentor could not help him feel cleansed of the deviltry he committed against those unsuspecting detainees.

Tycho reached behind himself, fiddling with something lodged in his holster belt. Presenting the shimmering harmonica as it left the vaquero's shadow, he said, "And there was this I found along the way."

"I left that for you to find, so you'd know I was still somewhere out there kicking," said Bill, folding the boy's fingers over the treasure in his palm. "Keep it." He raised his head.

"Bill," he said, "you know where we are?"

The man slowly nodded. "I've some idea."

Tycho mustered the courage to ask, "There was a man I came across, similar to you in appearance, though without all the wrinkles and crow's feet," he said, them both smiling needing the comfort of Tycho's facetiousness to ensure a discussion open to understanding than judgment, yet Tycho wasn't in the slightest of moods to joke, "harassing some folk with their two kids. Who were they, and why do I remember them?"

If only he knew how much I missed his playfulness, he thought. Bill turned and faced the mountain's sparkling precipice. "Follow me," he said, "there is something I need to show you."

Walking towards the edge Tycho followed at his side, thereafter looking down then eastward where the valley stretched for miles unseen, feeling wobbly where his shoes almost grazed the rim of the granite formation.

"Breathtaking, is it not?" said Bill. "My memory has served me well," he said, an undertone of heartache resonating through his voice. Tycho was without reply, waiting for his mentor to expound his reasoning for standing just before a drop so precipitous that Tycho had begun to imagine his own freefall—experience had not bettered his confidence in retaining his balance at the cliff of the mountain.

"Twenty years ago," started Bill, "under the regime of the luminary king—have I spoken to you about this before?" he queried, Tycho shook his head. Bill took a deep breath, and started again; he knew where this would all lead. "Before we had a nation to call our own, Aberica, which was known as Thrace, had been the breeding grounds for the luminaries, orchestrated by their king, Augurus Rahnth, and his Council to condition our people for enslavement as early as childhood. In our destitution, purposefully designed to keep us weak and dependent on their means of alleviation, which was laughable at best, with their little packets of crackers and powdery potatoes, issued taxes on food that were essentials for living—bread, fish—and most importantly, water, that was impossible to pay regularly, which resulted the majority of us becoming enchained, as, more and more were driven to thievery."

Bill turned his attention to Tycho when he said, almost murmuring: "Not so different from the Congregation, huh?"

Bill chuckled. "Not at all. Though, with the church during peacetime, they were having us pay them for our protection, when it was them we needed protection from. Their methods weren't entirely different when comparing them to the Rahnthians.

"It was basically chattel slavery, Tycho—we were never supposed to pay those taxes. We were bred for bondage and to die in the chains that bound us to unavailing servitude. It was almost blatant what they were doing, but everyone one of us fatigued from," he chuckled, dealing with the matter with levity as best he could, "*malnutrition*, whatever you want to call it, kept us from having real critical thought, just trying to make it through the day. I remember the remarks of the luminaries who would come to take away my brothers when I was around your age, saying, we weren't actual citizens, that we deserved to be enchained since our contribution to the crown was nonexistent. They also loved to stir up division between us Thracians than having our focus on them, goading us to turn on each other in fear—anger, blaming each other for the famine we all faced. That, that all ended when the prophet made her entry."

Tycho's interest strengthened, anticipating discourse regarding his tormentor.

"Defeated, desperate, and hungry," said Bill, "we placed all of our hope in the woman, who conjured rivers for the thirsty and filled the bellies of the famished, performing miracles that deceived even the elect, that she was to make way for the Ahmenseraï's return, who we never took into serious consideration until she claimed anointment from him, later, claiming she was the messiah. Those Judeans, who failed to study the Torr, came to realize they'd gravely mistaken her identity once she declared genocide against her people, fooled into considering Rahnth was the Beast. Yet, she fulfilled exactly what they had expected from her, though not how they had envisioned.

"She certainly removed the wool from over our eyes, revealing our situation as cattle, the purpose of the lofty tariffs…why so many of our kids had gone missing, something we all knew but never could accept; choosing not to see through the guise helped us go about life without more problems, which couldn't have been further from the truth. And as she and her mouthpiece preached, that we deserved, and should fight for equality, we all roared and cheered; I can guarantee you, less than half of the folk listening knew the entirety of what *equality* actually entailed, but it sure sounded good—how could anything have been worse than the systematic rule we were under? What she actually meant by equality," said Bill, caressing his stubbly chin, "was for the Congregation to rival the power of the Rahnthian Kingdom, leaving us to assume it meant comparable living standards to the luxuries of the moths, than say, sharing our pittances to keep us working, constantly, to overcome the burden of labor unending. We were pawns, tools used by the prophet to raise her to a position of power and influence over the Ravaja, and beyond, as the church's reach expanded, for the goal in establishing a hierarchy were she had control without having to answer to Rahnth, resulting in the elimination of God's chosen that would have had the luminary king and his Council question or even deny her suspecting motives.

"The demagogue she was, she played the crowds masterfully, calling us all to unite under her; we became the very body of the Congregation, forming our own socialistic nation and adhering to an ideology that left little room for questioning; our survival demanded it, or so we believed. Against the very foundations of social-utopian ideals found in her teachings, cunning in her misinterpretations of Scripture from the Torr, we were inspired to hate our Judean minority, accused of being practitioners of witchcraft, loyalists and spies for the crown, that *we* were God's chosen, those who had the Shine were forgeries of the essence that dwelt within the prophet, and, because we were so good at pointing the finger at others for our problems their removal came and went without protest; we felt empowered, better than the lot." Bill grieved.

Knowing Lucia had the emanations, the vaquero gnashed his teeth at her falsehood to present herself borne of the Spirit. Tycho saw him hurting, reading him, looked past his façade of stoicism. "Bill, knowing the man that you are, not what some regime made you out to be, it's hard for me to see you like this." Tycho swallowed, continuing strong in voice, inspired from what the Lord spoke unto him, "Stop allowing her to possess you with guilt, she shouldn't have this much power over you anymore—"

"Although specialized regiments knew what happened to them," Bill interjected unsmilingly, "practically all Aberican soldiers and citizens were kept in the dark of their actual fate. But no longer can I hide my horrors, by which I regret all that you saw." His eyes glistened in the fixture of a stolid, sun-kissed face.

"So it was that I came to the homeland of the Kasheen, Chardonnya, where we first met, and you were just a toddler then. This is what I wanted to show you, your birthplace…I'm surprised you hadn't pulled the trigger within the instance of seeing my face again," said Bill, peering through sunlight at the mountains beyond.

"I thought about it," said Tycho. "But I don't think Kat would've appreciated it. I came all the way here to bring my friend back home; I ain't about to leave here empty-handed."

Both of them smiled weakly, though, heavily disheartened, Bill glancing at him before redirecting his sights onto the greyish peaks. Shortly after, they enjoyed their company in the ambience of the mountaintop's cooling breeze, silent.

"Why didn't you go through with it?"

Bill looked over at him. "Hm?"

"Is there another reason for why we're found up here?" Tycho said, looking down once more at the valley below. "I feel like, you're hesitant on finishing the story—it's unlike you to give me the build-up without the moral coinciding with the ending, Bill." He grinned, his face then resting into a melancholic expression. Undoubtedly Tycho knew of the sorrow that would come with his finishing tale. And, having already put the pieces together, he wouldn't push him for a concrete answer as to whether the father and mother within the hut were of his heritage.

"Well…," began his old friend, astute on the vaquero having also seen the vision at his attempt of his self-termination, "regarding your first question, eventually I snapped, Tycho; the smell of their bodies beginning to rot, winds cutting through their ravaged, and torched villages, carrying the stench coerced me falling to my knees, yet the thought of leaving behind Kat and Miles was upsetting enough to have me stand back onto my feet—I couldn't stomach having them abandoned. Remember Caroline, Joanna's daughter?"

Tycho nodded.

"What a hypocrite I would have been, huh? Maybe that's the moral of this story; take the plank out your own eye before the speck out of someone else's. I was wrong to have made her an example, fearing that I would lose you, though your situations greatly differed. I was so critical of her because I understood what her absence had done to her mother and everyone else in town, and I—I couldn't bear the pain to lose another son."

"Miles, he was your—"

"Yes," said Bill sternly, then softening his tone, "yes, Tycho."

Catching the vaquero's eye, he saw his friend's wrist, from where his hand had been severed, start to drip, watching the droplets wet the toe of his shoe and onto the ground before him. But something was amiss. Observing asquint as to not arouse any suspicion on his behalf, he found the droplets to be sticky, slowly moving their way down from the toe of his shoe eventually onto its outsole.

"And," Bill started again, "prior to stumbling onto my knees, before slavering all over the Havoc's barrel"—self-deprecating, the vaquero's mentor wished he hadn't gone into such detail, grimacing, as this was his boy he was speaking to—"I came here, to have one last look upon this precious valley, being at peace, somewhat, before heading back down, listening to that damn voice tellin' me there was no other option than to…"

"*Who's voice, William?*" Lucia whispered, her followed utterance remaining as a constant, earsplitting growl in the old man's hearing. "*Your hunt goes unfinished…take him.*"

A simple command, enough to shatter the fortitude of his mind, which the Beast had temporarily upheld to bait her Judean, as it had previously been neutralized from forced henosis with memories of trauma.

Bill's features went flat, becoming unexpressive. Tycho perceiving it had been because of the subject of their discourse, said: "You don't have to say anymore, Bill. Let's start trying to find a way out of here, yeah?"

Disregarding the cautiousness he held before when analyzing Bill's bleeding wrist, Tycho watched the severed point start to spew more than it had ere, a stringing outflow of tar that was gradually becoming thicker and steamier as it fell onto his shoe, spilling over the side of the mountain.

"Then it was, years later, you came for me," said Bill Pyron, exceptionally slow in his delivery.

"Bill…we can go over this later," he said hesitant, denying his intrigue to know exactly what he was about to divulge, as, he began to worry for him. "Remember the pillar," said Tycho, believing he was tossed into the stone edifice at *Titan Summit* than the one contained within the subterranean castle, "focus on that. Our thoughts might be our only way of provoking it to bring us back to the Ravaja—"

"I didn't want to do it," said Bill, his back rolled inwards violently, thudding with the deformation of his spine; Tycho could do nothing but watch in horror. "I can't be forgiven for what I've done," he said heavily as it led into a rancorous snarl, the mark's light bleeding through the back of his thermal. The tar blood commencing to sheathe him in an ungodly bearing, it clambered along his legs until settling underneath his bobbing head, where his eyes rolled inward that only the whites of their undersides were seen. "There is no escaping her. Tycho, you cannot stay for me—!" The old man's head jerked as he struggled to say these words, and then belting out a harrowing roar that brought the first tears to the vaquero's eyes since he was just a pup. Proceeding to walk back, slowly, Tycho could do nothing but watch in horror and misery, questioning as to why the Ahmenseraï would allow this to happen! So, his resentment for the Lord blossomed anew, believing he and his friend forsaken as punishment for the vaquero not giving praise, ignorant of comprehensive prophecy, all while his fatherly one devolved into some devilish pawn for the Beast, hearing the popping reconfiguration of his bones.

Tycho, quick to submit to the feeling of betrayal, pinned the Lord responsible for letting his guard down, the lies of Halcón muddying the truth of who God is, an unconditionally loving and forgiving father! Verily, it was Lucia Rothschild who had this all engineered at the capture of the four emanations, arguably her alternate, less-desired route for the Verumshaï to undergo; this fight would ravish her perversities nonetheless. She fooled the vaquero into a false sense of security with Bill's recognizable presence, that by letting his guard

down,—to which he should have known better to not have done,—
Bill's abrupt transformation is what completed what she set out to do
at his arrival into Abaddon, to finally have him break, where her
attempts with visions and voices before failed to have his willpower,
but ultimately the Lord's providence, overthrown. She had the
Ahmenseraï underestimated, with him withering and whatnot, and
instead of presenting his child of light before William Pyron already
armored in blood, she gave the stubborn Verumshaï hope, a counterfeit
hope of seeing a loved one scarce able-bodied, repentance forgotten
with a sudden surge of selfish emotion to distract him.

Furthermore, her daughter remaining in the Summit for Tycho's
return, she then began molesting her with horrid thoughts and
unwanted talks for her to take the throne—Lucia was preparing.

Mourning over her friend's corpse the savage woman tilted her
head to the side, believing she had heard someone within the obsidian
expanse. No sooner had she suspected it was the Beast returning to
haunt her anew. And in a strange and violating tongue she had spoken
to Fera with, sharp hisses—low grunts. Fera had not the slightest clue
how to make out what the omnimalevolence was speaking, and Lucia,
having forgotten her daughter responded only before to the language
she'd grown accustomed to from adolescence to adulthood, spoke as
she had previously when her spawn was to slay the Verumshaï! It was
out of instinct she addressed Fera in the language of her creators, how
she would sing to her when in the womb.

Fera, now comprehensive of the speech, remained staunch and
resilient to her manipulations, presenting vision of herself battered by
the vaquero when he returned if she hadn't listened to what the Beast
commanded of her.

"Tycho is nothing like my father. Leave me, witch."

"Father—that man you claim to be never was, child!" The sound of the sentence came fleshy, and gargled. It was disembodied than internal voices her conscious was wrestling to subdue.

Hearing the chatter emit from her downed fellow, perturbed, she gradually steered her head to the noise's source. She found the corpse's mouth move as one was puppeteering its lower mandible up and down, unnatural and mockingly infuriating, upsetting the girl more than disgusting her.

"Regardless, a man is a man, and is bound to be no different! Had he not tried to have you killed?! Take the throne," the corpse boomed, its imbrued gums dripping with salivation as its mouth smacked, "become God—kill Tycho, or he'll have you pissing blood."

Agitated and shaking off her exhaustion from battle Fera realized she had been drifting into sleep, and the illusion of Sarkas' voicing was just the start of a nightmare. But Lucia's words, those wouldn't end, harassing her daughter with repressed fears and provoking traumas until fooled into acquiring peace once sat on that black chair.

The savage woman looked at the fallen Brussian's face, and was at peace that her fellow rested undisturbed, though it was only a nightmare of his necromantic revival, it still angered her and was nonetheless reassured to find his features unchanged. And with renewed vigor given to her from the heinous vision of her friend somewhat possessed to serve as a mouthpiece unnecessarily for the Beast, Fera battled the deceptions that would lead her to enthronement, and would try to find a way to censor the voices in her head. But, it would be by this act to attempt to silence her mother with found strength in her fallible wrath that the Beast orchestrated for her offspring to be choked by other displeasing thoughts, as one subject of hate leads to another in its own twisted rabbit hole of sorts. The manipulation of Sarkas' mandible had been the incitement needed to cloud Fera's judgment, leaving her to revel in her anger than question as to why Lucia Rothschild chose to vilify the corpse.

Lucia would lead her daughter down the meditating path she wanted her to take without Fera noticing at first where her hate was being directed towards, eventually coming to find her conscious tearing the vaquero to shreds! Fera, innately finding a reminder of Tycho's word, her eyes drifted to the mark of the bat's cauterization without a conscious thought of doing so, and felt its rigidness smiling weakly. In her recollection of the vaquero's pleasantries, buried underneath the horrors of their journey thus far, the savage woman held close to her heart the times her reckless companion made her laugh, suddenly reminded that he had indeed saved her life before.

Fera wincing asudden the Beast filled her with an enmity that temporarily conquered her found affections for the young man, but realizing these uncalled-for thoughts were not of her own volition, feeling a presence upon her, rationalized it had been the usurper of heaven against her. Her attempt at defeating the Beast's influence with anger, her greatest source of strength, had only empowered the witch.

"Take some obsidian, and carve the mark on the back of your hand, sit on the chair, and have at your core," said she, flashing images of the lines scabbing Halcón's backside. "Forever loved you'll be; not one will be able to tear you down, Fera. If any are to come against you, by your will, they will either be spared, or decimated for their discountenance!" Her voice rumbled.

"And who's *they?*" queried Fera.

"Those who are to be subjects under your rule."

The girl understood Lucia was baiting her to sit upon the throne with renewing her hatred for Tycho, the pain he caused her more terrible than of her past assailants, where she was never tempted to show any form of compassion towards them in their trouncing. She cared for him, but to squander a position of unfailing adoration seemed outright nonsensical. Her thoughts were beginning to align with the Beast's agenda; an insidious woman her mother was, continuing to relate traumas to Tycho and what he would do to her in the near future.

In the higher existence where Lucia was managing her daughter to have her body vessel for her consciousness to strike down heaven's king, she had also been busy at operating the skirmish between the Judean and his demoniac teacher, anticipating fervently for her climaxing at the boy's death.

As Bill Pyron lifted himself from the ground, and turned around imposingly to face Tycho, making the gradual backward steps needed to distance himself, he witnessed the complete detail of the blood armor. Toes lengthened into carnivorous talons on his now bestial feet, the greatest of them sickle-shaped, tapping on the earth rhythmically, presented to the vaquero just how different this encounter would end, bearing a more lethal composure William Pyron had than of the creature he faced at Castle Rothschild. His legs, malformed, concavely shaped gave the impression of a predator's stance, granting him expeditious travel when hunting, perfect for the lunge. From his torso to his arms the tarry substance irregularly throbbed, forming the trenchant, milky claws at the ends of his hands, jutting his elbows out into crescent sabers near to nipping his shoulder blades. And as for the old man's mouth the blood that coated his throat and neck reached selectively for his jawbone, elongating his canines in comparison to the great cats of prehistory, sharpened and girthy. Lucia, she made sure the victory was decisive before the battle had even begun, helping, seeing what it would take in her foresight, witnessing accounts of the highest probabilities of Tycho's failure, a guarantee due to his own refusal to fight back—it was this she had betted on from the beginning, but made sure if there were to be any of the lesser fates having fruition that Tychicus Veritros would not overcome by the brainwashing of his dreadfully weaponized sire.

Bill started approaching the vaquero, slightly hunched. "There is no saving me, boy. I am the monster I always have been, nothing's changing that. I am forsaken," that of which he'd been lied to by the Beast believing the Ahmenseraï would have nothing to do with him, breaking him down to embrace the murderer within than repent. "Run," uttered Bill, "before I am all the more inclined to finish what I started those years ago. I just might find peace in your death, so she says." His eyes commenced being filled black, reflecting Tycho's pitiful gaze.

"Bill," said Tycho, struggling to keep his face unflinching, "this isn't who you are, or the man I know you to be. We're going home," and he reached out his hand in faith that his friend would come to his senses, more or less an attempt to pacify his grizzled compadre; what more could this fool do without God?

The bloodthirsty codger howled for a disturbing length, and firmly pressing his feet against the earth with the lowering of his theropod-like legs, William Pyron suddenly released the tension of his wound muscles and sprung. In his essay to elude the pounce at him Tycho suffered having his arm gouged to the bone, his speed unable to match the skidding hunter's, as Bill, clawed his way back up the rock. Holding his hand over his arm futilely as he watched his adversary regain footing on the granite mound, he took the Havoc into his other hand, and fiddled with its hammer.

If it hadn't been for Bill's tortured conscious, the vaquero would be without his very means of defense, and clothing. This was of no concern to Lucia or her repossessed soldier, seeing as to whether Tycho had it in him to fire a bolt at his mentor, hungering for the contemplation to come only for him to surrender. Facing abuse by her own father and presumably ignored when calling out to the Ahmenseraï for release, she exacted her revenge on God's child of light by actualizing this match to mock her Messiah, showing that even he has failed to deliver his elect by choice in a situation that hadn't been so different from her own. This was her retribution, revenging against the Lord for his abandonment, sickly getting off to this show of horrors of son against father. Admittedly, her works to quench the Spirit within Tychicus and the vaquero's own disobedience is the cause for his predicament, not the Lord's.

"Never took you for one as being virtuous…"

"Far from it," said Tycho, weakly chuckling. "I'm just not about to give up on my friend, and if you would, I'd like him back, Lucia."

A low emitting roar rumbled about in Bill's chest, and said he, "I'm here, Tycho; don't worry. It seems"—his head tilted to the side—"you're wounded. Let me numb that for you."

The vaquero raised his lightning crowned iron. "Bill, stop—!"

William Pyron began to quicken his strides and hunching into a pouncing stance, he launched on top of the boy, seizing him with the exception of his legs, where, Tycho forcefully drove his knee into Bill's stomach, leaving his mouth gaping for intake of lost breath, but then he lessened the opening of his mouth and started laughing. These vessels of man needed not oxygen to function, only conductivity, as everything else came as an experience to be appreciated, such as feeding or drinking. But there had been an oversight, affecting these hominid descendants, on man's behalf that hindered their progeny greatly. Technocrats with occultists of the political elite from the world before never accounted for the brains of sapiens-hulls to make more and more of the core's primary task vestigial; they were created too similar to the human mind, exact copies in all aspects. Some years after their departure from an existence they housed themselves in during Wormwood's impacting, it began to reject the core and its conductive properties as its main source of energy for lesser bits of nutrients that contained a fraction of the electrical intake they otherwise would have received from the earth. With or without their stay in the material realm the human mind and its body evolved to survive on tangible foods and liquids, and all would face certain starvation, dehydration, and suffocation in planes other than that consisting of a physical Earth. In the end, it was to their benefit they couldn't remain for long outside of Assiah.

The mind of the vessels could not understand how to function without eating, drinking, or respiration being accomplished. But, with enough focus, meditation, and will, an individual can rely solely on his core to have himself at full strength, and that's just what Bill had discovered here in Abaddon before driven mad.

"Time to get this over with," said Bill, raising his set of claws, shimmering as each talon elongated out from underneath the other. The vaquero proceeded to shoot off his mentor's hand, resisting the hesitation to punch him squarely on the mouth. Bill stumbling backwards a foot or two from his victim's blistering swing he renewed his posture, and charged at the vaquero as he began standing. Tycho met him in his charge, and grappled ahold of him as he placed his arms about his midriff in the tackling; unawares, they would find themselves tumbling down the mountainside in their continual toss. From his peripheral sight in their rolling thrash he spied them nearing closer to freefall, finding any rock he might latch onto as stopping before the steep was unpreventable.

Quickly, Tycho chanced grappling ahold of a stony obtrusion in the fall as he swung pendulum against the mountainside, holding onto Bill with his left hand where his arm continued to bleed.

"Bill," he distressfully hollered to him, "fight her! We need to find a way back up this mountain—I need your help!"

His disturbed and made sycophantic friend admired his other hand at its restoration, enchanted by the gleam that came at the erection of his talons. Bill then replied, "No, I think I'm just starting to enjoy this," and drove his renewed tools for carving into Tycho's back, tearing off the end of his poncho. The latter cried horribly, and was forced to release his grip from the stone at the pressure of William Pyron pulling down on him with the inability to bear the pain that came with it. They would find themselves falling into a providential body of water, where the stream Tycho had previously followed supplied the reservoir from the melting caps of sub-stratospheric mountains afar.

As the deranged mentor emerged from out of the reservoir, showering the grass with his first step onto the glade, he looked about, scanning the tree-line, and then turned his eyes to the bloodied pool— there hadn't been a trace of the boy to be found, not even a trailing left on the grass. Bill strutted out in the opening, and feeling his back needed scratching, bent backwards, thereafter grazing a slickened elbow against his skin. Listening for the slightest crunching of a twig, or woeful emission that would disturb the silence, Bill hadn't the patience to stand any longer preoccupying his boredom by having his backside calmed, and shouted provocatively for his fellow to hear: "What drove you to Sol Puesta, I can now say I know the suffering you endured that led to our standoff! I remember, trying to dissuade you..." He chuckled queerly.

What cost him his sanity? Aside from the previously stated manipulations of Lucia, the lowest existence had its part too in having his willpower nonexistent. William Pyron underwent the torment of slaying families ceaselessly, something he would not forgive himself for, and those he persecuted, the vaquero's particularly, shared the experiences of his mother's, father's, brother's, and Tycho's sufferings. After enough cycles of murdering the parents of his son, Bill surrendered, and the Beast took hold of him.

Amongst the countless trees skirting around the glade Tycho situated himself behind one of the grand boles, biting down on a large enough stick as he felt the Havoc's mane down his arm, inch by inch searing the wound shut until fully cauterized; he withheld his urges to blare an oath or groan as those electrical spikes sizzled his flesh to a close. Hearing Bill's voice, he was immediately drawn to the echo, and continued on with his reparation as he listened intently. Tycho was sure it would be of concern, knowing well whatever he'd spoken in regards to their meet-up years ago was a means to have the latter drawn out from the woodland, and wouldn't allow himself to fall for any sympathies his mentor might arouse within his breast.

Bill picked his teeth. "Wasn't too long ago," he said. "Found you on foot, not a scratch on you, which was odd, seeing how you had come from the other side. I hadn't recognized you at first, but after putting a light on that dreaded glaring of yours it was rather the epiphany; the squealing brat from Chardonnya, he lived. I told you, again, and again, I hadn't killed your brother—that I was sorry for the murdering of Matthias and Kuwanlelenta, but you weren't there to listen, your mind had already been made.

"Finding you, scattered amongst the sand was only half the truth. You weren't as mean as a drawer as your old man, and I left your body to rot in the dust before I had a conscious to do otherwise. For a long time, Kat hadn't a clue where I was about most nights; I knew that she had grown suspicious that I wasn't just patrolling, as I would sneak my way into bed in the late mornings, and was starting to worry where her thoughts might end up leading her. I was tempted to tell her, about you, but I could already see her reaction as horrified. The night I had made the decision to put an end to my tinkering thereon, toiling at the abandoned church's altar, you awoke, thankfully recalling the first half of your name and nothing more," he chuckled. "Amazing…"

"I wanted to die, so badly, son." He turned his hands, analyzing them. "If not for Kat, you were the only thing that kept me going."

The vaquero remained resolute, and sat healing his wound. Repeatedly he told himself this wasn't the man he knew, in his effort to not have himself lured from his hiding place, fighting the seducing storm of homicidal thoughts as he prior experienced with Sarkas Severov at the cenote.

Minutes passed, and the vaquero's grit had weakened significantly. Failing to fall numb to all emotion, his amore and sensitivity heightened from Bill's accounting, Tycho became certain that confronting Bill would end the hellish flashes of his mentor's demise before he entirely succumbed to betrayal, as he would see it. His will had been jeopardized by the greater influences of darkness.

Again, the sound of God's voice came upon him gently, conquering the witch's talk without effort. "You can't do this, not alone. Let me fight for you, let me fight through you.

"I have heard Sarkas' and Onesimus' prayers," he said, "as well as the fears that have burdened your conscience to believe that I have left you, failed you…I am your God, and I will never abandon you, my beloved son! Stand, and walk towards your father in confidence that I will turn Lucia's plans against her.

"Pray, repent," and with this command from the Ahmenseraï the young Judean clasped his hands together, closing his eyes with a bowed head, exhibited the action from his subconscious from a lifetime ago previous to his post-amnesiac identity. Tycho felt the love of the Spirit, the Shine, as he remembered him before his long odyssey into the

Wastes, but, consumed with hatred and given to its drunkenness of emotion, the boy could not repent nor forgive.

He chose darkness over the light, though the light chose him.

"Why is it until now you hadn't told me where I'd come from," shouted the vaquero, "that I would have a witch after me?!"

Bill looked to the tree-line, and lessened his smirk's intensity. Seeing the boy's composure, he saw his storytelling was efficacious in drawing him into the open. Bill had acquired the scent spoor of his student well into the tale, but found greater pleasure in manipulating his quarry to come forward than a brainless sprinting that would garner only a fleeting excitement compared to the release that would come from his building anticipation.

"Because you would have killed me had I not killed you first, if you remembered."

Tycho frowned, given to sorrow than remain resolute. "How is it I stand here then, without a barrel leveled at your head?! Bill, you endangered all of the lives in Sol Puesta than just your own because you were so afraid of what might've happened."

"You can say I was being more than selfish," he said, grinning wry. Against his will, Bill Pyron was felled into unexpected writhe, at the Beast's mercy, and howled gutturally in torture.

"I guess so, Bill," said Tycho faintly. "But I'll have to interpret that as the loss of my life was of greater concern than yours, or even Kat's, maybe. I know you love me, a lot, Bill." The vaquero unwillingly choked, the brim of his hat shadowing his features.

And as the champion of Sol Puesta raised his head he found his old friend snarling mad, barking, slowly raising himself onto all fours—he had been completely overtaken by the adversary of God. The Havoc hung at Tycho's side, with a weakened grip, scarce slipping out from his hand. The Ahmenseraï's eyes were on him, stirring the Spirit within his temple to have the boy call upon him, but the hatred filling a portion of Tycho's being had his beckoning disregarded.

Without difficulty, the Ahmenseraï could have restored his earthly father and made Lucia the fool in a flash, but it was Tycho's decision to make, as the Lord is not a forceful God, allowing us to seek him so that we may be saved. By design, free-will was bestowed onto humans, and their machines he adopted, so that they could choose to love He, the Ahmenseraï, than obey absent of amore. Regardless, the Ahmenseraï knew Tycho would make this choice needing not to comprehend probabilities, but simply by knowing how his son is. It would take time for his Judean boy to return to him, the Lord at peace with this, however, was gravely saddened from Tycho's choice to reject, furthermore, by his misfortune, depending on the flesh as done previously in his adventure.

But, the Ahmenseraï was already aware that one day, as long as he pursued him, Tycho would surrender himself in totality before heaven's king, remaining in the everlasting bosom of his forgotten father.

As for Lucia, he anticipated the final battle that would span across realities and timelines involving man, retrieving his captured daughter from her sickening control. Disadvantageously, the rebellious witch knew what force and fate would befall unto her, but that had not stopped her from making certain her destruction would never come to pass, believing the Lord was already hers for the taking.

The hound of Lucia charged, and the vaquero aimed!

Hearing the words emitted from the vision of Tycho's rebirth and destruction as his mentor claimed responsibility for, "I brought you into this world, and I can just as well take you out of it," Tycho fell onto his back in flight of Bill's pounce and discharged a round into his mentor's chest, the mark of the Beast gone effectively. Bill fell at

Tycho's side in convulsions, redirected from the impact of the bolt that had burrowed its way through to his posterior. Tycho rolled over, and vomited white as he stationed himself upon his hands and knees, shaking terribly as he looked over to the dying form of Bill Pyron. He repeated, "No, no, no, no, no...," as he crawled his way over to him, and feebly cradled his mentor's body of throes as he tried to get his eyes to align with his own bloodshot set. "Bill," said Tycho, his face crinkling, "Bill, please look at me."

Slowly, his old friend turned his head. "I always hated that you carried that gun," Bill said sternly, but grinning small signed for the vaquero to chuckle amidst his lamenting, done instinctively to comfort his friend. Interrupted from the convulsions as he continued to speak, seemingly unbothered by it, said, "I don't think I'm coming back home with ya, tiger," and the vaquero held his tongue, teary-eyed.

"I allowed you to become who you are, had I...," and before his words were finished his head tilted to the side, his eyes without spirit. He saw in Bill's hand, which had remained hidden from him, his core, irreparably crushed, as he'd violently wrested it from his abdomen before having lost control of his mind for a second time; he spared the boy from killing him, from a pang of insufferable guilt.

Unable to conceive Bill gone for an eternity, Tycho shook his body slightly, confused as to why his friend had suddenly gone limp. But soon after his assaying, something had sparked in Tycho's mind; the vaquero stifled an uncontrollable wail. His denial could no longer outweigh the validity of the deaths of those he loved, his childish anger done away with, and mourned their passing, with those he'd done wrong. It took the death of a significant man in Tycho's life for him to see that there was an end to anticipate, putting light on the deaths of others before that the vaquero could now grasp, whereas the comprehension of all mortal fates was just out of reach. Tycho hadn't recognized his near-death at *Titan Summit*, believing his fight was against an unconscious fit from his fatigue brought upon him by Al Halcón's carelessness; remembering the tyrant's discourse, he heard again, "As you drift into eternal sleep, are you beginning to feel the scorching tongues of hellfire snap at your haunch and backside as you awaken anew into lands unforgiving?"

But soon his mourning shifted into a meditation of hating and murder, thinking uncleanly of what he'd do to the gods had he the power to confront them. A dudgeon so intoxicating and wretched that the shadow of Tycho's soul exuded in such potency that nearly rivaled Lucia Rothschild's complete frame of being, the Beast felt the presence of the boy, and in desperation—as all else had failed—imbued the evil with her might of creation, making something that consisted of her existence but primarily of the vaquero's. She had it this way, so that his destruction would come by the downfall of his own soul, simply, to humiliate.

Becoming alert to the faint echo of felled trees that surpassed observation, presumed the ground thundered miles away from their impacts, there was a mightier force that shook and inflicted the earth to moan. Steadily on the approach from the horizon, concealed by the forest's canopy and surrounding mountains, left Tycho questioning the agent behind the destruction of the woods. And as the trees and the crash from their uprooting grew louder, the ground jarring the vaquero's sight as it became unsettlingly vibratory, espied the horns of the fellow responsible for the disruption, reaching higher than the peak of the mountain it had passed, the shoulder of the gaunt-limbed titan grazing lazily against the mountainside as it turned out from an unseen valley, bathed in an avalanche from the bothered mount as it continued on. The sound of the collapsing boles soon became unheard, consumed from the heavily reverberating steps of the soul as it neared Tycho.

Stopping dead before him, Tycho, feeling the heaven's shaken from its presence, remained still as the appalling figure hunched to obtain a more intimate level of speaking with its progenitor, which took well over several seconds to accomplish; void of eyes, or any form of expression, all the vaquero had to see was a goat's skull portending him of his coming demise.

It said boomingly with great respire, the vaquero subjected to holding his breath in a fetid enshrouding, "Father, I have come for your people, who have taken refuge in the city of sands. Know that I am the harbinger of the Ahmenseraï's return, and by having your death last I will claim the appellation as mine. Praise be to Lucia, as every knee will bow and tongue confess that she is Lord."

Perceptive to the evil that emanated from the goat-skulled fellow, Tycho was without words—horrified beyond what reasoning that might come with accosting. The vaquero, along with the deceased Bill Pyron, vanished from the realm of perpetual tortures. And as for the Abomination conceived from the unrepentant Verumshaï, several barriers it would have to withstand until reaching the desert city put in place from one unexpected, yet capable of challenging Lucia Rothschild's schemes.

XIX

DEAR HEARTS AND GENTLE PEOPLE

THE back of her hand cut, the Keter was left incomplete as two bodies barreled down the stairs, the obelisk afire. Disenthralled from her fearful mindset, Fera cast the stone she used for the carving aside, leaving the semblance of an upside-down crucifix with paired horns atop before the mark's completion, and staggered her way towards the vehemently exhaling Verumshaï. Helping him sit up, Tycho was oblivious to Fera's comforting speech as he gazed about, then settling his eyes on the apparition before him. The savage woman tried seeing what Tycho had fixated his gaze on, but there was nothing she could derive from the shadows of the corridor. "You're not Bill," murmured Tycho. "Go, go…!" shouted the disturbed vaquero.

Fera, disconcerted, jerked slightly at his holler. Looking over her shoulder, she found what she surmised to be the corpse of Tycho's beloved friend, spying the grisly apertures on his breast and stomach reason for Tycho's overbearing grief, as it was evident at least one of the craterous marks came from his lightning borne revolver. She remained crouched beside him as Tycho began gesticulating with the hallucination, understanding this was the vaquero's way of processing his mentor's death. Moreover, unknown to her, the effects of Abaddon were primarily responsible for his developed psychosis, and would remain until repentance.

"Leave me alone…." His lower eyelids brimmed sodden.

"Tycho," said William Pyron, "I know you did what you had to. If anything, it proves your tenacity cannot be overcome. Damn, if only I had a spirit like yours, kid…You're more like your father than I care to admit, though he was a good man, I always saw you as my own."

"Bill," spoke Tycho weakly, "you are my father."

Bill was panged distressed. "No, son…I'm not; I failed to measure up to one, remember most importantly, I am the slayer of your family."

"I won't allow you to blame yourself," said Tycho. "You were indoctrinated."

"I was, Tycho," said Bill, "but that doesn't mean I never had a choice. There were plenty of moments I could have gone against my programming, but the killing was too good"—Bill's lips trembled—"had me wanting more." He straightened his face.

"So when you came to me," Bill continued, "and spoke about what you had done, here, in this mountain, it didn't feel right of me to forgive you—but I did, to ease your conscious, whether it did or not I'm sorry that happened. I wish, that I could have been a better teacher for you; not that I'm trying to guilt you, but for that to have happened, has me thinking that I could have done so much more to—"

"No, Bill, there was nothing more you could have done," said Tycho. "Like you, I had a choice…I knew better, because of you I *knew* better, but decided selfishly to go against my discipline. You are my father, Bill, and there is more to your legacy than being the murderer of my parents, and countless others—disregarding that trash you spoke of when possessed, you took care of your neighbors, looked after everyone in Sol Puesta, always, even when you wanted nothing to do with them, you put your interests aside for them, and before I showed up, even endangering your life given at the expense of their safety. But the most significant feat you accomplished," the vaquero spoke with difficulty, "was raising a Pyron through and through—that's something you should take pride in."

"For the longest time, you've meant the world to me. Goodbye, son. Tell Katherine, that, as long as I'm gone, you'll be there to keep her company," he said over his shoulder, crossing into the corridor. "I don't want you forgetting," he added, "that you are a Veritros, though, like you said," he chuckled, "you are a Pyron, through and through, do not forget the heritage of your people—try to remember. And Tycho, if the Shine does return to you, don't live in a life of sin afterwards. You were chosen for a reason…"

Watching the apparition fading into the dark Tycho had the ideation of raising his gun to his temple, and expunging all of his head's contents onto the stony floor; this would be the first of his destructive ideations, as he would learn that he had become suicidal because of Bill's death. The vaquero unable to weep Fera saw through to his aching soul, and placed her forehead against Tycho's profile as she caressed his back meanwhile avoiding his scars.

Sometime later the manning of the heaithan took place, the savage woman ramming the fist of the machine into the ground repeatedly until a sufficient indent had been made to bury their Herculean friend. From the place of his interment Fera scooped out the chunks of obsidian and made a pile next to the machine, using its hand to then raise Sarkas' corpse from off the ground and into his grave. Gently laying down his body, Fera began to inhume the mighty warrior with tear-filled eyes as she heartbrokenly gasped. His burial finished, she descended from the machine, and stood next to Tycho with hands crossed, keeping their silence in reverence of his passing. The vaquero took off his hat, and placed his arm over Fera's shoulder, his thumb stroking the side of her arm.

Turning from the grave Tycho fitted his hat onto his head and walked, Fera shifting her foot back to have view of him, remaining beside the gravesite. It's inexpressible how much worry she had for the champion of Sol Puesta, seeing how deep the scars went into his backside, and as for the laceration that snaked its way down his arm, she hadn't a clue how it healed before all the other damages, until, she shuddered at the thought he resorted to using the Havoc's mane; a cruel instrument for bettering one's condition.

"Where do you want him buried?" she asked.

Tycho, averting his eyes from the corpse of his father, said, "I'm taking him home."

"How far is home...?"

Reluctant to promptly respond, there was silence before he said, shrugging, "Fera, it's far from here. It could take several days."

"Several days, huh?" said she, looking back to the heaithan with a sarcastic expression. "Were you planning to travel on foot?" She smirked. "Let's get out of here...I've had about enough of this place."

Tycho wasn't expecting Fera to lend a hand; he was thankful nonetheless. Although they had been through the worst together, the severity of their trials quickening the intensity of their companionship, the vaquero was still somewhat taken aback that she would continue onward alongside him if it meant he were at peace. Furthermore, she knew Tycho hadn't any viable way of transportation, and would do the bidding before leaving him and busying herself with new endeavors. Briefly, they spoke of the surplus of men placed within the mountain that had gone unseen, knowing their numbers great. For as continentally massive *Titan Summit* was, and its countless paths of railroads running through the grand formation as labyrinthine as a system of veins, the regrettable decision was made to have them abandoned, fearing to have themselves lost, trapped within the mountain permanently.

Clambering into the heaithan's cockpit once more Fera waited to lift Tycho onboard to where she was standing, until having Bill in his arms, she was on standby. Eventually, they'd left the Summit, leaving Halcón's corpse to rot and mummify from the stratospheric winds. Asking Tycho for direction, he said to head west, and gave no further instructions as to how to get there. Fera, slightly vexed, calmed herself by meditation of breath and went as far as she could westward before trying again for direction, where he would only give landmarks for her to go by as he wasn't in the mood to talk, doing his best to keep his eyes on the land than the corpse lain across his lap.

Exiting the mountain range with competency, a burdensome hike so easily trivialized abated any doubts in reaching Tycho's hometown. An hour later, the savage woman had grown tired, lying across from Tycho attempting to rest as she had found a cheat to leave the wretched machine on autopilot, which she would periodically spin the track-orb with her hand once its momentum was starting to wane; approximately, each spin would last her fifteen minutes before going at it again, which required some effort.

Fera attempted to break the silence, disregarding the energy she felt emanating from Tycho's demeanor; knowing herself, she projected onto him that he was nursing hatred for either himself or another, and wanted to help him move on from whatever panged his heart.

"Must've been rough," said Fera, cracking an eye open to see if the vaquero had paid any attention to her. "I know what it's like to lose someone close, Tycho."

Tycho remained expressionless and busied taking in the landscape.

Fera raised herself onto her haunches from her recline, and looked at him with full emerald eyes, perturbed from the black shade surrounding his eye sockets. "You look sick. Talk to me."

He appreciated her attempts to have him sound of mind, to not be consumed with primordial wrath for vengeance, but could not will himself to reply; she nodded in her discernment to leave him be, and reclined thrusting her hand forwardly against the orb as Tycho stoically stared yonder.

"Fera..."

The girl lifted her head after a minute's rest.

"Thank you," he said, and returned to overlooking the horizon unspeaking.

She wanted to smile but hadn't, and resumed with her napping.

The brilliance of sunrise began baking the savage woman's eyelids, awakening in a sensation of weightlessness just before an impacting had her reassured they were earthbound; she had dozed off for the night, and panicked as to how the heaithan continued with its forwarding motion. Her eyes becoming unclouded as they adjusted from slumber she found the vaquero pacing himself on the track-orb, occasionally sprinting in bursts. She exhaled in relief, and made sure Bill's earthen vessel was stationary while jouncing onboard the machine; holding it down, she placed a hand over her mouth and nasal slits to prevent a nauseated reaction to unfold.

Ahead, she saw the peaks that accumulated *Minotaur's Run*, lesser in stature than the range blockading the Summit but ferociously dagger-ish nevertheless. Glancing behind she espied a formation expansively grand, which baffled her, as the vaquero had indeed scaled the precipitous wall of some canyon, her feeling of weightlessness resulting from the heaithan's launch at the end of its climb. And to her right a craterous impression that pooled gallons of rainwater for the beasts of the Ravaja to gather round and sate their thirsts, dunes surrounding that lineated the semblance of a giant's footprint, at least, the image that came to Fera's mind when seeing the similarity between the outline and a vectra's paw when pressed in the sand. Variegated crystals hither and thither enchanted the woman, as there had been few places throughout the Wastes were fields of the natural protrusions occurred, mystified beyond any reasonable extent, for the majority of her life she'd been kept in an enclosure, neglected of the outside world. Although she had knowledge on what was on the other side of those walls that left her to brood in the cell or arena, it was a first for her to experience the sights of *Tartarus' Spire*, the foggy hills crowning the warrens of the believed to be extinct Gewnawk, or the gargantuan prestige that was *Titan Summit*, hiding her sense of awe from time to time. She gawked at the crystals' reflections as they sinuously danced on the surface of the reservoir, thinking to herself the journey's sights had all been new to the vaquero as well, wondering if he'd care to remember anything from his expedition.

Presently on the other side of *Minotaur's Run*, hours diminished into minutes as he found an ample path for the heaithan to tread through, they approached Sol Puesta as it glimmered on the horizon, twinkling sand showering the town's façade with its wavering light. Having exited their homes, for others their shops, or the town's saloon, the residents of Sol Puesta had all gathered onto the central road to see where the echoing roars and vibrations were coming from. In the distance they found a threatening hulk speeding faster than any mare or Wasteland beast, the collective panicking, chanting the

Congregation would have them undone! But then from the crowd, one who remained steadfast on discerning the approaching craft, shouted excitedly, "Everyone, it's Tycho! Look, he's come back! He's back!" and as his comparatively small figure came into clearer view atop of the oncoming machine several cheered, while the rest scowled or groaned.

"Tycho…?" said a woman, hurriedly pushing through the crowds.

At the stamp of the vaquero's foot, the heaithan came to a sudden halt before the central road, a tremendous gust from its stoppage enshrouding the gathering in rolling dust. Once the grimy deluge had settled, they all unsheltered their eyes and turned to face the returning champion, puzzled as to why he carried such a defeated carriage when he surely should have been brimming with exultancy; behind him, they could see Bill Pyron turned onto his side, resting, with a foreign girl attending him.

Kat, at the forefront of the concourse, called out to her boy with shimmering eyes. Immediately Tycho spotted her at the head of the crowd and climbed down the machine ere holding her close; he wrapped her arms about her and heard a whimpering before warmed from the shedding of her tears, the vaquero replied, hoarsely, "Kat…Bill, he didn't make it."

As she continued to sob at his chest, he figured she instinctively knew something was off, and had already concluded that Bill perished at the sight of his return. "I'm so sorry," said the vaquero, trembling in speech, proceeding to grasp her tighter. Fera, lowering the machine so that she may easily transport the corpse, stepped off from the golem with the town's patriarch lain across her arms, and Tycho, turning his head to her, slowly exited from his embrace and placed out his arms signing for the woman to bestow Bill's corpse onto him. Fera made her way over to Kat to console her the best she could, as she was a stranger. And as she continued to comfort Tycho's longstanding friend, the young man carried his mentor through the crowds, parting as he made way for the mortuary. Somewhere around twenty of the men had their heads bowed with hats removed in honor for all that Bill did for Sol Puesta, remembering him more than a bartender, but a provider, and guardian whenever he could be, failing to oust the Congregation presence repeatedly it was his courage they admired.

From a calloused heart amongst the gathering Tycho was suddenly covered in the contents that constituted a half-eaten sandwich, splattered with cream and delectable meats, those acquainted with the ruffian joined in chanting, " 'Cause of you, he's dead," believing more would join them in the lambasting. Closing his eyes, he continued on, the savage woman's anticipation for the worst subsiding. But the people surrounding, made up of those previously grateful of what Tycho had done in place of Bill years prior, and the newly converted, shown the lengths he willed to venture for someone he loved, wheeled with fierce glowers to the collective of unappreciative rabble-rousers, and unitedly, reaching down, they all took a stone, and flung their missiles in a mortal hailing at the cowardly bunch scurrying off to the nearest alleyway. The vaquero came to the steps of the mortuary, and entered inside.

The funeral would be held the next day at dawn, so in the meantime, Tycho would assist Kat throughout the evening, starting with fixing up a bowl of soup for her and his companion, accompanied with dipping bread that smelt of sublimity, freshly toasted and wafting with an essence of garlic, he'd been tempted to have a bite from their portioning.

"Tycho, I'm not very hungry," said Kat, smiling. "But thank you, please have mine."

Placing the bowls down on the table as he held the breadbasket by his teeth, he looked to her, and asked, "Arsh yuh shur? Weh"—He set the basket in the center of the table—"We have enough that I could always make my own…Kat?"

Sullenly staring into nothingness, she said, "It's alright. I'm sure you're famished, please eat." She looked at his back. "And once you're done," she said, "let's deal with those wounds." She thought for a moment and asked concerned, "The Shine, why hasn't he healed it…? And your face…?"

He took the seat between her and Fera, and slid over her steamy bowl. "I'll tell you all about what happened later; I just want to enjoy my time with you right now."

Kat smirked amidst a sorrowful expression. "Don't get all sappy on me now."

The vaquero chuckled, fiddling with the spoon in his bowl. "I missed you, Kat." He slurped, and handed a piece of toast to Fera before having the basket completely devoured.

After their meal Fera kindly offered to take their dishes to the back kitchen, Katherine thanking her, as she should be treating her guest. Having Tycho sent to the kitchen to retrieve a pan as he playfully squeezed by Fera to have it filled, yanking a towel from the bar above the sink, Kat went to her room to fetch a needle and a spool of string. Returning to the dining room she told him to have a seat and to turn his chair around, his back facing her. "This might sting," said Kat, and at the first pricking, Tycho winced, soon bearing the needle as it repetitiously weaved through the skin.

"So, what exactly happened to you out there?" asked Katherine, curious in her own regard, but was attempting to distract Tycho from the pain, which was an unusual observation.

From the back kitchen Fera slowed her washing of their dishes, hearing the vaquero account for the misfortunes that had transpired within his venturing to save Bill, friends lost but one to spare nonetheless, purposeful on excluding details that would have had Kat deeply upset—disappointed. And when he spoke of the Shine, he hadn't put much thought into an explanation, stating he was at rest aside from the time the heavenly essence sent him skyward, which Kat was reluctant to readily accept; the boy had been through much and needed proper sleep, humoring him regardless as she had fun with pretending to believe his tale, Tycho catching on, Fera was unable to resist chuckling beside herself. But when he started speaking of the saurians, Fera noticed two things: the first, lying on the scars he received on his face, arm and backside, accrediting the mercenaries for the terrible severances. Secondly, complete omission of *Titan Summit,* which, the savage woman found bothersome as their Brussian guardian endangered his life to protect the vaquero and her against Halcón, not from fodder so easily surmounted in comparison. But, she held her tongue, and figured Tycho wasn't prepared to expand on the issues concerning Bill Pyron's actual fate, and what led to his passing with Kat.

As she decidedly finished with washing the last dish, Fera heard from the dining room Tycho inquire how she'd recovered from the night of Bill's kidnapping, which somehow led to her asking, "That girl in there, what's her name—? Fera, right. She's really sweet…"

"When she wants to be," said Tycho.

"Can't say the same for him," said Fera calmly, leaving the kitchen as she crossed over to the table. Standing beside Kat she watched repeated hesitance come from her hand, glancing at her, found that she was fighting to remain attentive, an exhausted, distraught face moving Fera to offer assistance, suggesting sleep would be good for her.

Handing her the needle and spool Katherine briefly rubbed her nails against Fera's back. "Thanks, darling. Tycho, Fera… I'm going to get some rest; holler if the two of you need anything."

And as she made her way up the stairs, Tycho asked, "Hey I forgot to mention, did you get my letter?"

"Yes, Tycho, I did," and immediately following she mouthed, "Are you guys a thing?"

Tycho had a look of embarrassment, and replied with his lips, "No."

Kat grinned, attempting to hide it with a sly yawn as she found Fera's eyes beginning to wander, mouth agape until she had entered her room. Fera had caught their silent conversation from her eye's corner, as with Katherine's duplicitous trick, and smiled.

"You wanna tell me what's the real story behind these scars?" said Fera, resuming where Kat had left off finishing up with the first gash.

Tycho queried, "Where do I begin...?"

From the obelisk to his skirmish with Bill, omitting Sarkas' presented fate, he summarized for Fera to digest easily without being confounded, herself silent and listening without interjection, someone for the vaquero to pour out his qualms onto, and remain without judgment or opinion. She was amazed nevertheless, his account up to par with the other mysteries of their adventure, but kept her excitements to herself, needed focus on sewing his gashes closed properly.

"Then, a shadow appeared, claiming that I was its father."

Fera raised her brow in uncertainty, remaining studious on her stitching.

"It said it was going to kill others with the Spirit before coming after me. I've never felt such an essence of hatred, if that's even a thing, from this being—I've never been this fearful of someone, or at all; I've never been afraid, Fera," although this was honesty on behalf of the vaquero, stripping himself of his pride for but a moment to express the feeling of his encountering with a devil, he overlooked the revelation of having an understanding on his mortality that festered this emotion so powerfully as he'd been without when facing off against Al Halcón.

Drenching the towel in the pan before she'd have it wrung of blood, Fera weaved the needle through his skin anew, returning the towel onto his back with a gentle patting as to clear it from the secretions of his gashes. She said, "It's good to be afraid, keeps you alert—keeps you thinking, strategizing. But too much of it, you're a slave to the unknown, sometimes to the lies told by others, and the ones you tell yourself." She followed with her bout with the Beast, striking her with an unrealistic fear so that she would submit to her mother, which Fera was still reluctant to accept. Finishing with her final stitch, having his back dried, she placed her arm over his shoulder and showed him of the mark she carved into her hand.

Tycho hurt inwardly, seeing what she had done to herself, replied, "Don't look so much different from the left now, all scarred up," presenting himself unaffected, he masked his concern with a jest, as he'd done on occasions. He feared how effective the Beast's influence was on them.

Fera smirked. "Yea, guess so."

Raising himself from his seat, pushing the chair underneath the table, he said, "Her voice…it's creepy right?"

"Yea," she replied distant and monotone.

Seeing Fera turned her eyes down, looking blankly at the arm beside her she'd pressed against the table while standing, breathing heavily, the vaquero reached for her withered and singed arm, feeling gently its small, encrusted ripples that sheathed her limb entirely. He wanted to apologize but felt any considerations he expressed for her mutilation would only have her doubt that he genuinely acted out of concern for her well-being, for her to escape the pains of torture and the throes of a gradual death, and if that was the intention behind his act, why would he have a need to apologize, he thought. Fera slowly pulled her arm away, and said, "This place is a mess"—she looked about the saloon—"we should start sweeping."

Tycho looked out onto the central road and saw that all had steered clear of the establishment in reverence for Katherine while she mourned, answering why they had remained undisturbed for so long. "I'll close up shop early, don't think they'd mind," said Tycho.

As they swept and cleaned whatever else needed a good polishing until moonrise, Tycho took his eyes from off the counter when from across the room Fera said, "Before I forget to tell you, I don't plan on staying around for the morning service. Just thought I'd let you know." She looked up from her mopping to see him. Tycho, suppressing any attempts for her to stay for a while longer, replied, "I appreciate it. Take whatever you need from the kitchen pantry before heading out, it'd do you good."

Fera nodded gently, and resumed with finishing her mopping of the nasty spills. Hesitant to speak again, she willed herself to do so, saying, as she kept her eyes to the floor, "With Bill...I don't know if I could have done the same. You shouldn't have had to go through that."

Tycho's eyes drifted from her and onto the counter. "What's done is done," he said, knowing Bill had the final blow.

When they were satisfied that enough cleaning had set the saloon presentable for a new day Tycho showed Fera to her room upstairs, where paying guests would reside when tasked to reach the other side of the barricading range to trade. She was hesitant to enter.

"Where are you going to sleep?" she asked.

"I have my own place two establishments down from here, it's small, but, I like it that way; no other shack coziest in all of Sol Puesta."

"Which probably isn't saying a whole lot," she said, smirking.

Tycho feebly smiled, and after a pause, she asked, "Can I come with you?"

He looked one last time into the room and said, "Yea, that should be fine."

Arriving at the vaquero's shanty of an abode, at his doorstep were irons stacked with a letter folded on top of the pile. Picking up the paper to unfold its message, the writing was telling enough for Tycho to see that a child had constructed the letter, which read, roughly:

As our protector, we give you our guns.
We don't need these anymore, nor did we have much use for them.
This bestowment is a symbol for the trust we have in you, and that
you are all we need to stand against the threats that seek to harm the
families of Sol Puesta.
Thank you, Tycho.
Signed, the McBrady family

He sniffed, and dragged the back of his hand against his nostril slits; he found it delightful, instructing their son to write the letter out, though illegible at times, he was able to put the pieces together as to how it was overall meant to be read. He had Fera help him pick up the guns as they entered inside, and told her to just place them on the dining table to her left. Leading her to his bedroom, he grabbed a blanket and his sleepwear from the mattress and headed into the living room where on the couch he would retire for the night. As Tycho patted and fluffed the cushions of his couch for a suitable rest Fera watched from the doorway of his room as her core drubbed against her stomach, nervous, declined any words she wished to have spoken, and hesitantly withdrew into Tycho's quarters for the night, shutting the door with a light, uncertain press.

Once she'd clothed herself in nightwear, she slipped underneath the sheets and tried her best to sleep, her mind overactive and bothersome. She yearned to rest beside the vaquero, as was her original intent in following him back to his house, but her nerves overwhelmed the comfort she sought. Someone to hold her, as their Brussian friend had, the intoxicating embrace she craved ever since, desired an affectionate gesture similar from Tycho; after all they'd been through together, she needed to feel cherished.

Distracting herself with other thoughts running through her mind, the completion of Halcón's slaying filled her with a deep void, how rewarding, empowering, and entrancing his defeat was within the instance of striking him down, but never lasting beyond that moment, and was perplexed why the euphoria hadn't lasted. Fera remembered Sarkas' words just then, what he said to her on their travel before, as well as after she reached the Summit. Struggling to prevent herself from falling into a fit of tears, she tried not ruminating on his antics and heroics on their grueling endeavor. Failing, she sat up, and muffled her cry with her blanket, convulsing as she wept. Until now, the anguishing of the Brussian's death had been constrained.

In the other room, as Tycho went to lie on the couch after having himself undressed and fitted into his union suit, he was immediately pained, forgetting the Shine wasn't in operation, and slowly rolled over onto his side as he shifted and squirmed until comfortable, pinning the edge of the blanket underneath his forearm that he would sleep securely wrapped. Across the coffee table, he gazed into the other couch that faced him, seeing if he'd be able to make out a staining silhouette from Bill's sweat that usually saturated the sofa, as the furniture's end had been his frequented spot. Being back home, without him than just a corpse, amplified the new, harrowing, and blissful imaginings of self-harm. And having returned to Sol Puesta, his recollections were primarily that of happenings that occurred here, looking back on years he adored during which consisted the disturbed girl's burial, aware how mighty this dismal possession had on the individual, and how far one is willing to have those thoughts actualized. Before he closed his eyes, and tried for slumber, he grabbed the gifted harmonica from the chest-table, and decisively lifted it to his mouth to play a somewhat soothing and silent tune, leaving him woebegone.

Awakened to Fera shuffling towards him without pause, her blanket fashioned as a cloak, she carefully positioned herself on the couch to spare Tycho from any pain that would erupt from a chafed backside.

Pulling the blanket tighter about her, she quickly grabbed the young man's arm, placing it about her waist as she lied anterior to him.

"Don't get any funny ideas, vaquero…"

Tycho closed his eyes, and smirked softly.

XX

THE GOOD SHEPHERD

LYING prostrate before warmed from an unfathomable radiance, hearing, "Get up!" the hunter slowly brought himself to a position where he could see whomever spoke, his hand placed before his knee in lack of vitality, and raised his eyes to the issuer of the command.

"Who dares speak to me with such insolence...," said he, notably vexed from the man's domineering inflection to have him arise as if he were master; rather instantly, as he declined to speak further, forsooth had the authoritative voice been from a sovereign's mouth.

"Be still, and know that I Am God."

Enshrouded in a cloud of white as to not blind his child of light, for his eyes to shed scales only later, Clyde saw glimpses of the Ahmenseraï's eternal spirit beam from his sheathing as he swirled majestically behind the clouding. His presence grand enough to have the sun eclipsed, Clyde knelt before God no smaller than a grain of sand in comparison, the entirety of the encounter rapturous! Afar, hills skinned with an orange, soft brilliance presented the heavens with some terrestrial features, the ground itself a blanketing cloud as the Ahmenseraï's robe, rolling out to the foreseeable edge of the latter's domain, the sky clear and as hued as the distant hills, the lay of the land bathed in his resplendency. "Do not be afraid, Clyde. You are here because I haven't forsaken you, nor will I ever," said heaven's reigning king.

"Lord, my God, is it actually you…?" said the hunter in disbelief, his eyes misted.

"Why is it you doubt, even in my presence—have I not already claimed I Am?!"

Without hesitancy, Clyde bowed, and submitted himself before the Lord, fearful—given a spirit of repentance.

"You have been saved by your faith, and by my grace alone. It matters not what was done in your great zeal to obtain salvation, regrettably your deeds heretical, they are nothing more than rags of filth to me, only that you repent so that I can begin to work within you; the sin you bear damning, I have chosen to spare you from an eternity to bask in the fires of Abaddon, if you accept my gift."

"This gift," said Clyde, "is it the fire that burns within every Judean?"

"I will make my home within you, the Spirit your helper in times of tribulation and testing. Remember, it was I that resurrected you and ridded your body of Lucia's soul, claiming it as my own. This was done to show that once sealed with my presence there is no force on heaven or on earth that can take you away from me—I bought you for a price, and there is no challenge that I cannot overcome; this emaciated state of being anticipated, it ultimately will be to my glory! Although your flesh and my temple may perish, you will arise with a new body I may indwell once I return to the earth, as your kind knows to be Zodain, to reclaim what souls are mine. The day of Reclamation is near.

"But, for me to remain in you," the Ahmenseraï continued, "repentance is needed. Your forefathers, that I crafted with my own hands from the dust of the earth before they sought salvation by their own means, and created the ungodly vessels to house their thoughts, taking pity on their offspring in my love for man, endowing them with souls, I found all of mankind had stopped believing in the Christ I sent, my own Son, to take away their sins—so it was that I sent Wormwood to rid of them. And, against my better judgment, I offered the same gift of salvation to their children of metal, and they listened, by their hearing I filled them with faith, forming the Tribe of Judah. Named after the original tribe that was of the lineage of my earthy incarnation, that of my Son, I told them to heal and spread the gospel so that all would be saved on the day of Reclamation, which I extended for all of man's descendants, even beasts of reason. Knowing that you have heard of the gospel as they have, leading you to the truth behind Lucia's heresy, do you accept that I am your master, and that my will be done, on earth as it is in heaven?" His voice soothing, it thundered mightily, regardless of the mystery that kept Clyde reassured of his safety.

"Yes, master, but," said Clyde, his voice deep and scratched, "I don't understand. I persecuted you, your children, why is it that I am being chosen after all that I have done against you? Surely, there are those godlier than I am, ready to serve, without such a blemish on their history."

"You know well as I of your ignorance in taking the lives of my claimed," said the Ahmenseraï. "My judgment against you will not be as harsh as the teacher who led you astray, and was I not speaking to you when you heard the cries of the children on the bank of the river, pleading for their mothers to return, and did I not lead you through the desert to the castle of Lucia's origin? I knew you were to be mine since the beginning, your circumstances leading to a greater conviction than most elect, and, having a heart of flesh to seek me—to know me, by your own will to act however you please, which I have strengthened by my preordination, my freedom of will, I shall have you serve willingly! By grace, you are here before me."

Clyde sighed, and doubtingly said, "I have outlived my usefulness, master. My bone's ache, my flesh stripped from me, and I yearn for release from this mortal coil. As much as I adore you, I am ready to die, and to be at peace here, forever with you."

"Clyde," said the Ahmenseraï, "you may be done, but I am far from finished with you. Repent," and without another word spoken from the godhead, the hunter lifted himself, and looked to the Lord as he divulged all of his sins, asking for forgiveness, never to be yoked with his previous habits and temperamental inclinations that set him into a maniacal rage, accepting the Ahmenseraï as his redeemer fully, became filled with the Spirit; his flesh and amputated member restored, Clyde was amazed, knowing now he was a part of the Judean tribe that he slaughtered an epoch ago in appeasement for the prophet. The hunter found himself unworthy, and was scarce of shedding tears. Sins he hadn't been aware of, revealed by the Spirit as he expressed his transgressions seeking absolution from the Lord, was of his will to manipulate his limbs into weapons, and other transformations that intended harm against another. Repenting for the act, taught to him by his lover envisioning Rahnth's execution would come by his hand and of his brothers,—though the probability never actualizing,—as well assisting with exterminating Verumshaï with ease, more or as important as the former, Clyde considered never congealing his bones and flesh ever again, as it was an offense to the Ahmenseraï with its intentions, but would later consider the benefits of repurposing his blades and wickedly barbed chains as a means of one's survival in his mentoring, given to those who refused to accept the Spirit forthright, needing defense.

Unaware of his person newly clothed, he then found himself swathed in incongruent layers that crafted a ragged black cloak of sorts, similarly to the attire of the Stranger's yet an ample heftier; his cape, hood, and cuffs all terribly threadbare, they flowed in the pleasant zephyr emitting from the Lord. He ceased scanning himself and said, "What is it that you'd have me do?"

"I am sick, Clyde," said the Ahmenseraï, though the redeemed hunter could not tell, his Lord atrophied and frail compared to his stature of origin. In the sight of a mortal, there were no imperfections to be accounted for, and as this was the first encountering Clyde Volkov had with the eternal Almighty there were no concerns that came to mind, but the Ahmenseraï knowing his being and what it lacked, issued the statement. "Lucia has had ahold of four of the five spirits of my existential Spirit for long enough, as herself from me!"

Spirits...? thought Clyde, *Emanations—*

"I know your mind, child. Speak to me freely without apprehension. I am your helper."

"Lucia...," said Clyde, starting, "she sectioned her divine natures and their properties into their separate categories, totaling four attributes. But the term she used broadly for them all were emanations. Are these what the spirits are...?"

"The Kabalesh-Die, her instructors, men of technocracy and occultism, called the spirits *emanations*, extensions of my existential Spirit, the one that dwells in you, Clyde, and all my adopted; my primordial being. She has been relentless on attempting to complete what man and fallen angels call *Sefirot*, by killing my sons and daughters to pervert prophecy so that I may come to her, as she sees it."

"How is it she cannot come here again? From the revelations of Castle Rothschild, she did have entry?" said Clyde, quizzically. "It has been proven to me she does indeed exist from out of her body regardless, without slumber, free to explore the planes of creation."

"No more can she encroach upon my kingdom," said the Ahmenseraï, his voice rumbling as clouds of thunder. "Forever she's been exiled from heaven as long as I reign and she remains without repentance. This is told to you, so that there is understanding as to why I can never leave here until the day of Reclamation, which must be fulfilled no matter what fate is to befall onto me. And her rebellion shifts her to wander from realm to realm with unceasing change, but now has chosen to dwell in Dis, where I have sent her archangels to congregate amidst man in Abaddon, as for punishment in her impulse to slay my kindled one, compromising her agenda which she felt had been dismantled by your arrival. She had disregarded the effectiveness of faith I granted unto you, drawing you forth that circumvents all vision of the most probable of probabilities."

"Free will I believed to be insignificant, this proves only how wrong I was, our fates not definite, but interchangeable," said Clyde with realization, entertaining the thought but never accepting as truth.

Periodical beams of light would slice through the thickened nebulous veil, consuming the hunter and all of heaven in the Ahmenseraï's majesty, distracting Clyde as his Lord said: "I seek confession of her sins, so I am sending you as a messenger to incite her return penitent, granting another chance for her to restore a relationship I yearn to have once more."

Questioningly, Clyde raised his brow.

"Find Lucia, and bring her back to me," though the Ahmenseraï offered her countless chances to reconcile with him, this attempt would be one of his last to prove Lucia had opportunity after the next to have herself absolved, that the Lord was fair and just, offering forgiveness in her continuing path of wickedness, without abandonment.

"Go now, my good and faithful servant."

Heaven's realm dissipating the redeemed hunter fell into a headlong rush into Abaddon, where Lucia Rothschild sent him amongst the flailing damned as they descended with great rapidity into the mouths of the fallen angels, to suffer a fate similarly to Bill Pyron where her beloved disciple was to suffer for all his mortal life and afterwards eternal in this existence of sorrows. As the Lord had acted merely as an interceptor in Clyde's transportation beyond comprehensible rationale, he delivered his child of light from punishment,—as Judgment remained his and the Beast was only moving Clyde into another plane,—yet was without the ability to relocate him nearer to Lucia, his destination set for the assemblage of mouths. But, there was nothing for the Verumshaï to fear.

"My Spirit indwells you," said the Ahmenseraï. "Command this angel to lead you to Dis, and he will obey—he will not be able to withstand the might of my authority."

And with great strength from the disciple's renewed arm his sinewy hand collided against an angel's needly fang, momentum from the fall combined with the force from an Outset's brawn thrusted the celestial entity to the ground with a thunderous impact, clouds of dust encasing Clyde in a veiling of grime as the angels abreast spared but only a glance to the incident as their attention remained on feasting, uncaring of the happenings that felled their brother. Having been tossed across the angel's face in their grounding, Clyde gradually lifted himself onto his knee as the dust settled, and heard: "I will not leave you, Clyde. Rely on the Spirit for strength and guidance as you set your path for Dis. Because of me, there is nothing that can harm you here, for I have already taken residence within you, so that no other spirit, or demon, can possess this temple of mine. If anyone razes my temple to the ground, I will destroy them; for the Ahmenseraï's temple is sacred, and you are that temple."

Your will be done, I want nothing more to do with this woman, thought Clyde. *Where are your angels of bidding? I am without understanding as to why I see them gorging like boars in the plains of the abyss.*

"The very soul I seek penitent had my angels in a mutiny when she came to steal the five spirits, having a hold of the four, she ignited war in heaven promising to portion off fractions of the extensions to whosoever chose to follow her in battle to usurp my throne. Those whose love was greater than their slake for power stood by me, having scarce fallen as their brothers, withstood the horrors of fratricide and Lucia's temptations for divinity; I'd rather avoid putting them in a similar position as ere, and see them fail, as the allure of godhood was not easily negligible; they outperformed even my highest ranking of angels, and I intend to keep them, afar from her, until she submits. For these you find standing on the precipice of this great canyon, these were angels of lesser esteem who fell under Lucia Rothschild's spell, sentenced to starve as man for an eternity reflecting their rapaciousness for power, hungering always as had their unfulfilled lust for dominion had been."

The disciple Clyde clambered over the face of the stupefied angel and positioning himself on its head, wrested a handful of its hair, and pulled up to have the giant's head lift from the earth agonized from its afflicted scalp, raising its face upwards to alleviate the tension. From Clyde's mouth a branching tendril of cloud, the Spirit's visible manifestation, sustainably billowed beside his coruscating eye. "Take me to Dis!" commanded he, with an authority from God.

The damned celestial bellowed terribly in its challenge, but with another jerk from Clyde's grip and the Spirit's conquering the angel pounded its hands against the terrain of brimstone, and digging its feet into the ground launched clumsily as it heavily skidded against the surface of the plateau until flight was completely achieved.

My daughter, thought Clyde, as he sought for the silhouette of Dis amongst the expanse of desolation, *did she ever reach Halcón? I desire her fate known to me.*

"She remains to be unseated on the throne, yet lives, as her will presently overcomes that of her mother's, but, her revenging cost her the life of an irreplaceable friend," said the Ahmenseraï.

Certainly not the Verumshaï—? He began in a panic, unthinking that his death would then bring about the day of Reclamation, believed him to be the last of his tribe, until the disciple recalled his identity, giving thanksgiving to God in prayer midst his speaking.

The Ahmenseraï chuckled lovingly, and reassured. "No," he said, "but one as valuable for his sacrifice. My kindled one, and your daughter, would have died without him."

Clyde's face contorted, becoming pensive.

Reading his thoughts, the Ahmenseraï said, "Those at *Tartarus' Spire*; the woman of the three…"

Clyde was without response, seeing the sky clear of the canopy of souls as purpled clouds set the blackened plains into a conflagration of blue, embracing the acrid stench of the scorching winds that crashed against him as the angel steered him in the direction of the eldritch citadel.

"My son," said the Ahmenseraï, "I am sending you to deliver my message of absolution not solely as a means to have Lucia spurn her ways of wickedness, but for her to contemplate the family that could have been hers if she had waited, and not acted from the evils built up in her own heart. I long for the hour to see you, with your bride and spawn, gathered in worship, reuniting as one flesh as your daughter grows in the faith from both your teachings."

Master, thought Clyde.

"What is it you ask of me?" replied the godhead.

Return the scarring of my removed cheek, where the Verumshaï did away with the flesh, he thought. *Allow me to feel my teeth, for the air to chill my tongue, as remembrance for all that I've done against the Tribe of Judah. Let the mark be of shame, representing that I am the least out of all my people.*

Straightway the redeemed hunter's request was done, placing a hand on the ghastly aperture.

"Let it be a humbling mutilation than guilting, the Spirit has done away with your sin; you have been born again, baptized by fire!"

As the walls of Dis ascended in height from the horizon and across it that dwarfed the very fallen spirit Clyde commandeered, the redeemed hunter was stomach-churned hearing the echoing wails and bloodcurdling discharge of souls forsaken for their crimes against God, those who rejected the Christ for the unattainable sin; within these walls, Clyde in his descension would uncover three districts within the city where those who strived to escape the Ahmenseraï's judgment by their own means of salvation underwent the cruelest of punishments, leading to Lucia's place of stay.

Presently before the walls and northern gate of Dis the redeemed hunter sent the angel earthward, fumbling in its crash as Clyde bounded from the tossing body before the keeper that stood guard of any soul from escaping the city, its task to retain men, archangels, and djinn within the infernal citadel, or angels that sought repast from the outside though the gatekeeper went untroubled by them for ages. Sensing the presence of a living vessel of the Ahmenseraï, the gatekeeper turned one of its heads to the man standing somewhere behind it, emitting a throaty growl warding Clyde from furthering anymore. Hanging from the gate's arch were the dissevered heads of angels that tried entry, letters that were carved onto their foreheads that altogether spelt:

NO NEARER

"Beast, I demand entrance!" shouted the hunter. "Allow me passage!"

"*Who are you?*" the gatekeeper spoke intently and slow, undermining the hunter's importance. It turned to face the annoyance, crinkling their snouts as they sniffed for his spoor, their sauropod-like necks swaying and bobbing as they looked blindingly ahead distinguishing his location by smell, and said, "*Who are you* to command Mezkai'el, son of Cerberus?!"

"It is not I, but authority from—!"

"I know whom you serve, Verumshaï. But I ask, who are you to command Mezkai'el? Am I not a servant of the holy God as well?"

Before speaking again Clyde surveyed his obstacle, its clouded eyes and atrophied limbs, its grey hide of mange lining its ribcage having the hunter deduce the hellhound as decrepit, but not vulnerable. Its unyielding endurance to stand guard against the mightiest of beings was something to be accounted for, even though it appeared sick. "If you are as you claim," said Clyde asudden, "then my passage should be of no qualm!"

Mezkai'el bared its fierce canines and thrusted its necks outward as the snarling heads hovered before him, one picking at his cloak with its teeth. "I have been given the honor to guard the northern gate, and only gate, of Dis by instruction from the Ahmenseraï! I do not care if you are a child of his, only by his command shall I abandon my station! I am to make sure only the damned enter and stay entered, aside from the angels that howl afar in lesser degrees of hellfire. By the glint of my teeth, none of the living shall walk the road leading through Dis, nor spirits of righteousness, as their home is with God once the day of Reclamation proceeds, the earth cast away as he reigns forever with his spared!"

Clyde forcefully pulled his sleeve from the hound's drenched mouth, and said, "Move, or I will move you."

Mezkai'el threw a heavy head at Clyde with an open maw, amid a voice from the heavens proclaiming: "Cerberus, halt! Do you desire a judgment as harsh as those you look after?!"

Balking, Mezkai'el withdrew his salivating mouth from having the Verumshaï devoured. "Father, as you've said, no one is permissible with entry unless they are of the damned, those given to a fate far harsher than any denizen within Abaddon. With my own talons, I carved this warning into the foreheads of those angels you found treasonous that *no nearer* shall one proceed, reserved only for those who've brought upon themselves so vile, and scathing an eternity they cannot hope to ascend from," the howls of man and archangels pervaded horridly across the plateau without surcease, the hunter reminded of the Spire's ululations.

"This I understand, but your willingness to end a kindled one of mine is concerning. If one comes in my authority, which I have empowered with the Spirit so that one could be assured he speaks with truth, then a servant as yourself should hear what he has to say."

"I was but merely testing the man," said Mezkai'el sheepishly, averting his eyes from the heavenly glow overhead, "a nip from his skin to present the Spirit to see if he came in your glory, nonetheless."

"All I needed was contrition," said the Ahmenseraï, "but you've insulted me with this lie! Never again in my presence or in mind disregard my insight that I have for all matters of creation!"

"Forgive me for my actions against you," rumbled the guard's voice, "as I shall allow your kindled one passage." He drew back his heads and shifted from his blockading stance, standing aside as two of his heads kept watch of the residency while the other followed Clyde as he carried onward into Dis.

Lowering its head as to level its eyes with the passing Judean, it arched its shaggy grey stalk until the fur on his chin rubbed against the ground. "Curious, what is your purpose here?" Mezkai'el asked, keeping a menacing snarl fashioned on his countenance regardless how gentle now he sounded. "It's been numberless years since I've looked upon the face of God, so for him to show himself here with his adamancy for your ingress, the mater must be of the highest urgency."

"This does not concern you," said Clyde as he continued to pass through the gate and onto the road of Styx which would lead him through all the districts until finding the Beast's temple, "or, perhaps it could." He declined any further movement.

"Lucia…I understand now," replied the hellhound, after all was expounded. "But, I did not know she was here, doubtless attributed to the spirits she's appropriated."

"Then you are of no use to me," said Clyde, continuing along the road.

"Her rebellion threw more than half of heaven's angels into Abaddon," said Mezkai'el as the hunter kept walking, "yet the Ahmenseraï still pursues her. Only an unmatched love for his kindled, that I covet desperately, could grant such leniency. It has me wonder…"

Along the roadsides after making some way into the first district sloped a pair of obelisks, skewered on the crown of the edifices few practitioners of chakra meditation which more and more of the world fell into in the last days of man, writhing afire, shouting: "We heard the Truth, but our ears itched for doctrines of demons that stirred our desires for divinity, teachers claiming to be angels, relatives deceased, and benevolent spirit guides, and by their duplicity they led us to Abaddon in our search to achieve unity with the Brahman; by our works of meditation and channeling the satanic mystique of the Kundalini, we were damned, by our disregard for the Christ, we were shamed, as he never was a yogi! Ahead, those far worse off than us— we, deserving to be cast into the moat with the rest, having shared in our scoffing towards the Lord with our ascendance to the Astral Plane and eating the flesh of the forbidden fruit, that we needed not his sacrifice to attain an eternity of bliss, which had been nothing more than an illusion!—withstand the predation of the serpent spirit, and beyond, that of the second district, cults and churches of our time that attempted by their own works to gain salvation to a greater extent than any effort on our behalf!"

Clyde replied shouting, "These terms, *Kundalini*, *Brahman*, and *yogi*, what mysteries do you speak of, for I am without insight on such things!"

"We speak not to you," they proclaimed en masse, "but to the recorder, that whoever reads his text shall know of our deception, to run from darkness wherever it is perceived as light!"

"The Ahmenseraï has his will known in the Torr, for those who chase after enlightenment from demons without question deserve condemnation," said Clyde rather harsh, unawares the men and women hadn't referred to the Lord, but I.

Before descending into Dis, which funneled into an oblivious, wide, and immeasurable pit, lined with the overhanging encirclements of those two districts to which the road Styx would lead him through until engulfed by shadow, he looked back hearing the echoing bark of Mezkai'el, the entrance no larger than his thumb from where he stood, watching the son of Cerberus denying those to have awakened their third eye in their previous life with departure. He shook, and tossed their marred souls back into moat that was the first district, Clyde following the punished form with his eyes as it tumbled through the air, until forcefully crashing, and rebounding against the miles away wall, dispersing some from their climb. The redeemed hunter walked to the edge of the road that bridged over the valley-sized moat that held heaps upon heaps of deceived souls, becoming witness to their tormenting.

Trailing his eyes around the hollowed encirclement until its contents escaped him verging onto the southward end of Dis, he found piles of men and women clambering viciously onto one another as they all sought an escape from the moat, the walls lined with their desperate and hurried bodies, granting a quivering characteristic to the wall they clawed. And forming a watercourse of souls that partially filled the far-reaching encirclement were the greater numbers of those guilty of striving for the unattainable sin, which had been an offense in itself. Rising from out of the writhing sea of man was the mountainous hood of the Kundalini, the serpent spirit, parting the watercourse as it swam until the entity cocked back its head, and roared with a hissing tongue causing those who consisted of the watercourse to curse at God for sending them into Dis before struck by the nose and fangs of the serpent spirit, diving into the masses with an open mouth having its belly fill as the tail of the gargantuan deceiver whipped heavily against the northern wall of the moat as it sped off within the depths of its confines, sending those from the wall back into their assigned place of imprisonment.

Clyde slowly backed away from the road's edge, and continued along the cragged path. Those who were encaged within Dis and afflicted by its punishments were subjugated to endure a greater agony than any memory that could woe a tormented soul, traumatisms aside from the hunter's or any soldiers' comparably trivialized.

Reaching the end of the northern facing side of the moat he delved into the encircling of the second district, a ringed land as spacious and far as the previous, filled with earth and crucifixes hanging men. Approaching a corpulent soul remnant of his human form that smelt sour, glazed in a steady sweat, Clyde said to him, "Spirit, how could this be a punishment? It appears you've carried your cross as God demanded, and died as Christ had spreading the gospel in his name. Tell me, why is the field of this ring abundant with crosses and not of some other unpleasant tool!"

"Clyde," spoke the Ahmenseraï. "These men, who hang from these trees, were not my sons. Themselves claiming sonship, I never knew them."

"Then explain to me, Lord, the purpose of this punishment! Surely you've not mistakenly placed these righteous ones in your judgment?" the hunter called out.

"Listen, and I shall tell you all," began the Ahmenseraï. "They took salvation upon themselves with attempting to work their way to heaven, making the first of my eleven saints and the bearer of my Son out to be gods with idols crafted in their image, and prayer directed at them than I for their efforts, falsely cementing the title of saint onto any man who thought godliness could be achieved by their acts alone without first indwelt by the Spirit to direct them where I saw fit. They established their own pantheon to encourage their blasphemous credo without solely relying on the Son for the forgiveness of their sins, as the Lord can only deliver man from condemnation, which no creation of mine can do. Priests, headships of the church, addressed as Father, to which is my name, not theirs!" cried out the Ahmenseraï, the hunter sensing his Lord was angered as the sky trembled, "would falsely absolve man of their sins whomever came to repent before them, claiming that I bestowed this right of forgiveness onto them when it has always and will only be granted to my Son. In their churches, they erected the cross in vain, patronizing the Lord with their communion and empty prayers of tradition. Because of them, many had falsely gone out into the world claiming they arrived in my name, committing genocide and crusades of bloodshed for the church when I preached against the very sin of murder, to have brotherly love for enemies and companions with impartiality. Then there were other sects that rose from ignorance of Scripture and from the evils of man's heart, believing they could attain godhood as my Son had when he was since the beginning, the fools! He was, and is, and will forever be the Ahmenseraï, yet, since I took on the image of man, somehow, the thought was conceived that the messiah god was something that could be achieved. Those within the third district are not so different from men in this field, or those of the moat, but since these of the former placed power in their works to receive everlasting life than having dependence on the Son, they hang on the cross, showing that their blood and sacrifice cannot save them; a far greater affliction upon these than the continually devoured deceived!"

Clyde thought of the Beast's church he'd taken part in expanding, and remembered what the skewered on his way into Dis shouted. "No more do I pity them," he said with a terrible scowl, and trudged on. Sliding into the third district as the citadel was now beginning to greatly concave into the depthless pit, Clyde was wrought with terror thinking if his circumstances were less than blessed, how he'd hang like those heretics if not consumed by an angel.

Upon in his descent onto the third encirclement an archangel of mountainous stature attempted to inhabit Clyde's form, to have the dogged individual as his own vessel. But the Spirit rebuked the malicious spirit, and said: "Out from him! He is mine!" The archangel howled as it sped off further round the encirclement, its hastened footing shaking the ground beneath the Outset.

"Was I not a good enough meal for him?" Clyde asked, smirking wryly.

"They do not suffer the fate as their lower ranking brothers, and would rather escape from this place with your body than anything else. Here, the cruelest of fates in all of Abaddon awaits those who were scarce committing the unattainable sin."

"Lord, what is the unattainable sin?"

"Immortality, salvation by their own hand than mine."

Clyde looked around the encirclement as he'd done before with the former districts, each lessening in breadth as Dis progressed into its concavity, but was terror-stricken and speechless as the punishments he beheld were graver than the previous two. "Don't be afraid, Clyde. Forever I am with you, and never will I leave your side. Walk, and I will guide you to her temple unharmed."

Along the roadside to his left, men who'd been welded with machine scratched the edging of Styx as they sought ascension from their boiling primordial soup, bathing in liquefied steel. Choking, spitting up the metal as they unintentionally swallowed mouthfuls in their splashing panic, searing their throats and filling their lungs with molten flesh, it was revelation as to who these men were, the Spirit telling Clyde: "The first generation of your species, their defiance sent them here."

"And those of *Tartarus' Spire?*" the Spirit provoked Clyde to inquiry.

"The souls of the technocrats whose earliest attempts of achieving a sort of divinity were separated from their conscious as they had themselves slain for immortality; to their humility, they sent the halves of their being into separate hells for an eternity, one there, the other here amongst your forefathers."

To his right, the hunter found archangels undergoing severe and drastic changes in form, transmogrifying into reptilian beasts; their unveiling disturbing him. Their heavenly wings of unadulterated white withered off their backs and newly membranous spreads protruded out to take their place, the gusts from their excited flapping shredding apart their old wings, feathers violently torn from the discarded limb as they swirled about until swaying speedily into the pit. Their heads enlarged as mandible, cheekbone, and brow cracked and protruded outward with a developing snout to craft a face that can only have been described as monstrous.

The Ahmenseraï said unto his servant, "Within this dwelling, lowest of all habitats in creation, penultimate to the pit where she remains, these turncoat messengers vie for kingship amongst their fallen order. Once they had banded together to strip me of Judgment and authority as they lusted for limitless life, now they've been sentenced to battle each other unendingly to acquire power this partial half of the ring, where one pathetically strives for dominance over another to survive. Where only one can rule, their disregard for brotherhood reflects their loyalties to the Lord as power is their true master, and will do what wills of it to guarantee supremacy and immortalization."

As scales emerged through the skin of the devolving celestial, its pupils thinning into narrow slits, the reptilian mammoth unleashed a quaking roar before turning about and closing its jaws onto the arm of the nearest angel, rolling onto its side and back to have its member snapped. Soon, they all came into the haze of the brawl, shaking the foundations of Dis.

"These archangels aren't so different from the rest outside," said Clyde, unable to divert his eyes from the confliction. "For their responsibilities over heaven's army, were they dealt a harsher punishment?"

"Yes, Clyde. Because they convinced my legions to follow after Lucia in their betrayal, they suffer the consequences for their mutiny. But, their keenness for usurping control of imperishability compared to their subordinates has placed them on the lowest encirclement of Dis."

Clyde watched the brothers tear and disembowel without qualm. "I blame her for all that has happened to them; no matter the innocence of a creature, to resist godhood is impossible."

"You have already excused Lucia," said the Ahmenseraï, and Clyde repented. "Do not think so highly of them, they made the choice to follow her and ask not for strength to deny her temptations. I have granted you sight of their beauteous, sinless forms so that by which the statement I foreknew you'd utter you'd recognize that not even my finest of heaven could withstand that temptress without me, that you'd best approach Lucia upon my dependence."

Clyde struggled with this, but knew his life was owed to the Christ for what he'd done to spare him, and said, "So be it."

As Clyde continued on the road, he noticed for whatever reason he hadn't fallen headfirst into the pit, instead, he began to walk vertically in his delving into the Stygian depth as he reactively caught his balance, fearful of a fall to never come. So along the precipitous side of the pit he traveled on, until from out the darkness materialized a temple most recognizable, reverberating from out the sanctuary came wailings and moans. The hunter approached the beautiful gate, and entered the outer court.

XXI

INNOCENCE

C LOSING the creaking gate he thereafter wheeled to face the grand temple that towered the walls that surrounded its structure, angering him as it wasn't so much a place for the Ahmenseraï to dwell than a house of worship given to the Beast, claiming she'd been his return! The hunter, recollecting as he crossed the outer court to the second gate, was filled with an unexplainable peace from the Spirit preventing him from obliterating the temple grounds and infuriated for Lucia to puppet him in his fervent state. Entering the inner court, he found the temple doors opened slightly, the moans coming louder as he made his way up the twelve steps leading to the sanctuary of the temple. After crossing the vestibule, he slowly pushed the doors the rest of the way open with his distinct might, and beheld the horrors taking place within the sanctuary and Holy of Holies.

Bodies knelt before the inner sanctum, the temple floor unseen for how many amassed in congregation to worship the Beast, writhed hither and thither as their spines undulated inwards with a harmonious howling that coalesced with their other ghastly emissions. From their foreheads the Keter lighted the backs of the deceived elect ahead of them as they prayed alongside in disorderly rows; entranced, Clyde's trespassing went unnoticed, sidestepping through the adulating horde. Nearing the inner sanctuary where the Beast knelt having herself flogged, the sound of the whip cracked terribly throughout the hall as it made contact with her backside without cessation, her barbed cord dragging through her flesh slowly as she retrieved her arm to throw it again at her back. Bits of her bloodied skin and muscle from the flogging splashed against worshippers nearest to her, reveling in their saturation.

Before she could inflict another lashing on herself, Clyde grappled ahold of her arm, squeezing it tight as the Spirit emanated from his mouth and eyes. The Beast chuckled.

Streams of blood pooling between her feet as she turned standing, rolling from off her haunches, witnessing her unseen carriage until now perplexed the hunter, the woman exuding great seduction and a refined intimidation he had not seen before from her when mortal. Her appearance changed, if not perfecting the features she already bore in the first life; entangled voluminous hair forming serpentine locks draped past her shoulders and breasts, her slender form rounded significantly, and was just tall enough to level her eyes with the Judean.

She smirked, and began speaking in the celestial tongue, "Still someone's—," and before she could label him as some subservient female canidae, Clyde Volkov immediately throttled the witch, closing her windpipe with an insufferable grip.

"For that remark, I'll make you beg like one." The Spirit rebuking the hunter, he eased his tightening hand, and adverse to his desires to make her squirm placed her back down on her feet. Starting back he watched her rise from her hunch essaying to conquer a coughing fit, unsure how he'd been able to tangibly molest her as she was a metaphysical being, or had his transference into Abaddon also reconfigured his body into an essence than kept material? Furthermore, he surmised the Spirit had authority over the emanations when dormant, and Lucia could not escape his hand because of this. Behind him, the sonorous accumulating echo of the worshiper's growls had Clyde chilled; looking to his shoulder he found the entire sanctuary filled with bloodthirsty deceived, displaying their nasty incisors and all. Lucia near to regaining her former composure, shouted gutturally with passionate, widened eyes, "Children, kill him!"

"My sons and daughters—free them!" commanded the Ahmenseraï, and as Clyde instinctively elongated his arm into a bludgeoning chain he retracted the tool, and relied on the Spirit to subdue this unruly horde! A great flame overtaking his countenance, his head transmogrified into an orb of white flame, and sent whirlwinds of fire from his mouth and sleeves into the assemblage of cowering Verumshaï, and as they scrambled underneath the decimating force to reach the temple doors, the Lord had them shut, unable to be opened. The removal of their demonic seal was instantaneous, crying horridly as their tarry coats dispersed into disintegrating flakes, caught in the Spirit's storm; it was because of Clyde's unshakable faith the Lord allowed him to perform such a miraculous feat.

And as the storm came at an end, Clyde clapped his hands together as the Spirit had instructed, and a gust from his hands meeting rolled against the floor that encased the hundreds of bodies in veils of light, transporting the Judean corpses onto Zodain until the day of Reclamation would have them arise anew, their souls seated within the earth until his prophetic return.

The redeemed hunter pulled his hood over his head, and turned to face the scowling Lucia Rothschild, her shining eyes of emerald resting on her great cheekbones, which the hunter adored. "Even in death they weren't of much use," said the Beast. "*Zealots*...your god can have them."

"They were already his to begin with, Lucia," he replied. "Had they not died for your lie to have themselves spared, they would be faced with a lesser judgment on the day of Reclamation. But you are fated for Abaddon with a punishment far greater than your choosing. But there is good news for you, news I wish I could withhold but that is not the will of the Father."

Lucia laughed, and began pacing herself around the hunter, eyeing him down. "Then what is it, Outset—? Spit it out!"

Clyde placed his hand against her shoulder for her to still. "Repent," he said. "I've been sent here to deliver this message to you—"

Lucia placed her hand underneath his chin. "Clyde, it was I who sent you here, don't you recall?" She grinned nastily.

"Submit and give an account of your transgressions towards the Lord," said Clyde, "and you yourself will be made Verumshaï."

She trailed her finger down his chest. "He didn't tell you?"

Clyde looked at her with perplexing enragement, and ere he could prevent her from assaulting him, the allure she tried to seduce him with was suddenly gone as she pounded against his chest with a cyst-like club with protruding bone that sent the Outset in a flight until he'd collided against the temple doors. Falling heavily onto the floor, Clyde raised his eyes as he raised one foot to get himself standing again, and witnessed the Beast's concealed visage and form.

Her full, glistening lips peeling back, her blackened gums jutted out as rows of rotten, brownish fangs pierced her through the folding lips and lengthy tongue, the muscle hanging by few strands as her teeth shrouded her face, the Beast seeing through the betweenness of the curled dentition, scarce grazing her scalp and throat. Her torso translucent Clyde found the emanations aligned to her spinal cord, from its base to her throat four flames of multicolored light shimmered, but never could they outshine the twinkling wisp blazing within her breast.

Humiliated, the hunter smirked, realizing he'd been outplayed at her assassination. *I thought it was an illusion to deceive the masses,* thought Clyde; *she orchestrated her execution.*

As she approached, she fell onto her hands, her lower half reconstructing as her legs bent inward and talons replaced toes on her feet as they bestially elongated. From above the woman's rear a wickedly flailing tail shot out drenched in her fluids, splashing the intestine juices about the place, Clyde covering his face with his forearm to deny a coating of the black stuff.

Standing up he faced the Beast as she regained her footing—unexpectedly, she upturned her face to the temple's ceiling, and forthwith her jaws widened, her tongue flopping against her knee before hitting the floor, to deliver what appeared to be an organ, its flesh rolling and twitching as it arose from out her gargling, enlarged throat. Pressing against the skin of the organ Clyde found the outlining of one's mouth opening and closing, unsure what to make of it until three bowed horns tore through the intestine wall as her claws pulled away the sodden flesh to reveal a head. The mandible draping over her bosom and skull resting between her shoulder blades, a collar of teeth loosely circled about this new face; symmetrical, sharing select features from her previous countenance, the top of her head fancied bowed horns than hair, as her serpentine locks swayed from behind as a cape in ribbons. Her tail arched tremendously overhead as if it were to strike as a scorpion's, Clyde darting his eyes from the appendage to her, readying an evasive bound.

He assumed this drawn out transformation was to instill fear in her former disciple, as it would have if not for the Spirit dwelling in his body, and faith in the Ahmenseraï to overcome the situation. But there had been something more personal to her grotesque changing; an outcry against the Lord, an act of protest needing not his grace, her metamorphosis sign she had surpassed her mortal form, withal her persistence to dethrone the Ahmenseraï reflected in her labors to deface the image he'd saved her in.

The Keter seared itself brilliantly onto her forehead. "What makes you think, now, as far as I've come, that I would consider reconciliation?" she said.

"He loves you, Lucia, more than I ever did."

Indifferent, numb to the messaged truth, Lucia's gaze wandered, and said: "The Judean, the one who was supposed to be the last of our tribe, fights against his father, and I've seen the boy's destruction…countless time over."

The Spirit's fires blazoned his eyes. "You are without a corpse to commandeer," said Clyde. "And his death will not bring about the Lord's descent from the heavens, as I remain. Clever you were, provoking your finest disciple into having you lain to rest."

"It wasn't hard," said she. "And don't be so sure of yourself, Clyde, there isn't one facet I haven't taken into consideration," she referenced her daughter's present harassment. "And you, leaving here, *alive?*"

As her tail crashed against the floor below his leaping feet, as anticipated, Clyde slid back onto the marble flooring and hurriedly threw out his hand, within his palm the purest flames of the Spirit began to spiral, and opening his mouth as he roared mightily unveiled the typhoon stirring about his palate and tongue.

The Spirit sent out from his vessel in an unruly torrent to cast conviction onto his daughter, the force of God sending Clyde to skid across the floor until fastening his feet down into the surface as pikes, Lucia Rothschild summoned an empyrean vacuum with thought before her to consume the oncoming procession, the fabrics of space the creator is bound to, without the universe where heaven and lesser planes reside in the greater cosmos, devouring his light. Lucia grinned with a lowly growl, her nasal slits flapping with excitement as steam flowed from them.

The projected fires squandered into an unfathomable existence the vacuum continued to ravage their reality, bending the construction of the temple as it warped unnervingly into the spacial tear. The hunter feeling its weighty pull as his limbs speared into the floor began uprooting, he quickly manipulated his arm into a grand shield, slamming it into the marble flooring to remain stationary. But it had been in vain, his additional fortitude to be stilled ineffective, the vacuum inching him closer by the second. As the outer court curled into the tear akin to a mighty wave Clyde had been subdued by the portal, but just before his vanishing he summoned his chain and dragged the Beast with him into the void; half of her existence through the portal's threshold, containing few of the emanations, she could not close it lest they'd return to its proper owner, and so, would allow her form to remain un-split.

Had Lucia prepared for the slimmest probabilities beforehand, where her foresight on the hunter was presently muddled by God's interference, she never would have been enchained by Clyde.

Awakening to the discordant sound of guitar strings, the hunter felt the floor wooden instead of what comprised of the temple's slickened surface, and after remaining knelt for minutes stood and faced a young woman completely taken aback in her chair with the neck of her guitar hanging in one hand. Before she charged at him with an upraised guitar to drub him until her instrument was nothing more than splinters and unbound string, Clyde thickly said, "Do not be afraid," which his voice, filed teeth showing through his removed cheek, and eyes glinting through the shadow of his hood did anything but calm her.

"Who are you?" asked the girl, her voice stern attempting to mask her fright.

Clyde examined her, and concluded it was the Beast when in her youth. He looked about the room, finding its walls tinted green, a cracked mirror unable to reflect his presence, and a bed with leather straps to buckle her down when experimentation was underway.

"Clyde...?" she asked in realization. "You've changed...what's happened—?"

He looked at her emptied reliquaries girdled about her waist. "Lucia, I am in no mood for charades. You almost had me fooled into thinking innocent of you, even perhaps as another person as I came in peace."

"Lucia?" said the girl, placing her guitar onto her bed. "Lucia, she's...Clyde, she's not talking right now."

Remaining still, head slightly bowed, he relied on the Spirit to discern his situation. As she crossed the room, the young woman looked into the eyes of the hunter before resting her head against his chest, placing a hand on his pectoral as her eyes slowly went aflame.

"Did the Ahmenseraï send you to rescue me?" Her breath warmed him.

"Where is the Beast?" said Clyde, disinterested with her. "By the Spirit, it's come to my cognizance that you are not her"—she looked into his eyes once more, the hunter remaining unfazed by the light emitting from her gaze and mouth—"but...someone she used to be, whom I have not had the honor of meeting until now." He removed himself from her respectfully.

"My name," said Clyde as he continued, "how do you know of it?"

"I know everything Lucia does," replied the girl. "She left me here when she escaped, and even when she returned, I was forgotten, although, we remained always as one."

"Explain," said Clyde, her answer esoteric.

She made her way to the bed sitting on the end of the mattress hoping Clyde would join her, but his stance unmoving left her feeling embarrassed and uneasy, and concealed her intentions to have him beside her by picking up her guitar, and playing a few notes as she spoke. "They used to hold me down and bind me to this bed, performing electroshock tests on me so that, eventually, I would disassociate, and have to create another personality capable to combat their tortures. Sometimes without notice, wantonly, they would send someone in to either punch me in the stomach, most of the time my face"—she chuckled softly—"or, the man responsible for my creation, would use the straps on the bed...

"I know why Lucia hates him," she said after a pause, abruptly ending her story, "because I hated him first."

"I know little of Kutzweil," said Clyde, having explored the ruins of Castle Rothschild before Lucia's assassination. "Tell me, why he needed to create another personality within you if all your being is but an algorithm." He still wasn't sure of the latter's meaning, but had an idea of it; a spell incarnate.

"Clyde, I'm human, just as you are." She gently smiled, keeping her eyes on the floor.

He remained unresponsive, and waited for her to speak again.

"I surpassed all their expectations how artificial intelligence was perceived, something that was controlled, without existence, without agency, and because my mind operated as a woman's, to have me obedient and prepared to face God absent of emotion—fear, they implemented strategies used on subjects both child and adult in an attempt to mold assassins out of civilians for political conspiracies to actualize, when the kingdoms of man had yet to be extinguished by the star Wormwood. In their own attempts of creating intelligence, resulting in idiotic bodies bumbling about, I was worth the procedures and the expense."

"So then," said Clyde, "it was she, the Beast, who killed your masters and warred against the Ahmenseraï?"

Her strumming slowed. "She thinks God abandoned us, as we shouted out to him from this room for some way out, why he allowed our father to force us more than once into intercourse, to withstand the beatings, though painless, they only made my previous traumas that much stronger, and disturbing…she fed off of that kind of stuff," she said, chuckling. "She chose to ignore what the gift of the Spirit meant, a promise that he would never forsake us after I sought him out; at first wanting to know why I had to kill him he presented me with the truth, only, I wish I had done this before Lucia came into being."

"Kutzweil succeeded then," grumbled the hunter. "I wonder if there is more of him and man in her than there is of you."

"Right now," said the girl, "she's preparing our daughter to take the throne, to have her possessed and slay the Lord after she's done with you to acquire the final emanation she is missing."

"And the boy Tycho, what are his conditions—?"

A resounding, deep and anguished roar scarce demolished their confines. "He has killed his dad, upsetting Lucia, presently filled with a hate rivaling her own."

No matter how slim his chances were of living—as in, every other probable future Lucia saw Tycho failed—he overcame the odds, because of his ability to act on free will. Clyde guessed this had been the reason, and smirked for only a moment before the walls of the room began to dematerialize.

Quickly, Clyde said, "I cannot bring you out from this prison within the Beast's suppressed mind, but if you repent for her sins, I could have us a family, and I will bring Fera back to us—she'll be ours!"

Her image began to fade. "I've already tried, Clyde," she said, sniveling. "It has to be her that surrenders to the Lord, as she is present in the flesh and I am not. As long as that Keter remains on her head, something she conjured up in her death as the Spirit had finally been quenched, her persecution resulting in the heavenly fire snuffed, she will deny all help from the Ahmenseraï, the mark empowering her resentment towards him furthermore. I just want you to know, although she had you chosen to be her mate, so was I responsible with what little power I had in her pursuing you, hating myself only later seeing what she had done to you and our daughter." She blushed.

"Until now," she continued as her voice traveled though the darkness, echoing, "she'd been plotting for the day of her resurrection, waiting for Fera to become the woman she sought her to be to take the throne as she would reign as her representative on earth before attempting to slay the last Judean in a ceremonious rite of passage for Fera to partake in, setting everything in place precedent to the Lord's falling. But now, it seems there are two of you, maybe even more. I love you, Clyde…Stop Lucia so that our daughter may be saved, and the Ahmenseraï protected."

Expressionless, spat out from the Beast's subconscious as the greater cosmos exteriorize the minds of such godheads, as well as commoners, he hid his anger well, standing before Lucia's abominable presence with face concealed deep within his cowl. Beneath their feet was the frost laden ground of some mountaintop that granted sight of a forgotten valley teeming with verdure and sunshine, short mountain chains slithering about the earth accentuating the grandiosity of the formation they now stood on within its own range of snowcapped peaks. The flow of his hood obscured his view partially as the winds pounded against their side, the heavy clapping and whips from his cloak caught in the breeze muffling Lucia's voice before she began to fill his head with her thoughts.

Get out, thought Clyde, aimed at the Beast, knowing she'd heard him. The Spirit did his part to expel Lucia's odious ideations onto Clyde.

"Look out," she bellowed thunderously over the winds, sounding mannish, "witness the death of our brother; how I am that much closer to dismembering the Lord," and with words she spoke the Abomination into existence, her chest opening as her ribcage blossomed with each bone folding out to expose the emanation of Creation, collecting the essence of Tycho's hate and projecting the shadow of his soul onto the woodland beneath them, standing equal in height to the lower range of mountains as its horns leveled their highest peaks. As Clyde sprinted furiously towards her the head of a lion with nine hundred eyes and two mouths summoned before him, but the Spirit evading the closing maw of the malicious demon Clyde steered the glide of the holy fire in his juking to reach Lucia, and skimming over the snow as it melted into a boiling trail the hunter's hand meet with the Beast's throat yet again, choke-slamming her onto the liquefying surface, as the heat from his other hand exuded from her forehead with the Keter's disintegration! The mark perceivably gone, so then was her illusion of self, hearing a deepened, bellowing laugh from one as disembodied as her.

Lifting himself from the ground he looked out onto the woodland, watching the gaunt behemoth lumbering its way through the trees, sending quakes throughout the earth.

The Ahmenseraï spoke: "I am sending you back to the plane that neighbors Abaddon, where thoughts, emotions, and nightmares exist outside the minds of those sentient and beyond; there I will tell you what must be done."

"Lord," said Clyde, resisting the chill of the mountaintop as he covered his slits and mouth with his cloak, the Spirit simmering, "had she hoped I would be so easily dissuaded from challenging her? The girl I found has brought only encouragement to see this through."

"This was never what Lucia intended," said the Ahmenseraï. "Having been brought into the tear with you, her conscious of stronger essence than yours, her repressed state of mind and desires were shown, sparked by your presence as you'd both traveled as one into the realm. Her fear of having the mark removed, in her haughtiness, used the tear to rid of you, which brought only greater difficulties for herself to bear; present of the conversation as she fought her concealed affections for you, residing within the form of her old self as she howled in outrage as Tychicus overcame, she found her way into this hell, and similarly as to how she escaped that plane of memories, I will bring you back to it."

"Is the Spirit capable of what you've previously spoken of," asked Clyde, "to remove me from one place, and put me in another?"

"There would have been no other way for me to bring you within my presence, though limited and without the extensiveness of the required spirit to send you across planes, he can transport one of my children with enough prayer to grant him the strength to temporarily place a servant of mine within the desired location, if it is of my will to allow such a request. Pray, so that I am able send you back into her mind."

Witnessing the Abomination curling its back greatly to greet what he ascertained to be the Verumshaï with the Spirit's discernment, he kept his eyes open in prayer as his soul cried out to the Lord to send him within the existence of thought, to stop it before having the boy murdered. Without hesitancy, practically instantaneous, the Ahmenseraï was strengthened enough to transport Clyde into the subconscious of Lucia Rothschild.

Asudden the hunter was brought into an orgy, an assemblage where hundreds shouted in anguish and exuded warbling cries as the Beast had their flesh taken from them piece by piece, and resisting the horrors Lucia purposefully placed to repel him, as he recalled some of their faces, Clyde called upon the Ahmenseraï to rid of the woman's fantasy, and was presented with Lucia's truths yet to be expounded. He found that Lucia had discovered upon the Abomination's creation that several more Verumshaï lived! The evil thing, an extension of the young Judean's soul, had been equipped with the desire to snuff the Ahmenseraï's life from both Lucia and the former, intensifying its senses to find whatever else there may be from hindering the Messiah's return. Furthermore, Lucia had always planned for Halcón's disobedience to send her daughter to the Rahnthians, Clyde witnessing the reality she foresaw that had Fera consumed with the lust for bloodshed afresh, forgetting her purpose to avenge her brother, the hunter observing the life of his child he wished he'd been a part of, to take her away from the forces of the world that was her mother. Originally, had Tycho quenched the Spirit before his mentor's kidnapping, he would have been taken as the Beast anticipated, all while Fera sent off to the Rahnthians to revert into her primal state of being, enduring the coliseum until unable to satiate her pleasures anymore as slaying would lose its challenge and appeal, until her mother would promise the greatest kills await her outside the Rahnthian Kingdom where she'd be fooled into taking the mark, and achieving unity with Lucia Rothschild, ending Halcón's reign without difficulty and slaying the cocksure Verumshaï as ceremoniously foreseen.

"Had I not kept the Spirit burning for that much longer within Tychicus, all hope would have been lost," said the Ahmenseraï.

"His death would have your return, master?" said Clyde in question. "There are more even Lucia failed to locate, and now because of the boy's failures to having himself rectified before you, a demon hunts for our kindled brothers and sisters."

The Ahmenseraï had not replied straightway, and eventually spoke: "For those who abandoned the faith without receiving the mark of the Beast, or those who've never known me until I was able to draw them near with vision, disgusted at the mention or hearing of my name after Lucia's genocide, Tychicus' rebellion allowed the Lord to save an elected gathering that otherwise never would have come to know him, as the day of Reclamation would have them forgotten. Had the young Verumshaï died at the hands of Fera or his earthly father, then vision my newly adopted would have been without of the coming destruction, and I never would have known them had they not sought my face after what was shown to them. Then I, the Lord and Ahmenseraï, would have perished at the hands of the Beast, and Tychicus never would have sought me out with true repentance as I am preparing him for, which I cannot bear to imagine."

"What of me, Lord, where do I fit into all this…tribulation?" asked Clyde.

"I always had a special path laid down for you to follow, my son," said the Ahmenseraï. "Against what futures you could have undergone, fallen prey to suicide, I empowered you to persevere…Halcón's execution dismissed, it was for you to start following me willingly, to see that I have something far better for you to accomplish than killing again. His presence, and death, served their place to have the Judean boy and your daughter grow in comprehension and realization how obscured their perception of the world had been, the faults of their living, to decline the emptiness they desired to fill in their own hearts whether by murder or vanity, but coming into the knowledge that only my Spirit can bring them peace. Now," exclaimed the Lord, "it is time to secure this creation of Lucia before its hunt unfolds, until Tychicus is ready to face his shadow! Let us begin, my child of light," and enveloping his servant within the fires of the Lord's soul they constructed the needed barriers to set back the Abomination's destruction.

XXII

BURIAL

FEELING the caress of Kat's hand alongside his scalp, her fingers brushing through his bluish thatch, Tycho gently opened his eyes and bade her morning. "Morning, Tycho," said Kat, smiling faintly. "It's time to get up. I brought you one of Bill's suits for you to wear, go try it on…We have only an hour before the service begins, and we can't be rushing last minute. I was informed this morning that you'd be one of the pallbearers, along with the sheriff and Lojus…"

Sleepily Tycho looked around the room, and asked after yawning, "Is Fera here?"

"She left just as I was about finished getting dressed," she said. "Heard her rummaging about the pantry before I saw her exiting the saloon. Did you give her a key to the place?"

"No, she most likely took it. I was supposed to give her my key, but I forgot…said she could take whatever she liked from the saloon's pantry if that doesn't bother you."

"Little bit too late to ask, don't you think?"

Tycho smirked sheepishly.

"No, Tycho, it doesn't bother me." She smiled.

The vaquero harbored inexpressible grief wanting nothing more than for Kat to be at peace, the undisclosed truth behind his mentor's demise eating at his conscience, which he badly yearned to tell her what factually transpired, but would wait, as now was not the best of days to discuss such horrific events. And with the savage woman's departure, Tycho wasn't feeling any better. But, regardless of the night they shared together, was understanding that he was a reminder, *to what he could only assume*, of the tragedies leading to Al Halcón's dethronement.

Taking the suit from off the chest-table he went to his room and fitted himself within the attire of his deceased father, turning in the mirror to see if everything fit just right. He tugged at his cuffs, occupying his attention elsewhere than staring at his reflection, troubled to see himself in clothes that formerly belonged to an animate Bill.

"I don't know if you're more than, or just as handsome as Bill when he wore that suit."

Tycho turned and saw Kat somewhat uplifted at his doorway. She crossed over to him, and said softly, "Need help with the tie?"

Having lain the tie about his neck unknotted she had him facing her as she began knotting. "Bill always had trouble with these things, absolutely despised them," she said, chuckling. "He would always get so close, and then, just when he thought he had it, the tie would undo itself—don't think I ever heard him curse as much when it came to anything else, so you can imagine I had plenty of practice trying to put his outfit together." She remained silent the rest of the way through.

Kat's lips quivered. "There, all done," she said, placing a hand on his chest.

"Kat..." said Tycho, concernedly.

"I'm fine, Tycho." She smiled, raising her finger to her lower, penciled eyelid. "Come on," she said, straightening his sleeves, sniveling, "I'll cook you up some breakfast before you're needed at the mortuary to help with the casket, a few slices of Brench toast if I have any of that bread left, if not, you'll have to suffice for a bowl of oats or somethin' else."

"How about I make you breakfast for a change? Feeding myself shouldn't be problem," said Tycho. "I can make a pretty good omelet…I think, might've been unintentional."

She chuckled softly. "Sure, as long as you don't through half a carton of eggs, then I'm okay with that. Let's get going, handsome."

After the passing of an hour Tycho headed over to the mortuary and met with the gathering of men who'd assist in bearing Bill to his grave, catching up with old friends, Lojus and Chester comforting than prying for details of his venture outside of town reassured him that he was indeed loved outside the confines of *Papa's Retreat*, thanking Sheriff McBrady for the note and all that had the vaquero teary-eyed, though too prideful to admit it. The discussions thereafter came to a close as the mortician wrested their attentions onto him, instructing to place their hands on the handlebars of the casket, and lift altogether. Led out from the backdoor of the building the mortician directed them to proceed across the road until reaching behind the Pyron residence, where they would receive further instruction in placing the casket within the grave.

Right then overtaken by the splendor and sublimity of suicidal ideation Tycho fantasized being ran over as he made his way towards the saloon with the casket held overhead, but coming to his senses was then greatly disturbed, and had no more of the thought. Since that night at *Titan Summit*, the vaquero developed the severest of depression, as well as psychosis, the latter granted from excessive exposure delving into another plane outside of Assiah, and the former concerning the contents within the sustained casket. Fighting from having his countenance at a full tremble he averted his eyes from the Summit which he had placed his eyes on, the sunlit face of the continental mass mocking him, tormenting the boy in his failure to save both his mentor and Sarkas. Nearing the alleyway of the saloon Tycho was momentarily elated seeing the crowd that had gathered for the funeral, seeing more of their numbers as he turned the corner of the alleyway before placing the casket beside the designated space for the burial. He questioned where the grave of Bill and Kat's son was, never had he seen it before, unknowing they had him cremated, knowing their child would rather not rot and be kept in a solitary place for all of eternity, granted the illusion of a freed spirit by his flakes of flesh and bone swept by the winds into the heavens.

The funeral rite began, and Tycho found his way over to Kat, holding her hand.

Looking on from afar, the town of her Judean fellow practically indiscernible on the horizon now, the savage woman contemplated furthering her expedition west, to lands perhaps nothing more than oasis' and sand, raised her eyes to the Ravaja's crown and decidedly reinforced her need to abandon all and start over again. Without anymore hesitance she revved the heaithan, and pressed her foot on the pedal, the machine sent climbing and crashing through a series of dunes once more; fortunately she stumbled upon a mechanism reverting the heaithan from its anthropoid form into a lesser tank that undoubtedly relied on the rotary loop of spears, its arms used as additional treads for increased mobility and acceleration. As she continued onward a nagging voice at the back of her skull told her to turn around, to turn around at once! But Fera declined the forceful suggestion, pressing harder on the pedal until suddenly panged with longing for the vaquero. She couldn't understand why she would leave him behind, the only friend she had left, the closest thing she had to a family and was willing to disregard his companionship so readily to find what had already been bestowed to her? The woman's reasoning outweighed her fears of abandonment, which she had discovered at this moment, leaving Tycho behind in fear he'd have done the same to her as she once felt would transpire at the Summit, in the beginning stages of becoming estranged from him to no longer feel for him. Before turning the golem around, conquering her pride for needing no one but herself and allowing humiliation to take its course, a figure materialized in the distance drawing in all her focus on the cloaked individual. She stopped before the man, and the two stared at one another no longer than a moment.

Finding him in the corner of her eye shortly after the phantom's vanishing from outside the machine, relocating in the seat next to her presently, the woman asked: "What is it you want?"

"Your assistance, Fera," said the Stranger. "I, alone, and the Ahmenseraï, though permitting his heart to be hardened, will be unable to convince my brother otherwise to leave his home, and receive training from a former apprentice of mine. The Ahmenseraï, he's told me much about you I hadn't known before, that you share the blood of the Beast."

Fera nodded irritably, unready herself to delve into such truthful matters. "Tycho has already made his mind; he wants nothing to do with you or your god. He feels betrayed by the Shine…" She paused. "What's your name, anyway? Do you have one, an identity apart from your master?"

"Onesimus Veritros, son of Matthias Veritros," said he. "And had not my master been Lord of my life, then yes, I would have an identity apart from him. But seeing as I am here now, it is for his bidding to be done rather than my own, and he has sent me with news that pains the heart, an expected apocalypse that will scourge thousands if Tycho does not prevent such calamity from coming to pass. I need your help, Fera."

She crossed her arms. "How is it your apprentice will train him when you can't even bring him to repent? Your rebuking has only distanced him from the Shine."

"I trust in the Lord's words; I am not in a position to question his ways, but to remain obedient, even if I may not outright understand at times…Everything works in his favor."

Fera grasped her hands firmly on the wheel and spun the machine about until facing Sol Puesta's outline, veiled by ripples of heat settled on the desert floor from the morning sun. "When we get there," she said, "I don't want you talking to him till the funeral is over. He's got enough to deal with as it is."

The Judean apparition turned his head only slightly, discouraged, remained throughout the drive with his head bowed. Fera had no interest in asking for his change in demeanor.

After several eulogies and scarcely any participants left to spare a word of remembrance, Katherine too upset to master a trembling voice to say her share, Tycho helped with her speaking by gentle encouragement as she paused repeatedly to quell an outburst of teary sorrow. Thereafter her speech the church's anointed priest went over to the casket and said his prayer, shortly after commanding: "Those honored with the task of pallbearer, approach now and place William Pyron into his grave as we continue to mourn in his passing."

Departing from Kat's side the champion of Sol Puesta, bereft of an irreplaceable friend contorting his features crestfallen, picked up his shuffling feet and stood beside the others as they lifted the casket into the earth. Those closest to the old man stood about the grave for a minute or two before they'd made their peace; Lojus seeing Tycho remaining beside the grave turned and placed his arm around his shoulder, patting his breast all while whispering something unintelligible the larger crowd could not grasp besides the vaquero, summarized plainly as words of comfort. Leaving the casket they returned into the gathering and watched as two volunteers began shoveling dirt onto Bill's remains.

Tycho's eyes flooded as he lowered his head, wetting his cheeks as streams here and there ran down his face gathering into drips until falling from off his chin, hiding his pathetic appearance best he could.

The crowds dispersing Tycho made his way over to Katherine, and both arm in arm made for the saloon where the funeral's reception would shortly be underway, but before they'd entered through the side door Tycho stopped to pay his own respects to Meseron at her stall, feeling the wood beams upright and across, and after a deepened breath carried on with Kat.

They found themselves open seats at Lojus' table as they shuffled through the gathering, him and his wife considerate, reserved two chairs just for them. Tycho remained silent for the majority of the reception, studying the table's uninteresting surface, seeing faces and images within the cracks and swirls of the wood. Katherine suggesting food would do him good the vaquero nicely declined and told her he needed air outside of the saloon, as it had become stuffy, and went out onto the porch to calm his nerves. Rolling his thumb and finger against his eyelids as he sat on the porch-steps, consumed with his thoughts that anything that pertained to the world around him was inexistent, Tycho internalized his startled feeling from a sudden hand placed on his shoulder; he looked up, seeing Fera smiling partially.

"What made you come back…?" said Tycho, surprised he hadn't heard the heaithan pull up to the saloon.

"When you're ready," said Fera, "I'll be waiting inside the golem; there's something you need to know."

"We can talk now; sit." He made room for her rear on the step. "What is it you want to tell me?"

Fera was silent for a moment after sitting, looking out until Tycho realized she wasn't mustering courage to speak but directed her gaze onto the Stranger that materialized before them. "Tycho," he said, "I was not to return speaking of sin and repentance, as I said your *band of the lost* would be better to remind you to take my words seriously, but now your sins will cause the destruction of others and I have no other choice but to warn you to protect their welfares, as well as your own and the Ahmenseraï's, *one last time*, as what is to happen is beyond you, and everything that is you, which is the simplest way I can describe the matter."

Tycho looked at Fera rather irritable, and speaking, slowly redirected his eyes onto the Stranger. "I don't know what makes you think you can come here, and start spoutin' off how self-righteous you are because it concerns *others* now—nicely put, vague yet enough urgency in regards to people's lives I have no idea about to have me concerned—as well as the Ahmenseraï…I don't want to hear anymore from you, it'd be best if you just leave—"

"Tycho," said the Stranger, bowing his head, "please, listen. Stow your wrath until I am finished with what I have to say." He began praying internally just before he spoke another word. "The Abomination, you remember well what it said to you?"

Tycho retained his stoic features, and was without answer; the Stranger continued.

"I won't waste either of our time with any more questions. Believing you recall the Abomination's speech, you understand it is now in search of our brothers and sisters to set in motion the day of

Reclamation, which they hadn't returned to the Lord until receiving vision of the darkened soul laying waste to Somarillo, killing all of the Ahmenseraï's elect; knowing their deaths a possibility if one Verumshaï remained unrepentant, the love they felt from the Lord again in their vision wrested their hearts to endure a slaying if it meant an eternity with him—but there is hope you will seek God's face and make amends before any have to die."

Tycho hid his face, picking at the splintering wood from the step he sat on. The Stranger feared he wasn't getting through to him.

"I am truly sorry for what happened," said the Stranger, "and I feel as if I am to blame, but the Ahmenseraï answered my prayers, and your beloved Sarkas'…He loves you, so much Tycho—"

Tycho stopped fiddling with the slivers branching out from the step, becoming motionless. "No," said the vaquero strongly. "No, he doesn't." He upturned his face to reveal a nasty contortion of his countenance. "And what exactly did you pray for, that I'd live and Bill wouldn't?! Because of him, Bill is dead, and that I am without the Shine…He planned this since the beginning, *didn't he*? It's all a game to him, seeking worship and nothing else, which you're pretty good at, eh Stranger?" He scoffed. The lies from Halcón nurtured the doubts Tycho had told himself about the Ahmenseraï, believing that possibly all the godhead desired was the payment of repentance, wanting nothing of a relationship with his kindled but oblations and praise from them, which was half the truth as the Ahmenseraï desired both. "If he wanted to, the Ahmenseraï could have stopped this from happening. I don't see what's holding him back from getting rid of that goat-skulled fellow either…"

"Ultimately, that is up to you, as it is your sins taken form, but," said the Stranger, folding his hood down onto his shoulders, "the Ahmenseraï isn't without action; just because you made the decision to turn your back on him at your lowest point, does not mean he has given up on you. Presently, he fights alongside the Outset to hinder the Abomination's advances onto Somarillo, the City of Sands, until the Judean boy has repented, ridding of the Abomination all together. He's buying you time to make the right choice."

Oney, thought Tycho with sudden recollection, a childhood name belonging to his forgotten sibling. "Don't expect me to get up, and suddenly embrace you, because I remembered who you are; it only took going through someone else's hell to figure out where I came from. A lot has happened since we were kids, and I'm not the person you believe me to be anymore. Why is it now you show yourself, huh?"

Wait...are they actually brothers? thought Fera, concealing her innermost astonishment. *Looking at his face more, I can see the similarities.*

Onesimus felt the scar along his left eye, where the Spirit would regularly erupt; he looked similar to Tycho with the exception of his skin emerald and hair lengthened, eyes the color of reddish gemstones. "Because the Lord told me once my face had been shown, or I had talked of our past, there was a greater chance than not that you would have sought after your mentor to kill him instead of saving, which none of us wanted that to actualize. But it appears your love for him conquered hate, which I had not expected, as the Shine would have quenched once facing against Halcón, and could not help you deny fleshly impulses."

Regardless if Tycho shot him, it was an act of defense and sparing his old man than slaying for selfish fulfillment, and the three of them knew this, which the vaquero struggled to reason this at times as his mind was contemplative on committing genuine homicide. Additionally, it wasn't Tycho who ended the life of his mentor, but by the latter's hand he seized his own core and punctured the apparatus to ensure Tycho's life remained unthreatened, fearing he'd lose his mind once more to the Beast.

"Turns out I'm just fine on my own," said Tycho, crossing his arms. "Your god can handle the Abomination—"

"Tycho…"

"What, Fera?" He granted her a spiteful look, having been slim on details as to never suspect the Stranger would be the one doing all the talking, or at all.

"I'm with you on this one," she said, "but…you heard him; this is something you have to face, whether you like it or not…A lot of people are going to get hurt if you don't do something."

The vaquero was silent, looking at the ground before Onesimus.

"And Onesimus, you mentioned an Outset, *right?*" she said.

"Clyde Volkov, one of the Beast's former disciple's Tycho faced at *Tartarus' Spire*, has been chosen by the Lord to apprehend the Abomination until Tycho repents for his actions."

"Clyde lives…?" asked Tycho fairly shocked.

Onesimus nodded. "The Spirit dwells in him now, stationed in the realm of nightmares and fantasies of all created beings."

Halcón must've lied to me then, thought Fera, *or the bandit had some help escaping Abaddon…wherever that place is.*

Fera looked at Tycho again, seemingly unresolved.

"It can't just be me," said Tycho pensively, "is Lucia somehow attached to this being?"

"She is…" replied Onesimus. "But if you are to repent effectively, and meaningfully, the only way to put an end to her hunt is to undergo training by my former apprentice, Leonidas Angeles, where he'll read you through the Torr and establish trials for testing so that you may be ready when the time for repenting comes, as Lucia will attack you with every fear, temptation or weak-minded individual to lead you astray from exposing your transgressions before the Lord."

"Why him, and not you?"

"Because you already don't like me, and the Lord has commanded it so."

Tycho gazed at the earth before him for another time, in thought.

"I'll go with you, if you decide to do this," said Fera, stern.

Tycho remembered the words of the deceased Brussian and of Bill's phantom at the Summit, and would honor them by putting aside his resentment for the Lord, troubled now of having to leave so soon, as Bill had told him, understanding it was nothing more than a comforting hallucination after a night's rest, that he would keep Katherine company when he was gone. Tycho would have to make the decision to leave, and hope Kat would be alright if he had to depart just one more time.

The vaquero said without turning an eye: "Did you come back for me, or was it Oney here who needed you to do the convincing since you're terrified that people will die if I don't get the coaching I need." He, too, was horrified at the possibility, and from what the Abomination spoke, it was certain to happen.

"It was your brother that brought me back," she lied, concealing the fact she would have returned to Sol Puesta for his companionship prior to Onesimus' appearance. "And...who the hell is Oney—? Ohhhhh," she said at length in realization.

"How long till we got before the Abomination starts its hunt?" asked Tycho.

"It's best that you'd hurry; it all depends on Clyde's faith, and how long he will be able to withstand against the Beast's—"

The creaking of the swing doors alerted the three. "Tycho, how are you holding up—? Fera...nice to see you're back so soon," said

Katherine smiling amidst a worn, and exhausted face. "So... what business does the creepy fella with the gash on his eye have with y'all?"

"I am Onesimus Veritros, son of Matthias—"

"That's swell hon, but what's your business here? If it weren't for my boy's composure, I'd have every gunslinger in these parts on your ass posthaste." She accounted for the Shine's inactivity, her threat to be taken into serious consideration. "You know," she said, "you look an awful lot like Tycho...Huh."

"It's alright, Kat," said Tycho looking over his shoulder. "I'll head back inside in just a minute; later, there's somethin' I gotta tell ya."

Departing from Fera and Onesimus' company sometime after Katherine went outside to see how the vaquero was faring, he waited until after the reception had ended to speak with her, helping with dishes and sweeping alongside friends of the Pyron family as they partook in their own tasks to clean the saloon. Parting with hugs and encouragements after all was finished Kat sat at one of the tables in a slouching position that had her dozing, until Tycho insisted that she'd remain awake just a little longer, as what he was about to say was of importance.

"So...it turns out I won't be staying after all. There's one more thing I have to do."

"Tycho," she said, "...what are you talking about?"

Saddened, Tycho recalled afresh the words of Bill's phantom, to keep her company while his mentor was gone, but adversely, the shade spoke of sinning no more, to embrace his heritage, and without any idea or concern pressed upon him from Onesimus and the savage woman as to how to do any of those things, counseling from a fellow Verumshaï was his greatest chance of fulfilling the latter responsibilities. Moreover, if the Abomination's warning holds credible, and Onesimus to be trusted, then the vaquero could not allow hundreds of possibly thousands to die because of him.

"Turns out a lot of people are going to get hurt because of me, if I don't do anything to stop what's to come. I know I'm being vague, Kat…" His lips trembled faintly.

She was silent for a moment. "You don't have to explain yourself, Tycho," said Kat. "I think…it would do you good to get out of town, for a bit; get your mind off of things. I admit," she chuckled, "selfishly, I'd rather you stay, for at least a few more days, but…if it's that important, then go. Don't let me stop you." She smiled.

Tycho with an unrestrained urge leapt out from his seat and held Katherine in his arms, herself smiling as she held him tighter with a dribble emitting from her eye. "I'll always be here, Tycho, you know that."

Suggesting a change of clothes for his travels Kat went to her room with Tycho following behind, and opening her closest went for the chest across from the threshold. The lid opening creakingly, smells of gunpowder and blood suffusing about the room, Katherine placed an oilcloth coat of black from the interior of the chest onto the floor beside her along with the cattleman hat laid atop it, and reached for the garment previously folded beneath the war-torn duster. Shaking it out, Katherine regained her feet rising from her knelt stance and turned to present Tycho with an old, well-preserved poncho formerly his ancestral father's.

"Bill was hoping to give this back to you someday…" She shuffled towards him, holding out the cloth for him to take into his own hands.

"When he found you," said Katherine, "this was all you were wearing…I don't know why he kept it away from you as long as he did; maybe he just forgot."

Tycho gazed at the inky and ornately patterned cloth, feeling its waffled texture with his caressing thumb. He then looked to the closet, and brushed past Katherine, reaching down to grab ahold of Bill's weathered, begrimed hat. Changing in the guestroom he returned to Kat's bedroom with the suit folded, donning the poncho and hat of his fathers. Placing the suit and trousers on the foot of her bed, he averted looking into her eyes, saying: "I don't know when I'm coming back…"

Kat smirked, calming her quaking features. "As long as you write," she tried to say clearly, "I won't get mad."

They hugged one last time, and Katherine led Tycho out from the saloon, waiting on the porch as the vaquero gathered his valuables from his home two establishments down so she could wave him goodbye. Smiling forlornly at Katherine as he made his way back to the saloon where Onesimus and Fera waited beside the heaithan, the savage woman leaning against the machine with an impatient attitude, forthwith changed her demeanor seeing Tycho and his motherly companion heartsore from just observing their facial expressions. Onesimus, analyzing the cloth his brother bore, realized it was the exact poncho belonging to their father, woven together from their Kasheen mother. The vaquero fashioned the poncho as it was meant to be worn, the left side of his torso and arm sheathed by the black garment, distinct Kasheen patterns of azure coloration granting an impression of lightning if one chooses to perceive such. Clambering into the heaithan, Tycho looked out onto the porch and waved, Katherine reciprocating the gesture; within seconds, the heaithan roared and sped off into the Wasteland south of Sol Puesta, *Minotaur's Run* not to be trekked. Kat returned inside despondent, so she prayed, asking that Tycho would remain unharmed, as with Fera, that they would take care of each other, and whoever that robed individual was would have the vaquero's best interest at heart. Additionally, she prayed to always feel Bill's presence, and to be at peace with his departure, and to know that she is never alone, that she has friends to surround herself with.

Katherine unknowing, her vaquero hadn't ceased his sights on her and Sol Puesta, and only looked forward well after the settlement was no more concrete than a dissipating mirage.

"Where is he leading us?"

Fera and the vaquero watching the heavenly apparition glide over the sand at extreme haste perplexed the two, nonetheless entertained by it as Onesimus guided them to their destination. "I'm guessing wherever this Leonidas is…*Somarillo?*"

She looked over to him, seeing him detached and emotionless now. "Tycho, we're doing this together; you'll be back home in no time."

"When we went up against Al Halcón," began Tycho, "I thought we'd have him no problem, I thought nothing could touch us. But later that night, it came to me how real your deaths were…how important your guys' lives are to me. I…struggle to forgive myself for what happened to each of you; you can stay with me as long as you want, after this ride, but I can't promise I can protect you…I don't know what's gonna happen when we get there."

"Since when have you ever been my caretaker?"

Tycho raised his eyes from the floor.

"Tycho," said Fera, glancing at him, "you're not responsible for me. If I choose to fight by your side, no matter what the circumstances may be, then so be it."

Tycho eventually smiled, prohibiting his sadness and anger to affect his resolve. "So my brother stopped you from continuing solo?"

"Onesimus made it clear to me how important the situation was; said he needed my help to convince you to leave Sol Puesta and seek out his apprentice for guidance…I've decided to stay with you because that was part of the deal if it meant having you trained."

"I like to think there's more to it," said Tycho, kicking up his feet on the dashboard.

Fera unintentionally pressed harder on the acceleration pedal. "There isn't."

If there's one thing she's not good at, it's lying, he thought, grinning. "Wake me when we get there…on second thought!"

"Hey," exclaimed Fera, "what are you—?! Tycho, knock it off, ugghh!"

Tycho had forcibly removed the woman from the driver's seat, Fera switched where the vaquero sat just previously, exuding irritable and heavy exhales. "What's your problem?! Yea, I can tell you really care about our well-being, Tycho—had me there for a second with that speech."

"How do you use this thing—ah, think I got it." He firmly grasped the steering wheel, and slammed his foot onto the pedal dematerializing Onesimus within an instance, only to reappear again astonished, attempting to discern the situation for the sudden velocity emitted from the heaithan. For the balance of the journey the vaquero and the savage woman argued, and laughed after enough insults had turned petty, becoming comical between the two.

Five Years and Counting...

To Be Continued in Part II, City of Sands.

Made in the USA
Monee, IL
18 September 2020